# ophelia ALIVE

# ophelia
# ALIVE
### a ghost story

## luke t. harrington

POST MORTEM PRESS
CINCINNATI

*For Julia*
*healer, hero*

*"Murder is a kind of love, a kind of possessing.
(Is it not, too, a way of gaining complete and
passionate attention, for a moment,
from the object of one's attentions?)"*

**- the diary of Patricia Highsmith**

I've sorted through the world (the human heart);
Encountered all its darkest crags and corners;
I know the taste of blood (I've drunk my part);
And yet—I count myself among the mourners.

I know that feeble protest falls on ears
Not primed to hear whatever tears I've shed,
But though my teeth still taste of blood and tears,
My enemy is Death, and not the dead.

And so—while no apology I've made
(Or ever make) could hope to set things right—
Still, after the one (only) prayer I've prayed,
I now can see why some hold fast to light...

...for with strange aeons, even Death may die.
Till all is new, my soul remains. (I cry.)

# mon. jan. 10.
# 1:32 pm.
# what's past is prologue

**After almost five years of college,** you start to realize that Christmas is a religion for you, and not in a religious way.

Throughout that first semester every year, you run on the proverbial treadmill, week after week, faster than ought to be humanly possible. There are a thousand sticks behind you—the threat of failure, the threat of losing your scholarships, the threat of looking stupid—but there's only one carrot. There's only one tangible concept you can use to motivate yourself to keep running forward, and it's Christmas.

After four months of staying up all night several nights a week, agonizing over every word in every paper, trying to jump through every hoop they throw at you, you finally finish finals and you can finally drop everything for a few weeks and do nothing. So even if you never liked Christmas before, even if reindeer and Santa and the baby Jesus and Will Ferrell in that stupid elf costume seemed a little too on-the-nose, a little too cloying, Christmas turns into your carrot, your pie-in-the-sky hope of not having the entire world breathing down your neck for just a few weeks. And you start salivating for sugar cookies dyed carcinogenic shades of red and green, and visions of sugarplums start dancing in your head, and you find yourself listening to that radio station that plays terrible Christmas music 24/7, and tuning into all the godawful specials on ABC Family, because even when you're in the depths of despair over that stupid Proust paper you can't get right, you know that Christmas is still waiting for you with open arms.

Three weeks ago, after the sun had set on the 25th, I was sitting in a ginormous leather recliner at my mom's place, drinking hot chocolate and eating those red-and-green cookies and enjoying the only Christmas gift I had wanted, a new H.P. Lovecraft collection to replace my old, tattered one, reading that *For centuries its lofty battlements have frowned down upon the wild and rugged countryside about, serving as a home and stronghold for the proud house whose honored line is older even than the moss-grown castle walls,* while my older sister Sara sat in the recliner nearby playing *Flappy Bird* on her phone and my mother smiled at me from behind the twinkling Christmas tree, and the moment was almost too perfect, and of course by "almost too perfect" I obviously mean "literally too perfect," because all three of us knew that it was about to come crashing down on me and chain me to the realities of the world I'd been doing my best to ignore for years.

Literal years.

Because eventually I looked up and my sister was gone from her chair, and my mother looked at me through the branches and the tasteful twinkling lights that lit up the snow just outside the two-story bay window, and she smiled. She smiled out of a desire to literally *put the best face on the situation,* which, by the way, is a saying that makes no sense. Situations don't have faces, and even if they did, it's not like making them smile would do a hell of a lot for anyone involved ("Let's try to put the best face on this global famine!"). People who try to make situations smile are no different, really, from construction workers calling out *Smile, baby,* as women walk by; they're just raping the situation with their eyes.

But anyway, she looked up at me and smiled, and in retrospect it may even have been a real smile, brought on by seeing how lost I'd gotten in this book that she'd known I'd been wanting, and she'd even taken the time to track down the right edition and everything. But then she sighed and the smile was gone, and she said, *Well, I guess we might as well have this talk now, Ophelia, since we've both been dreading it.*

And I sighed and I rolled my eyes, because as hard as I try to fight it it's damn near impossible to go home to my mom's place without suddenly turning back into a sulky teenager.

(She doesn't see me fighting the impulse, though—all she ever sees are the sighs and the eye-rolls.)

(Damn it.)

*We had an agreement,* she said. *We had an agreement that as long as you kept your grades up and maintained your scholarships I'd cover the rest. And, well—*

I should have interrupted her; I should have broken in and pointed out that *Mom, you know the reason that I got that stupid D was I was busy tracking down an internship and then after that I was reeling from being fired from it, and I can't believe you're cutting me off when your med-school-dropout daughter crashes here indefinitely and rent-free,* but I didn't say any of that because all I could do was sigh and roll my eyes like some idiot 16-year-old who just got told she couldn't borrow the car tonight, because I suck at life.

And she said *I've put up with a lot. I stood by you when the ed department turned its back, and I put up with that 11$^{th}$-hour major change, but we had an agreement, and I think I need to stick to it. Because if you don't learn now, well—then when?* And she sighed and said, *But anyway, I hope this doesn't affect the rest of your break. I want you to relax.* And then she stood up and walked out of the room.

And after that I couldn't sit in that big leather chair anymore.

I used to like the way it still smelled faintly of my father (booze and cologne) and the way that it felt like a giant, warm hug; after that, though, I just noticed the mom smell and the way it was swallowing me.

But that doesn't matter right now.

Because at the moment, I'm in a stiff, wooden chair covered in cheap fabric and a paper-thin cushion that forces me to sit upright whether I want to or not. And instead of my mother is my academic advisor, and instead of the glowing tree between us is a cheap desk where I've spread all the important-looking documents I could find. And after a long, awkward silence, she finally says, "Well, part of your problem is that you should have come in here years ago."

I tell her, "I know, I know, but please just tell me what to do."

She sighs and she bites her pen and says, "I guess that really depends on what you want?"

"I want my degree."

"Are you sure?" she says, skeptical. Chewing that pen like it's delicious.

"Why wouldn't I be sure?"

And typing away like a hacker in a movie from the '90s, she says, "Well, you have two-thirds of an education degree and half of an English lit degree. You're looking at maybe another year before you can graduate, if you're lucky."

I say, "Please. This is all I have left."

"This? An English degree? This is all you have left? You know the world isn't exactly clamoring to hire English majors, right?"

"It's not about that."

"It's not?"

"It's not," I tell her.

"So... what's it about, then?"

"It's about...pride? I guess? It's about not letting one more thing chew me up and spit me out? It's about finishing something, for once in my life?"

She says, "Well, I mean, here's what you need to take," and she highlights a few things on a page, and passes it across the table.

I snatch the page and the fluorescent yellow streaks catch the light glinting off of her window's melting icicles. "I know all this," I tell her. "I just—"

"You just what?"

"I just need to figure out how to pay for it."

"You know I'm not a financial advisor, right?" she says. "I mean, I could refer you to one—"

"Don't bother," I say. "I know what she'll tell me."

"What will she say?"

"She'll tell me to take out loans. Does that seem like good advice to you? Like we just discussed, I'm not likely to recoup the cost of a loan within my lifetime. I need better advice than that."

"...get a job?"

Part of me wants to throw a rich-girl tantrum right here and now. A loud part of me that smells like expensive mall body spray wants to stand up and yell *My dad is a doctor. My mom lives in a damn mansion. If you think I'll go flip burgers to earn a liberal arts degree from a state school, you're...*

(*...you're probably right, and that's what scares me.*)

But that's not me, and I don't want it to be me, and if I did I would have joined Tri-Delt five years ago. I know that instead I'll just slink back to my dorm and poke around on Craigslist looking for a help-wanted ad that's not actually a clandestine casting call for porn, and when I finally see an ad for a floor sweeper position at Walmart I'll spend the evening strategizing about ways to explain that *I've never swept a floor, but I'm a team player and I'm willing to learn!* just so I can get a job that probably won't even cover my gas money. And then instead of actually calling I'll get distracted by reading the history of brooms on Wikipedia before passing out and waking up late for class tomorrow.

So I tell her, "Thanks anyway," and I pick up my things and shuffle back into the hallway. And as I close her door behind me, I hear my phone buzzing.

And as it comes out of my pocket, I see the name *Sara.*

"Hello?"

"Hey, Oaf. You need a job, right?"

(binge)

**tues. jan. 11.**
**5:45 am.**
**despair**

*There once was this coed named Ophie*
*Who wore her life's goals like a trophy—*
*But then lost her job,*
*And got pinched by the mob,*
*And was stuck with a choice just like—*
 *Something.*
  *I totally had a rhyme for a second there.*

**Lately I've developed this habit** of writing limericks in my head. Not dirty limericks, at least not usually—just simple ones to convince myself I'm not completely brain-dead yet. It's a nervous habit, no different from cracking my knuckles, aside from the fact that it's a huge waste of space in my brain. It's weird to think about how much time and energy your brain wastes amusing itself—like if your computer had to be constantly playing solitaire in the background to keep itself from going insane while you worked on spreadsheets.

I'm still not sure why it's always limericks—why not sonnets and villanelles? If I'm honest, though, I think seventh-graders are to blame. If you tell a seventh-grader to write a poem and you give him a list of formats to choose from, he always decides to write a limerick, unless haiku is an option. If haiku is an option, he obviously picks haiku. But the point is that they always pick something short, because kids think if something is short then it must be easy.

They're wrong, obviously. But then, they're wrong about everything. Because, they're kids.

There was a time when I probably would have bought into the "short is easy" thing, but I'm starting to see now that short things have to be punchy, and punchy doesn't come easily for me. I always, always, always have trouble with that last line, because the last line of a limerick is supposed to be a punch line, and the thing is, life doesn't have punch lines. It just keeps going, long after it gets stupid.

Which, of course, brings me to why I'm standing here.

I'm standing at the back door to a hospital—the one Sara works at—and somehow it's falling apart a bit more than I expected. When someone tells you *Come work at my hospital,* you're hoping it'll be more Mayo Clinic than Danvers State, but I guess I shouldn't be all that surprised about my rotten luck, especially given my last few months. It's all true, by the way—all that stuff in my limerick— except, obviously, for that *pinched by the mob* part, and I don't even really know what *pinched by the mob* means, to be 100% honest—I was just looking for a rhyme, and it sounded badass.

And speaking of my ass, squeezing it into these bright green scrub pants just might have been the Ninth Wonder of the World (the Eighth being King Kong, obviously). It was only when I tried to put them on that I realized the jeans I'd been wearing every day for the last couple of years were actually my fat jeans back when I bought them. When you spend every free moment sitting on your butt in your dorm room reading, you don't really notice the weight gain, I guess.

Although now that I think about it, it's possible that Sara brought over pants that were a size too small just to make me hate myself a bit more. That actually sounds like something she'd do.

So... welcome to the exciting world of patient transport.

I'm picking at the temporary ID badge Sara gave me, the one I'm holding in my pocket right next to a tattered copy of *Hamlet.* Each time it stabs under my thumbnail it feels more real, until I feel that I've done enough thumbnail penance and it's finally real enough to use, and I pull it out and jam it through the magnetic scanner that hangs (floppy) next to the door.

It takes a couple tries to get it to scan right.

The thing's hanging by its wires and it's at a weird angle and honestly my hand is shaking pretty hard. It actually takes two hands, one to hold the card and one to hold the scanner, and the scanner's to the right of the door and I was holding the card in my right hand, and for some reason I grabbed the scanner with my left, and now my arms are crossed over each other, and even as I wince with pain from my wrists clashing together it doesn't even occur to me to switch hands, because I'm smart like that. But then I hear the telltale *click* and the door's unlocked and I pull it open and there's nothing in front of me but endless linoleum tiles and sparkling pools of fluorescent light. Stepping inside from the cold, I almost trip over a wastebasket that's overflowing with used gloves, facemasks, and hairnets—which probably tells me all I need to know about this place. (Isn't that a biohazard? Does anyone care? Apparently not.)

*Down the hall and to the left.*

That's what she told me yesterday after an awkward phone conversation—*You need a job, right?* she said, and I told her I did. *My place needs patient transporters. They're basically desperate. It pays well. Can you start tomorrow?*

*Uh.*

But now here I am, which probably says something for her powers of persuasion. Or at least about how desperate I am, since I would have taken a job scrubbing toilets if it would have kept me in school.

*You know the world isn't exactly clamoring to hire English majors, right?*

Yeah, student advisor, I know that. That's why you're stuck in grad school and working this student advisor job to cover your tuition when you'd probably rather be writing a book. Majoring in English is a limbo no one ever escapes from, a way of corralling those of us who are of no value to the real world into academia so that we can't escape and hurt the egos of productive people, sort of like how the lottery keeps stupid people from ever having too much money. *A fool and her scholarships are soon parted.*

But like I told her yesterday this isn't about employability. It's about being told *Don't major in English* by my mother who's never had a job in her life and my sister who couldn't hack it in med school and (indirectly) by the father who hasn't been in my life since fifth grade. It's about previously compromising with an education major (because *that* pays so much better than, y'know, nothing) only to have my ass handed to me on a silver ass-platter. It's about not retreating just because they all told me to retreat and I'm sick of retreating.

In other words, it's about pride (I guess).

But now here I am, standing outside of a room that's half office and half lounge. Some card tables and an Elvis dartboard and a half-finished solitaire game, plus a tangled jumble of gurneys. It smells like gym socks.

"You're late."

I might as well tell you now that the man standing in front of me is absolutely gorgeous. I know that sounds shallow, but what can I say, I'm human. It's those thick, powerful arms that grabbed my attention first, but as my eyes track up past his broad shoulders and perfect half-slouch to his boyband-worthy stubble and shy eyes, I feel my knees trembling just a little. God, what am I, thirteen? Has it really been that long since I got laid?

(Yes. Yes it has.)

"...yeah..."

"Ophelia? Ophelia Reed?"

"...yeah..."

"You're late. You're four minutes late."

"I...uh..."

"Hey." Snapping his fingers. Uh. Wake up, Ophelia. Say something.

"Sorry? Sorry. I, uh—I had trouble with—"

"Don't let it happen again," he's telling me.

"I—okay—"

"This isn't one of your English lit classes. You have to show up. You have to work. People expect results."

"That's, um, that's a little condescending—"

"Sara explained that to you, right? That results matter here?" He raises a perfect eyebrow—

"She also said you weren't in any position to be picky."

"That's not really your concern."

The silence that follows is long and it's awkward. I stare at his blinding-white Keds till his eyes stop burning my scalp.

"Anyway," he says, "welcome to patient transport. I'm Sam." He holds out a hand to shake and the sudden change in tone disorients me, and I quiver in my Chuck Taylors and forget to respond.

"I—uh—" Somehow I jerk my hand up and he grabs it and it wiggles like a string in the air while the lights buzz.

"You got an idea of how things work around here?"

"We...transport...patients?"

"That's pretty much how it works," he tells me, reaching into a box to his right. He's got a pager—because apparently pagers are still a thing—and he's stabbing at buttons on it with his thumbnails. "Here, take this."

I take it from him and it glistens sweaty in the artificial light, an overworked relic. Curves and contours that must have looked cutting-edge in 1992.

"This is how we communicate around here. When we need to move a patient from one room to another, you'll get the information on this screen. Other than that, it's just a lot of grunting and straining. Say, you're—"

He looks me up and down.

"—you're not exactly a linebacker."

(Um, thanks for noticing?)

"You're gonna have to be moving 300-, 400-pound people around sometimes. Are you sure you can handle this? Most of us around here tend to be big guys. I mean—I don't want you to hurt yourself. Are you—?"

"I'll manage."

I can see the words *discrimination lawsuit* flash before his eyes, and he shrugs his (beautiful) broad shoulders and the lime green fabric ripples (perfectly) over his pecs and he scratches the back of his neck, and he says, "Okay, then. Just—um—remember to, y'know, lift with your knees. I'll—I'll turn you over to Rachel. She'll show you the ropes."

Sitting at the table with the cards is a skinny blonde chick who looks up from a half-assed game of solitaire.

"Yeah," she says to nobody, "great idea. Let's put the only two women in the whole department together. Team Can't-Lift-a-Single-Patient, assemble!"

Sam says, "You're the only one around, Rach." And then, he adds: "I'll try to only give you patients who don't need to get out of bed."

She sighs.

And he adds, "...and I'm sorry for interrupting your solitaire game."

She says, "Yes, there it is. Thank you." She stands up and she looks like a model because of course she does, because I already feel awkward and lost standing here, so I might as well feel fat and ugly as well. She tosses an ace on the table and she stretches in a big, making-a-show-of-it sort of way, and she cracks her back and says, "Come with me, kid." She walks past me and squeezes through the door as Sam tries (too late) to duck out of the way, and gets playfully shoved, and it's suddenly obvious that that perfect stubble will never be mine to touch.

She's walking down the hallway faster than I can keep up, her perfectly white Keds flashing in the puddles of light. Why do people at hospitals always wear Keds, and how do they always keep them so white? Or maybe it's just the artificial light. (Somehow that stuff is worse than darkness.)

I half-start half-running.

"You know anything about patient transport?" she's asking.

"I mean—y'know, sorta."

"So basically, you don't have a clue."

"Uh—yeah."

"Well, it's really simple," she tells me. "Patients need to get moved from room to room—for CT scans, if their status changes—that sort of thing. And the nurses are too lazy to do it themselves, so they call us." She picks up the pace and I'm breathing a little harder. "Which, again, is why most of the people in our department are big dudes. But, obviously, if they're desperate enough, they'll hire anyone. Which is why the two of us are here."

She turns a corner and I run along with her and she keeps going: "It's usually not too bad. Patients stay in their beds, the beds have wheels on them, we push them around. It's a pretty good workout. I mean, unless you throw out your back."

And that seems likely. But I can't quit out of mortal terror now. Mom doesn't believe I can graduate, Sara doesn't believe I can handle this job.

Do the job. Graduate. It's all you have left.

And suddenly she stops and I walk into her back and my nose scrapes against her freckles and they feel just like well-moisturized sandpaper.

"You almost ready for us in here?" We're standing at the door to a patient's room and she's talking to a nurse who's behind a curtain.

"Uh—yeah. I think. Almost. Maybe."

And then I'm on the other side of the curtain, suddenly, without thinking, because I just kept walking (apparently?). "Oh, God, no!"

"What are you doing? What is wrong with you?" Rachel's screaming, but it's too late because all I can see is a faceful of old lady crotch—a forest of pubes, a wrinkly old labia— and a bloody tube being dragged out of her pee-hole.

And the nurse is yelling, "What were you thinking, what do you think these curtains are for, give this poor woman some privacy, oh my God!" and I'm running from the room (from the tear-jerking stench), and I crumple to my knees with tears in my eyes, just searching for air that won't smell like a buttcrack. I squeeze my eyes closed and the black turns to red turns to black, and the noise of the world turns to fuzz while the tile floor absorbs the sting. I'm here on my knees for an eternity and a half, till I feel Rachel kicking me in the butt. I'm scared to look up, but when finally I do, all I see is her face, and she's laughing.

"Okay," she says, "so that was...uh, wow."

I look up from hugging my knees into her face, half-haloed by the purple-green fluorescent light.

"Are you...I mean...what is this? What am I looking at here?"

"Uh—"

"I mean, are you sure working in a hospital is for you? You see a single catheter getting removed, and you're—I mean, wow."

I'm feeling the floor with my hands, on my knees, waking up, thinking *Wow, this chick's right, I'm embarrassed, and what's wrong with me?* The tiles are cold and they're rougher than they look from a standing position. They're weirdly familiar (the feel of linoleum), and all I can think is it's weird to remember the textures and feelings familiar to me as a child but forgotten as I grew. What was close became distant...

I stand back up. My knees creak.

"I...I'm sorry. That was... embarrassing. I'm okay. I..."

"Yeah, are you sure? Because if you need to go sit down or—"

"She's ready to go." It's the nurse who says that, pushing past us. "And get your trainee under control."

I scratch at my elbow and I laugh nervously.

She sighs, rolls her eyes, smacks her gum. "Okay, uh—let's—there's a...thing...we have to fill out..." And she picks up a clipboard that hangs on the wall, and checks several boxes and shows it to me. "You see how I did that?"

I don't, but I say yes, and she hangs it back up.

"Great," she says, and she leads me over to the bed. The old woman's awake, but Rachel ignores her, squeezing in between the bed and the wall. "There are brakes on the wheels," she tells me. "Make sure all four are released. Then we—" she moves some sort of lever underneath the bed that I can't see, and—"and we're off." She pushes on the bed and I forget to move and it runs into me and it stabs me in the gut and I gasp for air but she doesn't notice. I scramble to stay on my feet, and we head out the door, down the hall, and onto an elevator.

She hits a button for a floor.

"So..." she says, and then nothing, and the elevator rises in silence while I scratch my ankle with my foot, and the air is strangely cold. One of the lights is flickering, and she coughs. And then the doors snap open and she pulls on the bed, dragging me along with it, and I see that we're on the ICU level. Faces pass by, behind glass, under respirators and tubes and harsh, ugly lights.

Something is beeping. The beeps swarm around, between gasps of gray air, while the skulls with their skin falling off *snork* and bubble, and the lights are so bright, and she's dragging me along through the poisonous air, and this all needs to stop.

And then the bed stops. And I open my eyes.

"We're done," she says.

"What?"

"We're done. We have her where she needs to be."

"Oh. So I can—"

"Spend the rest of the day moving more patients around? Sure."

"I can't—"

"You're *really* not cut out for this, are you?"

"No—yes—I have to—"

"Oh, hey," she says, looking at her pager and stabbing at a button. "This is something you could probably do. You know where the morgue is?"

"The—the morgue?"

"Yeah, second basement? Just take the elevator straight down, and head to your left, and you can't miss it."

"Oh."

She says, "Yeah, I just got a message that they need a gurney down there. Just an empty gurney. Think you can manage that?"

"Uh—"

"Because I have another fire I need to put out," she says, poking at her pager some more. "Just grab the gurney against the wall over there and take it down with you. You'll do fine."

"Oh."

"You won't have to look at sick people. The thing will be empty, it'll be easy."

"Okay."

"Just come back to the transport center when you're done. It'll be great." And she checks some things on a hanging clipboard, and she jogs out the door, and I'm alone in the room.

Old lady opens her eyes.

And I run.

I'm out the door, and I'm grabbing the gurney, I jerk, and it's heavy, but I'm dragging it behind me, under flashing lights and back toward the shaft we came up through. I punch the button and punch it again, punch it over and over, just waiting for the door to open so I can climb on and get away from the smell of this floor.

Then they snap open and the mirror shows my face, scared and bedraggled, and I close both my eyes and step on and punch *B2*.

And I'm going down.

The elevator hits the bottom with a jolt and the doors snap open, spitting me out onto a concrete floor painted a splotchy red, and the gurney squeaks loud in the deserted hallway.

"There you are."

I jump because I didn't see her there, but there she is, just standing in the corner, her freckles lit up the same shade as the floor, and the lights above her are flickering while she half-smiles and taps on a clipboard. And this is the second time today I've been stabbed in the gut by hospital equipment, and I'm doubled over catching my breath till I can finally find the air to groan, "Hi, Sara."

"You having fun?"

"Um—" If by *fun* you mean *completely and repeatedly embarrassing myself,* then yes. If by *fun* you mean *injuring vital organs with hospital beds,* then yes. "It's fine. I'm—doing great. Yeah. Fun."

She half-laughs and the corner of her smile turns up a bit more.

"Anyway," I tell her, "I brought you this gurney. This is for you, right? They said the morgue wanted it."

"Yeah, it's for me."

"So...here?" I'm pushing it toward her, just hoping she'll take it, but she just stands there, tapping her red nails on her clipboard and smiling. And then, finally:

"Come on," she says. "I wanna show you something."
And she turns and heads down the hallway, leaving me here
with the gurney thinking *Maybe I should just leave it and
get back on the elevator?* Because I could, because I'm
thinking that it would be so easy to turn around and go
back to the transport lounge and pretend like I never even
ran into her. But for some reason I don't. Because she just
left me standing here, because she knows that no matter
what I'm thinking, no matter how long I stand here, I'll just
end up following.

Because it's always been that way.

And so I'm dragging the gurney, running after her as she
disappears into the red.

"Hey, wait up..."

*There once was medical thesis*
*That had fallen (quite frankly) to pieces.*
*I don't know the details,*
*But when my sister fails,*
*It's my own sense of self-worth it eases.*

(Hey, that one's not bad.)

And maybe that's why I'm following her right now.
Maybe that's why I'm filling the red and the flickers with
clicks and with clacks of a rickety gurney that's dragging
behind me and slowing me down, as she disappears further
and further and water-stained ceiling tiles fly by over my
head.

The air in the basement here circulates poorly, and
patches of cold, sweaty, underground air alternate with a
dry air that's stale from a dust-coated furnace. The chills
come in waves, interspersed between two-second fevers, till
I'm scraping my nose against freckles for the second time
today, because she stopped and we're both standing now at
a door that says *Morgue.* She scans her ID, turns around
and looks into my eyes with a smile.

A twisted, freckly grin stares down into my face, and I
can see her breath and it smells like medicine. Her hand on
the door, ready to open it, and she's running her tongue
over her perfect-white teeth. "Are you ready?" she says.

"Am I what?"

But she doesn't say anything. Just bites her tongue and closes one eye like it's somehow a trick to get the door open, and the air rushes out of the hallway and into the twilight that's waiting behind it. She says, "After you," because of course she does.

I wince and I step toward the door and she pushes me in, and she steps in behind me and closes it (hard), and I blink at the cold, bluish darkness. All I can see in the dark is a half-dozen rows of cold, metal drawers that are bathed in the light of a red *Exit* sign, and the air doesn't smell right, like an evil biology class.

As my eyes adjust to the dark, I can make out the gray, fuzzy shapes, tables with people on them. Most covered in sheets, but some grimacing wide at the ceiling. Bodies. I knew this was coming, knew where we were going, and I feel like that should have made it easier, but it didn't. We're standing in the dark, in a room full of flesh, and there's nobody here. No one living, I mean.

Cold hands on my back. Her breath in my ear. She laughs at me when I jump.

In the dark I feel her sharp nails tickling their way down my back, and she says, "Chill, okay? You're such a spaz." And then she walks past me, down the aisle between two rows of body coolers. "Anyway," I hear her say, "we're not here to gape at corpses." Her shadowy form is swallowed by the dark, and I run to keep up, and the night is filled with pounding feet. "Just leave the gurney anywhere."

I bump into her one more time because she's fumbling with her keys in the dark, one of those globulous key chains that's more fobs and toys than actual keys. Then I hear one of them finally slide into a lock and she throws the door open and orange light pours out onto the cold, dead faces.

I'm seeing something that's halfway between an office and a closet. A pitted concrete floor, with a stained orange rug that only half-covers a drain. A rusty filing cabinet, a cheap desk, and a bathroom scale. A dusty plastic plant. A computer that's old enough to be beige.

She pushes me inside. (Again.)

Then she closes the door behind us and leans against it and watches my face. She's smiling. The cheap clock on the wall is ticking, and she says, "Yeah, we all end up in the morgue eventually. I just got here sooner than others. Wish it came with a nicer office, though." She sniffs the air, like it's mustier than she expected, walks toward me. Instinctively, I sink down onto her desk, and her computer monitor stabs me in the back. "But hey, at least no one ever bothers me down here." Then she's on her knees, rifling through a desk drawer.

"You're seriously okay with this? Because, wow."

"It's only—ow—till I find a real job somewhere." Grabs something, slams the drawer shut, stands back up. "Or I'll be running this place." She leans in over me. "Open up."

"What?"

"Your mouth. Open up."

"Wait—"

She jabs me with a tongue depressor, the one she pulled from her drawer, and now it's in my mouth and it tastes like lipstick and dust and paperclips. She's pushing my tongue down and squinting at my tonsil stones with nothing for light but the orange lightbulb that hangs by a wire from her ceiling. And the splinters scrape my tongue as she pulls it away.

"What are you—?"

"Shh." Now she's got one of those things, one of those pokey-lighty things that doctors shove in your eyes and ears, and she's stabbing around my face with it. Holding my eyes open with her cold hands, squinting hard. And then she's sticking something in my ear, one of those ear thermometers with a loud beep that rips through my eardrum, and she pulls it out and looks at it and frowns.

"Stop—"

"Shh, I'm not done yet." Then her hand's up my shirt, pressing the cold, metal disc of a stethoscope against my chest. Fumbling around my bra, finding every possible inch of bare skin to touch with the icy metal and her sharp nails. She listens to my heart, and her eyes are far away, imagining the insides of my ventricles. Then she pulls the

20 ~ Luke T. Harrington

earpieces out, and then her hand is gone and my shirt feels cold and empty. "Get on the scale."

"What?"

She's nodding toward her bathroom scale. "Get on the scale," she says again.

I want to say *No,* but she won't look away, and her eyes, locked on mine, hold my tongue tightly closed in my teeth. And I look toward the door, and it's closed, and she's standing in front of it, blocking my path, while my sneakers hang over her bright, orange carpet, just dangling. I'm trying to look away, trying to think of a way I can teleport back to the hall or the lounge or my bed or a big, leather chair. But her eyes won't relent, and I shrink under them till my feet touch her rug and it squishes a bit of its orangey dye down the old, rusty drain as I step on a scale with a worn *Biggest Loser* decal on top of it. It's a cheap scale, mechanical, one of those types with a dial inside that swings back and forth, and it's clicking and clacking (it's mocking me), making me wait for my weight. I try not to wince when I see it and she writes it down on her clipboard, and says "Okay, you can sit back down if you want."

"If I want?"

"Have a seat."

Each step on her rug fills the room with a smell—an old-rug smell, mildew, I guess—and I look toward the door again, but she's leaning against it now, and I sigh and collapse onto her desk. "Sara, what's this all about?"

"Shh." She's back on the floor, shoving her hand around in a desk drawer again, like she's giving it a violent pelvic exam.

"And why do you keep shushing me?"

"I just—ow—just keep thinking I'm hearing someone coming, and—ow—there." Triumphantly, she slams a pill bottle down on her desk. It's one of those orange bottles, like you'd get at Walgreens, except without a label. It's full of chalky white pills that rattle around when it moves, and it casts orangey shadows in the orangey light. "Well?"

"Well what?" I say.

"This is it," she says. "This is my...miracle drug."

I snort. I can't help it. But she shoots me a look that withers my grin.

"What?" she says.

"That's seriously what you're calling it? 'My miracle drug'? That's, uh, overselling it a bit, don't you think?"

She frowns.

"This is it, though, huh? The results from that thesis that was going to change the world, but got you kicked out of Yale instead? I'm trying to remember why you said it fell through—"

She grabs it off the table and squeezes it in her hand till her knuckles are white. Bites her lip. "It just didn't work out." And she moves in front of the light bulb, and her shadow swallows me.

"Sara, 'didn't work out' and 'got me kicked out of Yale' are barely even in the same solar system."

"It was all bullshit," she says. "I lost my funding, I lost my advisor, and yeah, they kicked me out, but it was all just political bullshit. The science is sound, the stuff will work. I just need to prove it. I *should* be in a well-funded lab proving it right now, but instead I'm in a closet that smells like formaldehyde and mildew, trying to explain the minutiae of the drug development process to my English-lit-major little sister."

"You're not trying very *hard*."

"Just—don't. Just stop." Then her eyes close for a second while she unwinds her purple knuckles, and she sits down next to me on the desk and says "Sorry. Just—I just need your help."

"I...don't think I like where this is going."

"Don't you even want to know what it does?"

I look toward the door again—solid wood, no windows. "I mean, I guess you can tell me if you want."

Her eyes light up. "It's a diet drug."

I snort again. I can't help it.

"What?"

"A weight-loss drug? That's your miracle pill, Sara?"

"No, this is different from other weight-loss pills, okay?"

"I'm sorry, I have to—"

"Wait, listen." It's an order, not a plea. I was about to stand up, but I can't—her face is inches from mine now, lit orange by the room and the pill bottle, and the light pulses like a flame. "It's psychoactive," she says. "It's—well—how can I put this in terms you'll understand? Hmm." She's chewing on a hangnail as she thinks. "Well—first, it makes it so you don't want to eat. It shuts off your brain's pleasure receptors for food. And then—well—it gets technical, but— basically it activates your thyroid to burn energy several times faster than normal. It'll blow your mind how fast it works."

"So?"

"So, it could help a lot of people. Do you have any idea how many people there are out there who want to lose weight, but can't? It's going to be huge."

"What's any of this got to do with me?"

She smiles. "You're going to test it for me."

"*What?*"

"Yeah," she says. "I don't have the resources for a clinical trial. But if I can prove it works and it's safe for humans, someone will have to fund a serious study. Maybe Yale will take me back, maybe the for-profit sector will step up, but—seriously—*everyone* will want a piece of this."

"I'm just not—I'm not even a little bit—"

"Don't tell me you don't want to lose weight."

"I don't—"

"Because we both know you're the fat one."

Her green eyes, lit orange, won't leave me alone, and I was trying to stand up, but when she says those words, my whole body feels heavy. My muscles go limp.

"I mean, I'd try it on myself," she says, "but—obviously, I don't need it."

"I'm fine with the way I am," I tell her. "I don't need—"

"When's the last time you had a boyfriend?"

I breathe. Fast, through my mouth. "That—that's stupid. I don't need a boyfriend." But she's right, obviously. All I can think about is the way Sam was looking at Rachel, and how different it was from the way he looked at me.

"So you won't help me, then?"

"Help you play God? I mean, have you ever even watched a science fiction movie in your life? This is ridiculous." I get up to leave.

"That's too bad," she says. And there's ice in her voice—sharp icicles that stab at my nape.

My hand is on the doorknob. It's cold and it's hard like a stone, and when I squeeze it it hurts my bones. I try to turn it to open the door, but my eyes close and I bite my lip, and I can't leave because I still feel her eyes in my back. I try to say words, but they're whispers and croaks. (*Why won't you just leave me alone?*)

Finally, she talks again, just a few words: "I got you this job," she says. "You know I could take it away."

I try to think of something to say. She's bluffing.

Right?

Has to be. She's a mortician working out of a closet. She doesn't own the place, she's not in charge of anything but a bunch of corpses. She's lying. Has to be. (Right?)

But if I learned anything from my last couple of jobs (at the school, at the publisher), it's that office politics work in mysterious ways. I've seen the kind of power she has, I know how she can control people. Her eyes are raking over my back, and her smile wraps around me, and this is stupid.

"I can't—"

"Come on, Oaf."

When I hear my old nickname, the one that's she's called me for forever, my knees give out, and I almost fall down. I'm squeezing the doorknob until my hand bruises just so I don't land on my ass. "What if something goes wrong?"

"What is it you think is going to go wrong?"

"I mean—"

"Don't you trust me?"

*Why would I? Of course I don't.* "I—"

"Look," she says, "I know you're scientifically illiterate. I know you're one of the ones lined up to burn me at the stake for trying to make people's lives better—"

"I—"

"—but for once in your life, do something for humanity."

"Is *that* what you think?" I feel myself whipping around, picking hard at the cover of *Hamlet* in my pocket while my feet mush back into her rug. She smiles as I jerk the pills free from her outstretched hand and I say, "Give me those." I jerk on the childproof cap till it's off, and I think *This is stupid,* but now it's too late to turn back, I can't not do this now—"How much do I take?"

"Just one. Once a day." She's not even shaking. She's sitting there calm, smiling like God, while the pills rattle in my hand. I try to tap one out into my palm, but six or seven come all at once, and they're white in the orange air.

I pick one out and bring it to my lips, and it's chalky and dry and it tastes like Velcro and sand. I choke and I sputter. I had no idea it would be so hard to get down. But I swallow it, hard, and I finally remember to breathe.

"You need some water?"

"Nope. I'm good."

"You sure?"

I push down once more and the lump finally disappears into my insides. "I'm *fine.*"

"Good." She takes the bottle from me, screws the cap back on, and shoves it back into my hand. "Keep taking one every day around this time. And come down here before all your shifts, and I'll check your vitals and stuff. Oh, and—don't tell anyone you're doing this for me, okay? It's our secret. For now. Till we can prove it works." And now she's giving me a gentle push toward the door. "Listen—" she says—"this took a lot longer than it should have, so I gotta run. You can find your way back?"

"I guess—"

"Good." And she disappears out the door and into the hallway and I blink and she's gone. And then I'm alone in the dark.

# tues. jan. 11.
## 6:47 pm.
## exhausted

"No—that's not how that—" Rachel winces at me for the 99th time today as I jerk on the lever under yet another bed, and it grinds in the wrong direction, and I tell her I'm super sorry. "It's fine, just—just stop pulling on it—*stop pulling on it. Seriously.*"

"Sorry."

She sighs. Sits. Rubs her temples. "It's gonna be like this. Every day you're here. I can tell."

I wonder if I'm supposed to say something, but she's talking to herself.

"And he's gonna keep giving you to me, because of course he is, and it's gonna be my problem every time you break something or collapse on the floor sobbing. Great. I'm excited about this."

"Look, I'm sorry that—"

"No. *Stop.* I can't take another apology today. I just—I don't have the energy." She stands, sighs, pulls a clipboard off the wall, makes a few marks. "It's basically the end of your shift anyway. Did anyone show you how to clock out?"

"Uh—"

"Or *in*? Did you even clock in this morning?"

"I—"

"Yeah, okay," she says. "We'll just—we'll work on it next time you're here. You're pulling the night shift Thursday, right? Right. Yeah. We'll do it then."

"Oh. Okay. Uh—"

"For now, just—just go home. I'll finish up here. Just—get some rest and be ready to work Thursday night, all right?"

"Uh—yeah. Okay."

"G'night," she says, and I stumble down the hall and out the door, rubbing my eyes.

I'm not quite to my car when my cell phone rings. It's rattling in my pocket, and I nearly trip when I reach in to get it. Stupid scrub pants with stupidly deep pockets. "Hello?" My voice is a croak.

Hers cuts through the static. "Where were you tonight?"

"Uh—Mom?"

"Who else would it be? Where were you tonight?"

I'm fumbling with my keys. "Working."

"Well, you missed dinner."

"What?"

"You missed dinner," she says. "Sara and I ate by ourselves."

She's talking, of course, about our standing Tuesday night dinner appointment, which has been in place ever since I went away—across town—for college. "I didn't know I was supposed to come, Mom."

"What? Of course you were. Why would you not come?"

"Well, Mom, when you cut me off, I took that as a pretty strong signal that you didn't want me around."

"That's ridiculous."

"How is it ridiculous?" I'm still fumbling with my keys, stabbing around the lock. My fugly '91 Escort has more scratches than paint on it.

"Uh—" and then she has to think about it—"I don't know. But—" I get the key in the lock and it grinds like a pair of old dentures. The dome light flickers as I pry the door open, and when I climb in I'm swallowed by a musty smell. "But I do have some stuff I need to give you."

Ugh. "'Stuff'?" I sink into the sun-faded seat and crack my back.

"Yeah, important stuff. Can you come by?"

"I—" I inadvertently tap the horn, spooking a cat who was in the middle of crossing the parking lot, and it glares at me with its yellow cat eyes. "I mean, I guess I could."

"Great. Have you eaten yet?"

"When would I have had time to eat?"

"I'll fix you a plate," she says, and she hangs up. (People used to say *Goodbye* before they did that.)

I fumble until my hand lands on the hoodie in my backseat, which I jerk over my head; then, groaning, I pull down the visor with the mirror clipped to it and look myself over. Hair pulled back and sweaty, with roots that ache. A zit above my lip, no makeup. I pull my hair free and run my hands through it, a million pounds of grease and frizz. I don't have a brush with me, but maybe there's a compact in the glove box? I open it and it swings 180 degrees and dumps everything on the floor. (This is the only glove box I've ever seen that happen to, but apparently, every glove box in the world is just a single broken plastic tab away from dumping everything out whenever you open it. What I'm trying to say is, everything in the universe is stupid.)

(Anyway.)

So now I'm doubled over, crushing my guts, groping for the compact, and my blood runs into my ears and I can hear my intestines. In the dark, my hand fumbles over the car handbook, a pair of tweezers, the insurance papers, and a year-old Nutrigrain that's leaking.

Ew.

I go to wipe the fruit-tar on the carpet and my hand sticks to the missing compact.

I grunt as I straighten back up and flip it open and try to even out the purple splotches on my face. Then I squint at the half-lit results, and they're not great, and I can feel my feet swelling in my sneakers, but I guess I'm ready to go.

I turn the key, and it chokes, and I pump the gas twice, and it coughs to a start. I throw it into reverse, and I pull a muscle turning the wheel because the power steering hasn't kicked on yet. It jerks forward when I put it in drive, and I whack the radio but it won't turn on, and I pull (haltingly) onto the street. It's about a million miles from downtown to my mom's place. I drive by a Burger King that's always deserted at night, and the same kid is always mopping the floor (as if it'll make a difference). A grocery store that's always open and always has part of its lit-up sign burnt out. A pothole that's always full of oily water, even when it hasn't rained for weeks, and I always swerve to avoid it but always hit it anyway.

A thousand stores followed by a thousand suburbs leading to the edge of town, where a dozen farms were torn out to make room for a bloated glob of McMansions, shiny plastic houses that shake their fists at the cornfields across the street, cursing them for not being kale and lentils. I grind my car into park as I hit the curb, and I step out and slam the door and smooth the wrinkles from my bright green pants. I can see the stars and the moon in spite of the overpowered plastic lampposts, and they make the perpetually-wet-but-still-brown grass glow.

And of course the houses all look the same, but my mom's is the one with the perfect brown lawn and the gaudy koi pond that's an insult to the taste of carp everywhere. It's an enormous house, one that's taught me the benefits of marrying a rich doctor and then using his money to hire a pricey divorce lawyer. The pointlessly twisty cobblestone path leads up to a brick porch and an insultingly huge door, one that has a glowing doorbell I've never used and a lion-shaped knocker that's cloyingly majestic enough to embarrass C.S. Lewis.

I've found that every week it feels better than the last to pound on McAslan's face. I grab the knocker and pull it all the way back.

The door opens before I get the chance.

"Hey Oaf." It's Sara, leaning on the doorjamb, biting a dinner roll, wearing a nice dress because of course she is. She's blocking the way in, haloed by the yellow light from a cheap chandelier.

"Uh—hi." I'm trying to stand up straighter. The porch light is playing across my splotchy skin and she won't stop smiling.

"Does it work?" Whispering.

"Does what work?" I can see my breath, and it's cold outside, and I don't have a coat on.

"The drug! Does it work?" she says, the fog from her breath slapping me in the face.

"If you're asking whether I've lost 50 pounds in the last eight hours, the answer's no, Sara. Now will you please let me in? It's cold."

"Sssssshhhh, I know, I know." She sticks her head back inside for a moment and shouts: "Yeah, Mom, she's here. She'll be in in a sec." Turns back and says, "But, I mean, have you been hungry yet?"

"Like I said, it's only been a few hours."

"I *know*, just answer the question. Have you felt like eating?"

"Well—no—"

"See, I *told you* it works." She grins like the Cheshire cat, like she always does.

"Okay."

"Okay." And she walks away, leaving the door open.

I step inside. The foyer glows yellow, but it doesn't feel any warmer. Sara's three rooms away, bashing out some Duke Ellington on my mom's baby grand. I shift on my feet, watching my vaguely defined reflection in the oak floor. My mouth is dry and I'm too tired to think.

"I'm in the kitchen, Ophie," I hear my mom saying, and I take a deep breath and enter the house, fumbling with my keys. No matter how I shove them into my pocket, they're still stabbing me. If only I'd brought a purse.

Like the rest of the house, the kitchen is cavernous, and it's separated from the living room by only a bar with some stools. I lean on the bar, take a deep breath, try to ignore that she still hasn't even bothered to take down the Christmas tree. What does she do all day that she can't find the time to move a plastic tree to the basement?

At the moment, she's at the microwave stabbing at beeping buttons with a sharp fingernail. "Hi," she says, licking her finger. "You said you were hungry, right?"

"Uh—"

"This'll be ready in a second."

"I'm not really that hungry."

"What? You said you were."

"I said I hadn't eaten. That's not the same thing." I finally fix the keys in my pocket and climb onto a barstool, slouching, curled under the ten feet of hot, dead air between me and the vaulted ceiling. There's a border around the kitchen wall—stenciled farm animals, maybe in memoriam of the farmland torn out when the house was built. Sara's notes are still pounding in my head, sharp and punctuated with mathematical precision.

"Well, here it is, anyway," she says, and she slides a plate in front of me and sits on the opposite side of the bar. "I made it, so you might as well eat it."

"I'm not sure your conclusion follows from your premise."

That was a terrible thing to say, but can you blame me under the circumstances? She sighs and I poke at the plate, trying to decide what it's supposed to be. Some sort of...meat. With a mushy starch on the side. She's always been a lousy cook, but at least she tries, which is more than my dad ever did. And I'm in a foul mood, but I should probably make an effort, so I start swallowing some of it anyway. At least it's warm.

So much of this house is tangled in memories from my childhood.

There was an older house, one we used to live in, tiny and cramped and musty. Mismatched curtains and old dusty furniture and secret passages and a backyard covered in lush, perfect weeds. But then Dad got his M.D. and for some reason that meant we had to move into a big, square, beige-and-gray brick house, and we carried in hundreds of boxes and sat on our new expensive furniture and said *Now real life begins.* But "real life" (I guess) meant that he would be gone, and then Sara'd be gone, and then I was gone too, until nothing was left in the big-beige-brick-box but my mom, her divorce, and a study she always kept locked while the air went stale.

One Sunday, last year, when I was bored, I drove around and tried to find the old house with the secret passages and the green backyard and the magical smells, but someone had torn it down and built a grocery store.

(I never told her any of this. How could I?)

She's slouching like me, head in her hand, elbow on the bar, waiting for a conversation that I can't start. She's wearing a skirt.

"So." That was her. She said *So*. Just the word *So*, like a single conjunction will somehow fill the silence.

"Thanks."

"'Thanks'?"

"For the food." I got no pleasure from eating it (thanks, Sara), but I did manage to put some of it away.

She smiles weakly. Plays with her wedding ring, the one that's meant nothing for a decade now. I look at her face and study the lines, the same ones I can see appearing on my own face when I'm tired and squint in a mirror. Faint whispers around her mouth, sad crow's feet above. Blue eyes like mine, if a little icier. Add 30 years and subtract 30 pounds, and I could almost be that.

"This is weird, isn't it?" she sighs.

I stare at my plate. "What did you expect, Mom?"

"I guess—" she's saying—"I guess I thought we could just talk and be friends, like we used to, sometimes. But there's just the elephant in the room."

"I—"

"I mean, yeah, I cut you off. And I'm sorry, but you're going to have to learn to take school more seriously. That's all I'm trying to—"

"Mom."

"What?" She looks into my eyes, for the first time tonight. Then she looks away. Gets up. Pours coffee.

"I wasn't even thinking about that," I say.

"You weren't?" She sits back down, slides a mug at me. The kitchen counter's a disaster of gadgets, and all of them need cleaning.

"I'm way too tired for this conversation."

She pushes the sugar in my direction, but I just let it sit there and suck moisture from the air. She looks at her watch. "Well—" trying hard—"how was your first day of work?"

I drain the mug. "Do you really want to know?"

"I mean—"

"It was fine."

She takes my half-empty plate, drops it in the sink. "Ophie, I'm your mother. You can be honest with me if you want."

"It was actually pretty awful. There were old lady crotches. My pants were too small. Sara was annoying." And I notice the piano's stopped.

"Why is it so hard for you two to get along these days, anyway?"

"I dunno."

"Speak up. Why do you always mumble like that, Ophie?"

"Sorry."

"Ophie, we've been doing this weekly dinner thing ever since you started school four years ago, but every night we do it, I feel like I'm talking to a stranger. I'm your mother. I know you. You can tell me things."

I look around at the kitchen, well lit but poorly warmed, a faint glow in a dark house, in a dark neighborhood where no one ever goes outside, and it's so quiet I can hear the dew forming on the grass. I try to find something to say to her, to pick ideas out of the gray buzz sloshing around in my head and form them into something presentable, but there's nothing in there that she'll understand. "I—"

I start, but—

"—Mom, you said you had something to give me."

"It can wait." She picks at the sugar with the spoon.

"Wait for what?"

"I—I don't know."

I say, "Mom, if you want to talk, we can—"

"No, never mind." She sighs and stands up, walks off into the dark. "Come with me."

And then I find myself alone in the light. The dishwasher whines, and the clock on the wall ticks. I look down at my empty coffee cup, the dregs dried to the bottom. I hear her ascending the stairs, but she doesn't turn on any lights. Hollow steps on a hardwood staircase.

The light feels small, and the dark feels big, and I chase after her, up the stairs.

*There once was a dark, empty mansion*

*In a new (-ish) exurban expansion.*
*The floors were hard wood;*
*The acoustics were good;*
*And I'd finish this, but I'm totally stuck for a rhyme.*
*What's another word that rhymes with "mansion"? I'm*
*drawing a blank.*

Man, I felt so confident going into that one.

The landing is dark, but she's standing in the light of my bedroom, and there's a dull purple glow leaking from my door. She's inside, leaning, looking away. Biting a finger, casting a shadow that reaches into the dark and makes it darker. I fight my way through it till I'm standing in the doorway, and I watch her face as she looks from the bed to the bookshelves to her expensive leather boots. She knows I'm here, heard my footsteps, doesn't say anything, won't turn around. Her heels are four inches tall and I can hear the discs in her spine slipping. A new green shirt with cute stitching hiding perfect curves under the assault of age.

My feet hurt.

This was my room for years. It took me five years before I found the perfect shade of purple for the walls. Ten years spent buying bookshelves and filling them with books, and I've read them all, even though no one believes that I have. The perfect carpet, black shag that feels like weeds from another planet on my bare feet. An antique desk that I never sat at, but it fills the air with spiced cedar.

My bed.

A thousand years ago, back when Sara and I had to share a room in our old house, we lived in the attic with a low ceiling that sloped and our beds were side-by-side. But then we moved and they tried to give us our own rooms, but she held onto me tight and said *No, we want bunk beds,* and even though Mom said bunk beds were for boys, Dad stacked our beds together and she took the top one, and I'd lie underneath her and we'd share secrets late into the night, and I promised I'd always be hers. But then something changed and she wanted her own room, a newer and bigger bed, and she got them, and then forever after that she was down the hall in a different world.

But I kept the bunk beds.

I kept the beds stacked together, and I kept the curtains hanging around my bottom bunk. I still don't remember when we hung them, but they transformed my bed into a canopy like something a princess would have. I built it into a cave of pillows and stuffed dragons and unicorns, a niche fit to my body's developing contours and shut strong against the noise and people outside, where a stack of books and I could be alone.

But none of that matters right now because my mom is standing there, and she coughs, and she hasn't said anything this whole time. She's playing with her wedding ring like she always does, and I look near her feet, and there's a stack of boxes on the floor, nice ones like you'd get at Loewe's, and every so often she kicks them with her leather-covered toe, and it makes a little *thwack* noise, and I wonder if she even knows she's doing it.

I can't catch her eyes.

I made this room perfect, and left it that way—I didn't even clean when I went off to school—but now that I'm seeing her stand there with boxes and knowing what all of this means, that we've both crossed a line we can never uncross, and imagining this house without me, this room with no purple, no black, and no books and no canopy bed, and then I remember to breathe, and I stare at her, watching her biting her lip till she finally looks up, till her eyes come to rest (guarded) on mine.

She says, "It doesn't all have to be cleared out tonight. But soon."

I lean on my bedpost and study her face, hiding emotions behind freckles and expensive glasses. She's standing there, waiting for me to say it for her.

She says, "I'm sorry, I just need the room cleared out. It's nothing personal."

"You're kicking me out?"

"No—what?—of course I'm not 'kicking you out.' That doesn't even make sense, Ophie."

I'm pushing on the books, which are spilling out of my bed, trying to cram them behind the curtains.

"You can still come by any time you want," she says. "I just need the room for—for other things."

"For what, Mom?" I snapped a little. I shouldn't have. This moment has been coming for years, but it's worse than I expected. The air is thick.

"It's complicated," she says. "I—"

"What about Sara's room? Isn't it time for *her* to—to—"

I stop talking because I see tiny slivers of liquid in her eyes, the start of tears. Quivering lids, teeth biting a lip, trying to hide her eyes behind the glare in her glasses. Then I have to look away, and she turns to leave the room, and the darkness swallows her, and I'm alone.

It's cold and I'm tired.

I look at the boxes, and I look at the clutter, which is far too vast to fit inside them. A thousand adolescent hopes and dreams, not one of them realized and all of them silly. I'd forgotten this room. I'd forgotten this life, willfully, I guess. I run my hand over the books, paperbacks and hardbacks and plastic-covered library books I never returned. Globs of dust, collecting under my half-painted nails.

I wipe it on my pants. An ugly streak of greasy gray— what all memories come to, I guess. I start to pull books off the shelves, to stack them in the box, but I give up after a dozen or so.

This is *stupid*.

The book in my hand—*A Study in Scarlet*—gets thrown down in frustration, and I rub my temples and think that *I just want to hide.* Backing away from the light, I climb back into my canopy bed, the only comforting womb I have left, and I close the curtains so there's just enough light to read. And I pull the tattered copy of *Hamlet* out of my pocket.

I know it's strange, but I've been carrying this paperback with me ever since I found it on my mom's bookshelf more than a decade ago. I guess most 12-year-olds wouldn't have gotten far with it, but something about it grabbed me. Maybe it was just the shared name, but I spent that whole summer behind the curtains on my bed poring over the words till I finally understood them, while everyone else was out riding bikes and swimming and going to camp. Is it strange to say I'm comforted by a book where nearly every character dies? (Probably.) I don't know, maybe people are just comforted by the familiar, and what's more familiar than death? It's the inevitability—like when I was looking at those faces melting into the beds in the ICU and thinking *That will be me someday, even if I achieve immortality.* Because even if you find the Fountain of Youth or whatever, entropy always wins in the end. The stars will die out and energy itself will disappear and even the electrons in your atoms will stop in their tracks.

Or at least, that's what I gleaned from Physics 101.

I open the book.

It falls open to my favorite scene, the one where Ophelia finally snaps. She's handing out flowers to everyone else, singing songs with a lute and mumbling nonsense. *She speaks much of her father; Says she hears there's tricks i' the world; and hems and beats her heart; spurns enviously at straws; speaks things in doubt, That carry but half-sense.* She's got a bouquet and she's handing them out. *There's rosemary, that's for remembrance. And there is pansies; that's for thoughts.* I'm watching her fingers, they're picking at stems and at thorns in the light of the dawn. Thick-calloused hands but slender and beautiful; nails that were long but are worn down to stubs; a smoky black dress that goes on for miles and a smile that says *madness* that's actually knowledge. Thumbs picking thorns on the stems as she drifts past the king and the queen, speaking songs, mumbling flowers. *I would give you some violets, but they withered all when my father died.* Drifts down the hall, lace soaked in tears, and I follow her song. *And will he not come again? Will he not come again?* Following fast, across silent, white tile, hearing *No* in my ear, but her dress is absorbing the sun as he sets behind mountains and lights up the stream, and I follow her, barefoot, up into the arms of the willow that holds us and whispers that things are okay, with the water beneath us careening and sparkling and lapping at stones in the warm, dying light. We sleep in its arms till they're drifting apart, till we're feeling the air of the night on our skin, and slipping through breeze and through stars till we're wet with the sky and the moonlight and dreams, in cool, soothing memories (all dying away). I let the flow take me and pull me and bind me, a cool hand, a firm hand, a hand that's the color of night and it's sharp and it's prickly and won't let me go. It's got me, it's holding my hand, and my teeth, and my throat, and it's pulling. Skin I can feel with its claws in me, pulling, and screams in my ear, through door after door, through the hallway, the stairway, the moon and the stars, and then darkness takes everything, teeth in my eyes, by the throat, by the throat, and it pounds and I can't push the darkness away. I'm running and running, but can't get away and can't change what I've started, I'm lost in the dark with blood bleeding and yelling, She won't let me go—

And my eyes snap open and I'm waking up in my bed back in my dorm room.

(The light is deafening.)

## wed. jan. 12.
## 4:22 am.
## confused

**I'm tangled in sheets and the lights are on.** It's dark outside, and I'm still in my hospital scrubs. They smell, and *Hamlet* is stabbing me in gut, and my back is killing me, and I reach for my phone and my nails are chipped.

It's four in the morning. On the 12th.

How long have I been asleep? I retrace my steps. I was at my mom's place, and she took me upstairs, and gave me those boxes, and—

There's a box on the floor now, next to me, and it's filled with books that I half-remember running my hand over last night. Sitting on top is my old collection of Poe, a paperback with a raven on the cover who stares at me with red, glowing eyes. My roommate who never says anything and never turns off the lights is sitting across the room, on her bed, tapping on a laptop.

My phone has a text from Sara: "don't forget 2 take med"

(She sent it at three in the morning...)

It's not quite 24 hours since the last time I took it, but I guess it's close enough. I fumble around in my pocket for the orange bottle full of rattling pills and I twist the clicking lid till one tumbles out into my palm. I close my eyes and force it down, and my mouth is dry, and it tastes like chalk and mothballs, and it grinds its way down my throat while my headache gets worse.

I need water. Or aspirin, or something. I'm soaked in day-old sweat and twisted in a half-dozen sheets. I fight, jerking around until I'm halfway free, and then I yank on the sheet twisted around me until I push myself onto the floor, landing on my face. I breathe the cold air above the dry, dusty tile and I slowly push myself up to standing. What day did I say it was?

I glance at my phone again.

"Shit."

My roommate looks up. "You okay?"

"My paper." It was due yesterday, by midnight, and I worked on it for weeks, and I have to turn it in because I can't get another D, and my stupid professor hates email and only accepts hard copies. But it's only four hours late, and maybe if I slide it under his office door he won't know the difference.

"What?"

"I have to go."

It's there on my desk, and I grab it and run out the door. I hear her say something about how I might want a coat, but I'm already halfway down the stairwell, the gray-painted concrete steps flying by six at a time, and me barely touching the bannister till I land at the bottom and slam through the exit door into the dark, and it's snowing. The sky's cracked wide open, with white pouring out, catching the wind and slicing into my face.

I shove the pages up my shirt to keep them dry, and I can't see anything with the snow in my eyes, and it's catching my eyelids and melting down my skin like half-frozen tears. Nobody walks by. Campus is empty tonight.

The snow's getting deeper, it's up past my ankles, inside my shoes, melting and refreezing on my bare arms. But I'm here. In the dark and the white I can barely see it, but inches from my face is the door to the English building, a giant brick thing that smells of sweat and paper and incense, dark and cold and empty, and I grope for the handle and it's locked.

I jerk on it hard, but it fights against my wrist bones.

Not just locked, but it's chained with a padlock that's frozen with ice and with snow and it clacks and clunks against the door when I pull on the handle.

(I kick it.)

*I can do this. I know secret passages. I can get in.*

But now I see a glow, to the right, over my head. A bridge, a skywalk, lit up and warm and hanging in the sky. The building next door, the tall one with the coffee shop inside, stays open 24 hours, and it's joined to the English building by the skywalk above me. It's a long shot, but maybe I can get in that way.

I burst through the door, suddenly remembering what warm air feels like, and I charge past the coffee counter, vaguely hearing a voice that says *Please buy a macchiato or something I'm so bored*, and I leap up the stairs as fast as I can. Three floors up, to where the skywalk is.

I slam the door open.

It's quiet up here, and the lights are bright and buzzing. Empty, white hallways to my right and my left, and a glass tube of a bridge spanning off in front of me, its light pushing out into the white darkness outside. Three walls of glass and a tiled floor, and there's something lying in the middle of it, and I squint as I approach, my footsteps echoing.

I stop.

What is that on the floor? A person? There's a person lying on the floor of the skywalk. Just lying there. A sleeping bum? Sometimes they come in here to get out of the cold, and it's not like I blame them (I tug at my shirt that's soaked through with snow). I cringe at the thought of walking past a sleeping bum in the middle of the night (*one-in-five girls raped, one-in-five girls raped*), but I have to turn this in. I have to keep walking.

There's a window open somewhere, there has to be, because I feel a draft tugging at my frostbitten ear, and I hear someone breathing, but I have to keep going, have to get across the bridge. In the light and the dark, it's bouncing up and down, rolling in the puddles of fluorescence, rocked by the wind and the snow, and I close my eyes and push myself forward. "Hello?" I don't know why I said it, but I did, like I actually want to wake this guy up or something. It only came out as a whisper, and I'm glad it did, but I can still hear it echoing through the empty building.

He says nothing.

"Excuse me?"

Oh God, why am I still saying things? But again he just lies there, and my bones are fighting against my muscles, but I force myself to keep walking. I have to turn this in. I'll just sneak by him, he won't even wake up, and then I'll go back to my room where it's warm and stay in bed for a week and never go outside in the snow with the hobos again. *Keep going.* My steps echo like my voice.

I step onto the skywalk.

I swear I feel it bouncing and swaying like a rope bridge. *That's crazy, it's part of the building, it's steel and it's concrete, it's safe.* Steps behind me. Eyes on me. Just echoes. Just imagination. *You're just scared.*

I run.

I push on the bouncing floor (hard), and jump forward into the light and the dark, and I charge for the end of the bridge, and it's miles away but I'm almost there, thinking *just keep looking forward,* but I glance at the bum and his eyes are both fixed on me, staring.

I scream.

I scream and I jump and my head hits the wall and my hands both reach out for the railing and catch only air and my skin rushes into the glass, but he doesn't move.

He's still sitting there. Just staring at me with eyes that don't move, and there's blood on his face and it runs down his beard and it's caked on his shirt. And bruises on his neck and cracks in the glass and the back of his head is flat, bashed in, bashed hard against the cracked glass, his mouth hanging open. New torn plaid flannel shirt, backpack, beard, jeans, he's a student. He's a student and he's staring at me with his dead eyes. I gasp for air, I'm trying to breathe, and the floor's getting closer, and my eyes still can't focus, and I don't want to fall, but I'm falling. I reach for the rail but I can't catch myself and I fall onto him, breathing in sweaty beard air and stuck on his eyes, his dead-opaque eyes that reach into me and won't let me go and I choke and I choke. I'm breathing in the hipster blood caked on the hipster beard, and I push him away and I'm tripping hard over his worn, checkered shoes, and I'm running and running.

Colors fly by. Yellows and whites and blacks and drips and clicks and echoes. The stairs and then the door, and I almost trip over the hood of the Jag parked outside, and the night flies by and the snow flies by, and the lamps and the sidewalk and the trees and the door, and I'm back in my dorm and I'm running up the stairs, halfway up the stairwell, and my face smashes into her gut.

We collide. She's on her way down, and I just knocked her over, almost knocked her over, but I grab her and catch her and it's my roommate and she says, "Are you sure you're all right?"

"No—yes—never mind—come with me, come with me right now!" I grab her by the hand, pulling her with me, and I'm running, we're running, down the stairs, and we're back outside and the snow's stopped now, and the air is cold and black and full of stars and a thousand tiny lights ignite the white on the ground. It glows white like a sun against a black sky, and you can see everything but I don't see anything except the glowing bridge at the top of the hill.

She tries to pull away but my hand squeezes tight and she says things like *Ow you're hurting me* and *What is this about* and *What the hell is wrong with you* but I don't even hear her. I'm running like we're being chased, and maybe we are, and all I can think about is showing her the thing, the guy, the dead guy. She's keeping up.

Then we're back at the door, the one where the coffee shop is, and I throw it wide open, the barista is gone, probably in the back doing inventory, and roomie is trying to stand in the heat of the vestibule, but I can't slow down, I pull her inside and upstairs. Six flights of echoes and sweat and her saying *Just tell me what's wrong,* and we come to the door and I throw it wide open and stop.

I stop dead.

Because he's gone.

The skywalk is empty. Just a hollow glass tube that buzzes with light like it always does and hangs in the night and the stars. I'm breathing big, silent gasps through my mouth, and I drop her hand, and I squint in the light that's burning my tears with its silence. My ears pop, and I feel the cold air leaking through the seam between the building and the bridge as I stumble out onto it and the emptiness rushes at me like a train.

I look at the floor, at the ceiling, trying to think, trying to understand. She's behind me now, touching my shoulder like we're friends. "What's wrong?"

"I—" and my voice cracks and I'm gasping again, and I see the crack in the glass out of the corner of my eye. It's still there. Still cracked. "I—"

"It's okay," she says. "Breathe." She stands there, awkwardly, hand on my shoulder, in pajamas. She's in her pajamas. I didn't notice till now.

"I—saw something."

"Yeah, I got that much."

"It was right here," I tell her. "It's gone now." I'm rubbing at my eye.

"What'd you see?"

"Um—" I suck in more breath. "It was a body. A dead guy."

"That's—that's a hell of a thing."

"What do I do? What do we do?"

"Uh—" and she steps away, half-shrugs, looking out at the stars like she's on the bridge of a spaceship.

"But we have to—I mean, we can't just—" I'm still gasping.

"Hey, hey, calm down," she says, hand on my shoulder again. "It's okay. There's nothing here."

"But I—saw—"

"Are you sure you're all right?" She's looking me in the eye now, hands on my shoulders, biting her lip, thinking *What did I just get dragged into?*

"Okay—" I tell her—"this isn't what you're probably thinking."

She inhales through her mouth and forgets to close it.

"I'm not stumbling around drunk at 4:30 in the morning."

"I didn't say you were."

"But you were thinking it."

"I wasn't thinking anything."

"I was up here not ten minutes ago, staring into the eyes of a corpse. I know that's—I know it's weird. I know it doesn't make any sense."

And she shrugs. "Okay."

"You believe me?"

She says, "I mean, why not, right? It's not like I have any real reason not to."

"So what do we do?" I ask her.

"Uh—with regard to—?"

"Should we tell someone? Call campus security? The police?"

"Who was it?"

"Huh?"

"The dead guy you saw. Who was it?"

"I—uh—I don't know. Some guy."

"And where did he go?"

"I...don't know."

She sighs, and leans against the window, pushing on the stars with her shoulder and rubbing her temples, processing everything. Finally: "What were you doing up here at four in the morning, anyway?"

"I, uh, had a—" And I realize my *Hamlet* paper, which I hadn't thought about since I saw those dead eyes, is still shoved up my shirt, soaked in snow and sweat. I reach in and pull it out into the light, and the ink is running, but it's readable. "I—*ugh.*"

"Oh my God," she says, "is that your *Hamlet* paper?"

"I—what? How would you know that?"

She laughs at me and says, "We're in the same class, Ophelia."

"Wait, really?"

Rolls her eyes. "It's fine, it's a big class. Don't worry about it."

"Okay."

She sighs. Long and loud. "God *damn* it," she says. "I've been waiting all *year* to have this conversation, and now I finally get the chance, and it's...it's *now.* Four-thirty in the morning, and I'm exhausted, and we're talking about a dead body that may or may not exist. I've been rehearsing this conversation for months, and I finally have the opportunity, and...and *damn it.*"

"What conversation?" I say.

"I just...look," she says. "I know this totally isn't the time, but I've been saving this up for months, so whatever: I've literally known who you were since our freshman year. We've had, like, a dozen classes together over the last five years, and I think you've said maybe ten words to me, total. And this year we're roommates, and the two of us might be the only fifth-year seniors living on campus, and you probably haven't even bothered to learn my name."

"Uh—"

"It's *on the door to our room*. You see it *literally a dozen times a day*."

"Uh—"

Sighs. "It's Kate," she says. "My name's Kate."

"Hi, Kate."

"Hi, Ophelia," she says, shaking my hand. "Can we start there? Good, we've met. Can our room not be awkward and silent and weird for the rest of the year, now?"

"Uh...sure."

"All right," she says. "All right. Good."

The wind is whistling in the crack in the glass.

And finally, she says, "Should we go turn your paper in?"

"Uh...okay."

She opens the door to the English building, and we both step into the dark.

The hallway lights are on a timer, which means they won't come on for another hour and there's nothing either of us can do about it. But slowly my eyes adjust, and I recognize the familiar forms of the English building, which looks about like you'd expect an English building to look: no concern for aesthetics and no money for new furniture. The hallway is filled with old desks and ragged bulletin boards and a sofa that's probably been sitting there since the '70s. In the shadows, they're all jagged parodies of themselves. The dark swallows both of us, till she's nothing but footsteps and a voice beside me.

"So..." she finally says. "'Intro to Shakespeare,' huh? I guess you put it off as long as you could, too, huh?"

"Haha, yeah. Just couldn't work up a ton of enthusiasm for lectures about what sonnets and iambic pentameter are—ow." I say *ow* because I just walked into that stupid couch.

"Oh my gosh, so much yes," she says. "Such a dreary class. So many bored freshmen, right?"

"And such a bored professor. Sometimes I wonder if he's channeling Ben Stein on purpose as a private joke."

She laughs. "*Yes. That.* That *must* be it.

"Someday," I tell her, "I'm going to raise my hand and start asking him a bunch of really smart questions just to throw him off. Something like *Is Romeo and Juliet really about the inescapability of fate? I'm pretty sure it's just about how dumb teenagers are.*"

She laughs. "Are we on the right floor?"

"I think it's one down," I tell her, and we start down the staircase, our footsteps echoing loud. Somewhere a faucet is dripping.

"Okay," she says, "so now that we're actually talking, can I ask you something that's been bugging me for years?"

"Uh—I guess?" I'm feeling the walls and the doors, trying to find the right office number.

"How do you get stuck with a name like *Ophelia,* anyway?"

"Ugh," I grunt. "My mother."

"Been some tension there, huh?—ow." (She just walked into a drinking fountain.)

I sigh. "Only recently. Anyway, she's a big Shakespeare nut. My dad insisted on a normal name for my older sister, but *she* complained for years that everyone had the same name as her. So when I showed up he shrugged and told my mom, *Okay, give her whatever weird name you want.* And so now, here I am, trapped in a world full of strangers who think it's hilarious to tell me to get myself to a nunnery—oh hey, here we are. This is his office."

I crouch down, feeling for the bottom of his door, cold dust on the floor tiles sucking the moisture from my hand.

"Awesome."

"What?" she says.

"There's a whole stack of papers jammed under here. I'll just slide mine in the middle, and he won't even know it was late."

The pages, clammy and floppy as they are, don't really slide in as well as I'd hoped, but I manage to jam them in.

I stand up. I exhale.

"Feel better?" she says.

"Uh, yeah. I actually do."

"Be able to sleep tonight?"

"Uh—" In the dark, it's hard to tell how much she's joking. I hesitate, I blink against the shadows. The adrenalin I was running on is winding down, and I find myself starting to sway.

"Here, why don't you lean on me?" she says, offering me her arm. "You've clearly been through a lot in the last hour."

And it's awkward, standing here in the pitch-dark with a girl I live with but barely know, her elbow jutting out toward me, rising and falling with breathing that I can hear. But it's cold in here and her arm is warm, so I take it.

"Can we just go out the main entrance?" she says.

"I wish. It's padlocked from the outside. We'll have to head back toward the skywalk."

She helps me up the stairs. And as we climb, she asks: "So, you and your mom don't get along?"

"Not lately."

"Over the name thing, or—?"

I laugh. "Nah. Nah, not that. She's just in the process of cutting me off, kicking me out, and—I dunno, I guess I'm just—I guess I'm just kind of scared of turning into her? Y'know?"

"Oh."

"It's just—" I say—"here I am on the verge of getting a useless English degree, no idea what I want to do with my life, and I look at her, and she's got a master's in British lit, and she's done literally nothing her whole life. She just sits all day in her mansion. It's what she's done as long as I've known her."

"Well, you don't have to be like that," she says.

"I mean, I guess not."

"All you have to do is choose to actually do something."

"In this job market?—ow." (I walked into the damn couch again.)

"I'm not talking about a *job*, Phelia. Not necessarily. What do you want to do with your life? What do you want to accomplish?"

I hesitate—I mean, I try to, but she's pulling me along, so my feet just drag on the tile. "I mean, I can tell you what I used to tell everyone when I was a freshman."

"Monster truck driver, right?"

"Well, obviously. No, I used to tell everyone that I wanted to be a writer."

"What English major doesn't?"

"Yeah, yeah, I know." The glow of the skywalk is getting closer, and I can't get my mind off what we might find when we get back there. Finally she says:

"Well, what do you want to write?"

"I—I don't know."

"Well—" she tries again—"what have you written in the past?"

"Nothing. Papers for classes. That soggy wad we just dropped off."

She laughs. We're at the door now, the one that leads back to the skywalk, and I can only see some cracks of light around its outline. She leans on it, casually, because she's not the one that just came face-to-face with a murder victim out there. Her permed dreadlocks catch the light as she runs her hand through them.

"I try to write sometimes," I tell her, "but I just end up staring at a blank page for hours."

"Been there," she says.

"Yeah?"

"Yeah. I used to be the most constipated writer in the world."

"Ew."

"Yeah."

"But you're not anymore?"

She inhales. Bites her lip. "Not so much, no."

"What changed?" I ask her.

She winces. "I—" clears her throat—"I don't think I'm ready to go into that with you right now. We just met. I'm not quite ready to unpack *that* particular load of baggage yet." She pauses with her hand on the door, black freckles lit up in the blade of light. "You ready?"

"Uh—"

And then before I can say anything she pushes the door open, the light rushes in and I bite my lip, recoil.

There's nothing there. Just like before.

That crack is still in the glass, splitting the stars, but even the stars themselves are fading into the start of a sunrise.

I exhale.

"We good?" Kate says, finally.

"I guess."

She says, "Listen, I have an early class, so I guess I should get going." Sighs. "Wish I'd gotten to sleep a little first." Smiles. "Nah, I guess the night wasn't a total waste of time. You know my damn name now, at least."

"Hey, Kate?"

"Yeah?"

"What do we do about the—y'know—"

"What? Oh! The—the body, right?"

"Yeah."

She says, "I mean, are you even sure you saw something? It was late, you just woke up—maybe you should just forget about it."

"I mean—you don't think we should—tell someone?"

She crosses her arms. Cocks an eyebrow. "Listen, Phelia. I've had some bad experiences with cops in my past. So if you call the police, just leave me out of it."

"...okay."

She laughs. "I mean, come on, though. You have literally no idea what you actually saw. If something's going on, the right people will find out, I'm sure."

"I mean, maybe."

"And *if* something's going on—I mean—do you really want to get involved?"

"Uh—" and I pause, scratching the back of my neck, because I hadn't thought about it that way. She actually has a point. I'm just beginning to try to juggle a full-time work schedule and a full course load. I've got graduation, Sara's experiment, my mother to deal with. With my schedule and my stress already at the breaking point—"I guess not," I tell her. "Yeah, you're right. I'll let someone else worry about it."

"All right," she says. "Cool." And she's walking away, headed back toward the stairs.

I'm about to follow when she pauses, looks back, pulls something out of her pocket. It's a piece of paper, lime green, folded twice, and she's messing with it, debating.

"Listen," she says. "You might be interested in this." And she hands it to me.

"What is it?"

"You can read it for yourself," she says.

But now the sun's coming up, chasing the stars to the west and then out of the sky.

"Anyway," she says, "I need to get to class."

And she walks the rest of the way across the bridge, and I stumble after her.

thurs. jan. 13.
4:55 pm.
pensive

**It's only now that I'm realizing** what a strange night that was.

Not just in the obvious ways. Like, clearly, I didn't leave my room in the middle of a snowstorm thinking I was about to stumble onto a corpse. So *that's* not what I'm talking about.

And it's not so much that I think I imagined the whole thing. I can still see his dead eyes, smell his mothball breath, feel his moist beard on my face. I know the difference between dreams and reality. A dream was that thing with *Hamlet*. A dream can feel real at the time, and maybe even for a while after you wake up, but eventually you realize that *Oh, that made no sense, that contradicts everything I know, I think the laws of physics work a little different from that.* I know what I saw, and if it was a prank, it was a pointlessly elaborate one.

So no, that's not what's bothering me.

What keeps bugging me about the whole thing—what I can't get out of my head—is how my roommate reacted. She was all like *I believe you,* but then she wanted to just leave things like that. Don't normal people freak out about that sort of thing? All she wanted to do was calm me down. She wanted to spend the night chatting instead of freaking out, or calling the cops, or—I don't know? Literally anything else?

So really, there are only a handful of possibilities here.

Maybe she didn't actually believe me and she was just trying to calm me down because she thought I was nuts. But if that were the case, it seems like she should have been trying to get me back towards a well-lit, populous area, not following me into a dark, deserted hallway.

The second possibility is that what she said was true—that she did believe me, but didn't really see the point of doing anything about it. Like I said, though, that's a strange way to react.

No, the only possibility that makes much sense is that she was somehow responsible for the body being there. That she's a murderer. I admit that that presents some problems—like how she had time to hide the thing and then get back to the dorm before I did. And also, I kind of doubt she would have had the strength to slam a guy that size against the wall. But maybe she didn't actually commit the murder; maybe she just knows whoever did it and was covering for them?

I'm overthinking this.

I'm overthinking it because there's nothing else to do right now. I'm sitting in class, and it's that boring Shakespeare 101 one we were talking about that night, the one that Kate said she was in. I don't see her here tonight, though. Honestly, I haven't seen her basically at all since yesterday morning. I think she's been avoiding me. Which is weird.

I mean, not that weird, since the other night was the first time she'd ever really talked to me. But, y'know, still.

"One of the key themes of *Hamlet* is the Oedipal complex."

Oh geez, here we go. Professor Ben Stein is rattling off the clichés they've been teaching about Shakespeare for almost a century. The usual load of bullshit psychobabble that nobody buys anymore, except for English professors.

"The Oedipal complex, for those of you who have yet to take a psychology course, is the innate desire said to be in every young male to kill his father and marry his mother."

I'm thinking about what I was saying to Kate the other night. That I should ask a smartass question just to see his reaction.

"In this scene between Hamlet and Gertrude, we see there are geysers of repressed sexuality bubbling beneath the surface—"

I raise my hand.

"Uh—" he stops and gives me that deer-in-the-headlights look. Shock and disbelief because no one ever raises their hand, no one ever asks questions, no one ever says anything in this class. "I'm sorry, do you—do you have a—"

"Yeah, uh—isn't the Oedipal complex something that Freud just made up in 1910? How would Shakespeare have known about it 300 years before that?"

It's a softball question, something just to get things moving. But even this one makes him stutter. "Uh—yeah—well, Miss—"

"Electra. My name's Electra." It's a big class. I'm not risking anything at all by giving him a (hilarious) fake name.

He raises an eyebrow, but he doesn't question it. "Well, Electra, it's true that Freud didn't describe the Oedipal complex until 1910, but that's not quite the same thing as saying the Oedipal complex didn't *exist* until 1910."

"But Freud never provided any evidence for it, either—" I just interrupted him, not on purpose, but he jumped when I did it, and I'm trying not to laugh—"and modern psychology has discredited it. There's no reason to believe in the Oedipal complex, and there never has been."

Heads are turning. This is fun. I haven't been the center of attention like this in a long time. I'm hot and flushed, and I pull off my hoodie.

"Um, well—you're right about that, Electra, that mainstream psychology rejects the idea of the Oedipal complex, but it remains a recurring theme in literature—"

"Yeah, but I mean, do writers keep using it because it's a real thing, or just because they're lazy writers?"

"Um—"

"I mean, I'm just saying—you can name all kinds of works that turn on Freudian ideas, but almost all of them are from the last century. In other words, they were written *after* Freud's ideas became popular. I mean, obviously writers will use ideas that are *already* popular. It's easy. It's lazy. But besides *Hamlet* and, y'know, *Oedipus,* is there any evidence that the trope really resonated with anyone prior to 1911 or so?"

"Um—well—" I'm guessing that at some point in his career, he probably would have had an answer for these questions, but he's been on autopilot for so long that any question at all would have caught him completely off-guard. I feel bad for the guy. No, really. Teaching Shakespeare to a room full of engineering and pre-med majors is bitch work.

Wait, is it my imagination, or are there eyes on me? Like, not in just the *Stop wasting my time* way, but in sort of a positive way?

I look down and I remember that I'm just wearing a wifebeater, my bra straps sticking out underneath. And I don't look bad, either. I'm only down ten pounds or so—probably mostly water weight, I guess—but that's honestly pretty amazing for only a few days on the drug.

I mean, don't get me wrong, I'm still kind of a lardass, but I've lost some of the bloat, and it makes a huge difference. Not that I *really* care, obviously. I'm not shallow, but it's nice not to be so puffy. My boobs almost stick out as much as my gut now, which I'm pretty sure is the look they're seeking after for the Paris runways, right? Okay, I'm not quite what boys drool over (yet), but I think I could, eventually, potentially, be "hot."

I always figured that the hot girls of the world probably went home every day and stripped down to their lacy, expensive lingerie and stood there, admiring themselves in the mirror, thinking about how easy life is when your boobs and your ass are both the right size. And then they'd pull out their little pocket planners (because people use those) filled with lists of all the boys they were stringing along, and they'd laugh to themselves evilly (and hotly) and make little red marks in the margins.

So that's something I have to look forward to.

"Don't you agree, Electra?"

"What? Uh—" Crap. I got lost in my thoughts, and now he's caught *me* off guard.

"You agree?"

"Uh, absolutely." *I'll get you next time, Ben Stein. Next time.*

"Okay, then. For next week, read the last act, and we'll discuss it on Tuesday."

Everybody shrugs, grabs their bags, and heads toward the door, and I guess I should too. I have to go to work.

It occurs to me that I've barely eaten anything in the last 48 hours (thanks, Sara), and I'm about to pull a 12-hour shift, so I should probably try to choke something down. There's a snack machine right outside the door to the lecture hall, so I plunk in a few quarters.

I stand there. And look.

Everything inside is cold and sterile and not-real-food, wrapped in colorful plastic. Dry, dead plastic made from dinosaurs that everyone forgot about a billion years ago. Dead dinosaurs wrapped around salty fatty sugar that makes your blood vessels swell. Fatty salty sugar that people halfway around the world are fighting wars for so they can sell it to Americans and kill them with it. The fluorescent lights are a million times brighter than the sun and make the wrappers glow like a pukey rainbow.

I tell my brain that food is a good thing, that I have to eat it, that if I don't eat it I'll die, but it's no good.

*You have a 12-hour shift ahead of you. Eat SOMETHING.*

Ugh.

I steel my will and I punch in the code for a Snickers because everybody likes Snickers because Snickers satisfies, or something. I watch the spiral of twisted black wire turn and *clink* and *pop,* and the Snickers wobbles back and forth and stirs the air up with disgusting chocolatey fumes, till it slips and groans free of its little track and it hits the floor with a sick *thud* just like a body would.

I stick my hand in the slot, and it bites down on my arm, and I have to fish around until I find the log, and by the time I wrap my fingers around it, my arm is starting to bruise, or at least it feels like it. And I pull it out of the blinding, snack-selling light and tear the wrapper down the middle with a swipe of my nails.

I stare at it.

Just a brown, squarish blob in my hand, like a carefully machined piece of crap, forming tiny beads of sweat that dance iridescent colors in the off-white lights and mock my churning stomach.

*It's just chocolate.*

*And nuts. And caramel.*

*And "nougat," whatever the hell that is.*

I'm staring it down and swallowing sawdust while I climb the stairs and step outside and trudge through the half-melted snow to my car that's waiting against the curb down the block. I almost walk into a half-dozen people who roll their eyes at me because I'm acting so strange, but I can't take my eyes off the chocolate because it takes all of my concentration not to throw it away.

*You have to eat it. Quit putting it off.*

I take a few seconds to stab my key into the lock, adding some new scratches to the little sunburst around the keyhole. Then I pull it open with the hand that's holding my keys because my other one is busy hanging onto my Chocolate Oppressor. I slide into the seat and I somehow get the keys into the ignition and I start the car rolling forward, but I can't take my eyes off the ugly brown thing sucking the oxygen from the air.

I stop at a light, and the Snickers glows a moist, snowy red, while it slowly melts into a nutty sludge. I need to eat it because I need to get rid of it before my car smells like cheap, oily chocolate forever. So I close my eyes and I open my mouth, and I pull my lips back so they won't touch it, and my teeth sink into sticky, chunky slime, and I gag, but I push them together as hard as I can till they scrape against each other and the sound echoes through my skull.

Then the chocolate flashes green because the light has changed and I'm supposed to drive forward. My tongue is still kneading against the orphaned candy bar tip, and it sticks to the back of my teeth and I'm scared to chew.

I hit the gas.

I hit it too hard and now I'm flying along the empty street, but the sad, melty bar with its tip bitten off is still staring at me with its gooey nuts, accusing and angry and daring me to make a circumcision joke. *God*, I have to chew this.

It's awful. Like wallpaper paste mixed with the hairballs of a syphilitic cat. And it turns into goo that refuses to melt, and swells till it fills my mouth and sticks to my teeth and my gums and my tongue. It digs in and foams in every gap and crevice till my mouth is glued shut and tastes like charcoal and mucus. I choke and forget how to breathe, and the next thing I know, my window's half-down, and the Snickers flies out, onto the street, half-melted, half-chewed. It lands in the gutter, and sits there, flying behind me, as I hit the curb and jerk the wheel. And I choke again and my tongue rolls around in the strands of burning caramel till it gags its way down my throat and I slam on the brakes because somehow I made it to the parking lot at the hospital.

I'm here.

I step out and slam my car door behind me, and the gray sky's turned black and the air's turned to ice, and the stars that aren't hidden by clouds drip silver light everywhere. My mouth is coated in grainy, sugary salt that won't go away no matter how hard I swallow. I breathe the winter air in deep gasps, trying to flush it away, but the dryness only clings tighter. I can't see my breath in the cold.

My phone is beeping.

It's a text from Sara: "dnt 4get 2 cm down"

*From the Cloud comes a low, ugly growl—*
*My sister's IT skills are foul.*
*I don't need blinking lights,*
*Or a lacy invite,*
*But CHRIST, I'm at least worth a vowel.*

That one was pretty good. Call *The New Yorker* and tell them to stop the presses.

Actually, I'm kind of looking forward to a few minutes with Sara. Not that we ever have anything to talk about, but at least she's something familiar. In a week as bizarre as this one, something you've known for years can be a comfort, even if it's not something you're crazy about. And I shared a room with her for what, ten years? So 20 minutes with her feels like an oasis between that corpse and a 12-hour shift of pushing sick people around.

*We used to tell each other everything. Maybe I can tell her about...*

So I'm honestly feeling okay, considering, or at least that's what I tell myself as I force my temporary ID through the floppy scanner, jerk the door open, and take the elevator down to the second basement. Then the door jerks open to reveal a pair of red-glowing eyes and a grin and I jump.

"God, Oaf, don't be such a spaz."

I guess I'm on edge because it's just Sara's eyes, reflecting the glow of an *Exit* sign, and all I can think is that *No one has said "spaz" since, like, 1993.* "I—"

She rolls her eyes, and the red glint stays still while her pupils dance around in it. Then she says "Come on," and I follow her down the red-painted hall to the morgue.

"Can you get the door?" she says. "My hands are full." She's carrying a stack of books.

"I'll need your ID..."

"Nah, just use yours. The temporary badges open pretty much every door in the hospital."

"Seriously?"

"Yeah, I know, it's a huge security flaw. IT says they're on it, but from what I hear they've been on it for like five years now, and since IT is really just one old guy named Larry, not much ever actually gets done. If I were you, I'd hang onto the temp ID as long as I could. Never know when you'll need extra medical supplies."

She's joking, at least I think, and I don't want to know if she isn't. "Okay, then." I swipe my badge and I hear a *click* and I follow Sara through the door. She leads me down the gauntlet of toe tags, and it's dark like before. I ask her, "Don't you ever turn the lights on down here?"

She says, "Occasionally. When I'm working in the morgue. But I'm cloistered in my office a lot, so I figure, *save some energy,* right?"

"I guess."

"But anyway, things move pretty slow around here. Bodies come in and there's a butt-ton of paperwork before I can even start on them, and then once I have them ready, there's another butt-ton of paperwork before I can ship them out."

"I'd think they would want to get rid of a bunch of festering dead bodies as quickly as possible."

"Um, excuse you. My bodies *do not* fester. And yeah, you'd think so, but no. Think of it as a metaphor. You English majors like those, right? Metaphors?"

"A metaphor for what?"

"I dunno. Death, purgatory, whatever. You live for a little while, and you get dropped into the dark forever, and you're just stuck there, and you can't do anything about it, and nobody cares."

"Deep."

"Whatever," she says, dropping her books on an empty body table and jamming a key into her office door. "Not all of us spend every waking minute studying metaphors, all right? Get off your high horse, Oaf."

I really wanted to say *Speaking of death...* but now I can't. I don't normally tell her things, but I have to tell someone (anyone) about the body (those eyes, in my memory, I have to let them out...). But now I can't. It's something about that word *Oaf.* She's always called me that, ever since we were little. And I used to assume it was short for *Ophelia,* till I learned to use a dictionary and looked it up, and found out it meant *a clumsy, stupid person, a lout, a blockhead*—or in the archaic sense, *a mentally deficient child,* or even, weirdly, *a changeling.* Then I rehearsed for days, and I worked up the nerve, and I asked her to stop, and when I did, she leaned in close, eyes narrowed, and put her sharp nails on my arm and said *Stop what?* And I sat there, studying her face, watching her breathe, and searching my insides for strength I never found, and that's when I realized that somehow she had gotten inside me.

But these are just images. Jumbles of nonsense disguised as memories. None of it is real, it's just electrons swirling in my brain. Nothing is real right now except her hand on the key twisting 90 degrees clockwise and the clanking sound that it makes, like the elevator door, but smaller and louder. Nothing except the orange glow of the exit sign falling onto the tile floor and twisting up the table legs and over the dead people stuck here in purgatory. And she pushes me into her office and makes me step on the scale, and she nods with a smile and tells me she's happy to know that it's working. Then she bites her lip and says, "Have a seat."

I sit on her desk, and my stubby legs swing above the orange rug, and the single dangling light bulb is right behind my head, casting dark shadows on the closed door. She stands in the shadow, blocking the exit, depressing my tongue, sticking a stethoscope up my shirt. My heart shudders when I feel her cold steel.

She picks up the clipboard, one of those ugly brown particleboard ones that would go perfect with an orange hardhat, and she picks up a yellow wooden pencil and licks it with a tongue that darts out of her mouth and says, "Let's talk."

"Um—okay."

She stands there, eyeing me for a second, and finally says, "Well, how do you feel?"

"Uh—" *I'm freaking out, I saw a body, and it disappeared, and I can still feel its cold, sweaty beard on my face, and—* "fine, I guess."

"No hunger?"

"Not really. I'll tell you about my adventure with a Snickers bar sometime."

"What happened?"

"Um—nothing. Nothing, really. I tried to eat a Snickers on the way here, and it was disgusting. I can't get the awful taste out of my mouth."

"What's it taste like?"

"Um—seriously? I dunno, it's salty, and chemical-y, and cottony, and just really dry and gross. Why?"

"Just curious. Okay, what else? You feel okay physically? Still alert? Still energetic?"

"I guess. Do I seem alert and energetic?"

"As much as ever." Checks some stuff off on her clipboard. "Any feelings of anger or paranoia?"

"Why would I have feelings of anger or paranoia?" I'm thumbing the folded-up flier in my pocket. It's smooth and it's thick and chartreuse like my scrubs.

"It's just a question."

"I—well—maybe?" I'm folding it, unfolding it, looking over the printing. Black ink with a mottled sheen from a laser printer. A jumble of letters and shapes. Names and tomorrow's date and a bit of ironic clip art that probably looked like something before a dozen Xeroxings.

"What's that?"

My hand jerks to shove it back in my pants, but she's grabbing it away and holding it in the light, reading the words that I can see projected backwards. *FOLK NIGHT.* The name of a coffeehouse. Kate's name, followed by three others in a smaller font. Tomorrow's date and *8PM.* "It's nothing. Just something my roommate gave me."

She's picking at it with her perfectly manicured nails. Its giant green shadow shakes on the wall and her face flickers in the orange twilight. And she finally hands it back and says, "Lame."

"What? How is it lame?"

"A wannabe singer-songwriter going around, handing out fliers? What is this, the '60s?" She folds it up and slides it back into my pocket. "I can't stand people who are walking advertisements for themselves."

"It really wasn't like that."

"No?" She leans on the wall, crosses her arms, raises an eyebrow.

"Well—no." (But now I wonder if it was.) "She gave this to me as friend. Said that it was about writing. And how she learned to. And that it would help me—or—or something." This isn't coming out right, but then, why do I feel the need to defend either one of us?

"*God,* right? So she's Walt-fucking-Whitman? There's never any shortage of artists forcing their mediocrities on the world, is there?"

"Sara, why are you being like this?"

"I don't know. Rough day, I guess. You're not going, are you?"

"I mean, I was on the fence."

"Good. Stay on the fence. Good plan."

"Nah, y'know what?" I say, suddenly filled with inexplicable determination. "I think I will." And I get up and walk right past her and reach for the doorknob, but it sticks and I can't make it work, and I'm fumbling.

She pushes on the door above my head and it pops wide open and I stumble out into her morgue. Then the door closes and I'm alone.

# thurs. jan. 13.
## 7:03 pm.
## and then suddenly

There's shit everywhere.

I'm retracing my steps, the last seven seconds, the last three minutes, that led to this moment where I'm staring at a shit stain the size of a room, a starburst on the floor made of ass-juice and farts, and a nurse in the center who's drenched head-to-toe in the brown, with contempt in her eyes and a hand that's suddenly empty.

*Stay out of their way. That's all you had to do.*

And now, here we are. The bedpan I bumped sitting inverted on the floor, and everything streaked with the brown and the green and the yellow it used to contain. The TV is filling the room with bleeps from Gordon Ramsay's swears, and their eyes are on the brown and their eyes are on me, while the patient moans softly in her bed. We're supposed be moving her now, and she's laying there while we all just stand here and stare at each other and wish that I'd stayed the hell out of the room or my elbow had stayed at my side or my foot hadn't slipped or I'd just called in sick and I'd stayed in my bed for the evening and nothing involving my elbow, my foot, or my unbridled knack for just clumsily fucking things up had ever happened tonight.

And it's too late now. Too late for any of that.

Rachel's mouth's hanging open (she can't be all that surprised, right?), and my eyes trace her curves from her chin to her hips, where she changes from green into brown, and from there it's a blur where the line between her and the swamp of the floor is. All three of us look like we're mushrooms that grew in a mud puddle, legs splayed and standing in terror of what we've become, with flecks in our hair and our noses and eyes.

"I—" That little noise from my throat would have been some real words, except now there's no air in my lungs and my heart has stopped beating, I think. My run-and-hide instinct has kicked in, and all I can think is *Get out of this room.*

A dumb thing to do. Such a dumb thing to do. It'd be one thing if I were the one with the bedpan, or I'd had a reason to be in the room, or I were the nurse or the patient or anything else, but I'm no one at all. Just a charity case with no skills who has no right to be here, and I tripped through the door and then elbowed a bedpan, and shit's everywhere, and the smell is like nothing that's ever existed outside of a prison latrine.

"Well—" Rachel finally says, forcing the words through her throat—"Why don't you get a—"

I run.

I can't help it. I slip in the muck, and I push past the doorframe (I'm banging my elbow, again), and I half-slide-half-stumble through over-bright lights, just trying to outrun the stench of my failure, and gasping and choking on fumes made of vomit. I'm sure they're all staring and probably laughing, but I don't know what else to do, so I run. Brown globs spread out like a thick trail of breadcrumbs behind me, and I'm reaching out with my eyes both shut tight, pushing everyone out of my way, till my hands feel a door that somebody left open. I'm diving inside, and I slam it shut (tight), and I'm left all alone in the dark with my smell.

I'm in a closet.

It's one of those janitor closets filled with smelly mops and buckets and one of those cold, dirty concrete floors with a rusty drain in it. And I can feel the bile coming up in my throat, so I lean over the gigantic sink and let it pour out of my mouth. In the dark it slaps against the cheap fiberglass and flecks splash into my hair and it burns my nostrils. And I cough and I sputter and collapse on the floor. And I let the rusty concrete pull the heat from my pounding heart away. And I breathe.

I feel around.

I'm groping for a light switch, but there isn't one. Then I'm hugging my knees, hugging them tight, rocking back and forth on the floor, like a crazy person.

I can't stop thinking. I can't stop thinking about the classroom, the one with the bulletin boards covered in colored paper and the parts of speech, what a noun was, and what a verb was. How I sat observing for hours and hours while Mrs. Swift went over a grammar lesson and they talked about *The Outsiders* and I thought to myself *This looks easy.* Then I finally got up in front of the classroom, and I don't even remember what I said the first nine or ten times, but she buried me under a list of complaints that made no sense. But I kept standing up at the front of the room, telling them what a verb is, a noun is, an adjective is. Until one day she left me alone in the room, teaching all by myself in a roomful of sociopaths. *We're going to talk about poems,* I said, and I showed them a dozen, all in different formats, and said, *Now you try one,* but all of them wanted to only write limericks. I said to the girl in the front row, *Let's try something else,* but she told me no. And I said to her *Wouldn't you like to learn something that's new?* and she said, *No, just leave me alone.* I said *Just read this poem, I think you could do something like it,* and she told me *Why don't YOU read it if you really like it so much?* and all of kids in the room started laughing at me. And I said *Read it now, or I'll go get the principal,* and everyone laughed at me harder and harder. And then one of them, the boy in the back row, got out of his seat. I said *Why are you up?* and he said *I don't know,* and he pulled all the nouns off the walls. And I said *What is wrong with you, why are you all such idiots?* and the girl in the front row said *What's wrong with you, you're the idiot, you can't even teach us anything, and you wear the same stupid outfit every day, and you're fat and you're ugly,* and they all laughed at me again. And I said *Why are you so mean?* and she looked me right in the eye and said *Fuck you,* and I cried.

So many mistakes.

*There once was this failed student teacher*

66 ~ Luke T. Harrington

*Whose resolve just got weaker and weaker,*
*And she lay there and cried*
*While her third career died,*
*And considered becoming a...*
     *I dunno, a streaker?*
          *A motivational speaker?*

God, limericks are *so hard*.

Tears mingle with shit and it all flows down the rusty drain next to my head. And then I hear him say, *Hey, get up.* (What?) *Get up.* I feel the ghost of a shoe, an untied boot, nudging me so gently that I almost wouldn't notice, but I look up and through the tears and the dark I see a face like a hipster lumberjack that's somehow familiar. Long greasy hair and a beard and a red flannel shirt and he's saying *Get up.* And I say to him, *But I don't think that I can, I can't go on, and there's nothing out there I can possibly do.* And he looks in my eyes and he says *You belong here,* and I tell him *What? No I don't, I'm a writer.* But then he reminds me that *You've never written a word. So maybe just think about doing the job that's in front of you now.* I say *I could do so much better,* and he says *But now it's not time for that, Ophie.* Then he takes my muddy hand and he turns on the faucet for me and he says *It's time to work.* I say, *I don't want to, I can't,* and he says, *I know, but it doesn't matter. There's work to be done.* I tell him that's the most depressing thing I've ever heard and he says *Maybe it is, but we're here now, and we have to clean up the shit, because if we don't, things will keep being shitty. Everyone will get sick and it will be all your fault.* And so as he finishes rinsing my hair, I say, *I understand and I'm ready to go out and fix things,* but then the doors open and my eyes are burning from the fluorescent light.

"Ophelia?"

"Um—what?" I squint, trying to recognize faces and shapes in the flood of bluish yellow.

"Are you all right?" It's Rachel again, standing there and smacking her gum like she's trying to kill it.

"Something—about—what? Why?"

"You're sitting in a utility closet talking to a mop."

"Um—no—I was talking to—" but that doesn't make even a little bit of sense. There was someone in here, but he's a mop now. Leaning against the wall, greasy, and covered in a beard of dustbunnies. My head is throbbing.

"To be honest, I thought you were just kind of dumb, but now I'm wondering if you're schizo as well." Looking at me sideways, half-concerned. "Anyway, I came here to get the mop, since I had no idea where you wandered off to." She reaches past me and strangles the mop I was talking to, then drags it down the hall.

I chase her.

"Hey, wait, I was going to—I mean, I was about to—I was in there because—" I can't keep up, she's too fast. "Wait—I can—" I hate myself for stammering. And being so damn slow.

"*What?*" She's stopped now, turned around, looking me in the eye. Her pupils are black, and she's stopped chewing her gum, her jaw frozen halfway between open and closed. Breathing through her mouth. Flipping her hair.

"I was about to—"

"*About to?* About to." She's got her hands up now, somewhere in between shrugging, rubbing her temples, and strangling me. "*Uggh*—listen—" She stops, rolls her eyes, and bites her lip with her gum hanging out.

"What?"

"Ugh..." Crosses her arms. "Do you know where the child psychology wing is?"

"Um—no."

She gestures with her head toward a staircase down the hall. "Two floors up at the end of the building. Take the stairs, turn left."

And for a second she just stands there, like I'm supposed to know exactly what to do with that information. She breathes through her gum, and then remembers to add: "Listen, they took one of our gurneys earlier today, and we need it back. You wanna go grab it? And take it back to the dispatch room? Please?"

"I—okay. You're doing this just to get rid of me for a few minutes, aren't you?"

"Good call. Get moving." She walks off.

"Wait—who do I talk to when—" but she's gone, a million miles down the hall, practicing her swears.

I turn around and start walking.

And I'm glad.

Glad that I don't have to face that room again, glad that I can get a few minutes to myself, even if it's just to walk upstairs and get a stretcher.

Or a gurney. She said a gurney.

What's the difference?

*Damn it.* Not only am I unable to do my job without splattering shit everywhere, I don't even know the difference between a gurney and a stretcher. *That's, like, lesson one of patient transport. I'm the worst patient transporter ever.*

*(You're fired, Oaf.)*

I can't let that happen. I need to stay here, in a job, getting paid, need to finish my degree and write books and get published, need to show them all they were wrong.

I can do that. I can. Focus.

Sara told me she'd keep me employed if I took her dumb drug, and I'm taking it daily, the way that she told me to. So I guess I'm okay, except—

Actually, she said she *would* get me fired if I *didn't* take it. She didn't actually make any promises to keep me around if I *did*. Those are two different things, I guess.

I've the found the stairwell now, so I pull open the door and start climbing, slowly. Like most stairwells, it's a bland, yellowish echo chamber, perpetually empty because everyone is lazy and uses the elevators, and somehow it's quiet and loud at the same time. I listen to each dull slap from my feet fill the emptiness, amplified by the endless space above and below me. I start climbing even slower, listening to each tiny sound, because the longer I take on this task, the longer I can avoid work.

But I can't make the climb take forever, and soon I find myself at the top, staring down a heavy steel door the same color as the yellow-white walls. It's slightly ajar; it's the sort of door that's always too swollen to close and makes you wonder who designed it and hope he got fired. It doesn't want to move, but I squeeze through.

There's a giant, empty hall up here, one that looks like hardly anyone ever passes through it. The floor is immaculately polished like it's never been walked on, and the reflections from the lights overhead are bobbing up and down in waves. And across the hall from me, across the empty expanse of tile, is a wall covered with the faces of sponsors. Old, decrepit people with so much money that they decided to give it to a hospital, because why not make a sincere effort to cheat death? A grid of grinning half-dead (all-dead?) faces, with smiles that started flaking even as they were painted.

The hallway is so empty that it takes me a minute to figure out which way I'm supposed to go. For a moment I'm distracted by a library in the distance off to my right, a room filled with books and devoid of people. Through the dusty glass, I can make out stacks and stacks of bound volumes of medical journals, all in the same color, and a front counter that's covered in an inch of dust. A thousand medical articles, written over millions of hours, stacked on dusty shelves and never looked at.

Maybe the library is open sometimes, but now it's dark, and I wonder how often anyone climbs up those nosebleed stairs, just to read something that was outdated by the time it was printed. Twenty feet below are rooms full of people dying, and these books were here before they were born, and they'll still be here after they die, and probably never get opened.

I turn away. I have to focus.

Even if I've been sent on a snipe hunt, I may as well catch a snipe. There's a door in the distance, in the other direction, a plain beige door with no knob and a dull red sign that says CHILD PSYCHOLOGY, and I half-wonder why they hide the crazy kids all the way up here, away from all the other patients, behind a door that's four feet wide, with no knob.

I can't decide how to open it.

My first instinct is to knock, but of course my knuckles strike solid concrete and a shooting, silent pain rattles through them. They're swelling now, turning red, and I punch the door with them to punish myself for being so stupid.

(Sigh.)

It's only at this point (of course) that I notice the ID scanner, one of those magnetic stripe things that are everywhere in this place, hanging floppy from a handful of wires. And Sara says that my temporary ID will open pretty much any door, so I guess it's worth a try. I hold the thing steady with one hand and grind my card through with the other. It sticks, and I have to go back and forth several times to get it to work.

*HAL, open the pod bay doors.*

There's a sort of clunky-clicky noise, and the thing opens. I half-expected to see light spilling out, but there's only darkness behind it. Inside, behind my slightly ajar, concrete-filled nemesis, I can see a dark corridor that leads past several empty, unlit offices. And beyond that is yet another door, a glass one that says CHILD PSYCHOLOGY, in case I couldn't read the one out here, I guess.

The glass is frosted, but I see a light behind it. I don't hear any sound or voices, but I guess it's where I need to go. It's a short hallway, but the thick darkness makes it feel longer. Each empty office is dark and bare, with ancient, beige computers and greasy phones. Wires splayed across the desks, walls missing their posters, chips in the paint from old Scotch Tape.

Then I find my hand on the blackish handle on the glowing door, the one that says CHILD PSYCHOLOGY, and behind it I have no idea what to expect. A bunch of crazy kids, I guess. The hallway is cold but I steel myself and I yank. And the door *wooshes* by my face and almost hits me in the head because I wasn't paying attention.

In front of me is an empty room.

Well—mostly. It's mostly empty. Some of those ugly floor tiles of ambiguous color (off-white with flecks of everything) that you see on the floor of almost every room; a flimsy table with some of that awful-but-tolerable fake woodgrain; one guy seated at it. A massive mountain of a man half-drowning in his own manboobs. Seated awkwardly on one of those tiny plastic chairs with a square hole in the back, the ones that nobody likes to sit in but you still see them stacked everywhere, because they're cheap, I guess. He doesn't fit in it and his enormous butt is spilling over the sides. And the room is cold, but there are large beads of sweat running down the sides of his fat, shaved head, bouncing in between the spikes of stubble, while his eyes run up and down me and he twitches.

Behind him, around the room's perimeter, are heavy steel doors, each with a tiny window a third of the way up. They're covered in a wire mesh like the windows of the library, and they're dark, but I can still see in, and there's a small pair eyes in each one. Children's eyes, each pair staring out from a cubicle of thick darkness into the endlessly glowing room. No faces, just eyes—eyes that don't move or blink or smile.

One fat man, doing nothing, ringed by dozens of scared eyes, in a room that's too bright.

"Can I help you?"

Manboobs said it. It's not unfriendly, he doesn't mean it to be unfriendly, he's just asking, and I try to look in his eyes but I can't, and my words catch on the edge of my teeth, and they won't come out. I think I hear a rattling, like a latched door trying to open, jerked weakly by a hand that's too small. In the corner of my eye, a light flickers.

"Can I help you?" He says it again, and I'm backing toward the door and don't even know why. The eyes are familiar, but that's crazy, I can barely see them, they're behind blue glass, like they're underwater (drowning). "Are you new? You look familiar—"

Against the wall. I see it. The gurney, just sitting there, with its wheels out. It looks heavy, but my arm feels strong.

"You *are* new, right?" He's getting up, his greasy hands pushing against the table, and my heart is pounding. Why? I can't relax—

I run. I bolt toward the gurney, and I feel my hand latch onto the cold, steel handle, I yank, and I run, and it's dragging behind me. I run down the hallway through the darkness and toward the heavy door, while the gurney punches holes in the wall, and I'm not even sure how I get past it, but then everything's behind me and the door is closed and I'm in the bright, always-on light of the hospital hallway, but I can't slow down.

I tear past the faces, the library, everything, till I find the elevator and pound on the down arrow over and over and over. The door finally opens and I jerk the gurney on and I can't start breathing again till the doors are closed tight behind me.

I'm alone.

I lean on the gurney, heavy, cradling my head in my hands, gasping loud. My face is burning and I can't decide why. All it was was some eyes, some doors, a fat guy. It's sad, sure—those kids locked away. But it's for their own good. There's no reason for me to be reacting this way. The gasping, the panic. The way that I ran. It makes no sense.

I can't do this.

The elevator dings open, in the first basement, where dispatch is.

And everyone down here who was waiting for the elevator is staring at me now, their faces uncomfortable and ashen and awkward, unsure whether they should get on or stay off, say something or stay silent. *Who is this kid hunched over a gurney, her makeup running down her face and her hair falling out of her ponytail, gasping for breath and choking on the fart-filled elevator air?*

That's what they're all thinking.

I choke on my throat trying to breathe as I blow past them, dragging my half-shiny, janky-wheeled companion behind me. The gurney jumps and sputters, catching on the occasional crooked tile, and the lights are flying by over my head. I see the blue room with its Elvis dartboard out of the corner of my eye, but I just keep running, without even thinking, faster and faster, till I'm out the door entirely, and I crash into a hedge, dragging the gurney in, and collapse on the ground in a pile of leaves. They're cold and they're wet and it's dark but I don't care.

And I'm shaking.

I can't do this.

This is stupid. Am I six years old? A six-year-old hiding in the bushes because she's too scared? I'm looking up through the leaves now, at the stars glowing an angry shade of so-white-it's-almost-yellow, thinking *Get up. Take the gurney to dispatch. You still have half a shift left.*

But then I don't.

And all I can do is sit in the wet leaves, squeezing the bars of the gurney till my palms ache, crying. And I cry until my shift's over, while the stars flicker in between the leaves.

And then I go home.

## fri. jan. 14.
## 7:37 pm.
## numb

I open my eyes and I'm in my bed, staring at the ceiling. It's a cheap dorm-room bed that's so low I might as well be laying on the floor, except the bed is a tiny bit softer, so there's that, I guess. All my pillows are on the floor, and my head is wedged between a couple of wadded-up sheets. My feet are freezing and my boobs are sweaty. I pull Sara's pills off my desk, twist the bottle open, and swallow one, dry.

I spent all day in bed, and I don't remember large chunks of it, which I guess means I was sleeping, but I don't feel particularly rested. There are a couple of classes I missed, but I can probably get the notes from someone. I'm alone in the room; Kate might have been in here at one point, but she's gone now and the room is empty and cold and gray.

I throw off the covers and they fall on the floor. My mouth is full of sticky foam.

My eyes keep darting toward my phone, which sits silently on my desk. All day I've been waiting for it to ring, for it to be Sam or someone calling to tell me that I'm fired and not to bother coming back again. I spent all night last night sitting in that bush and crying, and nobody called me. Nobody noticed I was gone. I'm totally expendable.

I pick up the phone.

I know everyone has those moments where they pull their phone out and then immediately forget what they were going to do with it. They end up playing *Tetris* for four hours when all they meant to do was check the time. This is sort of like that, except I know why I picked my phone up but I can't quite make myself follow through with it. My thumb is hovering over the icon for the phone app—I could call Sam, tell him I'm sorry for wandering off, and beg him for another chance—or I could call Sara and tell her *I'm doing your stupid drug, you owe me, you can't let me get fired—* but the more I think about either one, the stupider I feel about it.

That first option would be suicide. I'd be calling attention to my own incompetence.

It's the second one that's bugging me, though.

It seems like it should be easy. People call their sisters all the time. *How are you, dearest sister?* they say. *I was calling just to catch up, dearest sister. I miss you and I love you,* and whatever the hell else people say to their sisters. But I know that that's not how it goes because that's never how it goes. So I just need to put the phone away and forget the whole thing.

And suddenly her face is on my screen and it says *Calling...Calling...*and oh God, it's ringing.

No, no, hang up, hang up. Your thumb slipped.

"Hello?"

My hand is shaking too hard and I can't hit the *End call* button.

"Hello?"

She saw my name on the screen and she knows it's me, but she's saying *Hello?* anyway. I guess I might as well talk to her.

"Hello?"

I hang up.

My thumb finally found the red button on the screen and she's gone. But her voice is still ringing in my head: *Hello? Hello?*

You *knew* it was me.

I slam the phone down on my desk. Just before it smacks into the fake wood veneer, I remember that *Hey, stupid, this is your only phone and you can't afford another,* but it's too late now, and all I can do is pray that I didn't break it.

I pick it up once more to make sure it's okay and I notice the time. That thing Kate wanted me to go to is in about 20 minutes, so I have that much time to walk a dozen blocks to the coffeehouse where she's performing. I climb out of bed.

My jeans, the only pair I ever wear (they're starting to smell), are hanging off my desk chair, and I slide into them. As for the tank top I slept in, it's good enough I guess, but I should probably wear something over it. There's a baggy sweatshirt (the kind I like) on the desk next to where my jeans were, but I'm wondering if I should make more of an effort. Nah, never mind. It's not worth it.

I throw on the sweatshirt.

This way I don't have to mess with a coat, and anyway, I'm just going to get a drink and hide in the back until this thing is over.

As I step out into the night, I realize just how insanely cold it is outside, so instead of walking I think I'll drive. My car is just a block down the street from my dorm anyway, so I jump in and instantly spasm at how frigid the seat is. Twenty years of existence have sucked every last twinge of heat from the upholstery. I turn the key and the vents blast cold air in my face.

I switch them off.

Now the windshield is fogging up and I have to duck to see where I'm going, and I switch the defrost on and it sputters and makes things worse. And I'd get mad about *that* particular cruel irony, except I'm already here, so I find a parking spot across the street from this place.

The cold air bites at my face, so I hurry inside. There's a bit of a line for the counter. I join it, and I glance around the place. I've been here a couple of times, mostly during my freshman year, but I decided a while ago that hipstery coffeehouses weren't really my thing. There was a time when I tried to be the scarf-wearing, MacBook-tapping, beard-stroking sort (chicks can be the beard-stroking sort, right?), but eventually I realized how completely insufferable that sort of person is. I took to just driving through Starbucks and then hiding in my room with my laptop instead.

But here I am again, so I guess I've come full-circle.

It's an older building in the "historic" district of town, a designation that in practice means the buildings have been allowed to crumble from the inside out and the beard-stroking crowd has taken it upon themselves to keep them that way, and then sit inside them stroking their beards and congratulating themselves for having lives that are *so much more real, man,* and making use of buildings that are, *like, totally retro and rustic and whatever else, dude.*

I tell myself not to think negative thoughts all night, because I do that sometimes and it just makes me miserable. And anyway, there's plenty to like about this place. The solid oak floor, the smell of cigarettes and burnt beans, the crumbling-but-thick walls that shield me from the cold.

And also, the line is moving fast. I almost trip over a box of checkers that someone left on the floor as I finally step up to the counter. A chalk menu and a barista with a bandana on her head.

"Can I help you?"

"Uh...yeah. I'll have a...coffee."

"O...kay?" She raises an eyebrow at me like she's never heard such a generic request before, but thankfully she doesn't ask me any further questions. She hands me a cracked mug of steaming black stuff, and I push my way through the crush of hipsters toward the back. There's one of those booths with high-backed benches that seems like the perfect place to camp out and hide. Across the room is a stage made of unfinished wood that looks like they've only brought it out a few times before. Shiny bolts, crammed full of amps.

I reach into my sweatshirt pocket for *Hamlet,* but there's a different book in there, one I must have grabbed when I was going through my old bedroom the other night. It's *The Poems of Edgar Allen Poe.* I start flipping through it.

It's a battered paperback, one with dog-eared pages thumbed by a hand that used to be smaller. Amid the various jeremiads is a poem that I haven't read in forever, one that haunted my dreams when I was 12, and I never understood it back then, but I think I might be starting to get it—at least a little—now. It's called "The Conqueror Worm."

*Lo! 'tis a gala night*

*Within the lonesome latter years!*
*An angel throng, bewinged, bedight*
*    In veils, and drowned in tears,*
*Sit in a theatre, to see*
*    A play of hopes and fears,*
*While orchestra breathes fitfully*
*    The music of the spheres.*

Now the crowd is filing in, taking seats, mostly students. I recognize some of them, I've passed them before, walking across campus. Giant pea coats and horn-rimmed glasses and bangs that hide faces. Moleskine notebooks with fountain pens clipped to them. As they find seats, the windows get darker till the winter air is pressing in against the glass, drawing ghosts on both the inside and the outside, and the lights on the stage fade in and out as some grimy dudes do a soundcheck.

*Mimes, in the form of God on high,*
*    Mutter and mumble low,*
*And hither and thither fly—*
*    Mere puppets they, who come and go*
*At bidding of vast formless things*
*    That shift the scenery to and fro*
*Flapping from out their Condor Wings*
*    Invisible woe!*

If I bury my head in this book long enough I won't make eye contact with anyone, and nobody will ask me to share my table. And that's a real concern, since this place is starting to look pretty busy. On the stage, they're plugging stuff in, tripping over cords. Something emits a *crack* and throws sparks, and one of them jumps back for a second. And then everything's hooked up and some smelly white kid with dreadlocks takes the stage to sing off-key about how war is evil. Thanks for the newsflash.

*The motley drama—oh, be sure*
*    It shall not be forgot!*
*With its phantom chased forevermore,*
*    By a crowd that seize it not.*
*Through a circle that ever returneth in*
*    To the self-same spot,*

> *And much of madness, and more of sin,*
> *And horror the soul of the plot.*

Smelly dreadlocked kid is gone now, and he says *Thank you* and puts his guitar down and goes outside for a smoke. I can see him out there, his cigarette a single glowing ember amid the snow and the smoke and the window ghosts. Some guys come onstage and unplug some stuff and then plug it back in, and then another act takes the stage, a duo this time, two skinny guys in bandanas with lots of tattoos. One of them straps on a guitar and the other drums on an upside-down beach bucket. Guitar Dude sings "Puff the Magic Dragon" with a wink and a nod while Bucket Guy closes his eyes and pounds. *Come on, guys, the song's not really about drugs. Snopes debunked that one, like, a billion years ago.*

> *But see, amid the mimic rout,*
> *A crawling shape intrude!*
> *A blood-red thing that writhes from out*
> *The scenic solitude!*
> *It writhes!—it writhes!—with mortal pangs*
> *The mimes become its food*
> *And seraphs sob at vermin fangs*
> *In human gore imbued.*

I'm starting to see what I missed as a kid, when I would wake up in cold sweats scared of the Worm, as if it were some sort of giant monster that would find me in the night. But it's not about that, it's about the inevitability of death, that we'll all be eaten from the inside in the end, by the entropic heat death of the universe, if nothing else. And maybe when we're huddled in bed at night as kids, glancing sideways at our half-open closet door, all we're really hiding from is the inescapable decay of our flesh.

> *But if the sun breed maggots in a dead dog, being a god kissing carrion...*

Anyway, it's not like rich white kids have much else to worry about.

Now that barista in the bandana is up on stage saying, "Please welcome Kate..." and Kate my roommate is up there now and suddenly things feel less awkward. Maybe because someone I actually know is here, or maybe because she can rock those dreads so much better than the white boys who just climbed down. She plugs in a few more things, and there are a few more sparks, and she starts playing some chords. Bendy, loopy chords, with a finger in a glass bottleneck, sliding up and down the neck of her guitar. And then her voice comes through, one of crystal and coal, one that barely needs a microphone at all:

> **Trying to forget the things from last year,**
> **Trying to push the night on through.**
> **Trying to forget the things from last year,**
> **Trying to push the night on through.**
> **Because I know that things won't last here,**
> **Behold, I'm making all things new.**

*Out—out are the lights—out all!*
> *And, over each quivering form,*
*The curtain, a funeral pall,*
> *Comes down with the rush of a storm,*
> **From midnight soil, a new shoot growing,**
> **It's small but strong and breaking through.**
> **From midnight soil, a new shoot growing,**
> **It's small but strong and breaking through.**
> **Something beyond my seeing or knowing,**
> **Behold, I'm making all things new.**

*While angels, all pallid and wan,*
> *Uprising, unveiling, affirm,*
*That the play was the tragedy "Man,"*
> *And its hero, the Conqueror Worm.*
> **A river flowing in the desert,**
> **A heartbeat in the carious rue.**
> **A river flowing in the desert,**
> **A heartbeat in the carious rue.**
> **Something that overcomes all effort,**
> **Behold, I'm making all things new.**

As she plays the ghosts on the windows fade and the lights in the bare rafters warm, and the room is filled with old friends sharing life over steam and biscotti. I didn't see it before, but I see it now; just people huddled together inside the drafty walls, crowding around tiny bits of the sun, trying to push away the ghosts for just a few minutes. I look back toward the door where I was waiting in line earlier, and I can almost see my hour-ago self still standing there, staring at my shoes and trying not to acknowledge anyone, ignoring that they're all just the same as me, looking for somewhere to hide, and that sometimes that takes a crowded room and a beat-up guitar and a four-dollar cup of coffee.

And I make up my mind that I'll just stop thinking thoughts about other people and thoughts about myself and just let myself get lost in the sound and the light and the warmth and for the first time in years I escape, if only just for a few minutes.

And then, before I realize it, I'm alone.

The music has stopped, and the crowd has left, and nothing lingers in the golden air except the clanking of dishes being bussed and the shuffle of the guys tearing down the stage. I look down at the bottom of my mug, and it's a sad, swirling halo of dregs that roll from side to side when I tip my fist back and forth. The almost-used-to-be-white bottom catches the light and shows a spiderweb pattern left from a thousand previous refills.

I push myself free from my slouch and find the place to drop off the used mugs. A brown tub stored under the cream and sugar that they leave out for the non-hipsters who drop by. And then I just stand here, looking around the mostly empty room, wondering what I'm supposed to do.

I reach into my pocket and pull out the flyer Kate gave me, the one I've been thumbing since that night on the skywalk, tattered and worn now, soft like a piece of muslin. Still warm from my body heat. Some of the deep black texture from the laser printing has worn away, but the name and the date still catch the light in a way that only the darkest blacks can.

I wander back toward the stage, where she's unplugging cords, loading speakers onto dollies. Her leather skirt obviously isn't conducive to all the bending over, and her dreads flop around, narrowing her field of vision to only the cable spaghetti directly in front of her. Still, she's probably done this a thousand times.

I don't know why I'm standing here watching her. I should just go.

"Here." Before I can turn away, there's a mountain of black cable flying through the air and into my face, and it almost knocks me over, but I catch it. And then she's throwing another. "Take this too." Then she grabs a dolly and she's flying out the door with it, saying "Follow me," and we're out the door and into the night, and I'm glad I wore my sweatshirt. She's far ahead of me, and I'm running to keep up. She's turned a corner with her stack of speakers, and now she's loading them into the back of an enormous van made of dents that reeks of cigarettes. It looks like it probably hasn't been cleaned out since the '70s, but she's clearly got a system for loading stuff into it. She puts the speakers in first while I stand here buried under a pile of black cable, only able to see thin slats of what's going on. Black boxes sliding into their slots, barely illuminated by a dusty dome light, *clunk*s and *clack*s, and then she starts digging me out of rubbery blackness. "Thanks for your help." She hangs them on some hooks, and then says, "C'mon, I have more to get," and drags me back up the hill to the stage, where she starts rolling cords and stacking speakers again.

"Kate?"

"Yeah?" She doesn't even slow down; she's stacking and rolling twice as fast as she was before.

"Kate, um...?" But what am I going to say? *Thanks for the show, but I have to get going?* Yeah, that's bitchy. I can't say that.

"What?"

"What am I doing...?"

"You're helping me tear down my equipment. C'mon." She throws me another stack of cords, and then another, and she and her dolly lead me out the door and down the hill and around the corner to her van again, where she starts sliding stuff into place and hanging cords up like before.

"Kate..."

"What?" she grunts, pushing a stubborn speaker into a tiny slot.

"Why am I here?"

That didn't come out the way I meant it to, and honestly, I'm not quite sure what I meant to say. "Because I invited you?" she says, staring blankly.

"Um—"

She sighs and she wipes the sweat off her forehead and says, "Look, I guess—I guess I don't really know why I invited you here, honestly. You just looked like you needed something to do with yourself that wasn't completely awful and depressing. And I had this coming up, and it seemed like an okay thing. That's all this is, really." She slides forward and sits on the bumper, her heels dangling above the frozen asphalt. "God, I need a cigarette. You want one?" Pulls some Camels out of her coat, grabs one in her mouth, and lights it behind her hand.

"No thanks, I don't smoke," I tell her. But I sit down next to her to escape the wind.

"Is there anything you *aren't* uptight about, Phelia?" she says, and I stare at my feet. She adds, "I'm sorry, that came out wrong. It's just—maybe you wouldn't be so down all the time if you were willing to try something new every once in a while."

"Yeah, maybe." She's still holding the pack out, so I grab one. "You know this stuff kills you, right?"

"*Everything* kills you." She sucks down a wad of smoke and her ember lights up the cold, dry air. I still haven't lit mine. Maybe I won't. I'm flipping it between my fingers in a vain attempt to look cool. She watches me flip it around for a while, and the finally says, "Look, I don't really know why I brought you here. Sorry if this is awkward."

"You said something about telling me what inspires you to write. Something about how you stopped being...what was it you said?"

"Constipated?"

"Ew. Yeah."

She kicks at the icy air. "God, I so didn't want to have this conversation. I guess part of me was hoping you'd just walk out the door and go home at the end. I just—I'm terrible at being honest about myself. I guess that's why I write songs? As long as you write songs, you can hide your words behind your music."

Wind and glowing embers. Silence like a vapor. "Who taught you to play slide guitar?" I finally say. I'm hiding the cigarette behind my back now, hoping she'll forget about it and stop trying to talk me into smoking it.

"Oh, that?" She laughs. "I wish I had an awesome story about selling my soul to the Devil at a crossroads or something, but I don't. I watched some videos on YouTube, taught myself. I just picked it up."

"That's still pretty impressive."

She sucks her cigarette down to the filter and tosses it into the street. An orange glow bouncing in the snowy blue, throwing sparks till it hits a snowdrift and its heat dissolves into the entropy.

She lights another.

"It's really not," she says. "It's talent, not skill."

"What do you mean?"

"Y'know. It's something innate, not hard work. Some people work their asses off to get good at something, and some people are just lucky and barely have to try."

"And you're—"

She laughs. "Yeah, I'm the latter. Some people can add huge numbers in their heads without using a calculator; I can pick up an instrument and figure it out without really working at it. I can't take credit for what I do. It's dumb luck, not hard work."

"That's still...I mean, I'm impressed."

"Don't be."

"Oh. Okay. I'll try not to be. I guess." Because what else can I say to that? "But I liked the songs."

"Don't get too excited about a little bit of 12-bar blues. I found something that works for me, that's all."

And we sit, staring at our shoes, till I finally say, "Were you going to tell me how...?"

"God, here we go."

I'm a little startled at how she interrupts. "Um—"

She sighs. "Sorry, I didn't mean to snap like that." Stubs out her cigarette on the bumper beneath her, lights a new one. "Sorry," she says again. "I was just really hoping we wouldn't have to have this conversation. I'm starting to understand why I used to hate listening to people talk about religion."

"Why?"

"Because it's *fucking annoying.*" And when I say nothing to that, she just leans against the wall of speakers behind her, and the van rocks on its broken shock absorbers, and she whispers:

**Remember not the former things,**
**nor consider the things of old.**
**Behold, I am doing a new thing;**
**now it springs forth, do you not perceive it?**
**I will make a way in the wilderness**
**and rivers in the desert.**

She says it to no one in particular. To the night. To banish the dark and the cold.

"What does that *mean?*" she says. "Making things *new?* It's such a weird turn of phrase, y'know? Things don't get newer, ever. You fix stuff up, you put a fresh coat of paint on it, but it's not *new,* it's just shinier. Things die, they decay, and eventually they give way to the same heat death as everything else in the universe." She sucks more smoke into her lungs, slowly killing them, and says, "Matter has been around for billions of years. It's *all* old. *Everything's* old, no matter what you do to it. Everything is gonna rot in the ground, and then the ground itself will rot away."

I'm thumbing the Poe book in my pocket, feeling each dog-ear, each bit of paper that rubs off onto my skin.

"Do I sound like a stoner?" she says. "Sorry."

I laugh.

"But, I mean, look at this," she says pointing to her cigarette. "If you stand outside in the cold smoking a cigarette, you look like a badass—but all you're doing is killing yourself. How is it badass to kill yourself, especially since the universe is already doing it for you? That's not badass, that's surrender." I'm still hiding the cigarette she gave me, and she adds, "I'm sorry, I'm really not trying to kill you. I was just trying to get you to loosen up. Not a perfect illustration, I know."

I laugh again.

She says, "I imagine you're not much of a partier."

"Well—I mean—I've been to a few—"

"It's okay," she says. "You don't have to be embarrassed of *not* doing stupid stuff. Isn't that weird? How you get social points around here for acting stupid? Staying up all night, binge drinking, that sort of thing? People admire you for being destructive instead of creating."

"Not everyone here is like that."

"Yeah, I know. But it's how I assumed everyone was, for sure. Maybe that's on me. I was buying into the party culture, rebelling against a repressive childhood that I never actually had, y'know? One last hurrah of rejecting adulthood as a concept. No, though, you're right—not everyone around here thinks that way. Maybe it was just me."

"It's pretty shallow."

"I know, right? *God.* And it's why I'm still *here.* It's the whole reason I'm still stuck in school, finishing up credits." She's waving her cigarette in the air now, trying to stab out her demons with the fiery ash. "I should have graduated by now, should be out in the world, *contributing,* or something, but here I am, still making up credits because I bought into a lifestyle that only exists in Axe commercials, or something. I mean, right?"

"I don't know." But she's not talking to me anymore. Just shouting at the night.

"I showed up here, told everyone I wanted to be a writer, but I didn't. Not really. I didn't even know what writing *was.* I wasn't ready to work, to bash a pen against a notebook for hours trying to make something happen. I just wanted to tell people I was a writer and feel really cool about it. And in between telling people I was a writer and feeling really cool, I just wanted to act stupid."

"You were a kid."

And she says, "Yeah, y'know, maybe that's it. Maybe it was just the last throes of adolescence." She sucks more smoke into her lungs and finally says, "You know that the very first teaching of Zen is to deny the teachings of Zen?"

"Really?"

"I dunno, I heard that on NPR once."

"Oh." I breathe in some secondhand smoke and swish it around in my brain. "How does that even work?"

"It doesn't, right? I think that's kind of the point. It doesn't make sense on the surface, but nothing spiritual does, I don't think. Anyway, I first heard that my sophomore year, and it occurred to me that any real pursuit of knowledge has to start with questioning what you already know. And that almost nobody actually has the balls—the ovaries—to do that. To question herself." A beat-up car rumbles by, and the moon comes out from behind a cloud, and she says, "It's probably not that brilliant of a revelation. It's just part of growing up, I guess—realizing that the stuff you were laser-focused on was just a tiny shard of an infinite universe, and quite possibly the tiniest and least important shard. And you start thinking that maybe you should chain your soul to something bigger, something that's outside the universe. So you start looking. And then, maybe when you find it, the poetry comes. And then the poetry turns into song."

She's fumbling in her pocket with some rosary beads. Trying to hide them.

"Anyway," she says, "I'm not trying to Jesus-juke you or anything, I'm just trying to be honest about who I am. Like I said, it's fucking annoying. I know it is. But I can't pretend that the big questions don't exist, or that they don't gnaw at me, just because nobody wants to hear my opinions on them."

She sucks more smoke down her throat.

"But don't let me act like I'm some sort of deep thinker or anything. I know I'm not. I just needed something bigger than myself and had a friend willing to take me to mass."

"And things got better?"

She laughs. "Better than what? Actually, they got worse. It's kind of depressing to know you get meaning out of something that's just an annoying cliché to other people. Kind of depressing to know that I'm pouring my heart out to you right now and all you're thinking is *God, she's so annoying.* But when a 2,000-year-old dead guy talks to you from a cracker and says *Follow me,* I mean, what can you do? It's like getting abducted by aliens, right? You don't believe it's a thing until it happens to you, and then you're the only one who thinks it's a thing, and you're like, *Well, either I'm the crazy one or I'm not.* But if it's *happened* to you, then you'll never convince yourself that it hasn't. It didn't matter at all before, and then suddenly it matters more than anything."

She hits her head on the speaker behind her. I hear the *thwack* and I wince.

"And then you have a bunch of teachings you're supposed to live your life by. And none of them actually apply to the real world, but I guess that's sort of the point." Takes a drag. "I mean, with Christianity. Not with the alien abduction thing. But maybe with that, too."

"I'm...not really religious."

She laughs. "*Not really religious.* Well, okay. *God,* what am I supposed to say to that? Why do people always say that?"

"I guess I didn't know what else to say."

"Man, I *hate* it when people say that. *I'm not really religious.* As if ignoring important questions makes them unimportant. It's like the people who tell me *I don't see race.* Well, good for you, but race sees me, whether I want it to or not. You might have the luxury of ignoring important stuff, but damned if I do. *I'm not really religious.* What else are you going to tell me? *I'm not really anything other than a privileged white girl?* Fascinating."

She takes a drag.

And she adds, "I'm sorry. I didn't mean to blow up like that. I can be a jerk, I know I can. It's just—what can I say to that? It's just a defense mechanism, and not even a good one. Nah, you've been sitting here, listening to my insane ranting for, what, almost an hour now? I'm not mad at you. I should be thanking you." She stands up, gives me a hand, and pulls me to my feet. "And anyway, I can't judge. I used to say the same thing to people. It's a useful line. A good way to deflect important conversations. But you can't do it forever. I mean, I couldn't, anyway."

"Why not?"

"I questioned myself for a second. Dealt with the possibility that I might be wrong about something." She coughs. "It was scary, but I highly recommend it." Drops her cigarette, grinds it out with her boot. "Listen, I gotta get back to the coffee shop. They're probably hoping to close sometime soon, and I still have a couple of speakers to grab."

"You want some help?"

"Nah, there's really only a couple things. You need a ride?"

"I drove."

She punches me on the shoulder, like a dude. "I'll see you back at the room, then, all right?" Her eyes catch mine for a second, a flash of white in the dark. And then she starts walking away, up the hill, toward the coffee house. And I'm a little dazed, but I feel like I should say something else. Not let things be awkward.

"Kate?"

She turns around. "Yeah?"

"Thanks for taking the time to talk to me. It's been a while since anyone bothered."

"Are you kidding?" she says. "Thanks for listening." Then she turns back around, and she rounds a corner, and she's gone.

And I'm standing here in the glow of her dome light, thinking *What just happened?* I think she's probably right about that *fucking annoying* thing, but it's not like I can hate her too much for feeling passionate about something. I mean, I wish I did. And the fact that she opened up to me like that when she probably didn't even want to means...something, I guess.

So I head back toward my car, and I realize that I'm feeling strangely okay, for the first time in a while. I'm not harboring delusions of *I just found my new BFF* (well, maybe a little), nor am I nursing a big, lesbian crush (well, maybe a little), but you can't have someone bare their soul to you and not feel—I don't know—uplifted, a little?

This will all seem really stupid tomorrow, I know. I'll wake up and say to myself *Some chick cornered you in her van and started ranting about Jesus and aliens. That's how serial murders start, you idiot.* And while that all makes perfect sense, especially given what I saw the other night, and while I'm sure at the very least I'll be requiring years of therapy to get over all of that, at the moment it just feels right, like I finally made a small connection with someone, even obliquely and imperfectly. Wasn't this what I wanted, back when I first showed up on campus? To stay up late into the night at coffee shops, talking with thoughtful people about life's big, important questions? Wasn't that what I hoped college would be?

But that was a long time ago. I barely even remember that girl.

And now I realize that I've been walking for blocks, away from my car, in the wrong direction, back towards campus. I'm already closer to my dorm than I am to my car now, so I guess I can just leave it. It's Saturday night, and no one will tow it till Monday at least, so I guess I'll just come by and get it tomorrow. It's nice outside, anyway, once you get used to the cold. The stars that have been fighting with the heavy blanket of clouds all night are finally out, and the windows of the downtown bars are vomiting their glow into the night.

There's nobody out on the sidewalks tonight; it's too late for the serious student crowd and too early for the bar crowd. The snow is stacked on corners and catching the muted halogen glow of the rare car that passes by. The cuffs on my jeans are wicking water off the ground, but I ignore it.

The traffic lights change, flashing red and then green. Each car that drives by is a blur, and the pavement shines wet from melting snow, while the water flowing in the storm drains spreads out and twists gray in every direction, till it tangles with the night and the snow into a soft, gray carpet. A Berber carpet like the one in the office I used to work in, after one failed career and before another. A soft Berber carpet supporting my shaky feet that were unused to heels. Every day it would rise to meet them when I stepped off the elevator and carry me to my desk where I would answer phones and sort through the slush pile. I'm back there now and it's morning and the sun is shining in through an enormous window. And the phone is barely ringing and my old boss in her skirt just like mine and her manicured nails is like *Hi, how are you?* and *Good morning, Ophelia,* her smile reflecting the gallons of sun pouring in, and I'm glad I got out of that classroom. There's coffee on my desk, not the fancy kind, just the kind that comes out of a stained carafe every morning, and I know because I make it myself because I'm the intern, the paid intern, so I don't mind. Sometimes I'm tired and sometimes it's work, but the memory of the monster children who made me cry is a thousand miles away. I tap at the keyboard, responding to emails, and my nails *click* and *clack* because they used to be pretty back then, back before I started biting them. And then I see it, far beyond the pens-with-flowers-taped-to-them, the elevator numbers rising, till it dings and the door opens, and I'm ready to welcome a guest, but she's not a guest. I see her step out, one bare leg at a time, heels higher than mine. Not even a skirt with those heels, just shorts that are white and hug hips, and her tank top is red. Not even dressed right for the weather, just like always, but she enters the room like she owns it. But she doesn't. She doesn't belong here, she never comes here, and I don't want her here, but she is, forcing her way into my memory and blocking the sun with her white-after-Labor-Day shadow. Her breath still holds the chill of the outside air, and she's breathing steam in my face like a dragon. *Hey Oaf,* she says, and I look up and try to see her face among the silhouettes, and it's the perfect shadow that won't leave my dreams alone at night. *Hi Sara. To what do I owe the pleasure?* I look away and pretend I'm alone, but even when I close my eyes I can still see her Cheshire-cat smile. She slams a book on my desk in front of my face and says *You left this at Mom's place last night.* It's *Hamlet,* the torn copy with the dog-ears that never leaves my pocket, except last night I guess. I breathe in bitter air and say, *Why'd you come here, though? You could have swung by my dorm or met me for lunch or stopped by one of my classes. Why would you come here?* (It was all I had left.) And the silence that follows lasts forever, broken only by the scream of an ambulance that rips through the sunlight outside and leaves night in its wake. She says, *I wanted to see where the magic happens. I wanted to see what happens when I'm performing a necessary function in the world and you're sitting here, daydreaming, or trying to forget your failed attempt to shape tomorrow's generation.* She takes one of my pens, the ones with the flowers taped on, and she sticks it behind her ear like she's a Bic Fairy Princess. The pink matches her tongue and I mumble that my work is important too, and she says, *Is it?* and I say nothing. *You're living the dream,* she says. I say, *'Living the dream'? What does that even mean?* She says, *While those of us doing real jobs are working our asses off, you come here and read words on a page and tell people why they suck. While I'm in a basement dealing with the trash we all leave behind no matter what, you're making ten bucks an hour pushing words around on a screen. You're living the dream of never getting your hands dirty or bloody, never having to leave that little cavity inside your skull. And I just wanted to see what it looks like when someone tells the whole world they can go to hell and she'll just sit up in her little tower judging them all. And it's as boring as I imagined.* And she sighs, and she coughs, and she turns around with my pen still behind her ear and starts walking away. I say *Why do you care?* She turns around and she's playing with the flower and she says, *Excuse me?* I say, *Why is it your business what I do with my life and my career? If you came all this way just to make me feel bad, you might as well tell me why it's so important to you that I do.* And she just stands there, planted on the spikes of her heels, her green eyes filling with the flame of her shirt. I finally say, *Oh my God, you're jealous,* and she stares and says, *What?*

and I tell her, *You wish you were me. You wish that you still had a passion for work. And it's not enough that you're better than me, you have to make sure I feel worse than you, too, all the time.* It's so hard to open my mouth and say words with her red/green eyes staring right at it. And she says, *Hey, Oaf, I was kidding,* but we both know she wasn't, she so fucking wasn't. I say, *Just go home,* and she tries to say *Wait,* but it's too late, I'm not even listening. And more words pour out from my mouth in a pile of regret-vomit, stuff I can never take back. *Just shut up, go home, Sara, nobody cares. So sick of the act, the 'Oh God, woe is me, the whole weight of the world's on my back.' So sick of the way you throw money around on these clothes and the Jag when we both know you're broke and your cash comes from Dad. And I know every mailing you've gotten from Doctors Without Borders has gone in the trash, so just please drop the whole Selfless Martyr routine.* Her mouth's gaping open, a hole in her face filled with dark disbelief that I said that to her. *Where's your lazy-ass boss when I need her?* she says. *Do you talk to everyone this way when someone comes in here? Aren't you the receptionist, Oaf? You think you can talk to your clients like that and you'll still be successful?* And she says *successful* as if she invented it, like she keeps it locked in a box and for one measly dollar she'll let you peek inside and feed it some breadcrumbs. I say to her, *Sara, you can't just walk in here and treat me like that and expect friendly service,* but now she's not listening. I say *Don't you realize how childish you sound? What you're doing's not normal—just—people don't do this.* She says, *No, they don't, and that's part of the problem. There's too many people (like you) who do nothing all day while the rest of us have to put up with your shit.* And she's yelling as loud as she can, which seemed strange at the time, but I see now she did it on purpose back then, that any excuse to yell would have been good enough. And I hear a voice, it's the same voice I heard on that day, it's my boss saying *Come to my office, please, Ophie.* She's calling me in, and it's all gonna happen all over.

Wait.

I remember all this. I'm back in a memory, living it over. I'm here. It's four weeks ago. This is the day I got fired. Laid off. She said *It's a layoff;* we both knew it wasn't. It was Sara. I see. It was her all along. She did it. On purpose? I guess; I don't know. But I'm here, back in time, and the plant by the window is still turning brown, and my boss is still calling my name. Sara's strutting away now, her heels stabbing carpet, the same way they did those four weeks ago back when she ruined my life, and her hands dethrone knickknacks from coworkers' desks, and they crash to the floor once again. The elevator door opens wide and she steps on, again, leaving me here to clean up the mess. It's the same. She'll be gone and I'm fired and back at the hospital, her hospital, where she'll force me to swallow her pills. And I can't let her do this again, not again. I get up, and I run, and my mouth's craving blood, and I'll make her pay this time. I'm out of my chair, leaping over my desk, the spikes of my heels digging into the carpet. I fly by the corpses of tchotchkes she knocked on the floor, and I reach out with claws that latch onto her hair, and I pull and she screams and her screams are delicious. I want more of them (many more), so I slide my nails down through the trickle of blood that they draw from her face, and I wrap them around her pale throat, and I squeeze. She chokes and she gags and I make her say *Sorry.* I make her say *Sorry* a thousand times more, little red-lipstick sorries in spit and in blood. They ooze down her chin and out onto my hands, and they spill out like warm sugar syrup. My claws taste the blood and my teeth become hungry and I can't control them. They reach from my mouth and sink into her skin and she runs as a liquid down into my throat. I taste the sweet-sticky, the salty, the life, and it's running all over me (warm), and I'm winning. *You hear that noise, Sara? The sound of me winning?* I choke her and choke her until she turns cold and my hands push through skin and through bone till there's nothing between them. I squeeze till the coffee dries up and the silver turns brown and the sun reappears and I'm back in my bed and awake.

And my lip is bleeding. And my pillow's torn open.

The sunlight is pouring into my eyes, and I'm fumbling around for my phone, looking at the time, and it's eight in the morning. Eight in the morning on a Saturday.

I honestly can't remember the last time I was up at eight in the morning on a Saturday. And I've got a headache, and there's blood running down my lip, so I probably won't be getting any more sleep. Kate's snoring at the other end of the room.

So I guess I've got the morning all to myself. Maybe I'll go to the gym, or something. That was another thing I promised myself I'd do as a freshman. *I'll go to the gym every Saturday morning.* Maybe I should actually do it this week.

Y'know. Since I'm already up.

I slide out of bed, disentangling a leg from a twisted sheet, bumping my head on my desk on the way. I pull open my medicine cabinet and fumble around, looking for Tylenol or something. There it is, behind the NyQuil. I need to get organized. (There's a pair of used socks in here for some reason.)

I try to swallow a couple of pills, but my mouth is dry and sticky and without water I can't squeeze them down. I should go to the bathroom and get some, but walking down the hall seems like so much work this morning. God, I'm lazy. I guess that's why I never made it to the gym.

But I'm going today. (I am.)

I shake my head, trying to clear it. That bizarre dream is fading slowly, but in the moment it felt real, like it was really four weeks ago, like Sara was really there, like I really...

There's a trickle of blood still on my lip, and I lick it off, and I try to focus on finding something to wear. Shorts and a tank top. Something like that.

I open my closet door, and I scream as a body falls out.

## sat. jan. 15.
## 8:13 am.
## can't breathe

**There's definitely a minute,** or an hour, no, a minute, when I'm standing here, just standing here, trying to push it all away and pretend that this isn't a thing. Hand on the wall, other hand on my throat, trying to breathe, to scream, but I can't. And then there's that silence when the room starts to glow and to sparkle, pressing in on my eardrums till they pop, and I close my eyes hard to keep them from exploding out of my head. I close them until all my thoughts disappear, and I open them again, but I'm still in the same place staring at the same body with the same dried blood on her face and the same pool of red underneath her. The twisted mouth, the torn-open throat, and the arms and the legs splayed in every direction. The glow. The darkness. The glow.

That moment lasts forever, but then suddenly it's over and I realize I'm falling, I'm losing my balance, I'm buckling from the knees up. I reach for the wall, for the cold, glossy paint, and my hand slips against it, leaving horrible red streaks, and my mouth's hanging open with sounds coming out of it, sounds I don't recognize, animal, feral. A scream, or a moan, or something more painful, a howling thing clawing its way up my throat. It's loud and it shatters the morning and I can't control it.

And then she's awake.

Kate's eyes are open. She hears me and sees me, and I'm crouching right here, on my knees, my hands covered in blood that's been drying to them, and a corpse on the floor lying there with her blue skin, her red teeth, her eyes that bulge open all yellow, just staring. It's not a secret anymore and I'm not alone anymore. She's jumping from bed in a thousand directions, shouting out *Oh my God,* or whatever you're supposed to say when you see something like this. Backing into the wall while she fights to find words in her throat, unable to run and unable to move, and she stands there while everything in here turns black and it spins and I'm listening hard for my thoughts.

Hours pass, or they don't. I hear her voice spinning deep in the blackness, quiet but somewhere. In darkness and stars, rushing by like a train and deep in my dreams. *Ophelia, Ophelia...* I hear her. I do; but my mouth is still miles away from my mind. I'm trying to cut through the black, icy numbness, but I yell and I tumble deep into the darkness of memories that I can't escape. I stare at the ceiling, the stars on the ceiling that glowed in the night, in that old, drafty house that I shared with my mom and my dad and my sister a decade ago. We'd sit up at night, every night, because we couldn't sleep, and she'd tell me the things that she knew about life, about school, about boys, and I'd lie there and stare at the green-glowing stars, in love with the night-wisdom Sara would breathe in the drafty humidity. Stories of school and how she got an A or she sat at the popular table at lunch, back when great news from *my* days would still all revolve around *Sesame Street* or an extra-good nap. And I'd hear her voice from the far side of night telling stories of sparkling-bright fantasylands filled with bigger kids (cool kids) and dream of when I could be her. And slowly the stars would grow dim and I'd drift off to sleep. But on nights when I couldn't, her voice would continue long into the night and I'd hear her say *Jeff was a bully again.* She'd tell me *He tripped me and called me a fatty, I hate him. I just want to tie him up down in the basement and make him eat rats for ten years.* I'd nervously laugh, little short bursts of laughs getting lost in the night, and I'd finally tell her, *That's silly. You're so silly, Sara.* And silence would drag, endless darkness and space between star stickers (light-years), and finally I'd hear her voice snaking across through the darkness again: *We could do it, y'know.* And I'd say *Could do what?* and she'd say *We could kidnap him, tie him up down in the basement. And then we could do anything that we wanted.* I'd want to say *Why are you stuck on Jeff, still?* but since kids don't have words like that I'd just ask *How?* and her tired, raspy voice filled the darkness with sharp, jagged stories of how we would give him a fake party invite, and when he was here we would drug him and drag him downstairs and duct-tape him to pipes. And soon I'd be adding ideas in, like big, gaping cuts on his skin that we'd fill up with lemon juice, making him into our hand-and-foot slave, prank-calling his grieving mom, making her cry, and I'd finally say, *But we're just joking, right? Sara?* She'd only say, *Don't you think it'd fun?* And somehow, eventually, smashing against all the odds, I would drift off to sleep, into dreams made of basements and duct tape and soft pleas for mercy, and then wake up (sweaty) at two in the morning, and run for my mom and dad's room, where I'd hide in their bed in between them and beg for a way to *forget, just forget.* And somehow the sun would still rise in the morning, and it'd peek at me (shy) through the slats in the blinds while my dad and my mom would snore loud just to drown out my presence. The past night would all seem so distant; yet somehow it clung to my ankles. I'd go back to playing all day like the night hadn't happened, but in late afternoon I still knew that I'd see her again and then she wouldn't leave till the cold night was over. The one way I had to keep clean was to stare at the sun.

The sun.

I force my eyes open. I force them to open, to focus, like twisting the lens cover off an old camera. I see her eyes like two brown orbs floating in a sea of morning and from there her face radiates out like it's forcing its way into the sunlight. She's still shouting my name, sunlit velvet smacking me in the face with ice water. *"OPHELIA...!"*

She's bent over me and I'm on the floor lying next to the body, a twisted grin with pink teeth staring hard at the side of my face while Kate looks in my eyes, but what can I say? I'm reaching for something, but my arms won't move. "I..."

"Phelia, what's going on? What happened? Who is that?"

Hands and knees now, everywhere, banging on the hard tile floor, and I can't quite stand up, and I'm falling back down before I make it to the doorway, and I lie there bruised and sobbing because I can't even escape the room (damn it). And everything's sideways and all I can see are the flecks of the tile and the scratched-up steel legs of Kate's bed and I sob and I shake and I tell her that "It wasn't me, wasn't me, wasn't me."

Retrace my steps from last night, just think back. I was sitting in Kate's van and watching her smoke. She went back up the hill, and I started walking, and then—then there's nothing till I woke up just now from hours of nightmares. What happened to all the lost time?

I can't control my face, my voice. And then she's crouching down next to me, hand on my arm, saying, "Hey, it's okay, it's okay." And I stare at her face, just mouthing new words I invented while her dreads catch the sun from the window. "Ophelia, relax, breathe."

Good advice. Good advice. I draw sun in through quivering nostrils, look into her blurred face, and trace freckles with my eyes till I can hold them steady. And when things stop spinning, her hand is there, and I take it, and she pulls me to my feet. Then I fall on my bed and she hands me the wastebasket while I vomit, and bile burns my nostrils while she patiently waits. The minutes tick by in hot breaths and cold sweats, and when the spinning finally slows down, she says, "Phelia, what happened?"

I swing a pointing finger toward the body and say something that makes no sense. Gasps escaping over the acid on my tongue, fouling the air and making me wonder how she's holding it together. "I just—opened the closet—and—" More gasping and pointing. The gray winter sun is pouring in between the blinds, on the shredded throat of the girl. Her highlighted hair is spread across the floor, her fingers twisted in impossible, conflicting directions, jagged, broken nails darting out like scared rodents. Bluish tongue scraping the tiles. Pools of blood drying into gray-brown smears. I look away.

"Who...who is she?" Kate's biting her lip, screwing her chocolate eyes into stern focus, fighting not to let them roll back into her head. She's holding it together. I should try to calm down, as well.

I rise from the bed, except instead of rising, I mostly flop onto my hands and knees and inch toward the body. Then with hesitating knuckles, I nudge her face until it's in the light, looking up at me.

Oh God, her eyes are open.

I turn away. Squeeze the vomit down into my gut and force myself to look back at the cold, bloodshot orbs. Eyes that used to be blue, turning red in the gray light.

"I don't know her," I say.

Honestly, she could be pretty much any skinny white chick on campus. Mousy brown hair with obligatory blond highlights. Button nose, a handful of freckles, Gap jeans, Ugg boots. People still wear those? Whatever. She's in a pea coat and a scarf, so she must have come in from outside.

Kate is next to me now, on her knees, pajama pants collecting dustbunnies. Patting her down, reaching into her pockets. She pulls out a driver's license. "'Cyndi Johnson.' You know her? Unless it's a fake ID, I guess." She hands me the ID, because I guess she thinks looking at it will help? Whatever. Picture looks like the body. She's about 22, if the birthdate is right. Address around here. A student, maybe. She looks like one.

And my hand falls by my side because I can't hold her ID up anymore, it's too heavy. Seeing a picture, a name, an address, I can't ignore that this thing that's in front of me once was a human, a person, a girl with a life and a family and friends, and that now she's a torn, twisted pile of meat, and she's here on my floor and she's real like a D on my transcript or a box filled with books and won't disappear like that one that I saw in the skywalk.

My eyes are darting everywhere around the room, and then suddenly I'm looking into Kate's eyes and I can't look away. Like a mirror made of flesh and blood and skin and freckles. The same fear in her eyes that I'm feeling in mine. The same short, panicked breath, the same hard-grinding teeth. She's scared just like I am (it's clear, you can't fake this). The air in between us is fear and mistrust with the smell of bad breath and B.O. and a mint body spray. And we stare at each other for a thousand years or maybe a second, and I see we've got no one but each other.

I run.

It happens too quickly to stop or think. My arms and my legs all start flailing at once, till I burst through the door and I fly down the hall and I'm closed in the elevator, sinking down toward the ground level, while Kate is left kneeling in the room with a body and blood on her hands, thinking *What can I even do now.*

I left her there.

*I left her there...*

sat. jan. 15.
10:43 am.
alone

**Halfway to the front door** of the dorm complex is a restroom—a shockingly nice one with granite stall dividers and an arched ceiling and a door that locks. A paean to peeing that somehow got included when they were building this place a century ago, and then, against all odds, survived the onslaught of additions and remodeling and general modernization. It's something that almost doesn't exist: a public restroom that invites you to lock yourself in, breathe deep, and forget about the world. You'd think a line would form at the door, but actually, one almost never does, since there's a full-sized restroom down the hall—one with a dozen stalls and a beige floor and ugly mauve dividers. So whoever gets to this one first gets the royal pee treatment, while everyone else gets herded through the mauve stalls like cattle.

It's a good place to hide.

I'm not sure why I came here now, though. Just to think, I guess. It's been my go-to since freshman year, when the still air and arched ceilings put me in the mood for quiet contemplation, which is what I assumed these hallowed halls were for; and it still seems appropriate now that I realize how full of shit I was.

I'm watching the square patch of light cast by the window, the one filled with frosted-glass convolutions, because apparently someone (God bless her) decided we needed sunlight to pee. It's crawling over the floor, and the tiles it's passed over are cold again, leaving behind it an inevitable darkness. I lean back and I close my eyes and I run my hands over them, over the crust of seven months' worth of urine, and when I open my eyes I'm not alone anymore. Someone familiar is here, her blond highlights peeking around the edge of the stall, her blue eyes catching the drops of winter sun. A swinging scarf as she inches closer, sits next to me, takes my hand, and says, *Can I ask you a personal question?* and I tell her, *Sure, why not.* She says, *What are you doing at a state school anyway? A rich girl like you who's passionate about writing—aren't people like you supposed to end up at NYU or someplace?* And I say to her, *This was my safety. Don't think I didn't try. I filled out the NYU app, got confirmation, but I never heard back, one way or the other. Then I called them to ask, and they told me I'd called a month prior and retracted my app. I said I'd never done that, but it was too late, and, well, now here I am. But I guess that that's life, right? We all start out starry-eyed, thinking that it'll be awesome, and then it's just one disappointment right after another. But you learn to deal. Sara wanted to graduate summa cum laude from Johns Hopkins; instead she got kicked out of Yale. I wanted to get my degree, be a writer, now it looks like I'll get charged with murder and hauled off to prison. So you learn to deal, right?* She says, *Yeah, about that. You think maybe you should go up there and help out your roommate? You left her alone with my corpse on the floor.* I say, *Why would I help her? I'm sure she's a murderer now. Before I was on the fence; now, though, I'm sure.* She says, *But you're ignoring that from her perspective, things look just as bad for you.* I say, *But I was the one who freaked out!* and she tells me *Emotions are complicated things, though, y'know? People react to things all sorts of different ways. Maybe she's freaking out now. You don't know. Maybe you should go back and see.*

And she turns to dust in the sunlight. She's gone.

She's right, and I know that she's right. The body upstairs in my room is too real to ignore. It's concrete (like a concrete block, dragging me down). And where else can I go, and what else can I do?

Do I really think Kate is to blame? She seemed so damn nice last night. Last night was the first not-completely-depressing thing to happen to me in weeks.

I should have known better than to hang out with someone who lured me into the back of her van to yell at me about Jesus and aliens. I should have run away the second she started offering me cigarettes like a pedo. (I always make the worst decisions, though. First I majored in English, now this.) But there's nothing I can do about it now.

It's weird how those tipping points—single, small moments—can change everything in your life, and you can't take them back. In the back of my mind, there's a moment like this one—a thin, vague impression of how the first chasm began in my life. We would play in the backyard (my sister and I), with dolls or with cars, or pretend to be spies on the lam. Or we'd stack up the blocks in the playroom together, with her blocks on mine or with my blocks on hers. And then Mom would get up from her keyboard (which she almost never did), come to the room, and say, *Wow, what a tower, you built that one all by yourselves,* and then *Maybe you'll build one for me?* We knew she was joking, but still the words hung in the air, while the staircase would creak from humidity, rising. I said *Or we could build one for your bully, Jeff, Sara? Lock him inside and then feed him on rats?* And before I was done, Sara shot me a look made of ice, one that said *That was our little secret,* and I knew that I couldn't take back those words. I'd let loose a monster that used to be ours, one that used to be secret and live in the dark of our room, but I'd thrown on the lights and I'd thrown the door open, and now it was loose in the house. And for some reason, then I said, *Sara, I think I should play by myself for a while.* Then the sun slipped behind a small cloud for a second (just one), and an afternoon thunder that shook sunny streets till it reached my feet (up through the carpet) came through. And then I was standing there, all by myself, watching cloud-shadows track across frays in the couch, while Sara played all by herself in the attic, the door tightly shut. And so was my mother's door—it was shut too—while behind it I heard her nails tap on the keyboard. So I hid until night in my usual place, the old secret passage that only I knew about. The one full of boxes that led from my parents' room out toward the laundry, and it was all mine because I was the only one able to squeeze between boxes enough to fit through it. I sat in between them, straining like always to listen to voices that filtered toward me through the air ducts. A voice on the phone speaking dark second-thoughts. The boxes of Yahtzee dice rattled sometimes under feet that passed over, and slowly the darkness of night hid the sun and I knew that I had to emerge. I looked through the laundry room window at starlight reflected on puddles (how strange that the light still exists in the nighttime), while loud snores like monsters would drift down the hall from my parents' room. But when I went to warn them of strangers asleep in the dark, it was just them in there, just my two normal parents, precarious, balanced on opposite sides of their mattress. I lay in the chasm between them and nudged them until they both snorted awake, and I warned them, and they told me, *Go back to bed.* Then I climbed the long staircase, and lay in my bed, and I listened to inhuman snores. They were Sara; I knew that this time; all my fears had been silly; but somehow they still didn't sound like her. I knew when I woke she'd be different, that somehow the late nights of sitting up talking about bully-torture were over. Her cold, sterile breath in my ear with white noise, pounding like hail on the roof, or the dying stars floating above my head—

"Ophelia!"

And then I'm back in the bathroom, and the sun's gone down, and Kate's pounding on the door.

"Ophelia! I know you're in there!" More banging.

Kate's pounding fists jar me back into time and space, and it's evening now. The night is spilling in the window, where the sun used to be, and I hear girls in the hall shuffling off to the bars. Kate's still yelling at me, and I'm thinking, *Do I answer?*

"Ophelia! Ophelia, I know you're in there. I've looked everywhere else, and this door has been locked all day. Let me in!"

I press my back against the cold wall, trying hard not to breathe. I'm looking toward the window. It's screwed shut, but maybe I could find a way to open it and climb out? Let her clean up her own mess.

"Ophelia—I—I didn't do it. It wasn't me. You *know* it wasn't me. Just please open the door. Please?"

All I have to do is wait here and be quiet. As soon as she's gone, I can go to the cops. Or to Sara. Sara would know what to do.

The pounding's getting slower, desperate, and then I hear a forehead hit the door with a choke and a sob. "Please, Phelia. Open the door. I'm scared."

I heard her that time.

I don't know why, but I believe her. The fear, the desperation. It caught me off-guard, that she's as scared as I am—that, in a weird way, maybe I'm not alone. There's someone outside the door that—

(But what if she's a killer?)

(But what if she's not?)

"Phelia, please?"

I open the door.

## sat. jan. 15.
## 11:13 pm.
## tentative.

**We're back in our room** now and I can still smell her on me from when we collapsed into each other's arms at the restroom door and we both cried. I'm embarrassed by it now, but at the moment it seemed right, and I guess she and I both probably needed it. But now we're both wedged awkwardly back into our room, and I'm sitting on her bed, and she's in the black mesh chair at her desk, slouching in a way that looks weirdly unrelaxed, like someone who's trying to look at ease for my sake, even though we both know she's not. The lamp on her desk, the small one with the red shade, is fighting with the fluorescent lights in the ceiling for control of the room. She's absentmindedly picking at her teeth with her black nails, rocking the chair back and forth and sliding it on its wheels with the one foot she has planted on the floor. I'm hugging my knees like a girl at a slumber party. I'm in jeans but not shoes, and now that I think about it, I don't even know where my shoes are, and the days are flying by, running together, even as the moments drag on. I can't decide if I've been sitting like this for an hour or for five.

Took another one of Sara's pills when we got back to the room. I can still taste it on my tongue.

The cold tile of the floor has been cleared of blood and vomit and bodies. She says she picked Cyndi's body up and shoved it back in the closet and then cleaned the floor with water and paper towels from the restroom, and she might have also said Lysol, which I think I read somewhere used to be marketed as a douche, which is pretty much the worst thing I've ever heard. No, what's actually worse is that there's a body in my closet. Like, a literal skeleton in my closet, which I always thought was a dumb figure of speech, but, well, there you go. A body in my closet, and a roommate I barely know sitting across from me, just three feet away.

I look at her face.

The same dark freckles on dark skin, but her lids are narrowing while her mouth hangs slightly ajar. Words are dissolving just behind her teeth, words that never make it into the dry air between us. And just as I open my mouth to talk, she says, "Do you know Augustine's *Confessions*?"

"What?"

"St. Augustine? There's a famous line in his *Confessions*. You've probably heard it. It goes, *God, make me good, but not yet,* or something like that. I think *Make me chaste and celibate, but not yet* is probably the better translation."

"I think I've heard the line," I tell her.

She bites her tongue. Bites it too hard, winces in pain, continues. "Anyway," she says, "that's kind of how I feel right now, y'know? I think we both know what you're supposed to do when you find a body."

"You report it."

"Yeah," she sighs. She takes her glasses off and chews on one end, twisting the earpiece so it won't ever fit her again. "The only thing about that, though," she says, "is that if we call the cops to say *Hey, we found a body in our closet,* it just looks really bad for both of us."

I glance toward the ceiling, an ugly mess of tiles with water stains at more than half of their corners, and I finally rest my head on my palm and my elbow on my knee and say, "I didn't even know her."

She says, "I know, neither did I. I found her on Facebook earlier, and I don't even have any friends in common with her. But that doesn't matter. We still have her body in our closet. It really doesn't look good for either of us. I know I didn't kill her, and you say you didn't kill her, but who's gonna believe us? You probably don't even believe me."

I can't think of what to say to that.

"I mean," she says, "I don't think *I* believe *you*.

"Wait, what?"

"Well, here's what I know," she says. "We were together last night in my van. Then you left before I did, and yet somehow I got back here before you. I was asleep before you even came in. As far as I know, you could have been doing *anything* last night."

"I—"

"Plus, I mean, you've been acting really strange lately. Dragging me all the way to the English building in the middle of the night, ranting about a dead body? I mean, you have to admit that's—y'know—"

"Uh—"

*But this proves I was telling the truth!*

No, actually, I guess it doesn't. It doesn't really prove anything, except that she thinks I'm just as crazy as I think she is. I really want to say *But you're the one who lures people into her van with cigarettes to yell things about Jesus and aliens and Zen at them,* but really, does that even hold a candle to imagining dead bodies in the middle of the night? Not really? I guess? Those things are a little hard to compare.

"What time did you get back here last night?" she says.

"Uh—" I'm trying to think, but all I can remember is that dream with Sara at the publisher. It replays over and over, no matter what I do, and somehow it's different each time. "—I don't remember."

"Ballpark?"

"Um—what time did *you* get back?"

"Uh—I think it was one-ish. Something like that."

"And I wasn't—?"

"You weren't here, no."

"Weird."

She sighs, stands up, shuffles toward the window. She's looking down into the alley, at the dumpsters and rain puddles. "Do you even remember getting back?"

"I—it was late. I was tired—I—"

"So that's a no, then. Yeah, cops would love that." Breathes deep, sighs, leans hard on her elbow. It can't possibly be comfortable, with the metal frame poking into it like that, but she stays there. She's really trying hard to piece the night together. Maybe I should help.

"Did you lock the door?" I ask her.

110 ~ Luke T. Harrington

"Huh?"

"When you got back last night—did you lock the door?"

"I—no. I figured you were right behind me, and I didn't feel the need to keep you out. Did *you* lock it?"

"Um—"

She sighs and says, "Right. You don't remember." Runs a hand through her permed dreads. Sits on her desk, her calloused feet dangling. "You realize this looks really bad for you."

"Or *you*."

Laughs, joyless. "I know, I know. That's why I was saying—well, y'know. I'm just not excited at all to go to the cops with this. Especially considering how cops tend to treat people with my particular shade of melanin."

"I'm seeing your point here." I'm busying myself by playing with the sheets on her bed, which hasn't been made since the first day of school. There aren't quite as many crumbs in it as you'd think.

"And you agree?"

"I mean—um—"

"Come on, Phelia. You can't stay on the fence forever. It's not an option here."

"I know, I know, I'm just—I'm trying to think."

"Did you lock the door when you left for my show?"

"I—I think so."

"You *think* so?"

"I mean," I tell her, "I guess I don't think about it all that much. It's something I do automatically every time I leave, so I never remember it consciously."

She sighs, gets down, sits on the bed next to me, and tilts her head back, counting ceiling tiles. "It just doesn't make any sense, though."

"No argument here."

"I mean, right? If neither of us knows her, there's no motive." She lies back, rubs her eyes. "And even if we had one, we'd both be idiots to stick the body in the closet."

"So you think someone snuck in here and hid the body while we were sleeping?"

"Yeah, except that makes even less sense."

"And it kinda freaks me out."

"Yeah, no duh," she says. "And again, I'd say *Let's call the cops,* except the whole thing looks so deliberate. Like we were set up or something."

And then I sigh and sit up, because we have to figure this out. My back is against the painted concrete wall, and it's cold and it hurts, which is just what I need to keep myself awake and focused. "Well—maybe if we could figure out who killed her..."

"What do you mean?"

"I dunno, we could do some amateur detective work, or something. Is that such a terrible idea? Dig around, see what we find?"

She sits up. Leans against the wall, almost in the corner. "And while we're playing your detective games, we—what? Just leave her in your closet? Let her rot and stink until she oozes out under the door?"

"Okay, eew."

"Um, *yeah,* eew—that's what dead bodies do, Phelia. They rot. They stink. And they give themselves away really fast. They don't wait around for you to solve their murders. This isn't an Agatha Christie novel."

"Is that—?"

"Yeah, that was dig at your book collection."

"Oh." She's got an entire shelf of Nicholas Sparks, but I'll bring that up some other time.

"Anyway, I wouldn't even know where to start with this. I've been Facebook-stalking her all day, and she's *boring.* I can't imagine who would want to murder her."

"A rapist?"

"She's fully clothed."

"A...mugger?"

"She's still got her wallet. And let me remind you that *her throat has been torn out.*"

"So...bears?"

She sighs. "Yeah, that sounds right. Yogi came down from Jellystone, stole her pic-a-nic basket, and dumped her in our closet."

Okay, okay, point taken. "So..." I finally say, "I guess we're dealing with whatever sort of sick bastard violently murders people for the hell of it, and then shoves the bodies into random closets while the occupants of the room sleep soundly."

"...yeah."

I jump up from the bed and twist the lock on the door to the room so hard that my hand aches.

"Look," she says, "we just need to get rid of the body, however we can. Whatever's going on here, we don't want to get involved in it any more than we already are."

"Okay, fine, Kate, you win. What do you suggest we do with it?"

She's pacing. "I—I honestly hadn't thought that far ahead."

"Oh."

And we stand there, and she wrings her hands, and we stare at the floor. And the wind catches one of our windows and whistles like it sometimes does at night, and it rattles our closet doors.

And I finally say, "I have a thought."

## sun. jan. 16.
## 1:57 am.
## still awake

*Been working on this rhyme now for hours.*
*With each minute ticking by, the air sours.*
*Past that door, near my coat,*
*Is a girl with no throat,*
*And her scent is distinctly not like flowers.*

**Obviously, I'm not happy with that last line.**

Of course when I started, my first line wasn't *Been working on this rhyme now for hours,* because at that point I hadn't been. I originally started with *There once was a corpse in a closet,* but that seemed a little too on-the-nose, and besides, it turns out that pretty much nothing rhymes with *closet,* anyway. I tried *faucet* for a while, but that wasn't a real rhyme, and besides, I didn't have much to say about faucets. I had an image in my head of a bunch of faucets squirting out blood, like something from a cheesy horror movie, but that was just macabre for the sake of macabre, and didn't really have anything to do with my situation, since I haven't actually run into any blood-squirting faucets.

(Nor do I plan to.)

So, anyway, after I tried thinking up rhymes for *closet* for way longer than I should have (*posit? pause it? crawfish?*), I realized that I'd been working on the stupid thing practically forever, and that's how I ended up with that line about *hours* that I'm currently using. All I've really learned from the experience is that I was right all along, and those stupid seventh-graders didn't know what they were talking about, not that they'd ever admit it, because of their stupid stupidity. Limericks are *so damn hard,* just like everything in life is so unfairly hard, and it's a huge bait-and-switch and it's not fair. Parents and teachers and everyone else tell you you're special and you're amazing and everything you do is great from the moment you're born till you hit adulthood, and then it's like *Yeah, just kidding, you're not actually amazing, have fun working three pointless jobs just so you can make rent this month.* And then you realize that *Oh, wait, I'm not really that great, I'm barely even adequate.* And I can't help but think that maybe—*maybe*—the people who actually aspire to greatness should have to work hard, but I'm not one of those people, I just want to be adequate. I'd be fine with adequacy, but even adequacy takes *so much goddamn effort* that it's not even worth it.

Anyway.

Kate and I both changed into my hospital scrubs around midnight, and since then we've both just been sitting here. For hours. Me on my bed, and Kate on hers. And a lot of dorm rooms are little cubes designed to be conducive to hanging out and socializing, but this building is different, and our room is more like a long, skinny shoebox, where each half is a mirror image of the other. Our beds are staring each other down, with their heads against opposite walls and their feet almost touching opposite sides of the doorframe, and there's nothing between us but a dozen feet of empty, sweaty air.

It's almost two now, late Saturday night, or early Sunday morning, or something. The time of night (morning?) when the only real reason to be awake is that the bars won't close for a few more minutes. But here we both are, not at the bars. Not quite awake, but a million miles away from sleep. The lights are still on, the crummy fluorescent lights that make purple things look green, but we still haven't turned them off because we both know we won't sleep anyway.

My left eye is twitching.

She's sitting at her end of this private little tunnel, and I'm sitting at mine, and we just stare at each other because there's nothing left to say. We talked for hours, agreed on a plan, signed a blood pact (not literally, but sort-of-literally), and now there's nothing but silence in the air, because there's nothing more to talk about. Just a plan that we made up only two hours ago, but it already feels so old and ancient, and it's starting to sag in the middle, but what can we do except prop it up and try to make it work? It's too late to think, and there's nothing to do but wait for 2:30, when no one will be awake, we hope. Her eyes are red now, deep red, and they've grown another layer of red with each hour that's gone by, like rings in a tree trunk, and I know because I haven't looked away from her eyes this whole time. And I know mine are red too, because I felt each layer of red form, like the crusty skin you get on top of soup when you don't stir it.

She has her laptop open in her lap like always, but she hasn't even touched it in two hours, and I saw the screen go blank a while ago. I know because the light from the screen was shining reflected in her eyes, and then it disappeared. And when the screen went blank, her lips dried out and they cracked until I almost stood up and screamed *Get some goddamn ChapStick,* and the pores on her nose swelled up with black oil from the sweat that's been beading on her face. Her nose is whistling and she's tapping on her bedframe with a rhythm that keeps switching between a waltz and four-on-the-floor.

Then:

*BONG BONG BONG BONG*

It's her phone and it's ringing. Our red eyes snap open at loud, angry noise, and they meet, just half-cleared, and she jumps and I jump, and she's swinging her head left-to-right, trying to find it, her phone, half-alert, like she just woke up out of a coma. I see it right there, it's under her butt, folded up in the sheets and the blankets and crumbs, and I try to say *Hey, it's right there,* but my mouth's stuck together and dry. Then her hand slaps down onto it, a splash in the deep waves of sheets rolling under the lights, and she holds it up stupidly, trying to find an on/off switch. She punches it (somehow), and finally it turns off, but we're sweating and cold, and I stare at her eyes like they're headlights.

"What the hell was that?" Gasping. *Get it together.*

"My phone."

"I *know* it was your phone. I mean, who's calling at 2:30 in the morning? Why do you have the ringer turned up so high?"

"*God,* chill, Phelia. I just—I set an alarm. In case we fell asleep, or whatever." She's brushing a dread behind her ear.

"You were planning on falling asleep?"

"I was—I mean, just in case, y'know? Anyway, ssshhhh." Puts her finger to her lips.

"It's a little late for *that,* don't you think? Now that your phone's woken up the entire building?"

"*Stop shouting!*" She grabs my arm.

"God, fine, chill." She's locked on my eyes, hand clamped on my tricep.

It takes forever for her grip to relax. "No, you're right," she says. "I'm sorry, I just—I need to relax. I know. I'm sorry." She's whispering now, hot breath in my ear that mixes with the chills. It's a simple plan. We take the body to the hospital, to Sara's morgue. She says it takes forever for the bodies to get moved, anyway, so no one will notice one more. Then we stick it in one of her body coolers, which will keep it hidden and fresh while we try to figure things out from there. Should be easy.

I shake my head, trying to clear it. "I just—why did you have it so *loud?* Turn it off."

"I can't turn alarms off."

"What?"

"Even if you switch the ringer off, the alarms still—"

"Just make sure it doesn't go off again. You have any more alarms set?"

"I—what? Of course not. It's the middle of the night."

"Uh, *yeah,* it's the middle of the night."

"What's your point?"

Ugh. "Never mind. Let's just get her out to your van." It's nice of her to volunteer her van for the cause, since my Escort wouldn't fit the thing, and anyway, it's still stranded over by the coffee shop.

"Yeah, let's do that."

I get the box of latex gloves from my desk, the one I took from the janitor's closet two hours ago, and we each slip on a pair. I've always hated that powdery, clingy feeling.

"Okay," she says, "let's do it."

I nod.

She nods.

I nod again.

"Well?" she says. "Go get her."

"Why do *I* have to get her?"

"Because—because she's in your closet."

"But *I* didn't put her in there!"

"Neither did I!"

"What? Yes you did!"

"Not the first time!"

"But that's—!" I stop because I realize we're almost shouting and I thought I heard something, and I probably actually *did*—it's a big building, and there's always somebody awake, which is another reason to whisper. "Look," I say, "this is stupid. Neither one of us could carry her by herself, anyway, so let's just both go over there and get her, together."

"Yeah. Good plan." We both shamble sideways toward the closet door, and then we stand there, staring at it, a thick panel of wood holding back a flood of stinking carrion. And—somehow—I ended up on the side with the doorknob.

*Damn it.*

"Well?" she whispers. "Open the door."

"I—just gimme a second." My hand's on the knob, and it's cold and it's sweaty. I haven't seen Cyndi since early morning. Up until this moment, I could pretend she wasn't real, and I kind of want to go back to that.

"Well?"

"Shut up, shut *up,* we need to stop talking so much. We're gonna wake someone up, they're gonna hear us—"

"Phelia."

"What?"

"Just open the damn closet."

I close my eyes, and I count to three, and I twist the knob, and the door swings open, dumping a body onto my shoulders, and I hold my breath tight to muffle the scream. Arms around my neck, cold and stiff, goo against my face and an awful smell pouring out of the mouth that won't close, and I squeeze my eyes shut and push her away.

"Not at me, not at *me!*" And Kate's got her now, pushing her back towards me, yelling things I can't hear, and we juggle her back and forth. A hundred and fifty pounds of coed (give or take) hangs on both of our necks and squeezes us together till our faces are smashed between stiff, clammy arms.

Kate's nose is grinding into my cheek, and I catch her eye in the corner of my own and say, "What do we do?"

She gapes at my cheekbone from point-blank range, mouth hanging open. "I—let's—"

"Can you maybe—?"

"Here, put your arm around her back—"

"Okay—"

"No, not like that!"

"Sorry."

"Okay, and I'll get her feet, and—"

And then somehow with some twisting and some rolling, I've got her by her armpits and Kate's got her feet, and her chest is sagging on the floor, but we've got her, at least, and I say, "Okay, let's get out of here."

We waddle sideways, toward the door, like a beast with three backs, and Kate puts her hand on the doorknob, half-twists it, and "Wait."

"What?"

"How will we—how do we get her down to my van?"

"What do you mean? We just take the elevator, and—"

"Really. The elevator."

"...or the stairs?"

She's wincing from the weight of the body. (*Please*, I'm holding the heavy part.) "Come on, Phelia, you really can't see the problem with that plan?"

"Well, I mean—"

"You're talking about going right out the front door with a dead body," she hisses. "There are *other people here*. I mean, you know that, right?"

"Uh—damn it." How is it we didn't think of this? We spent literally an hour planning out exactly what we would do once we got to the hospital, but we didn't spend a second discussing how to get the body there in the first place. "What do we do?"

Cyndi's dead legs are dragging Kate lower and lower, and she leans against the wall, leaving me shouldering almost all the weight. "Well, uh, we can't go out the door."

"We *can't go out the door?* What does that leave? A window?"

She bites her lip and drops her end, and Cyndi's weight jerks me toward the floor as Kate wanders absentmindedly toward the window. "That's actually not a bad idea," she says.

"*What?*"

"The window. We'll get her out through the window, and then—"

"You want me to *climb out the window?*" I say, and she stares at me like I'm an idiot, and maybe I am. It's so hard to think straight.

"No. We *drop her out,* and then we *go pick her up.*"

"We're *five floors up.* She'll *splash.*"

"Bodies don't splash."

"*Hers might!*"

"Look, c'mere."

"Come over there? But what do I do with—"

"Just drop her."

"On the *floor?*"

"Yes—no—look, just drag her, if you want. Or something. Look—what I'm trying to tell you is there's a dumpster down there we can drop her into."

"And then what?"

"I'll pull the van around, we fish her out and throw her in the back, and we're in business."

"What if someone sees us?"

"You have a better idea?"

I don't.

"Look," she says, "I'm gonna go down there and pull the van around. You see if you can get the screen off the window."

"Uh—how...?"

"There's a screwdriver in my desk. Just make it happen." And she runs silently out the door and the next thing I realize is that I'm half-squatting in the middle of the room with a corpse hanging around my waist, tongue dangling out the side of her mouth, whitish pupils staring straight into my eyes. I'm sweating and cold just like she is, and the lights are too bright, and I'm wondering, do I drop her and go look for the screwdriver or do I try to pull her over there with me and let her hang onto my waist while I'm combing through Kate's drawers, or what?

*White eyes filled with cold accusation*
*And a tongue that knows no satiation;*
*Her boobs drag on the floor*
*While I pick through a drawer*
*And I prep for a defenestration.*

I always wanted to use the word *defenestration* for something. Anyway, Kate seriously needs to organize these drawers, because I can't find anything. There's makeup piled on top of pencils and pens next to dirty dishes and junk mail, and so far I haven't come across anything you might find at a hardware store, not even a rubber band or a nail. In the fifth drawer I try, I see a nail file sitting on top, and I figure that's better than nothing.

There are only four screws holding the screen onto the window, and they're Phillips heads, which makes it awkward to loosen them with a pointed file—I have to hold it mostly sideways and sort of crank it—but eventually all four screws fall loose onto the floor, where they disappear into her rug. I stick my head out the window and I see that she's standing in the dumpster, waiting. She whispers something up at me, but she's so far down that I can't actually hear anything she says. I say, "Are you ready?" and she says something, and I shrug and push Cyndi out the window.

I watch her body topple end-over-end through the night while Kate screams and jumps out of the way, followed by a muffled *clang* when Cyndi hits the dumpster. Then the dust settles and Kate's standing there, dirty and scared, staring up and me and gritting her teeth. "What was *that?*"

"I thought you said to drop her."

"I said to *wait.*"

"Just now?"

"Yeah."

"That's what you were saying?"

"Yeah."

"Oh."

"You didn't hear me?"

"Sorry."

"Why didn't you ask me to repeat what I said?"

"It, uh, seemed rude, I guess."

"Seriously? Just get down here and help me. We need to stop yelling."

"Yeah."

As I crank the window shut, I realize how sore my arms already are. I guess I've been running on adrenalin up to this point (how else could I have lifted a body out the window?), and I'm starting to realize just how hard it's going to be to keep this up. I'm seeing spots, but I catch my breath and I stumble toward the door. I lock it but I leave the lights on, and I trip down the stairwell and out into the security lights in the alley, where Kate's waiting in the dumpster.

"Over here!" She's whispering, but still loud, and it's kind of annoying (to be honest) that she feels the need to tell me where she is. I can actually see her, even from way over here at the door—she's just a head, bobbing down above the lip of the dumpster, while she grunts and strains trying to pull the body out, and suddenly I feel pretty good about myself for being able to move the thing on my own. Her curly dreads are flipping up and down in the harsh shadows, and she grunts and pulls with her back. "Gimme a hand?"

I'm sore and my arms feel like they're dragging on the ground, but whatever, this needs to happen. I'm looking the dumpster up and down, trying to find a way in. It seemed like a good enough idea to drop the body in here, but now I'm honestly wondering what we were thinking. It's not like I didn't know that dumpsters were big, but at the moment I'm looking at having to scale a ten-foot vertical wall made of rusty metal, and I'm realizing that there's no such thing as a simple plan. I'm trying to think back to the time when my dad made me take gymnastics, but it's been so long. I'm reaching up, grabbing at anything, but there's nothing but sharp, jagged rust.

"You having trouble?"

"No. Yes. Shut up."

"Would you like to know how I got up?"

"Uh—I can—yes." So humiliating. I didn't ask to be a fatass, it just happened. Damn Snickers bars.

"Look over at the wall of the building. See how the bricks are sort of uneven?"

"I can—uh—yeah."

"I sort of shimmied up that way. Y'know, put my back against the dumpster and pushed against the wall with my feet—"

"Were you raised by mountain goats?"

"No, I was—just get up here, please?"

I look the bricks in the wall up and down—they're actually rocks, yellow limestone with mortar in between, so it's a little bit like mountain climbing, which coincidentally is something I've been avoiding my whole life. I grab a brick and lead with my right foot.

I'm thanking God right now I was smart enough to wear my Chuck Taylors. Honestly, I really felt like wearing flip-flops, but it's good to know I was smart enough to realize that was a bad idea. This wall would cut up flip-flopped feet pretty bad, and I'm about to jump into a rusty dumpster. I'm not sure how current my tetanus shot is, either (it used to be my mom's job to keep track of that, but I imagine she's given up on that sort of thing lately). I give one last push against the wall with my foot and jerk the rusty lip with my hand, and I land facedown in garbage juice.

*Now I wish I had gone to the gym more.*

*(If my swimsuit still fit, I could swim more—*
*'Cause the lifeguard there's hot,*
*And I like him a lot,*
*And I think I might like to see—*

"Phelia!"

"Uh—" I'm trying to pull myself to my feet, but the goo is sticky and all I can see is brown. I think I'm standing on something sharp. And I need to stop with the limericks. They're starting to get compulsive.

Also, that lifeguard's not even that hot. I was just looking for a rhyme.

"Are you all right?" Kate's saying. "You look like you're spacing a little."

"I'm okay, I'm sorry, it's just—y'know—"

"I know. Just give me a hand with her."

"Yeah." I grab Cyndi's armpits—again (why do I always have to get the heavy part?)—and we inch our way up the dumpster's slope. Kate's going up backwards, pulling (jerking) on her knees, and I'm stumbling forward, pushing like Sisyphus, and Cyndi's dragging her butt on the metal.

*CLANG*

I dropped her arm. I dropped her arm and it hit the metal and it was loud and we freeze and we stare. Kate's eyes jerk left and then right, like she's trying to see behind her without moving her body, and we listen, but there's no one coming. Nothing but silence in the air, swirling around us like the steam from our sweat that I can see rising, even though it's a cold night.

I crouch down, slowly, reaching for the arm. That *clang* left me on edge, and now every little sound, even the pop of my knee from crouching, makes me sure someone's coming. I wrap my fingers around the cold skin, and I stand back up, and we start shuffling toward the metal slope's crest once more, until finally we're looking down at the wide-open hatch of Kate's van, where the yellow dome light illuminates the Peavey amps and the cigarette burns.

"So now we just..."

And we stand there and look at each other, because we're slowly becoming aware of the thousands and thousands of details we never once thought of when we were making this plan. The dumpster is huge, and the van is ten feet below us, and we're wondering now, what do we do? Just throw her?

(Or...?)

I say, "Maybe I could hop down there and you could toss her to me?"

"Are you kidding? You'll die."

"Yeah, probably." A cold breeze whistles by, and we both shiver. I say, "Maybe we could just...toss her in."

"Into the hatch? Like, directly into my van?"

"...yeah?"

"But my shocks!"

"That van's like 40 years old. Does it even *have* shocks anymore?"

"Yes—I mean—I don't know. I don't know anything about cars. But if we wreck my van, that's the end of my music career."

"Uh—?"

"Oh, and we're stuck with the body," she adds.

"Yeah." We stand here looking stupid, till I finally say, "I can't come up with anything better. You?"

Sighs. "No."

We both swallow hard, and I say, "Count of three?" and she nods, and we swing her once, twice, and then three times, and try not to close our eyes too tight, and let her go flying, down toward the faint-glowing light. And I hear a *clank* and a *thud* and Kate's busted shocks squeaking, and when I look I see a stiff, gray corpse lying on the stack of amps, a single arm sticking out into the night over her bumper.

It looks totally metal.

That's not a thought that I want to hang onto, because there's nothing funny about this situation, nor is there anything funny about the noise we just made. We're staring at each other, wincing, waiting for someone to come running out the door shouting *What's going on,* but the door stays closed.

And then, suddenly, she jumps down onto the pavement, and I wish for a second that I was as in-shape as she is. Then, blindly, I grab at the edge and jump off. And with my eyes closed I feel my feet swinging in the dark and my hand shredding flesh through my glove on the filthy, rusted metal, till I let go and wait forever for gravity to work its magic. And my face and my hands feel the asphalt.

"You okay?" She yells that over her shoulder because she's already in the driver's seat with the engine running, and I trip over my hands and feet running for the passenger door, which I jerk open. I hop inside and the torn vinyl of the passenger seat is cold on my ass, and before I even get my door closed, we're rolling forward. "Put your seatbelt on," she says.

# sun. jan. 16.
## 2:51 am.
## putting my seatbelt on...

"Seriously?" I say. "My seatbelt?"

"What?" She turns onto a back road with no streetlights.

I reach around for my seatbelt and say, "We're out in the middle of the night to dump a dead body, and you're worried about whether or not I'm wearing my seatbelt?" I'm reaching around for it, but I think it might be caught in the door.

She says, "You gotta take care of yourself first, right? If you die on the way there, I'll have two bodies to get rid of."

"Thanks for your concern." I finally have the thing dislodged from the door, and but I have to slam the ends together several times before they latch.

"I'm just saying." She turns down another residential road. We're weaving, doubling back, trying not to leave an obvious trail. "If you don't look out for your own health, you won't be able to look out for anything else. I mean, why do you think we have a gym on campus? Just so shallow people can get laid?"

"That's what I always assumed, yeah. Well—that and it's an excuse to jack up student fees."

She makes another random, arbitrary turn, and says, "God, you're cynical." Her headlights catch a cat crossing the street, and he freezes for a second, and his eyes glow yellow and green before he disappears into the dark. "How does someone get so cynical, anyway? If I were Freud, I'd guess you were abused as a child."

"Worse. I was abused *by* children."

She laughs, but then she realizes I'm serious. "Wait, what?"

I bite my lip. "Ever been cussed out by a room full of 12-year-olds?"

"No, but it sounds hilarious."

"God *damn* it," I say, "I knew you'd say that. You open up to someone and they just think it's funny. Every. Damn. Time." I pull my feet up on the seat and I hug myself.

She sits there silent, gearing up and down as we curve in between some HOA-funded parks and swimming pools, and I hope she actually knows where we're going and isn't just waiting for me to give her directions. Her headlights catch someone, and we both jump, but he's just a jogger, a pudgy old guy with a sweatband on his head and a dumbbell in each hand. If I looked like that, I'd run at night too. (Maybe I should.)

And she finally says, "You're right."

"What?"

"You're right. I shouldn't have laughed. I'm sorry. I thought you were joking."

"I wasn't."

"I know," she says, her eyes tracing the shadows. She takes a deep breath, and she adds, "And you're right. Abuse is abuse. It doesn't matter who's doing it." Houses fly by, houses with gnomes and votive statues in their gardens. "It's like—well, like with rape, I guess." She's biting her lip, thinking hard about whether she wants to continue with that thought. "If you get raped by a guy, there are support groups, and *You're so brave,* and stuff, but if you get raped by a girl, you're just a freak."

"People get raped by girls?"

"See? *That.* Exactly that. That's the reaction you get, if you're *lucky.* But I had a guy friend, and this chick slipped him something one night and then had her way with him, and for a long time he was just too embarrassed to tell anyone." She gears up and adds, "And finally, he told me, and I just laughed at him. Like his pain somehow meant less because someone weaker than him had caused it. And then—" She turns right. "What I'm trying to say, I guess, is I'm kind of an asshole. I know I am. I've hurt so many people, and not even in a fun way. Just by being a callous bitch when they tell me about their pain, y'know? And, y'know, I'm sorry."

Streetlights whipping by. Wind beating on the side of the van. With every bump, Cyndi's hand slaps on the floor, and one of her jagged fingernails is tearing at the carpet. Kate's driving faster now, barely paying attention to the road. And finally, I say, "This really isn't the same as that."

She says, "But it *is*. Pain is pain, y'know? It's not a competition. It's not like, *Oh, he was hurting more than you, so it's okay for me to make light of your pain.* That's not how it works. You're feeling what you're feeling, and I have no business dismissing that, and I did, and I shouldn't have. I just—*God*—I see patterns like this in my behavior all the time, and it's not okay, and I'm sorry."

The *tick-tick-tick* of the fingernail in the carpet. The mist of the night in the streetlights. The side mirror rattling outside my window. I say, "It's all right, I get it." I pick at a thread in my seat and add, "I mean, it probably *is* kind of funny. When I hear kids cursing at each other on the street, I crack up, because they don't know how to do it. It's just kind of embarrassing for them. But when you're trapped in a room with 30 other people, and they're all abusing you, it really doesn't matter how old or intimidating they are, y'know? It hurts."

"So what happened?"

"Well—y'know. I was doing my student teaching, right? Seventh grade? So I thought I'd teach these kids to write poetry. I show them some different forms, but all they want to do is write limericks. Honestly, I was probably lucky to get them to move beyond haikus. But anyway, I'm begging them to try something else, something a little more challenging, and the teacher's not in the room, and they all just go nuts. Out of their seats, destroying things, cursing at me, calling me stuff I can't even repeat. So, anyway, I never went back. Changed my major the next day."

"Geez."

"Yeah, I know. It's lame."

"Well, I mean—that *is* really awful. But that doesn't seem like typical seventh-grader behavior to me."

"What are you saying?"

Shrugs. "I dunno, just that it's weird. And that, I dunno, maybe you shouldn't have given up on teaching after a single bad experience? Like I said, I doubt that was typical."

"Yeah, I know. But it's like with your rape metaphor. If the first boy I ever met had raped me, I probably would have been turned off to dating for the rest of my life."

"Gotcha." We're getting closer to the hospital now, and the fingernail scraping through the carpet is getting louder.

"Anyway, it's just as well," I tell her. "I never really wanted to be a teacher. Got a lot happier once I embraced my identity as a writer."

"Except you don't write."

"Yeah, that's true." I bite at a hangnail. "I guess it's just easier to do nothing."

"It sure is." She turns into the hospital parking lot and gears down. This is it, we're actually doing this thing. "Anyway," she says, "you might be right about the gym thing."

"The gym thing?"

"Yeah, I think you're right that it only exists to wring student fees out of us. God knows I never make it over there." I laugh, and she says, "Where am I going, exactly?"

"We need to park around back. In the shadows, if you can."

She parks the van and crosses herself as she jerks the gearshift back and kills the engine. Then we sit in the dark. The lot is deserted, and a streetlight behind us flickers off. The air in the van's getting cold, but we just sit, breathing stale, congealed smoke, each of us waiting for the other to open her door. Waiting for a *click* to assure us that this is really happening.

I open mine.

She follows my lead and then our doors *clunk* shut and the yellow dome light blinks out. The sky is mostly overcast, but the black clouds glow around their edges with the weak light of the stars.

"Wait here a second," I whisper.

"Hold on," she says, grabbing my arm before I can run off. "Are there security cameras?"

"In the lot? Or inside the hospital?"

"Uh, either?"

"I haven't seen any. And if there are, they probably don't work."

"How would you know that?"

"Call it a hunch? This place is decrepit. And Sara was saying—"

"Who?"

"Uh—never mind. Just—just wait here for a sec."

Unless someone found it and moved it, the gurney should be right where I left it Friday morning; in the dark of the night, though, the hedge where I hid it is just a mass of jagged shadows. Thorns and branches and broken bottles sticking in a thousand different directions, stabbing the night air with a sickening enthusiasm. I duck down below them and reach blindly into the dark, feeling for the cold metal or the soft foam. Thorns scrape against my arm and blood leaks out, but I keep stumbling forward till my forehead bumps against something icy. I curse, but I grab the thing and start pulling.

Now that I know where it was, I feel like an idiot for not seeing it right away. It was only stuck halfway into the bush, its back end hanging out like a pedo's ass in a public park. The metal frame digs into my hand, and the wind whistles through it, but I grit my teeth and drag it around to the back of the van, where Kate is waiting. She says, "You ready?"

"I guess."

She opens the hatch and again we're drowning in yellow light and looking into the half-closed eyes of a dead coed. We each grab a random limb and pull as hard as we can because the sooner we get her out the sooner we can close the hatch and douse the light and take her inside and hide her away and be done with this mess. Kate's got an arm and I've got a leg and we pull till she lands slantwise on the slab, with an arm hanging off one way and a leg hanging off another, and she slams the van shut, and we close our eyes and wait for someone to see us and yell *Hey what are you doing,* but no one does. All we hear is the wind picking up again, and Cyndi's hair blows around and catches the streetlights in its blond streaks.

We head for the door, and for a few horrible seconds, we're out in the open, under the streetlamps, where anybody could see us. But then finally, we're standing at the back entry, the one I stood at for the first time less than a week ago, shaking and nervous about my new job. Now I'm shaking again, and so is Kate, but I grit my teeth because this has to happen.

I reach for the ID scanner, which is hanging even more floppily than the last time I saw it, and I jerk my temporary card back and forth in it until I hear the door *click*. Then I pull on the cold handle, revealing a hallway full of whitish tiles dripping with fluorescent light. But—

"Damn it."

"What?"

"Just get her inside," I say. "Hurry up." I pull hard on the gurney, dragging Kate with me, until we stumble in the door and catch our breath.

"What's going on?" she whispers, and silently, I point ten feet down the hall, where a security camera's light is glowing red. "I *told* you," she says.

"It probably doesn't work."

"But what if it *does?*"

"Uh—" I look down, at the wastebasket that tripped me on my first day here. As before, it's full-to-bursting with hairnets and facemasks. The smell isn't great, but it's something? I guess?

I reach down gingerly, trying to touch the used safety gear with as little of my hand as possible, which is ridiculous considering I'm about to put it over my face, but I guess you do what you can to make the awful things you're doing seem slightly less awful in your own mind.

I snag two facemasks and two hairnets from on top of an empty Lunchables box, and I toss one of each at Kate. "Put these on."

"Are you—?"

"*Just do it.*"

I tie my own facemask over my nose and mouth, noticing that it smells of ham and cheese, and then I tuck my hair into the bouffant. Kate does the same. Then we look each other over, and we look like extras from a movie about a zombie outbreak, and it occurs to me that that might be exactly what we are. "We need to cover her up," she says.

"Huh?"

"We need to cover up the body. We can't have anybody seeing what we're carting around here."

"Well—" I'm thinking—"it's a hospital, so there's gotta be sheets everywhere."

"I thought you said you worked here. Don't you know where anything is?"

"I've only worked, like, two shifts."

"Okay, well, just—"

I open the nearest door, hoping for a linen closet, but I'm met with a patient's room, dark and filled with snores while a monitor beeps. I panic for a second before I realize there's a linen closet just inside the door, and in one motion I open it, grab a sheet, and toss it over Cyndi. For just a second it catches in the air and hangs like a dirty plastic bag in a breeze, and then it flops onto her face and her knees, leaving a single cold foot sticking out in the ham-and-cheese-scented air. Kate grabs the corner and jerks it hard over her foot like she's hiding a monster under a bed. Then I say, "Let's go," and we start down the hall, wheels clacking loud.

One wheel on the gurney squeaks, and the squeak seems loud, but I tell myself that squeaky things must coast down these halls all the time, and no one will notice us. Just two patient transporters moving a body, is all. A nurse walks past us but she stares at the floor, and I wonder how long it'll be till I'm like her—someone who's seen death squeaking by on a cart so many times that she won't even look into the eyes of the living. Out of my eye's corner, I see Kate watching her, craning her neck to make sure she keeps walking, and I want to say *Stop that, you'll just draw attention*, but I can't bring myself to say anything. She's watching so closely she trips on the gurney and it skips and it squeaks, and I swear I hear Cyndi moan under the sheet, but that makes no sense, and I tell myself *Chill, just keep moving. You're almost home-free, just keep moving, it's this way, down this hall, you're almost to the elevator, just don't slow down.*

And then there it is. A recess of gray-painted steel in the beige-painted wall, with a cobweb-filled corner, because nobody cleans down here, ever, I guess. One floor and we're there. Just an elevator ride away from freedom.

"Ophelia."

"What?"

"Are you going to push the button?"

"Yeah, sorry."

But then, three hallways back, there's a voice and some footsteps. "Yeah, I found someone. So far it's been interesting." It's Sara's voice, coming this way. My hand bursts forward and hammers the button, again and again, trying to drown out her footsteps. *Clickclickclickclickclickclickclick.* "Nah, I'm not really worried about double-blind. I just need to prove that it works. And it *does*, and we can work out the bugs later. I just need to show that—"

The door judders open and I yell-whisper "Move!" and I jerk the gurney forward as I leap on, dragging Kate behind me, and pound the *Door close* button over and over again. I duck behind the wall and close my eyes and pray.

The door closes.

And then for a breathless moment I'm shut in a tiny room with Kate and a corpse, and the air hangs sticky while the fake wood paneling on the walls sweats, and the dust and the cobwebs fill me with sneezes that never come. The floor sinks beneath us.

"What was that about?" she says.

I try to say something, but what is there to say?

"Who was that?"

"The—the mortician—"

And there's more, and we both know there's more, but both of us stand here too scared to make noise, while our guts both drop lower and then finally the door groans back open. I jerk on the cold steel again and drag Kate down the dark reddish hallway behind me, saying, "We have to hurry," but I'm not sure if she even hears. We fly down the hall till we get to the door of the morgue, and I scan my ID and it opens.

Darkness.

As always, the lights are off in here, which is just as well, I guess. Cold, wet, dark, with row after row of sterile steel tables covered in sheets with hands jutting haphazardly out from beneath them. Behind us the red glow of an *Exit* sign, and somewhere from in front of us the cold draft of AC, cranked up by some bureaucrat who doesn't know it's January. As my eyes adjust to the dark, Kate's masked face comes back into view and our gazes catch in the icy air. Then we both look away.

The door shuts behind us and we slide the gurney in between the rows of coolers, and I pick one at random, blindly in the dark. A cold, shriveled face, a naked old man. I slam it shut, hard. And the next one has more human flesh. It's a woman's, a shriveled old bag, belching gas in my face. They're all naked, all of them, covered in droplets of water or I-don't-know-what, and my stomach is turning while the room spins around me (the black, and the red, and the cold, clammy flesh).

Then, a voice in the dark: "I know, I know, but I'm making progress with it, I'll just keep tweaking things, and—" Kate grabs me, pulls me down, behind the coolers, as Sara steps in the door, tromping through the dark, still talking on her phone. "And what if it *does?* No great loss to the world." Then the door to her office closes and it's quiet again.

Kate whispers, "I think I found an empty one," and she pulls a drawer open. I brace myself for cold, wrinkly skin, but it's empty, just like she promised.

"How'd you know it was—?"

"There's no name card on it."

"What?"

"Never mind. Now help me out," she says, and I pull the sheet off and I reach to pick Cyndi up and Kate does too, but then she stops and says, "Wait a second."

"What?" It's cold in here and we're whispering loud, and I just want to be done, to go to bed, but of course she's overthinking it.

"We're going to have to undress her."

"*What?*" Then I realize I said *What* so loud that Sara had to have heard, and I duck low again, and I shiver.

"Look at all the bodies in here," she says. "They're all naked. We're going to have to undress her too, or she'll stick out like a sore thumb. There's no choice here."

"What do we do with her clothes?"

"Throw them away? Burn them? I don't know. But we need to get them off of her right now."

Ugh. "You're right."

She's already pulling a boot off.

I swallow hard and start pulling on her earrings, dangly things that catch on her flesh and tear it like meat. There's a necklace too, but I'm done being careful; I grab it and pull and the clasp breaks apart like it's made of foil.

I shove it all in my pockets.

Now Kate's got her boots and her socks off and she's working at undoing her belt, and I need to catch up, so I start working on the enormous buttons on her jacket. Then I grab the cuffs of the sleeves and yank toward myself, and I punch myself in the jaw when it finally comes off. The draft from the vent is right behind me, and shivers are running up and down my spine, but I force my stiff hands to grab onto the hem of her sweater, and her arms flop over her head when they come free.

Her bra gives me a bit more trouble since she's lying on her back, but I manage to slide my hand under her icy skin and twist the fabric till it comes unhooked and she pops out, and then it's just a flick of my wrist and she's totally undressed. Kate doesn't even blink, just says, "Okay," and then we lift her and drop her lopsidedly into the drawer, and she pushes it in and it shuts with a *click*.

And she's gone.

136 ~ Luke T. Harrington

And we never have to see her again.

We stand there together, in a pile of clothes, the gurney between us, and I look at Kate, and she looks at me, and we finally both smile a little. We smile, I think, because neither of us really thought that this moment would come. We've had Cyndi now less than 24 hours, but somehow it feels like it's been weeks or months, like death has been dragging behind us for years. Now the weight of that death is all gone, and we smile at each other with big, ugly smiles, and then I'm in her arms and then she's in my arms, and it feels like forever since I've hugged anyone. She's sweaty and so am I.

Then I break away, and we pick up the clothes, and we pile them back on the gurney, with the sheet on top. And we start for the exit.

"Get down!" Kate's pulled me back onto my knees behind the coolers, and we sweat and we hold in our breath while Sara stomps back through the room, whispering on her phone again.

"Don't worry, I've got a backup plan. Look, this is my only chance to leave my mark on the world, so—"

The door clicks shut and she's gone.

Our breath hangs in our lungs, but we're alone, finally, and Sara's gone, and Cyndi's gone, and we might actually make it out of this. We wait till we don't hear her footsteps anymore, and then we wheel the squeaky gurney out the door and down the hall to the elevator. I push the button and we wait and the doors jerk open. And the gurney squeaks on, and we follow, and the doors slam shut and we rise, but my eyelids are heavy and sinking. The ragged red carpet is pushing us up toward the sky, which is still a full hour from sunrise, and relief in my gut is swelling to modest ambition. To be fully honest, it's kind of a strange feeling to suddenly have motivation. I see now that all that it took was a single accomplishment under my belt, even if said accomplishment only consisted of hiding a body. First thing on Monday, I'll see my advisor again and we'll figure out how I can graduate in a semester or two (I'm sure that it's possible); then I'll get started on writing that novel that's bouncing around in my head and has been there forever, and then I'll check Craigslist and find a new job that's far from the corpses and bedpans as soon as I can. The glow lights the threads in my scrubs in a green-yellow sheen, and the air's feeling fresher. We rise and we rise until Kate melts away and it dumps me out into a gray cell that's strangely familiar. A cell that I've seen from the outside, but once, long ago, it was mine. The eyes of the children that looked through the windows and pleaded with me while I ran for a gurney—but those eyes are mine now. They're mine, and I'm inside and standing behind them with them in my head, surrounded by walls made of concrete, the frame of a cold, metal bed, and an icy steel mirror. My eyes behind glass, looking out through the diamond-crossed wires at a brightly lit room ringed with eyes just like mine and a thumb pressing hard on the pages of *Hamlet*. And Sara stands outside the cell, looking in at me, mouthing sharp words like *I win* and *You know that they'll never believe you again from now on.* My mother has hands on her shoulders and leads her away, and says something to her, but I can't hear anything inside my cell. A memory that I had forgotten—this cold, concrete cell with the ugly steel fixtures and one tiny window that spills in gray sunlight and casts long, black shadows of bars. I seethe and I choke on my tears, and I plan for the day when I'll make her cry back all the tears that she gave me. All day and all night everything that I see is through one tiny window that bleeds bright fluorescence and rows of the staring eyes into my tiny, square box. Eight tiny corners of ugly concrete that twist in forever and press on my eyes, and one-thousand nights ago, I still remember when she got the curtains she hung on our bunk beds—the dark, heavy curtains that blocked out the light of my nightlight and let her do to me whatever she wanted. The long midnight sessions of her playing doctor, till I begged her to stop and she mouthed the word *No*, every night, for six weeks or six years. Till I grew up and finally got her alone, and I reached out to hurt her as much as she'd deep-wounded me, and that's when we were found. My mother screamed (loud), and she carted me off in the back of her car, and I finally woke up in these four hard, gray walls, with the light pressing in from the hole in the door, and the huge man outside with the sneer and the twitch, and he'd bang on the door and he'd force his way in. And I run from him over a sea of gray eyes and dark curtains and hot, sweaty palms, and grinding concrete turning thumbnails to stumps, and the midnight, the endless, dark clarity bleeding from walls, tearing me from the inside and screaming its screams in my ears till I beg it to stop, and I'm falling. I fall into memories lost long ago till I tear through the wall and I'm back in my bed with the sun again.

**sun. jan. 16.**
**10:43 am.**
**anyway**

**I've been thinking a lot lately** about what Kate said, about things being *made new.* Like she was saying, it's a strange turn of phrase, one that the first time you hear it you say *I know what that means,* but then you think about it for a minute and you realize *I guess maybe I don't know what that means,* and then you think about it for a couple of hours and you're like *I actually have no idea at all what that means.* People talk about buying "new" shoes, but the shoes are always made from old, dead animals. People talk about a "new" baby, but the baby's always made from recycled DNA and whatever crap its mom has been eating. Then it comes out into the world smothered in old blood and old gunk, and pushed headfirst through a sweaty vagina.

Kids are gross.

I'm not saying I don't like new shoes, just that Kate might have a point. I can't stop thinking about the possibility of *starting*—not just, like, *starting over* or *starting fresh,* but just plain *starting.* Is that possible? I remember reading once that even Big Bang cosmology can't account for the first $10^{-37}$ seconds of the universe's existence, whatever that means. We talk about newness like it's a thing, like we see it every day, but it's not and we don't. Everything is made from old, recycled stardust.

I think I'm starting to understand Kate's fascination, at least a little.

Last night in the elevator, before the nightmares started, I remember standing there, thinking about all the things I would do tomorrow as soon as the sun came up. Graduate, find a job, write that book. But this morning, now that I'm sitting in my room with the blinds half-open, in the glow of a stale sunrise and the last vestiges of evaporating frost, all that seems secondary. To really fix things, to really start over (there it is again), I'll have to track down my father.

I don't know where that thought came from, to be honest. I haven't given the man a thought in years, and it's not like I feel particularly hung up on the guy. It's just a bridge that's been burned, and when something is lying broken, you fix it. You ever feel like you don't *want* to do something, and maybe you can't even think of a good reason for it, but you still *have* to do it? Because it's, y'know, the "right thing" (whatever that means)? Yeah, this is that.

Is that stupid?

I've been poking around online this morning, trying to find a phone number for him. There's a name that matches my dad's on several of those shady "white pages" websites that people only use when they're desperate. I briefly thought about looking at Facebook, but no one ever puts their phone number on Facebook anymore, plus it doesn't seem like the sort of site my dad would spend a lot of time on. But anyway, all the white pages listings match up, so I guess the number here is legit. There's no picture, just one of those silhouettes with a question mark over it, but I guess that shouldn't surprise me too much. Actually, it'd be scarier if this sort of website had more people's pictures, right?

And now that I think about it, I could probably get the number from Sara—I'm pretty sure she still talks to the guy (he's paying a lot of her bills right now, I think). But whatever, if I call her, I know what'll happen. It'll be just like last time, where she answers and I realize I can't say anything and then I just hang up. I still wish she didn't have that sort of power over me, but one thing at a time, right? I've been staring at this number for almost an hour now, and I should probably either call or give up.

And I need to stop giving up. That's not something I'm going to let myself do anymore.

I carefully punch each number into my phone, and then my thumb hovers—for too long—over *Call.*

Then I stand up and walk out the door, locking it behind me. If I'm going to be awake, I can at least get a late breakfast or something. And somehow, that momentum, moving forward, even just toward breakfast, gives me the spark I need to let my thumb fall. I trip down the stairs, putting the phone to my ear. It rings.

I close my eyes (hard). I can't see where I'm going, but after four-and-a-half years I know the campus by heart. I burst out into the winter air, and it's cool and it's dry with the smell of brown grass and mud. A third ring, a fourth. Then the fifth is cut off halfway through and I swallow my breath and I squash the impulse to throw the phone into a snowdrift and run, and I clench my fist till the handset bleeds silicon, but then I hear his voice.

"Hey, sorry I missed your call, leave a message."

I open my eyes and I breathe. Voicemail. I can do that, sure. "Hey, uh, Dad. It's Ophie. Ophelia. Your daughter. Sorry, uh, sorry I missed you. I just thought we should catch up. Or something. Give me a call back at this number."

It's weird when you gear up for something awkward and possibly contentious and then it's not. He might not even call me back. Would that be so bad?

Ah, damn it.

He's gonna think I was calling about money.

I could kick myself for leaving that message now. He'll call me back with a lecture about being responsible and not wasting my time, and I want to chuck the phone again, but I shove it back in my pocket, so hard that the seam tears. But I'm at the door to the dining hall now, so I guess I might as well have something to eat.

It's dark inside, even compared to the clouded-out sun. I haven't felt like eating in days (*O, true apothecary*), but I know I should probably try. I swallow the cottony lump in my throat and scan my ID badge (guy at the register doesn't even look up), and step into the garish bazaar of assorted foodstuffs.

The room reeks of industrial-strength dishwasher soap. If I can find something bland, maybe I can force it down. The specials are waffles and omelets and sausage, doubtless all frozen from a factory, and I can't stop thinking about them rolling off the line on a sanitized conveyor belt. I turn to the old standby, the breakfast nook, where cereal comes out of a faucet. Froot Loops and Lucky Charms and other grain-sugar pellets that scrape your tongue like sand. I reach far away from the sugary stuff (toward the cardboardy stuff) and my hand lands on the knob for the Cheerios and jerks it back and forth fast, trying to get as little as possible into my bowl. The loathsome rings bounce rustily down the chute like a knocking car engine, and they smell like old newspapers. And the milk from the machine next-door smells like a foot, but I put some on them anyway, and it erupts out of their little white O-holes with a bubbly, white stickiness. I grab a spoon and collapse into a booth and stab at the floating things, trying to work up enough hatred to make them worth grinding between my teeth.

Maybe I should just give up and go back to bed.

A tray clatters down across from me, and it's covered in waffles and eggs and bananas, and I struggle not to vomit from the smell. "Hey Phelia."

It's Kate.

I say hey back, and I throw down my spoon, and it bounces on the tray, throwing gray-silver sunlight back out the window. She sits and she bites her lip and plays with a fork.

Hesitates.

"You feeling okay?" she says.

"Yeah, sure. Just a weird morning so far."

"Weird how?"

I slouch back against the seat and I shrug. "Called my dad."

"Your dad?"

"Yeah."

"That's what you think is weird about this morning? That you called your dad?"

"Well, I mean, I haven't talked to him in almost ten years."

"Oh." She's slowly peeling a banana, but won't take her eyes off of me. Her brow is wrinkled, and she's staring, like maybe she's afraid I'll run off or pull a knife.

"Sorry—I still haven't told you much about me, have I? My folks divorced when I was in fifth grade. I'm still not sure why."

"Oh. Sorry about that."

"Yeah, I mean, it's all right. I guess. Except, it's not."

"Oh?"

"Yeah, I just, have this feeling, y'know? That I need to fix it. No, I don't mean *fix it,* not like that. I'm not trying to pull a *Parent Trap* here. I just, y'know, need to see him. I mean, I haven't talked to him in forever, but, like, he's my father, and I need to. Even if he's a total dick and it's a miserable conversation, I feel like I just can't leave the wound sitting there."

She picks up her orange juice and sucks at the straw, slowly. She still won't take her eyes off of me. Narrow and skeptical. "That makes sense, I guess."

"Does it?"

"Yeah, I think so." She stabs at a waffle with her fork, again without looking down. "I've been there. I think. That's a big step, though. Ballsy."

"Yeah, I guess."

"What'd he say?"

"Nothing. I mean—he didn't answer. I left a message."

"Oh." She sits there, looking me up and down. Barely eating. Finally: "You sure you're okay?"

"Okay, Kate, you wanna tell me what's up? You've been acting weird since you sat down."

"Uh—" she says—"it's just that—I mean—" leans forward, and under her breath: "—do you even remember last night?"

I lean in as well. "Of course I remember last night. It was awful, but now it's over, and I'm trying to move forward. I mean, what else can I do?"

She grabs my wrist. Stares into my eyes. Drops a fork with a *clank* on her tray. She says, "This is important, okay?

I need you to tell me, from the beginning, what you think happened last night."

"What?"

"Just do it, okay?"

"Um—okay. And I push the bowl of soggy oat mush aside, and I take a breath, and: "We left the room around two-ish, right? We threw the body out the window into the dumpster, and you pulled the van around, right? Hey, I never found your screwdriver, by the way."

"It's somewhere. Go on."

"Okay. So, once we got her into the van, we drove around for—a long time."

"Yeah, I took a lot of twists and turns."

"Okay. Then we got to the hospital, took her down to the basement, stripped her naked and put her in a body cooler, and then we got back on the elevator."

"And then?"

"And then—uh—"

She finishes her orange juice and says, "That's what I thought."

"What?"

"You don't remember anything after that."

"Well—" and I stop because she's right. A dozen nightmares ago I'm in the elevator with Kate and a gurney full of clothes, and it rises and it doesn't stop. Then the thrashing and the sweating, the waking, the phone call, and then I'm back here in the dining hall, eyes stinging.

She's silent, her deep-black eyes holding back something—a dark, heavy thought that feels out-of-place here, with the plastic benches and tables built out of cheap particleboard and stumbling, gray sunlight that pours through square holes in the window shade, casting prison-bar shadows across her black freckles.

"Well, what happened?"

She's playing with a tater tot now, mashing it into ketchup over and over again, not looking up. She says, "I saw things last night I wish I could forget."

"Kate, you're kinda creeping me out."

Laughs. "*I'm* creeping *you* out?"

"Kate, would you please just tell me what happened?"

She breathes deep. Sighs. "Okay—well—we were in the elevator, right?"

"Yeah."

"And we were going up, and you looked over at me, and suddenly—"

"Suddenly what?"

She bites her lip. "It's hard to explain. The look in your eyes got weird. They got—distant. Sort of...grayish? I guess? Then the doors opened, and you ran off."

"I ran off?"

"Well—sort of? You weren't *running,* exactly, it was more like—shambling? That's a thing, right? But, y'know, weirdly fast. It was—I've never seen anyone move quite the way you were. Anyway, I guess I thought you were messing around, or something, not that it made a lot of sense for you to be messing around at that moment, but whatever. So I was like, *C'mon,* and I grabbed the gurney and started back toward the door. But the next thing I knew, you were gone. I looked over my shoulder, and you weren't there anymore. So there I am, standing in the middle of a hallway with a gurney full of bloody clothes, and I have to decide: do I try to find Phelia, or do I try to get out of here while I still can?"

Deep bags under her eyes, bearing down on her freckles. The mashed tater tot finally finds its way to her mouth.

"What'd you do?"

"Well, obviously I went after you."

"What'd you do with her clothes?"

"I threw them down a trash chute. Probably wasn't the best move, but what choice did I have?"

"Yeah, I guess," I say. (That'll come back to bite us in the ass.)

"Anyway, I just left the gurney sitting along the wall, and then I went off in the direction that I thought I saw you go."

"And you found me?"

"Eventually, yeah. Took me almost an hour."

"And I was—?"

"You don't remember any of this?"

"Sorry."

Starts mashing another tot. "You were five floors up. I found you lying in front of a door."

"Like, lying down?"

"Passed out on the floor."

"Oh."

"It was weird."

"Yeah."

She bites her lip, looks away, picks up her fork and plays with it. There's more, but she doesn't want to say it. "It was—" she says—"it was one of those heavy steel doors? Like, a painted metal door? Anyway, it was covered in scratches—deep gouges that went all the way down to the metal. And there you were, at the bottom, with your fingernails still dug into the paint."

I look down at my fingernails. Jagged, flayed, still filled with paint chips. Orange, and under that, beige. Bleeding. "So—what? I'd been scratching at a door for an hour?"

"As far as I could tell, yeah."

"Why would I do that?"

She shrugs, looking down at her food. "Anyway," she says, "you were lying there, passed out and bleeding. I managed to wake you up—I mean, you opened your eyes, anyway."

"I did?"

"Yeah, but again, your eyes just didn't look like you. It was a weird, faraway look—gray, y'know? And I couldn't get you to talk. You just gurgled at me." Her tater tot is basically liquid now, so she gives up and leaves it in the ketchup-potato mush and starts wiping her hand on a napkin.

"What'd you do?"

"What *could* I do? I did my best to get you back to your feet, and then you shambled with me back toward the van."

"I didn't say anything?"

"Not till we got back to the van. Then you collapsed in the passenger seat and mumbled all the way back."

"I mumbled? What was I talking about?"

"Nothing that made sense. I picked out the name *Sara* a couple of times. Does that name mean anything?"

"It's—my sister's name—"

"Oh."

"What?"

"There's been some drama there, then?"

"I—I mean—that's not really your business."

Once I say it, I wish I could take it back. It sounds so unfriendly, so hostile. Like I'm shutting out the one person who's listened to me in years.

"Listen," I say, "I'm sorry—"

"No, I get it. Listen, though, Phelia. I've known enough druggies to recognize drug-induced behavior when I see it. I don't know what you're on, but you really need to get off it."

"But I'm not—"

She raises an eyebrow. Just one. Just a bit.

"I mean—"

"Was that her last night? The one following us around? The mortician? Was that Sara?"

"How could you possibly know that?"

"Just a lucky guess." She leans on her elbow. "No, I saw the way you recognized her voice. The look in your eyes while she was still around the corner. It was obvious you two had a history. An uncomfortable one."

*Don't tell anyone.* "I'm not *angry* at her. I mean, I needed a job, she got me a job—"

"—which you complain about every day."

*It's our secret.* "Well—I mean—I need it, though. I was in a rough spot."

"Uh-huh."

*For now.* "What?"

She says, "I don't know. There's a missing piece here. Something you're not telling me."

*Till we prove it works.* "Maybe you should mind your own business." I said it again, and I wish I hadn't said it again, and I wish I could take it back, again.

"I just think it's weird to see someone who's obviously young and ambitious working in the morgue in a public hospital. And that she got you a job, even though you two obviously don't get along, and she didn't ask you anything in return—"

"Kate. Stop." *Don't tell anyone.*

"I'm just concerned, is all. You're sure you're not taking anything? Maybe a prescription? Ambien or something?"

"*No.* Leave me alone." *It's our secret.*

"Look, Oaf—"

"DON'T EVER CALL ME THAT."

And she's suddenly quiet, and I realize I just yelled, and she shrinks back against her bench, eyes shining in the crisscross shadows.

She sighs and I'm shaking. "I just—if something's wrong, I want to help."

"Nothing's wrong," I tell her. "Just drop it." And as I stand up I bump my bowl and milk splatters all over her food. Soggy Cheerios in her ketchup.

"Phelia, don't be this way. I'm just trying to be a friend—"

"*Maybe I don't need a friend, okay?* Maybe I can live without the condescending bullshit you call friendship. Maybe I—maybe I don't need you to rescue me."

I shouldn't have said that, either. I don't know why I did, but I did, and I can't take it back. The eyes in the room are all staring at me, and the noises of forks and glasses have stopped, and there's nothing to do but run for the door.

So I do.

"Phelia, wait—" (and I stop)—"I'm sorry," she says, "for whatever I said. You just don't understand. You think I'm condescending, and maybe I am, but I'm trying to help, the best way I know how. I can't save you from drowning if I'm treading water myself, and I can't pretend to understand, I can only try."

(But I can't turn around.)

She says, "I know—I know it's fucking lame, and I'm sorry, but I can't dress up the truth. And the truth is we all need friends to pull us out of our shit, and maybe I can't be that for you, but—what am I trying to say? Find *someone?* I guess?"

I can hear her voice choking on salt, but I can't turn around, won't be weak, won't be wrong. I knock someone's tray off their table and throw the door open and run.

I don't know where I'm going, but I have to escape all the eyes, all the people who are wandering around campus. People on sidewalks, standing in crowds. I run back toward my dorm, trying not to make eye contact, trying not to breathe, not to think. Cop cars parked on the street, walkie-talkies and officers standing and talking with horrible mustaches, sunglasses years out of date. Dirty piles of snow melting fast in the sun. Soggy squishes from wet mud, under my feet. Yellow tape, yellow tape.

I throw open the door, the one that leads into the stairwell, and I climb under the staircase and hide, like a troll waiting for someone to cross her bridge. I hug my knees and I squeeze out the light while my cheeks burn with tears, and I pray hard for silence and let painted concrete suck heat from my body. I breathe. And I breathe and I breathe.

It's horrible, completely awful, but everything is starting to make sense now. The bodies, the nightmares, the gaps. The way that she found me last night.

And I just hope she doesn't see it. I hope she hasn't put all of this together.

But what if it *is* me?

An hour ago, I would have said that was the stupidest thought ever, but now it seems like a real possibility. The nightmares started a few days ago, and that was about the same time I started finding the bodies. And as they got more intense...

The killer is me.

Is that even possible? Real murders woven through my dreams and enacted while I slept? Is that a thing? Can that happen? Kate was talking about drugs, but I'm not on drugs except—

Yeah...

It's so stupid, but that has to be it. Sara said the drug was psychoactive (whatever that means), and she was banned from human testing, and she's avoided every question I've asked her about it, and she's been questioning me about my moods and behavior, and—

I look at my nails, the ones with the paint chips, broken and flaked and bleeding in places. Kate's telling the truth, she must be. No, this is the only possibility that makes sense of everything—the nightmares, the sleepwalking, the bodies.

*It's weird to think that I'm a killer—*
*That my theme song should be Jackson's "Thriller"—*
*But the facts all align:*
*All the bodies are mine—*
*Something...*
   *Something...*
      *(This last line's just filler.)*

I'm telling you, limericks are *so freaking hard.*
I guess the first thing to do is quit the stuff.
Wow, what will Sara say when I tell her I'm done?
I guess I'll have to look for another job, or—
But I can't think about that now. People's lives are in danger.
Do I turn myself in?
What an awful question. Either answer is terrible.
My cheeks are stinging and my eyes are burning.
I shut them again.
*It's not your fault,* she says, and I feel her hand on my shoulder, with the manicured nails and the pea coat that scratches my ear. I say *But it is, I never should have listened to Sara, I should have refused, I'm so weak.* And then he's there, the one with the flannel and beard, at my other side, saying *We have to move forward.* I say, *But where's forward? Where can I even go from here?* and she says, *Get up. There's something upstairs that we need to get rid of.* I tell them *I'm not sure I can. I'm not even sure I can stand up at all. My legs are both burning from thousands of sleepless nights spent spilling blood*—and he says, *Don't exaggerate, it's only been a couple.* And he takes one hand and she takes the other, and I'm back on my feet, and my phone is ringing.

Vibrations and ringing. A buzz in my pocket. My phone ringing, for real.

An unrecognized number that looks familiar. "Hello?"
Silence, then a crackle, then: "Hi, is this Ophelia?"
"It is."

"Ophelia, this is your father."

The words are tiny in my phone's little speaker, but they fill the yellow-gray glow of the stairwell, and I swallow.

"Hello?" he says.

"Yeah, I'm here, sorry—I just—I just didn't think you'd actually call me back." I'd actually forgotten that I had called him. It was so long ago.

He says, "Listen, I uh—I don't know what you were hoping for, but —I dunno, we could go grab a beer, or something. That's not weird, is it?" And when I say nothing: "Is it?"

"How's now?" I say, on top of his words. Anything to get out of here. Anything seems like a small problem compared to the blood on my hands.

(Anything at all.)

## sun. jan. 16.
## 2:34 pm.
## waiting.

**I'm sitting on the curb now**, waiting outside my building, still in disbelief this is happening, that he's actually coming to get me. And I can't believe I'm doing this either, can't believe I'm meeting up with a man I've barely given a thought to since I was kid. The wind is blowing gently, whipping a stray wisp of my hair up and down, and it tugs at my scalp. Everything outside is muddy and warm and waiting to freeze over again.

I jump every time a car goes by, thinking *Maybe this is him and what do I say and what do I do?* but each car slides past me, kicking bits of gravel at my knees.

Maybe he won't even show up.

An hour or two ago that would have been a relief, but now that this rendezvous is my only escape from the realities I just discovered, I'm kind of dreading his absence, the way I used to at night when I would lie in bed awake listening to Sara's snores. I'd lie there and stare at the glowing star stickers on the sloping ceiling, shining green and bending over like the supernatural trying to kiss the real. And every moment without a click from the screen door downstairs was another spent listening in fear to the breath in the room, praying it wouldn't turn into snorts and invade the air with its words. And after the clicks, when the snores would fade into low, simple breaths, the stars would burn out, a chemical death, repeated each night, inevitable for all glow stickers. And yet—when mine would burn out, I would witness it live, every time, as the masters of galaxies dwindled to red dwarfs, then brown, and then turned to black holes in the darkness. Then nothing was left there in front of my eyes except dull, faded stickers veneered with a salty, green crust. They still might be stuck to that ceiling somewhere in a landfill, yellowed and cracked but still there, because stickers cling on, even once you outgrow them. If you keep your old stuff and don't throw it away, the stickers stay glued to it, fading in sunlight and wearing off slowly when your sweaty hands rub against it, till faces you loved are distorted and grins become mocking. Somewhere in my bedroom at Mom's place are drawers of old notebooks all covered in grimacing, torn Barbie faces with blinding-white skin and gray, fuzzy teeth, black grease in their hair and their shoulders ripped off. I can't open the drawer without looking away.

A door clicks open.

"Ophie?"

There's a car in front of me, a yellow Beetle, not the new kind but one of the old ones from the '60s—repainted and running smoothly, but definitely one of the old ones. And inside is a man I haven't seen in years, stubbly and wrinkled, but not all that different. A starched white shirt and pleated pants, a stethoscope hanging around his neck for no good reason. He's wearing a lab coat, but it's open and splayed over the seat.

"...Dad?"

"Hi."

And I stand there for a moment looking into a tired pair of eyes, blue like mine, but he's skinny like Sara, lanky and crammed comically into this car, hands refusing to leave the wheel and argyle socks showing. He's biting his lip. I stand in the wind, adjusting my coat and noticing that my shoe's untied. The wind is warm and dry and it's chafing my lips. "Well," he says, finally, after too long, "would you like to get in?"

I stoop into the car, pulling on my coat to keep it from shutting in the door. "Nice wheels."

He steps on the gas and we're moving. "Well, y'know. Keeps me humble." Hits the turn signal, makes a right.

"No, I mean I really like it. It's unique. You don't see a lot of old-school Beetles anymore." He coughs and I slam the ends of my seatbelt together until they click. "Anyway, I was expecting a Porsche or something. This is fun."

"Well, it used to be a Porsche. Before alimony payments."

I don't know what to say to that. I reach inside my coat and scratch my arm.

He says, "Sorry, that probably wasn't the right thing to say. I didn't mean to insult your mother. I—"

"It's all right," I tell him. "We're not getting along right now, anyway."

He says, "Oh." And I hope we get to the bar soon, because *God, I need a drink,* and he adds, "You two always seemed like you were on the same wavelength."

"Yeah, well."

"Anyway, I only drive this because it was cheap. I have a friend who restores cars for fun, and he got this thing street-legal for me. Barely charged me anything."

"It's nice." We're stopped at a light. "Actually, I kinda wish I had one."

"Yeah?"

"It's a lot more interesting than the '90s Escort I'm stuck with. Blah. The '90s were the dark ages of cars."

"'The dark ages of cars'? Really?"

"And also movies. I was thinking about that the other day."

"You realize you were born in the '90s."

"Yeah, I'm still trying to live that down."

He laughs. It's a laugh I haven't heard in years, one that would shake the floorboards in the house as I drifted to sleep at night, wrapped in warm blankets. "But '90s movies suck, huh? Hmm."

"Come *on,*" I tell him. "*Forrest Gump? Bram Stoker's Dracula?* Even the award-winners were terrible."

"*Fargo?*" he says. "*Shawshank Redemption?*"

"Name a third."

"Uh—" and he bites his lip and makes a left and laughs. "Okay, you win." Pulls into a spot in front of a bar, adjusts the gearshift, yanks on the parking brake. I open my door and step out into an almost-puddle. The road is wet from all the melting snow, which is flowing (loudly) into storm drains. "You ever been here?" he says.

"Uh—yeah. I used to come to concerts here in high school, sometimes."

"High school. Huh." He stops for a second, standing there in the breeze, gray strands of hair flipped vertical. "Well—" he opens the door for me and I walk into the smoky darkness. It's a place I used to know well, with a bar up front and a stage off to the side. Black walls crusted with guitars and neon beer signs. Dangerous and safe, tacky and real, the sort of place that truckers and hipsters both pretend to like. Where the sound system will play Nirvana, then Enya, then Miles Davis. The sort of place I used to come all the time, back when I needed a fake ID.

But I've never spent much time on the bar side before. I've never seen the stage empty. I've never been here on a Sunday afternoon to see all the sparsely filled tables of middle-aged guys picking at nachos. Somehow it's darker when it's emptier, even in the daytime. The tables are crowded haphazardly, casting jagged shadows against the black paint that joust with the guitar necks and jut up against the bar like encroaching ivy. It's strange to see it like this, when my only memories of it are concerts with friends. Crowded rooms and loud music, youth and rebellion, back when I thought those words meant something profound. Back when rebellion was easy and cheap.

I study his face. Like the bar I used to know it's familiar but more worked-over, and more vacant. The strong lines I remember chasing monsters from closets now clash with jagged wrinkles and five-o'clock shadow. The strong arms that once held me have atrophied some.

He sits at the bar and asks for a Guinness. I join him and ask for the same.

"Same beer," he says. "Cool."

"Oh come on, everybody likes Guinness." I shouldn't have said it. Shouldn't have shot down his stumbling attempt at connecting. Should've given him a fist bump or whatever. Should've done a lot of things, but the moment is gone now, and we're sitting in silence. His blue eyes (like mine) are looking down, scanning the bar for something to play with, and he finally picks up a peanut from the bowl.

Rattles it around in his fist like he's rolling a die, and then flips it between his fingers. "Here," I finally say.

"What?"

"Here." I'm making mirrored "L"s with my thumbs and forefingers to form football goalposts, laughing at my own lameness. "Go for a field goal."

He laughs, and he turns the peanut on its end on the bar, pinning it down with his left pointer finger. Then he starts whistling my school's fight song in a goofy, piercing tone, and he jogs his fingers up the bar, pauses, and flicks the peanut through the smoky air. It sails, end-over-end, till it flies perfectly between my goalposts.

My arms shoot into the air. "It's good!" I make some of those throaty crowd noises that people always make even though they don't actually sound much like a crowd, and he laughs, and he grabs another peanut, and I laugh too. I swallow some beer and I say, "I bet you can't do that twice."

He shrugs at the peanut he's got now—it's crooked and lopsided, with a point at one end—and he sets it up on the table, backs up his little finger-person, whistles some more, and glances up at my eyes for just a second. "You ready?"

Finger-person charges up the varnished cherry, dodges the puddle from the condensation on his glass, and kicks like it's the fourth quarter of the big bowl game.

This one pulls a little to the left—I blame the weird, pointy shell—but it easily slips between my fingers. "Another lucky shot."

"I could do this all day," he says, and grabs another, sets it up, and flicks it again.

I barely have time to get my fingers up, but it sails right between them and smacks me in the forehead, and I feel the shell crack with a sudden, salty sting. "Ow."

"You okay?" he asks, putting a hand on my arm.

"Yeah, I'm fine," I tell him, rubbing my head. "I'm just a whiner." And he laughs, and I laugh. And he gives me a hug—the first in ten years, and it's weird, but I like it.

"Sorry, I was caught up in the moment."

"I could tell." And I add, "You're pretty good at that."

"Yeah, well," he says. "Years of putting off studying for med school exams."

I laugh.

"I used to take your mother here all the time," he says. "Back when we were in grad school."

"A dive like this?"

"It used to be nicer."

"Yeah, I thought I remembered it that way."

"That's so weird that you used to come here." He picks up his beer.

"This used to be where all the really good shows were," I tell him. "I used to sneak in here all the time for concerts when I was in high school."

"You'd sneak in?" he says, and I see worry flash in his eyes, but he knows it's too late to be a dad.

I say, "Yeah, a lot of the shows were 18 and above. But so what? I'm 23 now and I turned out okay."

"Twenty-three...?" I see him counting years, adding in his head.

"It's been a while, hasn't it?"

He says, "Yeah, but it's not just that. I'm just wondering why you're 23 and you still haven't finished your bachelor's."

"I, uh—" I better drink for this conversation—"taking a fifth year isn't that all unusual."

"Oh no?"

"Uh—no."

"...but?"

"But I also had to change my major." (Here we go.) "I mean, what can I say? I started in education because I thought I should do something with a clear career path, or whatever. And then I tried teaching and got my ass handed to me."

He laughs. "That happens to all of us when we start in a new field. Didn't I ever tell you about my residency?"

"When would you have told me about that?"

"Yeah, good point," he says. "Anyway, it was day after day of being elbow-deep in bodily fluids, with doctors and nurses both screaming in my ear. I went home crying more often than not."

"That's manly."

"It's the truth."

I immediately regret saying what I just said. I try to make amends by forming the goalposts again, and his fingers kick another peanut between them. And I stare at the bar, tracing a pattern in the puddle, and say, "What kept you going back every day?"

He sighs. "The knowledge that maybe there were more important things than being liked or respected. The realization that even though hard work sucks, you still have to do it because there are people who need your help."

"Didn't realize you were such an idealist."

"Well, there was that, and then there was the fact that after so many years of med school, I didn't know how to do anything else." He clears his throat. "And, y'know, my folks would have killed me if I gave up medicine."

The silence after that hangs heavy in the air, while I push the water around on the shining wood. "Mom cut me off."

I don't know why I said that. I shouldn't have. Of all the things I could have said, that was probably the worst choice. He says, "Oh."

"Please don't think that I mean—"

"No, I get it," he says, and reaches for his wallet.

"Dad, I don't want money. I'm working for a living now." (Crap, now I'm committed to *that*.)

"Yeah?"

"Yeah, I'm in the family business. I work at a hospital."

"No kidding." He's looking up again, back at my eyes.

"Yeah, Sara got me a job at her place," I tell him.

"That was good of her."

I shrug. "Yeah."

"A little out-of-character."

"Yeah."

And an old classic blues song starts playing on the speakers:

*Don't you mind people grinnin' in your face;*
*Don't you mind people grinnin' in your face;*
*Just bear this in mind:*

*A true friend is hard to find,*
*So don't you mind people grinnin' in your face.*
He says, "How is Sara these days, anyway?"
"I thought you guys still talked."
He's tapping on the table with a peanut, keeping time with the drums and the bass. "We did, yeah, for a long time. And then we kind of just...stopped. Right around the time she got kicked out of Yale. I send her a check sometimes, but that's it."
"Oh."
*You know your mother would talk about you;*
*Your own sisters and your brothers, too.*
*They don't care how you're tryin' to live—*
*They'll talk about you still;*
*Yes, but—bear this in mind:*
*A true friend is hard to find,*
*So don't you mind people grinnin' in your face.*
He says, "Yeah, what happened with that anyway?"
"With what?"
"Yale. How'd she get herself kicked out?"
I shrug. "She had some sort of drug she was developing as her thesis. It didn't work, she made herself some enemies, something like that."
"Huh."
*You know they'll jump you up and down;*
*They'll carry you 'round and 'round.*
*Just as soon as your back is turned,*
*They'll be tryin' to crush you down.*
*Just bear this in mind:*
*A true friend is hard to find,*
*So don't you mind people grinnin' in your face.*
I say, "Yeah, the whole thing was pretty weird." I slam my empty glass on the bar. "Anyway, she moved back in with Mom and she's working in the morgue now."
"What is it with you two and giving up?"
"What do you mean?"
"You, giving up on teaching the first time you hit a bump. Her, giving up on medicine because she's been kicked out

of one school. I mean—maybe it's none of my business. Maybe that's the wrong thing to say."

"You're damn right it's the wrong thing to say. Y'know what? Maybe it's because we had such a great example from you and Mom. You wanna talk about giving up?"

"Come on, that's not fair."

"No, y'know what's not fair? Walking out on your kids and your marriage. That's what's not fair. And now you're going to lecture me about *my* life?"

"She kicked *me* out," he says.

*Don't you mind people grinnin' in your face;*
*Don't you mind people grinnin' in your face;*
*Just bear this in mind:*
*A true friend is hard to find,*
*So don't you mind people grinnin' in your face.*

Those four words—*She kicked me out*—hang in the air, in the smoke, and I try to decide what I'm supposed to say in response as the song changes to a Christina Aguilera number I haven't heard since grade school. He flicks another peanut and I barely get my fingers up in time. I don't know why it makes such a difference to hear those words (didn't I already know this? didn't she keep the house?) but somehow it does, as if I've been harboring the wrong grudge for years, as silly as that is. Like maybe I should have said something one of those Tuesday nights when my mother would pick at her terrible cooking and complain about him.

Not that I would have had much to say. I don't even know this man.

But I have to fill the silence. "I've been thinking a lot lately," I tell him, "about that old house we used to live in— remember it? Where Sara and I slept in the attic?"

"Of course I remember it. I had to fix part of it every single day we were living there."

"Good memories there."

"Yeah...a few." Now he's finished another beer. He sets it down on a coaster.

"I was just thinking—y'know—that place just had so much soul. All those secret passages and hidden nooks.

They don't make houses like that anymore. The house we moved into, the one Mom lives in, it's nothing like that. No secrets. No soul."

He laughs.

"What?"

He says, "You do know *why* it had all those passages and compartments. Right?"

"I..."

"You really don't?"

"I guess I thought that people were just more interesting in the past."

He laughs at me again. "The house was built in the '20s, Ophie. The 1920s. You know anything about them?"

"Uh—flappers? Flagpole sitting?"

"I'm talking about prohibition, Ophie."

"Oh."

"Yeah."

"So you're saying that—"

"The nooks were for hiding hooch, and the passages were for escaping from cops."

"Oh." He sets up another peanut, and I give him the goalposts, and it pulls to the right and bounces off my finger, but it's good. "So much for soul."

He shrugs. "One guy's soul is another guy's sin, I guess." He pays for the beer. "Listen, sorry if I'm cutting this short, but I have a 24-hour shift coming up, so I should probably get going. You need a ride back to campus?"

"Actually, I think I'll hang out here a while longer."

"You sure?" he says.

"Yeah," I tell him. "I have a lot to think through."

He pauses, half-standing, fixing his coat. "Okay, if you're sure." He takes a step toward the door, but then he turns around. "Listen, would it be weird if I hugged you again?"

"Uh—"

"I won't, if it'd be weird."

I hold out my hand, and I give him a handshake. It's weird and it's awkward.

Then I change my mind, and I pull him down to my level and I put my arm around his back. It's not quite the little-girl-in-her-daddy's-arms fantasy I remember from years ago, but it feels like an important first step. And he smiles awkwardly and he just barely says, "Thanks." He heads back toward the door; pauses; turns around. "You really think '90s movies were that bad, huh?"

"Have you thought of a third yet?"

"Nah, I guess not."

And he leaves.

## sun. jan. 16.
## 5:17 pm.
## not drunk. yet

**I spent the rest of the afternoon hiding** at the bar.
I know that's stupid, that I need to face my problems, but
whatever, it's what I ended up doing. My head's been reeling,
spinning in and out of the now, dizzy from everything I've
learned today—first Kate's weird story about last night,
then the sudden realization of what I've done, and now all
this stuff about my dad.

(He looked so lonely.)

I'm sitting exactly where I was when he left, staring at
the same fingernails with the same sticky paint chips under
them. And the dim lights are shining the same way, casting
jagged shadows in the same places. Everything looks
exactly the same as it would if he had never been sitting on
the stool next to me.

People are starting to filter in now, grasping desperately
at the last vestiges of the weekend before the sun forces its
way back over the horizon. I guess I'm doing the same thing,
really—sitting here, on my fourth beer, trying to put off life
for as long as I can.

But the thing is, I know what I have to do.

The obligatory course of action here is so obvious that
part of me can't believe I'm just sitting here. I need to walk
back to my room, find the whole supply of Sara's wonder
drug, and flush it down the nearest toilet. Then I need to
tell Kate everything and ask her (very politely) to watch me
carefully. Or just tie me up, or call the cops, or something.

*God.*

It's that last bit, the part about Kate, that's got me glued
to this sticky barstool, wasting my time. She *must* have put
two and two together by now, *must* have figured out where
the bodies are coming from, can't possibly still be giving me
the benefit of the doubt. And yet, she looked at me so

innocently at breakfast. *You sure you're not taking anything? Ambien, or something?*

Maybe she just really doesn't know.

Is that possible? I mean, because if she doesn't know, I don't have to tell her anything. The bodies are gone, and there's no harm done otherwise (right?). I go off the stuff, things go back to normal, everything's fine.

Of course, *normal* is a relative term, and at the moment it means half of a degree that I care about less every day, a job that I suck at, a mother who's banishing me from my own bedroom, and a fat ass that diet and exercise can't seem to get rid of (mainly because I hate dieting and exercising, but who's counting?). So what is it I want?

I mean, really want?

It's a question I haven't asked myself in a long time, and having it at the front of my thoughts is strange and a little scary. The more I turn it over in my head, the more real it becomes, till it's concrete, an object that's floating in the foam of the beer in my hand, bobbing and spinning till it's coated in sticky, brown sweetness, making rims on the glass. It's a jagged idea with sharp angles that sparkle like stained glass, igniting the air, till it turns into sun, an early-March sun, one that lights up the wisps of the cold afternoon with the laughter of kids and feet pounding on grass. And the sky is a blue-yellow white, while I awkwardly cradle a black walkie-talkie in my hand and watch seventh-graders chasing a dull, pockmarked soccer ball up and down patchy lushness. The crush chases after the white-and-black leather till the knee I remember comes sliding out (hard). The one knee, the one I can't scrub from my mind, skidding hard across grass, across gravel, mixing blood with the dirt and flesh with the green. Drags a girl behind it, a small one, attached to it, scared and alone, breaking off from the crush in a bloody mitosis that pushes this small, crying, scraped, sweaty thing up against me. Two eyes, deep and brown, looking at me through tears, and they're so far below me. She begs for a hand to reach out toward the muck (which is her). The sun hangs in the south, still refusing to rise to the blue-yellow dome's center (though it's high noon), and the breeze makes me shiver in lingering dew. The face at my feet, attached to the knee, with jagged adult teeth wedged awkwardly into the mouth of a child, and bangs not-quite-grown-out, and small bits of acne assaulting its jawline, looks up at me (desperate); I feel my gut sink and my eyes fill with fear. A thing like a human, but smaller and awkward, with parts where they shouldn't be, dreams that are nonsense (naïve) and no thought past *I wonder what lunch is today* and *I hope this pain stops really soon.* My past and my future collide into sparks in the big, yellow (dying) star caught in her eyes, and in them I see nothing but life marching down into death for eternity. An endless parade of our wombs all ripped open and filling the world with more of this pain, all stretching from now to forever. With every one born, there's a thousand new ways to create pain invented, but one way to stop it (just one). And it's then that my hand reaches out—and I see it, stretched out there in front of me, piercing through thin strands of mist, reaching down into hers with its black, half-chewed fingernails, thumb with red ink stains, and shaking (still shaking!), but reaching out, down, on its own somehow. Pushed by a fire inside me that burns with a blue and a yellow that's brighter than sky, and it burns through my fear and my panic and pride. In front of my face in a downward salute, cells standing alert in full battle formation, a phalanx of fingers with cavalry (muscle and bone) spread out toward the horizon. It's fighting for life, even just for one moment, an army that stands to paint *Life!* on the sky and the sea and the air and the land in bright yellow and blue—life that fights and that struggles, made perfect in fighting for nothing beyond what just *is,* life that's breaking through pavement and shattering, cells in cells, light in light, and a hand in the mist, and it's mine. Reaching out, and it's mine, shaking hard, and it's mine, and she takes it. Crooked fingers reach up from her small, desperate frame, seeking nothing but hooks she can hang her resolve on. The heat of a thousand and one suns exploding between our two hands, mine calloused and full and hers small and still-smooth. Exploding with *life!* that's refusing to die in the shredding of dirt and crushed rock. And I pull her up. Her feet are too big and her frame is too small, but her eyes soak up light and she smiles. I say *Are you okay?* and she tells me *Yes, thank you,* but still her knee's bleeding. Blood spackles the ground, leaking out in defiance, and catching the wind to approach shining blackness (my shoes). My hand fumbles into my purse, its black nails and its callouses searching (a mind of their own) for a Band-Aid I know that I have, left over from hiking two years ago, while I say, *Hold on, you're bleeding.* She holds her knee still while I crackle the paper, till SpongeBob comes free, and he's just big enough to fit over her scrape. The red disappears into cool, healing calm, and the next thing I know there are arms around my neck. Just two tiny arms, squeezing me in a hug that shines brighter than sunlight and brighter than life. And for one perfect moment I don't even care about later today, when the principal tells me to come to her office and yells at me, saying *We never give medical care to the children* and *We could get sued* and *If you were a teacher I'd fire you now* and *Hey, while you're thinking on how you should never give Band-Aids to students, perhaps you should think about how you should keep your hands off of them too. Maybe spend your few months here developing lesson plans rather than trying to make friends.* I don't think of the tears or the weekend spent crying in bed watching SyFy and eating Trix in my pajamas. I just hold her until she stops crying, and life pushes the sun to the top of the sky, and my life is what life should be, just for one moment, in blue and in yellow, the beer and the cigarettes, voice getting louder and louder...

"Ma'am?"

What?

"Ma'am? Are you all right?"

I'm facedown in a puddle of beer, breathing in bubbles and hops. Cold cherry wood against my face and a headache in just one temple.

"Ma'am?"

"Yeah, I'm sorry. I guess I just fell asleep. I, uh, had a late night. Last night. Sorry."

He picks up my glass and puts it in a bus tray and says, "Maybe you should head home."

"Look, I'm not drunk, if that's what you're thinking." But my speech is slurred. "I had, what? Three-and-a-half beers? I just fell asleep."

"Well, but someone with such a low bodyweight can—"

"Wait, you think I'm skinny?"

"I didn't say that, just—"

"But I look small to you."

"Well—yeah."

"So it works. I'm finally skinny. Thank God."

"What?"

"Never mind. Give me another."

"Are you sure?"

"Look, I'm walking home. What does it matter to you how many I have?" He pours me another Guinness, and I smile. This drug may have some crazy side effects, but at least it works as advertised. (Two people dead, but it's too late for them, right? I may as well get *something* out of this clusterfuck.) And now that I think about it, my clothes have been fitting looser than they used to, and maybe I finally at least have one thing I wanted. I made fun of Sara when she tried to sell me on this stuff, but you know what? It works. It feels good. I don't count that exchange with the bartender as the sexiest I've ever had, but it was certainly a compliment.

Y'know. Sort of.

And now an idea crosses my mind. There's a vintage clothing store next-door to this place. Maybe I could go in there and find something that fits my body a little better. Wear it in here, see what kind of attention I get. It might be fun.

Nah, that's stupid.

It's stupid, but it does sound fun, and with each ring on the side of my glass, it seems like a better idea. And finally, head swimming with suds, I slam the empty thing down and say thanks with a 20, and half-walk-half-stumble out the front door. I think the bartender was right, that my lower bodyweight makes me more susceptible, and the fact that I haven't eaten anything in days doesn't help either. And also, who knows what sort of drug/alcohol interactions I'm experiencing. Who knows. But this makes sense, it's a good idea. I'll need clothes anyway, I can't just wear sweats every day, and I might as well have something that fits my body, my new body. It's a good body, it's fun to have a body that people pay attention to, and maybe it was worth it, even.

No. Don't say that. That's horrible.

But maybe it was. I didn't know those people, and I don't even know for sure that I killed them. The whole thing could have just been some weird coincidence, and even if it wasn't it's just a couple people, shallow people (probably) that no one will ever miss (probably). And I'm going to go off the stuff now anyway, and it will all be over, and don't worry about what happened because now I have the body I always wanted and everything else will work out. I mean, maybe now I can finally get started on writing and people will pay attention to me and care about what I have to say. Didn't Dad just give me an hour of his time, and he's never done that before, ever, and if my dad who's ignored me all my life listens to me now, then I must be worth other people's attention too. Right? I mean, I'd like to lose a little more weight, but now I can do that with diet and exercise, I'm done with the pills.

Yeah. I'm done with them.

And now I'm outside and the stars are bright with a white that's so white it's yellow, and they're spiky and accusing, jagging into my eyes, saying *Liar, liar, liar*. But I ignore them and they're wrong, and I throw the door open to Vintage Clothing, Inc., and the girl at the door, the one dressed like a flapper, says, "We close in half an hour," but I just walk right by her because she's stupid and she doesn't know what she's talking about and she's stupid. And I go to the racks and I pick through the clothes, and there's yellows and blues and there's sequins and lace. Bellbottoms and skinny jeans, hot pants and miniskirts. I grab what looks good and I cram it all into a fitting room cubicle made out of plywood that's tiny; its curtains are thin and a sticker that clings to its wall says *This cubicle's so fucking small* and I laugh. I fumble my way out of jeans that just slide off my hips and the sweatshirt that's drowning my boobs in its scratchy and over-washed fabric. They sit in a pile, down there in the corner, and catch dots of light that reflect off a small, holographic peace-symbol sticker, and I try on some shorts that are sparkly and leave nothing at all to the imagination (but wow, does my ass look great). I peel them back off and they fall (wadded) on tile and shag carpet (half-on, half-off), and I'm thinking these orange bellbottoms (full '60s proportions) might turn out to be less ridiculous. I slide into them and they fit on my thighs like they're molded for me (just for me), and I mean, yeah, those short, sparkly shorts were pure fun, but these tight pants are better. I only have ten minutes for picking a shirt, but a glittering one that I grabbed seems okay. It's got one of those big-foldy-plungy-type necklines (what are those called, anyway?), and it shows off my boobs. I leave my old clothes on the floor, and I charge to the checkout without even taking the new ones I'm wearing off. Flapper girl rolls her eyes back in her head like she's thinking *The weirdoes we get in here sometimes.* But she takes my credit card, scans it, and somehow it clears, and I thank God for credit cards, burst through the doors wearing clothes like I've never put on before, shaking my fist at the sky, shouting loud (in my head), *Hey! Fuck you, stupid stars!*

And I burst back into the bar.

Are all eyes on me? Are all the guys, in the booths, at the bar, looking at me? Are they looking at me like I thought they all would, or do I think they are because that's what I was expecting? Is it strange that this mood is exactly the way that I thought I would feel once I turned myself into the center of attention? Like my feet carry red carpet everywhere with them, and outside, in black, every star in the sky has been shining for me, filling all the room's windows with light that reflects off the sway of my hips. Like I'm wearing a ten-thousand-dollar makeover, not just the foundation dusting I put on this morning? Like each move

I make sends deep shockwaves throughout the whole room?

I'm exaggerating, I must be, probably. I can't look that good, I can't be that pretty. It's just the beer, just the novelty, but I'm not *that* drunk and I'm not *that* shallow. Am I? I mean, every girl wants to feel pretty, every*body* wants to think they're attractive, that people enjoy looking at them. Right? It might not be deep. It might not be important. But everyone wants it. Everyone.

I stand in the room's center, absorbing the looks and enjoying the glow from the stars and the lights and the faces and me. For the moment, I own this bar.

I take a seat.

I climb up on a stool next to a guy with big shoulders and a tight t-shirt, and he's there with a girl, but I don't even care, and he's looking at me. I say hi.

"Uh, hi." He's cute and he's shy and I know he wants to talk, but she grabs his arm, and she's skinnier than me, but I've got his attention and she knows that I've got it.

I lean forward, and I say "Buy me a drink," because that's what chicks say in bars, right? It's just an experiment, really. He's a little rat in my Skinner box, and I'm pushing the buttons and taking notes. I've had too much beer, really had too much beer. Need to stop, need to quit, this could go anywhere. I could regret this.

He says, "I, uh—"

It's so cute when they stutter. I didn't even know. I push the button again. "Please." I lean forward just a bit more, squeeze my arms together around my tits. Do I look hot or ridiculous? I guess I'll find out soon—

"Um, excuse me, who said you could talk to my boyfriend?"

It's happened. That bomb that I dropped? Just exploded. Just ripped wide open and showered the room in acid-estrogen that melts skin off bones. This is what I was missing. All those nights I spent wrapped in sweats and pajamas, highlighting Piaget, Dickens, and Austen, this is what I was missing. This is the jungle, the meat market (life?), where the beer and the sweat and the hormones combine into a cocktail of violence and sex. It's stirring new things in me. Time to show claws. She's a skinny, blond bitch, I could take her. I'm a killer, and she doesn't even know that about me. I'm awesome. She's not. And she knows, if I wanted to, I could leave now with her cute little boytoy. You can deal with it, bitch.

I say, "I'm sorry, I didn't realize you owned him." There's no good answer to that one. Smart.

Her mouth is wide open. It's pretty much got flies buzzing into it.

He says to her, "Hey, come on, she was just—"

"Tell her to go away."

"What?"

"Tell her to go away," she says.

He stutters some more. So cute. "W—why?" Guys are so dumb.

"'Why'? 'Why'!? Are you serious?"

"What did I do wrong?"

Oh, dude. It's adorable watching you throw your girlfriend away like this. And you don't even know what's happening. She's sitting there, seething, leaking boiling-hot fumes that smell like her gross watermelon-flavored drink into the air, and you don't even have a clue.

(Why are watermelon-flavored things always green? Wouldn't that mean that they taste like the rind?)

(Anyway.)

She's grabbing her purse. It's not even a purse, it's a clutch, and it's sequined and way too tiny to hold anything. Useless. Impractical. "Either she goes or I go," she says. Her eyes are unblinking and stabbing at me with their green-watermelon-estrogen-venom, through the beer and the smoke and the dark. And I laugh.

She stands, in a sort of awkward way that only an angry, skinny, blond chick in five-inch heels can, sort of rocking from a full-on-slouch to a hunchback-on-stilts, and trying to look dignified, but you know how those things go. And she storms out the door in a way that's the opposite of intimidating.

Now I'm sitting here with this guy I don't know, and he's got a beer mustache and he's staring down my top, and I'm suddenly thinking, *What did I just do?* There's something in my hips saying, *Go, girl, keep going,* but my headache says it doesn't feel fun anymore. She's waiting out front, I can see her through the window, fumbling with a bra strap that keeps falling off her shoulder and clutching her clutch (as one does).

I sit up. (He's disappointed.)

"You know she wants you to chase after her," I tell him.

"What?" His face is buried in his beer while he buries his eyes in my cleavage again. Are guys really this clueless, or is this something they do to mess with us?

"She's leaving because she wants you to chase her."

"Oh." He swallows more beer.

"Well?"

"What?"

I sigh. "Are you gonna go after her, or not?" I can see her still, standing there just past the window, green and boozy against the stars. Still out there, still waiting.

"I dunno." I'm sobering up now, and he's looking less cute, like he could just really use a shower and a shave. College boys, y'know? I can't do this anymore.

"Look, idiot, she's asking you to make a choice here. Don't you get that?"

"Uh—"

"You can't just sit here and watch things happen. It doesn't work that way. The *world* doesn't work that way. You're not allowed to just sit on your ass and say 'Yeah, I'm just gonna see how this all plays out' when you're *one of the players on the damn field.* Sports metaphors. Boys understand those, right?" By now his girl has already stormed off, but whatever.

"So, she's, like, testing me? This is a test?"

"A *test?*" I take the beer right out of his hand, I don't know why, I just do it, and I down half of what's left, and I slam it on the bar. "A test, like she's some sort of mob boss trying to see where your loyalties lie? No. It's not a test, genius, it's *life.* She wants to know if you're willing to *fight*

Ophelia, alive ~ 173

for her. It's basically the only thing that matters *at all,* and you don't even *get it.* What do you think she is, just a drinking buddy plus some free sex? There's a *human being* attached to that vagina."

"Ugh," he says, shifting uncomfortably in his seat. "I liked you better when you were just trying to get free drinks out of me."

"If it makes you feel better, I did," I say. And I finish his beer and slam the glass so hard on the bar that it cracks, and everyone looks, and I push off the stool, and I stomp toward the door, throw it open triumphantly, and immediately bend over, puking my guts into the bushes. And the thin, foamy strands catch hard on the jagged thorns, while the stars beat down hot, laughing, *Fuck you too, Ophie.*

mon. jan. 17.
1:49 am.
not sure

**The stumble back to my dorm** is taking longer than I thought it would. The beers probably account for some of that, but seriously, it was only three beers. Or four. Some number of beers.

It's true that I drank them on a very empty stomach, but nobody ever acts the way I just did because of four (five?) beers, regardless of stomach contents. And it's possible, maybe, that the night sky is swirling the way it is at the moment because the alcohol interacted with the pills somehow. I'm not sure. But this feels different.

And now I realize that I've actually been off the pills for more than a day. Twenty-eight, 30 hours? Something like that. It wasn't planned, not entirely, but staying away from my room all day did the trick. Does that make me officially off of it? Was the habit really that easy to kick?

I mean, if it's strong enough to turn me into a sleepwalking murder-zombie, it just seems like maybe I should be expecting some withdrawal symptoms. It's possible I'm already having some. The swimming in my head, the cackling stars, the weird, impulsive behavior (what was I thinking in there?). Sara obviously put zero effort into safety-testing this stuff, and I know she was barred from testing it on humans (go fig?), so who knows what'll happen to me. And it's that thought, right there, that sends chills down my back, from my shoulders to knees, while a cold breeze blows by, and I wish that I still had my sweatshirt. The breeze is blowing harder and the stars are shining brighter and everything stretches to ribbons of color. My dorm's up ahead, but each step that I'm taking is pushing it farther away, pushing hard on the bricks that sink into each other and swallow their mortar for thousands of miles. They twist and they turn till they're long as my arm, and she's there on my arm, it's the girl with the pea coat and Uggs saying *Why are you leaving me? Why?* and I tell her *I'm not, hey, I'm not going anywhere, everything's fine,* but he's there too, the one with the beard and the flannel, the hipster; he says *Won't you miss us? I thought we were friends,* and I tell them, *We are friends. We are.* They're both grabbing my elbows and pulling, and saying *Your made us yours, now we're yours, now we won't leave you.* I say *Let me go,* but they won't say a word in response, they just squeeze. They squeeze and their sharp nails are claws, and their teeth shine like steel and their arms are on strings made of starlight that reach all the way to her eyes, Sara's eyes, and she stares down at me from above while she pulls on them, hard. I run and reach out, but I'm tangled in starlight. It's thin and it's sharp and it digs in my throat while I run for the building. I reach for the door, but it's moving away, and I'm reaching through sweat on my face and through blood on my arms, and they won't let me go. Their claws sink through flesh and they pick at my bones, but I throw the door open and charge up the stairs. And their mouths are black holes now, deep, sucking black holes filled with razors of teeth that are hungry for me and each step tumbles into them, growing the jaws into shining-bright-silver barbs, closing around me and laughing while fires keep blazing below. And my burning, bruised legs push the stairs one last time, and my hand finds the knob and the door throws wide-open. I reach for a leg and grab hard and hold on, and it's Kate.

It's just Kate.

My breath's coming out hot and sticky onto the cuffs of her Supergirl pajama pants, and she sits up and jerks her legs away and says, "Ophelia, what's wrong with you?"

I look down at my arms, and my arms are okay, and the pain is fading, and the spinning has stopped and the flames and the dark and the teeth die away. It's just Kate, and she's on her bed reading a book, and I'm squeezing her ankle, and it's starting to bruise, and I say, "Uh—"

"Are you all right?"

The things I just saw, and the things I just felt, are fading to black, and all I can see is the light from her lamp, a small lamp with a glowing-red shade, casting light on the sky full of Supergirls.

I loosen my grip.

"I—" (I choke. I whisper.) "I think I owe you an apology."

"What do you mean?" she says.

"We had a fight, right? This morning?"

"Yeah, it was sort of a fight—"

"I mean, I yelled."

She says, "Yeah, I might've as well."

"I don't know—I don't know why I was so defensive." I'm still breathing hard, still choking on sweat.

"Are you sure you're all right?"

I say, "Yeah, I think you're right, though. I haven't been myself lately. I'm not sure why." (Well, I've got an idea, but—)

"I've only known you for a week, so I can't really confirm that."

"Well, still. I'm sorry."

She leans forward, and her arms are around me, in a sideways hug, across my chest and behind my back. At first I jump back, but the warmth draws me in, and my head's on her shoulder, and she smells like smoke, and tears start to flow. I choke them back (embarrassing), but I don't push her away.

We sit in the glow of the lamp and we breathe.

Till she finally lets go and she says, "I'm sorry if that was weird."

"No—"

"You just looked like you needed a hug. It's—y'know. It's sort of my go-to when I don't know what else to do. I just—"

I roll my eyes and I say, "Thank you."

"Yeah?"

"Yeah."

She hands me a pillow and grabs one herself, and we lean up against the wall and slouch in the reddish dark till she finally says, "You wanna tell me what's going on?"

I sigh. "What *isn't* going on." My orange bellbottoms and sparkling shirt catch the light as I sink deeper into her mattress.

She notices my outfit and says, "Did you have a date, or something?"

I say, "I'm pretty sure I just did something awful."

"Oh no, what?"

"Um—" (she sounds really worried)—"probably not what you're thinking."

"Why, what am I thinking?"

"Listen, I don't mean *awful* like *robbed-a-bank awful*. It's more like *insulted-somebody's-mom awful,* or something."

"You insulted somebody's mom?"

"No—no, I mean it was *like* that. In, y'know, magnitude. Magnitude of awfulness."

"Oh."

"Yeah."

"Um—why don't you just tell me what you did? And then if you want, I can tell you how awful it was."

"Um—okay. Well—the short version is, I think I just broke up a couple."

"That doesn't sound so bad."

"Yeah—I mean, it could have been worse, right? But I did it so *deliberately,* y'know? It was weird." I push myself onto my feet, and I go to the mini-fridge and grab a Coke. Then I sink back into her bed and say, "I'm honestly not sure whether I'm more embarrassed that I did it, or that I feel so guilty about it. Y'know?"

"Well—I mean—what'd you do to break them up?"

"It was so stupid. I just started flirting with him, and—y'know, I don't even know why I did it. I was just having fun. Blowing off a little steam."

"Is that why you're all dressed up?"

"I guess. I just—I don't know. I've just lost some weight lately, and I thought that maybe I should finally have some of the fun that skinny girls get to have, and—the whole thing was just idiotic. God, I'm embarrassed."

"We all do stupid stuff."

"I guess." I sigh. "Anyway, I guess I must've had too much to drink, because it seemed like a really good idea at the time, y'know? I went to the vintage clothing store and I bought this outfit, and then I went to a bar and started flirting with this guy just to see how he'd react. He was there with a girl, though. I don't know why I chose him, there were plenty of single guys in there. But anyway, I flirted with him till his girlfriend got pissed enough to leave. And now I feel really bad about it."

"What'd he do?"

"Nothing. That's what really bothers me. He just sat there smirking like an idiot. Wouldn't go after her, wouldn't put moves on me. Just sat there being amused."

"That's guys for you."

"Yeah?"

She says, "Yeah. They think life is just something that happens to amuse them. They don't realize they're supposed to be living it. Playing life on easy mode'll do that to you."

We laugh.

And finally, she says, "You don't need to feel bad. You were just having fun."

"So why do I feel so awful about it?" I say, and she laughs again, but I don't.

She says, "Well—" and she hesitates.

"Well, what?" I say, and she awkwardly scratches her butt against the sheets.

"I *guess* I have some thoughts," she says, "but they're not fully formed. Just a handful of ideas bouncing around in my head, if that makes sense."

"Run them by me."

"Well—okay." She pulls herself to her feet and then climbs on top of her desk, perching there with her calloused feet resting on a drawer that hangs open, slightly askew. Eyes screwed up and distant, trying to push thoughts without words out into the air. "I guess the more I think about it, Phelia, the more convinced I am that there are only two forces in the universe, y'know? There's life and there's death. And everything you do—like, *everything,* including brushing your teeth and remembering to breathe and whatever—is in either one direction or the other. I mean—does that sort of make sense?"

"And you're saying that...?"

"I guess I'm saying that a relationship is sort of like a life?"

"So I just destroyed a life? Ugh."

"Sort of. I guess." Sighs. "I mean, if you want to think about it that way."

I lie back on her bed, put my arm over my eyes, and shut out red light. "But it wasn't a *good* relationship. I could tell just from those few minutes with them that they were both shallow, terrible people. She was controlling and clingy, he was horny and boring. I didn't destroy anything worth keeping."

She leans back against a stack of books and papers, a pile of learning that's coming unraveled. "You're probably right about that," she shrugs, "but a life that's not worth keeping is still a life, I think—I mean, because the essence of life is potential, isn't it? Death is just nothingness, but life is growth." She laughs. "Toddlers are shallow, terrible people, but it's still wrong to kill them."

"What about seventh-graders?"

"I think those are open-season."

"Thank God." And we laugh again. It's a stupid thing to laugh at, we both know it is, but we'll take what we can get on a dark winter night like tonight. "So what's that mean, then?" I say. "Like, for us?"

She says, "What do you mean? Like, in terms of *What do we do now?* or something? I don't know. I guess I'm just describing the universe the way I think it *is*, not the way I think it *should be*. Life and death are two insurmountable forces, and you can't fight them—you only latch onto one and cling as hard as you can, I think. You either jump into the dark or you jump into the light, and they're both swirling pits, and they'll both eat you alive."

"That's, uh, depressing."

"Yeah, I guess," she says. "But the thing is, there are things in the universe that are a whole lot bigger than you, and there's not a whole lot you can do about it." She plays with one of her weirdly perfect dreads, turning it back and forth in the dim light. "You were born into an ocean, Phelia, y'know what I mean? We all were. It's so much older and so much bigger than us, and if we pretend it's not real, we just drown. But you can also find the current going in the right direction, y'know?" She coughs, intentionally, I think, to fill the silence. "Does that make any sense at all? I mean, that's the way I see things, is all I'm saying."

I say, "Yeah, I get what you're saying, I think. But—I mean, that's not really what I was asking."

"Oh."

"Yeah, I mean—I was talking about last night. Like, what we did. Last night."

"Oh."

"We took a dead body, Kate, and we hid it, like a couple of murderers."

"But we *weren't* the murderers..."

"Well—" *You* weren't.

And I want to tell her. I want to tell her so bad. There's something in the air, an incense almost, a not-quite-stale scent hovering around her form and glowing yellow in the red that makes me ache to confess, makes me want to tell her everything, but I can't. Secrets, not sounds, globs of sticky emotion congealed in my gut, buried in niceties and nothings. And finally, I say, "But we still covered it up, didn't we? Isn't that, like, sort of *capitulating* to death?"

She says nothing.

"...giving in?"

She's looking down, studying the floor. Scratches at a calloused foot.

"I mean, right?" I say, finally.

She sighs, "Yeah, you're right."

"I am?"

"Yeah, I think. I mean—we did it because we were scared, right? And we did it because we didn't know what else to do. But no, it wasn't the right thing—just the easy thing."

"Wait, you thought that was easy?"

She laughs. "Easier than calling the cops and saying, *Hey, I've got a dead body in my closet, and also I'm black.*" She laughs. "*That* takes real balls."

"And, arguably, stupidity."

"Like there's a difference, right?"

"Yeah."

"You've got a good moral compass, Phelia," she says, trying to toss it off like it's a casual, unimportant observation, but the words are heavy from her gravelly smoker's voice, and they stick to the air.

"I do?"

She says, "Yeah, I think so. And honestly, that's more than I've ever had." She jumps down and opens a desk drawer, starts slamming stuff around in it. (Looking for that screwdriver? Yeah, probably not.)

"Well, I mean—"

"I mean it," she says. "You know when things aren't right. When you've screwed up. That's further than most people ever get in their lives. You've never been to catechism, and you might understand the Gospel better than I do. Definitely the part about *needing* it. I'm still trying to wrap my head around that much. It's hard to fit the whole ocean in your head, but you're halfway there, y'know?"

There's so much I want to say. Two corpses (more?), tugging hard at my ankles and dragging me down, and I can't get away from the past. I can try to ignore it, or just not to repeat it, but it's still behind me, and dragging me down like a current. A pile of the dead, melted into a salty, thick brine, dragging me to dark places I don't want to go. I could end it all, maybe, by opening my mouth.

But I can't.

She says, "Listen, I don't want this to be weird." (Too late.) "But I can tell you're going through a lot. I'm not sure what all, exactly, and I'm not looking to make you tell me your life's story. But I'm thinking you might need this more than me." And then out of the dark, her hand is in mine, and it's pressing her rosary into it. It's the one she had earlier, the blue one that was hanging out of her hand that night in the van, now catching the light from the lamp, turning red into blue, with a tiny cross dangling.

I should say something, but I don't know what. I have no idea how to pray a rosary, and I'm pretty sure this one's important to her. A few weeks ago, I would have said *You keep it,* but the cold fingernails digging into my ankles tell me I should probably grab it and hold onto it tight. So I squeeze till the beads leave deep tracks in my palm and say, "Thanks."

She's exhausted.

I can see it in her eyes now, deep brown spirals crisscrossed with jagged red thorns that stab at her pupils, and her gravelly voice fades to a croak. That last reach into the dark, that final Hail Mary pass, took everything out of her. I'm holding a piece of her in my hand now, and it's long and it's stringy like entrails, and it hangs loose in my hand while its reddish-blue shadow draws swirls on my bellbottoms. And it's three in the morning, and tomorrow is threatening to come right on time, pressing the darkness into my face until it almost bursts out with a blinding, bloody light. She feels it too, that the room is breathing, twisting into swirls of red and blacker black, shutting out dreams with hypnotic nothingness.

She says, "I don't mean to cut this short, but I have an early class and I should probably get some sleep."

"Yeah, me too."

I stumble to my bed and pass out into the black, clutching the beads till my hand goes numb.

## mon. jan. 17.
## 3:49 am.
## confused

**The scratching at my ankles stopped**. The swirling faces, the aching memories, the insatiable thirst—they all stopped. For the first time in days, the sleep was nothing more than a black nothingness, a deep gray fuzz that buzzed in my head and pulled my eyelids shut with ten-pound weights. But now I'm awake, and I don't know why.

My room fades in from the sparkling nothing, and everything seems normal. I'm not twisted in the sheets this time. I'm not drenched in sweat. The room is real, the dark is quiet, and my hand that held the rosary is empty. The indent of each bead sits cold in the winter air and I can hear my skin drying out. I glance at my hand and see it hanging over the side of the bed, empty and limp, and the beads must be lying somewhere on the floor below, wedged in between the bed and the wall, buried in dustbunnies and Cheeto crumbs.

I try to roll over to pick it up off the floor, but I can't move. My hand hangs there, limp, and my body refuses to roll. I've heard of sleep paralysis before, but this is the first time I've woken to a dark room that refuses to let me up from my bed. I can't move.

Why?

But, actually, I *am* moving. I mean, I'm not moving myself, but something's tugging at my arm, the other arm, the one I can only see out of the corner of my eye. Someone is tugging at my arm, again and again, while they rifle through the things on my desk. Shuffling through papers, slamming pens into pencils, knocking my phone and my purse on the floor. I push my eyes all the way to the edges of their sockets, trying to see what's going on through all the fuzz.

There's no one there.

No one standing there, and no one tugging at my arm. And yet, the noises continue. The shuffling continues. The tugging continues.

I'm struggling to move. I really am. But all I can do is lie here and feel the tugging get stronger.

I push. I twist.

Using all my strength, I manage to turn my head—and inch or two—and slowly I realize what's happening.

And then everything turns cold.

Through the fading gray static, I slowly make out the shape of my own hand, completely numb and violently stabbing at the things on my desk, slamming them to the floor one-by-one. Dragging itself drunkenly from corner to corner, like a spider tied to a lead pipe, searching, looking for something. My lifeless body is glued to the bed with icy sweat, watching my own (cold, dead) hand tear apart the stacks of homework just above me, like a cop rifling through a crack house. I try to scream but my tongue is just as dead as the rest of me, limply choking air out of my throat, while my tingling arm jerks hard on its socket.

Across the room I can hear Kate snoring softly, unaware of my silent distress, till her snoring is drowned out by the buzz in my ears that mingles with the silver in my eyes and drowns all my senses in waves. *What are you doing (hand)? Why are you like this?*

More sweat bursts out in another chill when I realize the answer. She—it—my hand—is looking for the pill bottle, and she's almost found it. I see its translucent silhouette, just out of reach, where she can't get to it, halfway to the window and glowing with yellow streetlights. And I can't fight. I can't do anything to stop it. I'm trapped, just a mind in a cadaver, watching as my fingers finally brush the plastic and stiffen, aroused and determined.

And they pull.

They pull from the fingernails out, reaching into gray ink, jerking desperately against my knuckles, my elbow, my shoulder. She—my hand—jerks into the night, clumsy but determined, ripping against tendons, till she lands on the bottle and the rattle is muffled by sinuous flesh and angry bones.

And the first thing I can feel her do is squeeze.

I feel her fingers, my fingers, press in against the plastic, tearing at polymer strands with a strength wholly not my own, the strength of needles in my bones and fire in my blood. I jerk back on my arm, command her to return, but still nothing moves.

And I feel it all now, every single ridge of the white cap is quaking through my arm as she digs her nails into them, shredding plastic into splinters and grinding her claws into ruptured stumps. The childproof cap, the flimsy locking device that keeps old people away from their prescriptions—for one moment, that's my hope, my only chance of getting through the night without being force-fed by my own zombie hand—but then it gives way, too, just a latch, nothing but two sticky globules of pseudo-liquid slipping through each other like ghosts, tearing apart like the shrapnel of a car crash, crushing bones in the goo.

I can see the bottle now, glowing orange like a flame inside the gray, a twisted, broken mass of waxy fat, shreds of terrible light and heat that burn my hand. And the pills inside rattle loud, tasting sweaty air they weren't supposed to taste and whispering my name while I beg them to stop. Chalky, unfinished pills with rough, pockmarked surfaces that breathe in the air and swell with humidity and push it back out as angry whispers. *No, you don't own me. I put you away. I'm done, it's over, I'm done.* But the pills don't listen (because pills can't listen). She's angry (my hand is), she's desperate and hearing the call from the rich, creamy insides of chemical nuggets. Demands them with anger and violence and sharp, jagged claws I feel growing, claws prying the bottle wide open and dragging it in toward my mouth, which won't close. And my eye tracks the flame as she floats over the bed, a will-o'-the-wisp, a jagged ball of lightning floating stiffly toward my mouth at the end of my spindly zombie arm. And it cracks, like sticks breaking, as the flame shoots straight downward and burns on my lips while its fire pours into my mouth. I try not to swallow, but you can't not swallow when something's already in your throat. And now it's inside me again, sinking into the gaping cavity in my middle that dictates my survival, and it burns all the way down till it lights me aflame from my gut to my eyes, and the dreams start again. The dreams again, the ones I've had, the ones that come and go, but this time they're instant and they're brighter and louder and realer, and they're not even dreams. They're not even dreams, just blocks of concrete that stack on each other, till they're miles above my head. And gray paint slathers over them, and the window ten feet above me glows dull with the sun, casting shadows of cold iron bars on the floor and the stainless steel mirror and the toilet. I desperately look through the door's tiny window till the diamond wire pattern is pressing itself deep into my face, among wrinkles that come early from too much experience. Small child's wrinkles on a small child's face, but no one ever notices them, ever sees them or asks me why. And a room that should heal them, a room that should smooth them, but instead it's a cage, it's a prison for the battered to be battered again. Every day they all find me, collapsed on the floor, on my face, with my nails dug deep into the paint, and each day I make scratches a little bit deeper, and they say that *She'd better stay here one more night, maybe two, just for close observation.* And each night the fat man, the one with the twitch and the bald head and cold, meaty hands and wild eye, he would unlatch the door with a *clank* and a *clunk,* and his big, meaty hands would be on me again, and oh God, he's still there, he's the man at the table who looked me up and down, I remember the strange way he twitched when he did. His one wild eye traced my curves from the floor to the ceiling, I know he remembered them, I could see drool on his lip like I used to. And now here I am in my cell and can't breathe, I can't breathe, and I'm trapped in my body, the old one I used to have, a frail child's body that's tapped out and used. And I have to get out, and I have to escape, and the concrete is thick and my nails are unsharp, but they're all that I have, so I tear at the walls. The thick sound of smashing surrounds me in noise while I strip away paint till my dull, jagged nails scrape against cold concrete that's been shutting me out from the sky. And my hands don't stop moving. I'm digging, destroying, escaping. Blood mixes with paint, and the shrapnel keeps falling, till the latch on the door, the one on the outside, unlatches. It's *click*ing and *clunk*ing and stabbing inside itself, and he's coming inside. He beats through the cold and steel gray of the door, and he forces his way into my square of concrete, through ten-foot-thick walls that still can't keep me safe. And a million old memories flash through my mind of the heaving, gray floor and the pain and the shame while I bled. He won't touch me again. He can't touch me again. And my hands, with their claws, both still burn with the flame of the substance inside, and I know he won't touch me, because I have strength now, and no one will hurt me again. The blood and the paint that are under my nails all cry out for death, for a blood sacrifice, and I spring from the floor, dirty nails in the sun, crying out in a voice that's not mine but belongs to the flame that's inside me. I land on his throat with my jagged nails ready; my fingers sink into his fat and firm flesh. And I squeeze. He chokes and his eyes fill with fear when he feels all the power in my hands and the flame in my eyes. And I'm not a small girl anymore. I'm not the weak one that you once used to play with, not just a doll you can throw to the floor when you're done, toss away, toss aside, just use up and throw out. I'm not that! I've discovered my strength, I've discovered my voice, and my strength is a flame, and my voice is a cry prepped for battle. I'm dirty and bruised, but I shine like the gray of the sun, and the bars aren't for me, they're for you, and you're mine now, you won't get away, won't escape till I squeeze every last ounce of breath from your throat. And he begs through his chokes and, and his giant, fat throat's folding over my hands, and my beaten nails sink into flesh till his voice is closed tightly away from the world.

And he's saying my name.

"Ophelia!"

She's saying my name.

"Phelia!"

What?

"What are you doing?" A choking voice. A voice that I know, and it's saying my name, and it's Kate's.

It's Kate's and she's right there in front of me, sat up in bed with my hands on her throat, and she's sweating and scared and she pulls at my hands while her eyes look around at the things on the floor and the shreds of the wall paint and posters (all torn) and the vases (all smashed), and I'm standing there stupid and gaping (her face!) with my hands on her throat thinking *What the hell happened?* and *What do I do?*

I loosen my grip.

Her face in a stare of confusion and anger and shock, just a huge, gaping hole asking me the same questions.

It's our room, our dorm room, and I never left, and I'm still 23, and my 23-year-old body is standing in the middle of an enormous, horrifying disaster. The paint hangs in shreds from the walls and the vase from her desk is smashed on the floor and her guitar sits broken in the corner. And my nails are ground to stumps and the posters from the walls hang in jagged ribbons and the sun is peeking over the horizon to reveal it all, and she's sitting there staring into my eyes with bruises on her throat and her mouth hanging open in silent disbelief.

And the sun keeps rising.

I watch the yellow morning spread through the fibers of her shag rug, now wadded up under my feet, while we stand there just staring at each other and breathing through our halitosis-mouths. I watch her face while her hands run over the gouges in her throat and she catches her breath and she tries to decide what to do. If she's smart she'll run. She'll bolt out the door and she'll call the police and they'll drag me away and she can maybe get on with her life. But she doesn't do that. She's just sitting there, studying my face while I'm frozen three steps away, hands raised in the air, half in fear, half in half-assed surrender. Tears run down her cheeks, from the pain and from cold resignation. A look of acceptance at the carnage in front of her, and a final exhale that says *What do I do with it?*

I don't know how long.

I don't know how long we stay like this, but the yellow stripes of the sun crawl slowly down her bedposts and we're still just standing here and gaping at each other and trying to remember how to breathe in the stale, sweaty air.

And then, finally, she speaks.

It takes her voice a few seconds to escape her mouth. I can hear it—feel it—stabbing its way up the collapsed maze of her throat. She sputters, she winces, but she speaks, and when she does, her voice is a croak that juts out into the air with ice and with fire. Her eyes don't leave my face, and she forces out just a handful of words:

"Are you ready to tell me the truth now?"

# mon. jan. 17.
## 7:49 am.
## tentative

**We're sitting on the steps to our dorm,** shivering in giant hoodies and wishing we had some coffee. Watching the sunrise fight against the mist and counting the cop cars on campus. I can't look at her, but I feel her eyes studying me, and she's ready to run but she's ready to listen.

(I'm not ready to talk, though.)

I'm thinking back to what she said just yesterday, something about needing a friend to confide in, even if it's not her. Touchy-feely-girly stuff, the sort of thing no one would ever say to me if I were a dude.

(But maybe she's right.)

I don't see it that way. Talking about my problems isn't going to change them; it'll just make me relive the pain over again. I'll still be a murderer, sitting here and passively watching the cops close in on me (three cars that I can see), and I'll still be powerless against this addiction. The only difference will be that someone else will know about it. There's no universe where talking about this problem won't make it worse.

Oh, Kate. You want to pull me out of my shit, but you have no idea how deep this shit goes.

(It's too late.)

Some guys in t-shirts with the sides cut out are playing half-court across the street, dodging and ducking between the fingers of mist. Under other circumstances I might enjoy the view, but it's hard to distract myself from my situation at the moment. They're bros who think they're a lot better than they are, and their fumbling's moderately cute, but it's not enough to lighten my mood. The arrhythmic pounding of rubber on concrete provides a soundtrack to my sweatshirt as it swallows me whole.

"I met up with my dad yesterday," I say. (I don't know why I'm bringing this up.)

"What?" (She wasn't prepared for me to say anything.)

I say, "I met up with my dad. Remember yesterday when I said I called him up? He wanted to meet. So we did." The words hang in the air, and she rolls them around in her head.

She lights up a cigarette. "That can be really dangerous."

"It can?"

"Meeting up with somebody you barely know?" she says.

"Uh, yeah."

"He's my father."

"But you don't *know* him. You haven't seen him in a decade."

"Yeah, I guess you're right."

She sucks her cigarette down to ash, stubs it out on the step, and offers me one. I figure I'm damaged goods already, so I let her light it and I take a drag. It's every bit as awful as I'd imagined, but also strangely calming—easy to see why it becomes an addiction for so many people. It's the perfect mix of pleasure and pain. (It's not hard to turn down pure pleasure, but when you can punish yourself for enjoying something, it's somehow easier to accept it. Maybe that's weird, but I see it all the time in people.)

"I thought you didn't smoke," she says.

"I don't have much to lose at this point."

She doesn't ask what I mean, and for a moment we sit there sucking on the glowing ash. It swirls hot in the air, chasing the mist away. "Well, what'd your dad say?" she says.

"He said the house I loved was built by bootleggers."

"What?"

Across the street, one of the bros drops the ball and chases it into the bushes. "We used to live in this house when I was little," I tell her. "It was one of those quaint old bungalows, and it was full of hidden compartments and secret passages. I thought it was the coolest thing in the world. I thought people just used to build houses that way, y'know? I thought people just used to be cooler, that they just put a little more effort into what they built, to make it interesting. It, uh—it sounds stupid now that I'm saying it out loud."

"You were a kid."

"Yeah, I guess. Anyway, he told me yesterday that all the passages and compartments were only there because bootleggers built the house during prohibition. It was like if he told me that Cookie Monster was only funny because he was tripping LSD."

"Isn't that what they said about Pee-wee Herman?"

"Or something." I can't make myself laugh this time, and my throat is soaked with tar. I tell her, "I'm starting to realize that nobody ever does anything cool or interesting just for the sake of doing something cool or interesting. Nobody does anything unless they stand to make a buck from it, y'know?" I suck down more smoke and I choke out: "Is that the difference between being a child and being an adult? Seeing the profit motive?"

She says, "Maybe. That and taking responsibility for your actions."

I sigh, and it's a smoky sigh. I could get up and leave right now, but what would be the point? "I guess you want to know about the bruises on your throat," I say.

She nods.

"Why are you hanging around waiting for an explanation, anyway?" I ask her, studying the muscles on one of the clumsy basketball dudes and watching his sweat turn to steam. "There are cops everywhere. You could just run to one of them. Or you could be at the hospital getting your throat looked at. But instead, you're sitting there, waiting for me to explain myself." My mouth tastes bitter from smoke. "Why are we doing this, Kate?"

She shrugs. Heavy shoulders that aren't easy to lift. Stubs out yet another cigarette and finally says, "I guess I'd rather fix the disease than the symptoms. Y'know?"

"Yeah."

"Sometimes you just do something because it seems like the right thing to do, even if it doesn't make a whole lot of sense." She's trying to light another smoke, but her lighter won't cooperate. "Like I told you before, Phelia, I'm not a great thinker. I can't pretend to be one." She coughs. "Now you can either tell me the truth, or you can lie to me some more. But if you lie to me, at least make it an interesting lie."

I lie back on the landing, my arm under my head. The cold concrete drains the last bit of fight out of me, while I suck the dregs from my filter. The last tower of ash falls to the ground, narrowly missing my cheek. I say, "I guess it all starts with my sister."

"Uh-huh." She's not trying to sound condescending, but there's an *I knew it* in her voice that's driving me nuts. I guess it's to her credit that she's trying to hide it.

"When I lost my last job, she told me she could get me another one, one at her hospital. But there were strings attached. There always are, with her."

"What sort of strings?"

I close my eyes to the foggy sun and I hear voices in the dark, but I ignore them. "That's where it gets complicated. See, I don't keep up with my sister all that well, but somehow she managed to get herself kicked out of med school about a year ago. But she had been doing some research on a drug—"

"Uh-huh."

"—and I guess the whole thing sort of blew up in her face. She doesn't talk about it, and I never wanted to know the details, but I guess it ended in a really ugly way." I hold out my hand, and she fills it with another cigarette. I'm gonna need it to get through this conversation. "My mom and dad both know more, I think, but no one talks about it. Anyway, she moved back in with my mom and picked up a job as mortician, which she doesn't seem too happy with."

"It's not a field a lot of people are dying to get into."

I ignore the pun. (The only way to win is not to play.) "So, anyway, I show up for my first day of work, and—" I take the lighter from her, light up, and fill the sunlight around me with smoke.

"And what?"

"And she's selling me this weird, Faustian deal. If I want to keep the job, I have to help her test her drug some more."

"You're saying that—?"

"Yeah."

"That's sick."

"Is it?"

"How is it *not?*"

"Um." I take a drag, a deep one this time, and I'm starting to feel sick to my stomach. I need to take this smoking thing slower. I say, "I mean, I guess it's unethical. Probably illegal. But sick? I mean, she's just trying to get back in the game, right? Just trying to prove that the pills work and win back some respect from her colleagues? Right? Or something?"

"Really?"

"I dunno."

"If that's true," she says, "why not just test it on herself?"

"She says I'm the fat one."

"What?"

"It's, uh, a weight-loss pill."

"A weight-loss drug? *Really?*"

"Yeah, I guess. Is that weird?"

"It's just—just a weird thing to stake your work and reputation on, is all."

"Well—I guess that's where the money is, right? People's vanity? No one's going to get rich developing antibiotics."

"I guess."

"Anyway," I say, "I didn't really ask questions. I needed the job, so I took the pills. I've been having weird nightmares ever since."

"And sleepwalking."

"Yeah."

"And being...violent."

"I guess."

"And—"

She stops. I think we both know what she was gonna say, but we sit silent because neither of us wants to admit that we know what we know. It's obvious to me, of course, and she might have an inkling, but she won't say it out loud, won't admit that she's thinking it, maybe even to herself. Doesn't want to acknowledge just how deep the shit is.

(We've all been there, I think.)

We sit here, both pretending we're just two friends enjoying cigarettes and watching the sun rise. I think about how I probably needed this and maybe she did too, so she won't say what I'm thinking, won't draw the obvious conclusion, won't shatter the mist. I feel her eyes on me, pondering what I'm capable of, trying to find a reason not to run away.

She finally says, "What I can't figure out is why she has this kind of power over you. You've been hired, you've got the job—why not just back out of the experiment? What's she going to do, get you fired?"

"She's done it before."

"She what?"

"She was the reason I lost my other job. The one at the publisher."

She's gumming her filter, trying to eke out the last bit of nicotine.

I take a drag, and my gut swims some more, and I say, "She's got this weird power over people. She always gets what she wants."

"Except when she got kicked out of med school."

"Yeah, that was surprising. Whatever happened must have been awful."

She says, "People who are used to success don't handle failure well."

"I guess not."

"Listen," she says. "This is not healthy."

"What's not?"

"This relationship. You and Sara. She's got you putting chemicals in your body, and you don't even know what they are—and even though you're obviously suffering from it, she's blackmailing you to keep doing it. And—for some reason—you seem pretty okay with it."

"I'm not *okay* with it—"

"Really? I don't see you fighting too hard. Are you going to keep working at the hospital?"

"I mean, I guess—"

"And you're going to keep taking the drug?"

"Well—"

"Sounds like you're okay with it to me."

"That's not fair," I tell her.

"Why not?"

"I mean, I'm—" I start, but there's not much I can admit to her. "It's not *that* bad. My behavior's been a little weird, I know—"

"A *little* weird?"

"—but, I mean, look how much weight I've lost. In, like, less than a week. The drug works, you have to give her that."

"Oh my *God,* Phelia, why are you defending her?"

"I—I'm not defending her, I'm just saying the drug works, is all."

"Okay—" she says, grabbing my arm—"do me a favor and just listen to yourself for two seconds. Just two seconds. You're talking about someone who's blackmailing you to put dangerous chemicals in your body, who deliberately got you fired from your last job, who managed to get herself kicked out of med school—and all you can say is *Look how much weight I've lost, teehee!* I just—"

I know she wants to say more, but she's trying to let me breathe. I'm trying to breathe, and I'm trying to think. There are nails in my back, sharp fingernails like from last night, and it's her, it's the girl who's been following me around in the pea coat and Uggs. She's saying things in my ear, and they're loud now. *Don't let her tell you what to do. If you throw away the pills then I can't be your friend anymore. You want all the pills and you want me to stay. Don't you? You do. I know that you do.*

"Shut up! *Stop!*"

"What?"

"Not you." I'm not talking to Kate, but she thinks that I am, and she shrinks away. Sharp nails in my back, strong hands on my arms. Strong hands from the bearded boy, the one with the flannel and the knit hat, and now both of my ghosts are here, but I know Kate can't see them. He grips my arms tight and he squeezes and tells me *I won't let you do that, I won't let you send us away. You know it meant something, you know that it did, when I washed your face clean in the closet.* I say, *You're not real—*

"You're not *real!*"

"What?" He's not real, Kate can't see him. She thinks it's just me, that we're just out here talking on the steps like we have been all morning. No one but the sun and the smoke and the bros. Just alone. No one else. They're not real.

"Listen, Phelia—" Kate's voice again—"I don't know anything about you and Sara. I've never met her and I barely even knew you until recently. But you need to understand that *this is not normal.* She's not treating you like a normal sister would. She's treating you like a—like a lab rat. A piece of meat. Maybe you don't understand that because you've never experienced anything else, but it's not normal, and it's not healthy." The claws go deeper. The hands squeeze harder. I open my eyes, but Kate's fading into the gray. *Don't listen to her, don't*—"I can't tell you what to do. It's not my business. But please think long and hard about what you're doing and why you're doing it." And I hear her walk away while I'm pulled into the darkness by strong hands.

# mon. jan. 17.
# 11:13 am.
# and now i'm

I open my eyes and I'm back in my room.

This needs to end.

I'm lying on my bed, on my back, wondering how and when I got here. Scratches up and down my arms, gleaming reddish in the late morning sun from the windows. Kate's right—what she said about Sara treating me like a lab rat. Unethical. Immoral. Illegal.

So why is it so hard to say no?

I'm watching the pill bottle on my desk. Twisted and shredded open, but still half-full, catching the light and flicking orange flames at the walls. I still have memories of Sara that aren't bad. When we moved into the big house, the McMansion, we both could have had our own rooms but we insisted on sharing anyway. We stacked our beds into bunk beds over my mom's protests, and when she started dating I'd stay up at night waiting for her and make her tell me every detail. But somehow every story blurred together and ended the same way till I tired of asking, and then she hung up the curtains around our beds, and—

I can't remember much after that. Not until she moved into her own room, and shortly after that she was gone. All she ever talked about was how she was going to be a doctor like Dad, when I could barely remember the man. The second she was done with high school, she was rushing through her undergrad work to get into med school, and we barely spoke once she was out of the house. I'd listen to her sometimes when she was home for a weekend or a holiday, sitting across the table from me, and her stories all struck me as the same, simple tales of how she'd been pushing hard for success, and the latest classmates she'd sabotaged, and ephemeral romances, all one-dimensional bits of a life I had no part of. But despite my ennui, I would still come to dinner whenever she was there and I'd sit at the table and listen to every word she said. And later, in the hallway, in the dark, when I saw her smile flash as she walked past, I'd follow the teeth with my eyes, unable to look away, like I was watching the Cheshire cat disappear into the yellow glow of the kitchen. Then I'd be left alone in the naked dark, unable to get to the warmth of the bathroom fast enough. I'd close the solid but too-thin door behind me and press my back against it (hard) while I caught my breath and tried to banish the flash of white from my mind. The bathroom was always the same just after she'd used it, with the hiss of the just-flushed toilet spraying an angry calm into the air until it dissipated to nothing, and a small puddle of water just in front of the sink—the calling card of someone who still hasn't figured out how to wash her hands without making a mess. I'd always marvel at how an obligatory cleaning ritual could result, in the end, in a mess, even one as small and mundane as this one. Somehow a mess so unspectacular was more of an insult than total chaos would have been—an odorless insistence that anyone after her was somehow not worth considering. And once I caught my breath I would always find myself unable to pee, and when I finally went to wash my hands I would find she had already thoroughly soaked the single hand towel, leaving me to dry them on my pants and sit in my own graywater for the rest of the evening.

I roll over.

My bed is wedged into a corner of the room, which means that if I face the right direction, all I see is a cold, gray wall—a smooth nothingness that on some nights will lull me into unconsciousness. Except this time upon turning, I'm greeted not by the immaculate gray, but instead streaks of color that perfectly match the gummy paint underneath my fingernails. Shreds and flakes hang from the wall, piling onto my mattress like dandruff, getting lost in the folds of sheets. I study the streaks in front of me, paint piled on top of paint that tells stories of a wall trying to hide its concrete. It's gray now, but under the gray is pink from the '90s, then brown from the '80s, burnt orange from the '70s, green from the '60s, and gray again from the '50s— all of them trying in vain to hide the truth: that this room is nothing but a concrete box poured by the lowest bidder, a holding tank for human beings while their heads are filled and their pockets emptied. But when colors get old, they get ugly as well, and the ugly thing they hid shines through again. I wonder if they knew, I wonder if it ever occurred to them, even a little bit—a fleeting thought in the minds of the painters as they enjoyed their beers after work—that each time they added another layer of paint to the wall, they made the already-tiny room smaller. Not much smaller, I guess, but smaller. Walls closing in a bit more on each generation, till the room is nothing but paint. Till the walls exist only to hold the paint that hides them.

But I know that before that actually happens, the building will be gone. That it'll be told it's no longer good enough to hold its occupants, either because prospective students with real money are applying to schools where the dorms are nicer, or because some neglected routine maintenance is threatening to result in condemnation from whoever it is that condemns buildings. And then, rather than fix or improve it, they'll tear it to the ground and rebuild on the same spot, this time with cheaper materials and trendier colors.

And now here I am, lying on the fifth floor, trusting my weight to a structure that sometime in the future will be nothing but some shards of concrete lying in the mud, naked and stabbing up into the sky.

Because everything dies.

It's not a deep or original thought, but it's a true one, and it's overwhelming as I lie alone in this wreck of a room I destroyed. Every poster in shreds, her computer on the floor, all her books torn apart. It's chaos—a swirling death of paper and glass, spread out on the floor and the walls for everyone to gape at and know that *Destruction is inevitable*.

I should get up and start cleaning, but why bother when everything comes to this end, anyway?

My 23-year-old frame is fully formed. I've achieved the Holy Grail of adulthood, and now the universe will spend the next 60 years (if I'm lucky) slowly grinding me to dust. Maybe those are just the thoughts of a rich white girl feeling sorry for herself, but am I wrong? This is what happens. We take things that are new—our things, our bodies—we use them until they're destroyed, and we throw them away.

*The hero, the Conqueror Worm.*

On the floor, between the bed and the wall, Kate's rosary catches the light and my eyes for just a minute. A flicker of blue amid the gray of the dust and the orange of the Cheetos, sitting where I dropped it in the middle of the night.

I pick it up. Because what else can I do?

I turn it over in my hand. It's nothing special. Some blue plastic beads and a dangling cross. I don't have a clue how to pray a rosary, and she must know that. And it was obvious last night that giving it to me took everything out of her, though I'm not sure whether that was due to a reluctance to part with it or a general embarrassment that she actually believes in something. Probably both.

(Her habit of deflecting criticism—*I'm no deep thinker,* etc.—makes me think she honestly wishes she could be something other than what she is. Maybe it's a pain in the butt to deal with, but I sort of wish I had the same problem: believing in something so thoroughly that I couldn't shake it, even if I wanted to. She'd probably laugh in my face if she heard me say that—*You have no idea what you're wishing for, Phelia*—but is it so much worse than existing just to exist? Being chained to *something*—even something insane—sounds a lot better to me than being chained to *nothing.* Maybe if you caught me at a stronger moment, I'd feel otherwise.)

So I'm left here holding a rosary that's useless to me, and that she obviously didn't want to hand over.

Why?

I've been turning that question over and over in my head. Last night, she said, *You might need this more than me,* but she must have known that I wouldn't know what to do with it. So she just wanted me to have it, I guess, just to possess it, as an object. A talisman, like it has some sort of power. A superstition.

But it seems kind of mean to dismiss it that way. Everybody calls the beliefs they disagree with *superstition,* which is a word that really doesn't mean anything except *You're stupid and I'm not.* Am I ready to do that to Kate—to write off sincere convictions just so I can feel like I'm better than her? It seems unnecessarily harsh, as if it would actually mean something to embrace my own nihilism. *There is no hope. Take that. I'm superior to you, and then we both die anyway, and then universe itself dies, and nothing mattered, ever.*

*But I'm smarter than you!*

And the alternative is just as cruel and insulting: to embrace hope, but only out of a desperate, generic need for *hope* itself, not because I think there's any truth to it. Kate gives me the unmistakable impression that she never *chose* her beliefs, but that they "chose" her, sort of. That she believes them because she has no choice, not because she wants to. And I didn't *choose* this nihilism, either. I was forced into it by years of attrition, disappointment after disappointment. And the knowledge that my life could easily be worse than it is does nothing but aggravate the emptiness I feel. We're all the products of our own experiences, and if I believe in emptiness, it's only because mine have been so empty.

Haven't they?

Now I'm thinking back to that lone memory, the one I'd almost forgotten (like everything else) till my dream at the bar. My hand reaching out, stretching down toward the tiny pile of life on the ground, pulling her up into the sun. A connection of flesh and bone, uniting old to new and life to life, filling the air with a brightness that screams *We will go on!* at the yellow-blue sky.

And then it was over.

I hadn't meant anything at all by it at the time. It was just a reflex—a simple, automatic one that represented nothing more than a cavemanlike instinct to avert injury—and yet, somehow, in memory, it means something entirely other. A monument of flesh and sinew, a determined affirmation of the *new,* a digging in of my heels and a resolution to stand up against death in all its manifestations—even something as unthreatening as a scraped knee.

Am I dissecting this honestly, or has Kate just brainwashed me into thinking in arbitrary dichotomies?

And then in my mind I'm there in the principal's office, with her bright orange carpet and blank, windowless walls. I remember her lecture so much better than that moment on the soccer field—how she yelled at me and yelled at me, just for giving a Band-Aid and a hug to a hurt, crying child, and then threatened to send me home for good, to block me from certification (as if that matters now). And I remember the long-but-not-long-enough weekend of sitting in bed watching TV and eating cereal and just thinking, over and over, *She's wrong.* I took no pleasure in the thought—there was no joy in imagining that I was right and yet would still be trampled by her wrongness (a wrongness born of slow strangulation by bureaucracy and a profound ennui for reality). I kept trying to tell myself *It doesn't matter* and *I don't care what she thinks* and *Life goes on,* but I just couldn't silence the open wound screaming *She's wrong* and *She's wrong* and *She's wrong.*

*You've got a good moral compass, Phelia.*

I can't get Kate's words out of my head. They feel ancient and musty, but they're less than 12 hours old.

I keep using that word *nihilistic,* but I can't call myself that, not really. Not as long as I believe in right and wrong, and I guess that I must, because Kate says that I do, and I can't get the idea of them out of my head, no matter how much I want to. I can't destroy thoughts like *guilt* and *life,* because even when the universe dies, ideas will go on (won't they? how do you destroy an idea?). I can't imagine they're imaginary, even though reality tells me—*screams at me*— that they are. I want to. *God, I want to.* But I can't.

*And honestly, that's more than I've ever had.*

Kate denies she has a moral compass, but do I believe her? Can I believe her? She's tied herself to a system of thought with rigid, inflexible standards of what's right and what's wrong, but she doesn't seem to quite believe it inside, doesn't seem to quite *feel* it. And then here *I* am, trying my damnedest to doubt any meaning in the universe, but I can't shake *right* and *wrong*. I just can't. I want nothing to matter, but things keep mattering.

I roll over to face the reality of my destruction, and I let the rosary and its cross dangle over it, a golden ratio coming into focus in front of the entropy, like a hand reaching out to a scraped knee. And I see now, by the layers of paint scraped off the walls, that I can't just get lost in the gray anymore.

*You were born into an ocean, Phelia, y'know what I mean? We all were. It's so much older and so much bigger than us.*

What did she mean by that? That I can't escape history? That there's nothing new under the sun? That I'm not really separate from others?

I don't know.

What was the other thing she said, though, about finding a current going in the right direction? The right school of thought? Which I'm sure she'd tell me is hers?

All I can see is matter bumping into matter until it dies (but I wish I saw more). She sees a world filled with magic, where spirits are everywhere and objects can have power and a string of beads can shield you from evil (but I gather that she wishes she saw less). Am I ready to step into that world?

(Am I able?)

I can lie here pretending to be tentative all I want, but if I hang onto these cheap plastic beads, I'm essentially buying into her outlook, whether I want to admit it or not. I'm buying into not just the possibility of a spiritual reality, but a particular one (which I honestly find a little ridiculous). I'm not ready to do that.

The blinds on the windows cast black, bar-shaped shadows across my face and I know that somewhere outside it are two bodies of people who I killed with my bare hands, plus one living person with my thumbprints dug deep into her throat. And wandering around campus are a bunch of cops looking for me, even if they don't know it's me yet. And my career and education are a disaster. Half my possessions are destroyed. And my mother wants me gone. And yet something inside me, my lizard brain, I guess, says *Keep going,* because your lizard brain always says *Keep going,* even when that doesn't make sense.

Keep going for *what,* lizard brain?

I hold the beads up to the light, and I squeeze them in my hand, and I don't feel any different. I don't feel stronger, or safer, or anything—but then again, I'm starting to realize that the way I feel rarely has anything to do with reality. I slip them around my neck, and I think I heard somewhere that you're not actually supposed to do that, but whatever. I guess this means—I don't really know what it means. I still don't know how to use them, but I guess I can hang onto them for now.

There's a mirror above my desk, one that always looks dusty, even right after I've Windexed it. I stand and I take a look at myself, still in jeans and a sweatshirt, still looking frumpy but finally a little bit skinny. The beads look gaudy and obnoxious around my neck, so I tuck them inside my shirt and the cross tickles me between my boobs. My eyes are a dull gray (they used to be blue), but I think I can still see a sparkle of sunlight.

And I know what I have to do.

The twisted, broken pill bottle is still sitting on my desk, scattering orange flickers of light around the dried-out husk of our room. It's been 24 hours now since I realized I had to do this. So I guess it's time.

Picking it up is like catching a flame. I hear the pills rattling around inside my hand, but it's lighter than I thought it would be, and it feels like a toy, like a baby rattle with some weird, jagged edges. This is what I'm scared of?

No, I can't start thinking like that. It's like a black hole, tiny but with infinite gravity, pulling me in. I remember from high school science that weight changes depending on where you are, but mass stays constant, and this is like that. Long after the universe collapses, this pill bottle will still be a million times stronger than me, a weird reality that exists beyond matter, a current I can't quite fight against.

But I'm going to try. I look down at the rosary, just some blue beads almost like from Mardi Gras, and I say *Help me?* and start for the door, and yank it open. The hallway's deserted—

"Hi Ophelia! How's the semester going?" And my RA's smile is in my face, so close I can count her pores. Where did she come from?

"Uh, fine." I jerk the door closed behind me so that she won't see the destruction inside. Let her find out at check-out in a few months.

"Everything all right?"

"Uh—yeah. Absolutely." She's blond and she's skinny and I swear her face is going to fall off from all that smiling and I'm trying to decide whether she's on her way to or from the gym. My eyes dart from her unchanging face to the restroom door down the hallway, and I just want to run. *Just move her out of the way.* (Why does she only acknowledge me when I need her not to?)

"Listen," she says, "I don't want to make a big deal about this." (She doesn't want to make a big deal about anything.) "But I got a complaint this morning. Something about loud horror movies in your room around three a.m. Any truth to that?"

"Um—yeah. That's what it was. Sure. Sorry. Kate and I were watching—uh—something—scary."

"Oh."

"Yeah, like—that one movie. With the vampires." God. I've seen a thousand horror movies, but my mind is blank.

"Oh."

"Yeah, we'll, uh—we'll keep it down—uh—next time."

"No problem! Good talk!"

"Okay."

"I have to get to the gym, so I'll catch you later! Have the *best* day, okay?"

"Uh—yeah."

"Great!"

As she jumps down the stairs, I call out, "Have a good workout!" which is weird, because I've never said anything like that in my life. And then I'm thinking maybe I should go to the gym too, get in shape, whatever, but then I'm like, *No, stay focused, you have one thing to do.*

Just one thing.

Let's do it.

I walk to the restroom, barely blinking. I stop at a toilet (determined) and pull out the bottle, the orange pill bottle with the chalky, white pills. I swallow and, biting down hard on my tongue, turn it upside down. The pills take a second to work their way out through the broken, twisted top, and they rattle and bounce, but I watch them all drop in the water, one-by-one, and they swirl in the white.

I always thought this restroom was weirdly overlit, as if whoever designed it was worried that we all needed to get a good, close look at our bowel movements. And now the bright light and harsh shadows paint me a sickening picture of white-on-white, drowning chalk that leaves little trails of bubbles as it sinks into the crystal-clear foulness, and my nostrils are filled with the strange mix of chlorine and feces that only occurs in a freshly "cleaned" restroom. For a moment there's an urge to reach into the water, to pull the pills back out—*Save them from drowning!*—but that doesn't make sense, I tell myself, and I close my eyes tight, and I reach for the steel handle and flush.

I hear the swirling before I see it, because it takes me a second to work up the nerve to open my eyes again and watch the white solids disintegrate into powder before twisting into a cloudy cyclone that snakes its way down the drain. It's strange how, when you watch a toilet flush, it always seems like it takes forever for the water to actually stop running. The pills themselves are gone in a second, but I stand here, still watching, eyes half-unfocused, listening to my pulse till the bowl refills completely. Then the rushing of the water slowly fades into a hiss that inches its way down the trails of grout in the floor and up the walls and finally into the air till the whole room is filled with a new, blank freedom.

And silence.

It's a calm, ambiguous silence, the sterility of the scent mixed with the yellow light and an air that feels sweaty and dry at the same time. And I feel weirdly and completely alone, till the line between my skin and the air disappears and my body dissolves into mundanity. Then the sparkles take over my head because I've been forgetting to breathe, and it's all dark and there's nothing.

The blackness is one I can barely remember, one from a time before everything happened, and it echoes last night maybe a bit, but it's deeper and darker, a swampy ink with no dreams or unrest, and my arms and my legs dissolve into night, till I'm left as a kernel, an idea of myself, something less than a body (but more), just a blinking light adrift at sea. And the black of the waves pounds harder, seeping into my pores till my pores disappear, and my brain's finally nothing. No fears and no hopes and no yearnings or thoughts, just a hum in the night like an old TV with the volume turned off. A low whine. A dreamless nothingness I've needed forever.

And then, even before it began, it's over.

"Hey."

I'm looking up into Kate's face, haloed in the restroom lights and bouncing dreads, looking worried.

I feel the floor again. Hard tile, digging into my back at weird angles and mashing the stickiness that never goes away into my sweatshirt, and I'm numb from the waist down. "You okay?" she says.

"Where am I?" I ask, and she laughs and gestures with her hand, like *Look around,* and I'm lying on the restroom floor feeling grimy and numb and my ponytail hurts and my ass is sore. "Was I—?"

"You were passed out," she says. "I mean, I guess. Unless you're taking naps on bathroom floors these days."

"No—well, maybe." And then I add, "I did it."

"You what?"

"I dumped the pills."

"Well—good," she says.

I wait for her to add something else, but that's all she has to say. Just *Well—good.* "Now what?" I ask her.

And she bites her lip, and she studies my face, and she says, "I guess that's up to you."

"Oh. Ow." I'm trying to get up, but my arms can't find a floor to push against, and my feet are ten thousand pounds of dead weight. She helps me up, and then I collapse onto the nearest sink while the room spins.

"You sure you're okay?"

"Yeah, I guess. I just—I really thought I'd feel better once I got rid of them, y'know? And all I feel is...tentative. Empty."

She helps me stand up again. "You want a guess as to why?"

"Sure. Why not."

She squints in the yellow light and says, "Once you finally beat your demons—that's when the real work begins, y'know?"

She just leaves it there, hanging in the sweaty echoes, looking over my face with her chocolatey eyes, and she sees the rosary around my neck, and I know that she does, because her eyes stop on it, but then she looks up and says nothing.

"What do you mean?" I say.

She says, "You're back to zero. Your life isn't about the *wrong thing* anymore—now it's just about *nothing*. Now you have to make it be about something positive."

"Oh." My knees buckle from the numbness and I almost fall over but she catches me again and she helps me back up.

"You sure you're okay?"

"I'm fine, I'm just—I'm a little numb. I've been sleeping on a hard tile floor."

"Well, why don't we get you into bed—"

"No. Wait." *Stupid.* "What day is it?"

"I think it's Monday. The 17th. Why?"

"Dammit. What time?"

"Almost six, I think. What's up?"

"I'm late for work."

mon. jan. 17.
6:20 pm.
almost late

I pull my car into the last slot near the door, and shake my head, trying to clear it. I can sort through Kate's existential questions in twelve hours, but right now I just need to make it through the night. It doesn't even matter what I'm doing with my life if I can't make rent. Or tuition. Or whatever.

The reality is that, most days, there just isn't time or energy for life to have anything like "meaning." Saving orphans and rescuing puppies is nice and all, but they're not things that normal people can do, not when we're still wondering how we're going to stay awake all night and then sit through class in the morning. There are orphans who need saving and there are the saints who save them, and then there are the rest of us: boring people who get trapped in the middle, running on a treadmill until we slip off and die. *You were born into an ocean, Phelia, y'know what I mean? But you can find the current going in the right direction.*

*I once had this roommate named Kate,*
*And the stuff that she'd say sounded great—*
*Till I breathed in the air*
*Of a world that can't care*
*Whether I save the cat or sleep late.*

Someone told me once, I think it was in a fiction-writing class I took freshman year, that the hero of your story always has to "save the cat" early on—she needs to do something to make herself likeable. I don't think the world works that way, though, even if fiction does. When you meet someone, you don't decide if you like him based on how many cats he's saved or whether he volunteers at a soup kitchen or whatever. You like him because he's funny or he dresses well or he likes the same things as you—stupid reasons.

And they definitely won't be giving me a bonus check at this place based on whether I feed any orphans. All they care about is whether I'm on time and whether I get my job done. In real life it's never about whether you're a good person, it's about whether other people can get something out of you.

But thinking thoughts like this is a luxury—a luxury for the people who can see the treadmill because they don't have to run on it. And I used to be one of them, thanks to my mother's bottomless pile of alimony, but I'm not anymore, so I need to start running, and now is as good a time as any, I guess. What was it Kate said just before I left? *Your life isn't about the wrong thing anymore, now it's just about nothing. Now you have to make it be about something positive.* I guess I can give that a shot.

I look up at the building that I was standing in front of, waiting for my first day of real work, just a week ago (but it feels like a lifetime). Back then it was nothing but a giant, brick ogre, a monolith of death and disease masked with the odor of disinfectant and breathing its financial halitosis in my face. And now I'm here again, looking up at the height and the shadows, but now I see something else, something hiding behind the thick brick and the windows that won't open and the stacks of death in the basement.

And—weirdly—it's life.

There's a twinge in my gut at the realization that death and life can exist within the same space, share the same bodies, use the same toothbrush. It's a sickening twinge, sort of an angry one, but there's more to it than that, and I think it's what normal people call *resolve*. What Kate was saying earlier, about resolving to side with life over death, and the realization that this space, horrible as it may smell, is where death and life literally fight their battles. And the battle lines are drawn directly onto human bodies, and the infantries charge, and it's disgusting and ugly and terrible and glorious. And it doesn't even matter whether I belong here or I want to be here, because this is where I *am*. All that matters is that I fight.

And it doesn't even matter who wins, I don't think, because after all death always wins in the end. But if there's a line drawn and a battle fought, it still matters which side I'm on, and even if the war is unwinnable it's still worth fighting.

*You were born into an ocean. Find the right current.*

I think I can at least do that much.

And now I'm standing nervously on the threshold yet again, thinking that what I'm about to do is tiny but in its own way it's huge. I jam my ID into the floppy scanner and jerk it up and down until the door clicks, and I yank it open to reveal the familiar basement.

"Hey, Oaf."

*Dammit.*

With a breath every thought falls flat, and the five minutes I just spent psyching myself up were for nothing. Just two bodies standing on the grimy, salty tiles, and her eyes are deep red and her mouth smells like cinnamon gum.

"Hi Sara."

"You were on your way down to my office, right?"

"Um—I mean, I guess—"

"Don't tell me you forgot about our standing appointment."

"Uh—yeah. I mean, no. I was thinking—"

"Great. Come downstairs, then." And she grabs me by my shirt and pulls me down the nearest staircase and down the red hallway and to her morgue, and I smell the flesh and chemicals decaying in the endless chill, and I close my eyes till we're inside her office and again the air's warmish and the lights aren't quite bright enough. "On the desk," she says.

"What?"

"Have a seat on my desk. We've done this before, haven't we?"

And I sit, and she takes my pulse. "Take your shirt off."

"What?"

"Your shirt. Take it off."

"Why?"

"It'll just be easier to take your vitals. Hurry up."

"I'm gonna be late for work, Sara."

"Then maybe you should hurry up and take your shirt off?"

"Um—" and her eyes flash veiny red at me and I sigh and strip off my top.

"What's that?"

"Huh?"

"That." She's nodding at my throat and I look down and realize I'm still wearing Kate's rosary. I'd forgotten it was there—once it warmed up to my body temperature, it felt like nothing.

"It's, um—a rosary."

Rolls her eyes. From my vantage point, her pupils seem to disappear for half a second. "I *know* it's a rosary. Just, why are you wearing a rosary? You know you're not even supposed to *wear* them, right?"

"No—I mean, yeah. I know that. I just—it makes me feel better, I guess. My roommate gave it to me."

"Your roommate." She jabs me in the ribs with a cold stethoscope.

"Um, yeah?" My arms fold in around my prickly boobs as my chest turns into gelato.

She turns her back, shuffles things in her desk. Somehow she's still blocking the light from the bulb. "Why are you suddenly talking about your roommate constantly?"

"I just—uh—" and I look toward the door, but it's far away, and I have no shirt, and where'd my shirt end up? "We, uh, weren't close before, is all."

"And now you are." She doesn't look up from the drawer.

"I—well—I guess we've been talking a bit more lately? I don't see why it matters."

She turns around, and the swinging lightbulb makes shadows on her face like she's telling a ghost story. "And now she's got you wearing a rosary."

"I mean, I guess. Who cares? It's just a stupid necklace."

"It's a superstition, Oaf. I just thought you were better than that, is all."

"It's not hurting anything."

I barely notice when she pulls it off, over my head. "Oprah's not hurting anything either, but her channel still sucks." She turns around.

"Like I said, it just makes me feel better."

"Better about what?"

Nothing. "I'm just—depressed, I guess."

She's flicking at something. "Which do you think is a bigger problem—" she says—"that you're depressed, or that superstitions make you feel better?"

"I—"

"You should focus on what's real," she says. "Your problems won't get better until you do."

"I don't know what's real anymore." I shouldn't have said that, but it's too late.

"This—" she says, and she jabs me with a needle—"*this* is what's real. Chemicals reacting with other chemicals. That's it."

"*Ow,* what was that?"

"Just something to calm you down. You seem a little upset."

"You could have warned me, at least."

"What would have been the point of that? You would have tensed up more and worried about the needle-stick."

"What? No, I wouldn't have."

"Yeah, you would have. You're always freezing up and freaking out when you're worried about something. That's why you can't hold down a job." She's across the room, talking away from me while she tosses the needle into a hazardous waste bin. "You really need to learn how to handle stress, Oaf. Can't go through your whole life being all PTSD." She grabs her clipboard and stands in front of the light again. "Anything to report?" she says.

"What?"

"Y'know, weird stuff. Side effects? I mean, you've obviously lost plenty of weight, so it works—but, I mean, I need to know if anything weird is happening."

"Um—"

"It's not."

"What?"

"It's not, I know," she says. "I mean, look at you, you're the picture of health. Why do I even ask?"

"Uh—Sara?"

She stops, surprised to hear my voice intrude. "What?"

"I think I'll be going off the stuff. I mean, if you don't mind. I mean—"

"You what?" A flash in her eyes in the dark again, like from the hallway at my mom's. A spark in the darkness that doesn't say much, but what it says it says hard, like the stare of a threatened animal or a knocked-over block tower. Like King Kong's grip on Fay Wray—a tiny squeeze that's a bit more than love and a bit less than a threat.

"I—uh—I mean, you can *see* the stuff works, right? What's the point of going on with it?" It's strangely difficult to keep my balance on her desk with her shadow pressing down on me like this. The air is dry and it cracks my lips.

She leans in close and studies my freckles and my graying eyes. All I can smell is cinnamon gum, and she could say anything, but she just says one word: "Why?"

"Uh—" and I realize, too late, that I should have said nothing at all. That I should have said nothing to her and just stayed off the pills and just crossed my fingers and hoped to God she didn't find out. That now she wants an explanation, a really good one, and that I can't sit here and say *I kill people and I think your stupid pills are to blame.* That I'm trapped now between the truth and myself and my sister, thinking *There must be a right thing to do here but I don't have a clue what it is.* Thinking *Why do I have this compulsion to be honest when there's nothing to say except I've fucked everything up and I shouldn't even be allowed to walk free anymore?* That knowing the truth doesn't do a damn thing for me except chain me to a past I can't do anything about. *The truth will set you free* my ass.

"Why?"

"I just—" and I bite my lip while her teeth and her eyes do that Cheshire cat thing again, and I swallow the words that I really want to say, and—"it just—it gets in my head. The pill does."

"It's supposed to."

"No, you don't understand. I mean—I see things."

Nothing. Just looking at me. Waiting. Chewing her pencil.

"I mean—y'know—hallucinations, I guess?"

"What sort of things do you see?" She's writing now, and her pencil scratches are sharp stabs, and I hear the clipboard buckle under it just a little.

I swallow. "People."

"People?"

"And...memories."

Somehow that word changes something, like a distant crack of thunder in the dry air that I know she must have heard, and instead of at me now she's looking into the distance, somewhere beyond the beige of the wall, while the air hangs heavy with the moisture of an impending storm. The little twist in the corner of her mouth has disappeared.

But she shakes it off.

"What sort of memories?"

"Forgotten memories. Stuff I'm not even sure happened. I get trapped in them, and I can't get out, and—"

"And what?"

"And—" and there's so much I want to say but nothing that I should. The storm in the air is headed back toward me, and I shiver. "It's just scary, is all."

"I see."

And all I can do is look down at the floor and wait for her to look away long enough for me to breathe.

"I'm doubling your dosage."

"*What?*"

"Take the pill twice a day from now on. I saw this same sort of thing in the animal trials. The solution was to increase the dosage."

And that's her answer. And I'm sitting here thinking *How stupid do you think I am?* but then I see that having her think I'm dumb maybe isn't such a bad thing, that maybe if I just say *Okay* that maybe that will buy me the time I need to figure things out. (That maybe the whiteness of her knuckles from squeezing the clipboard isn't meant for the clipboard at all.)

"Okay," I tell her.

"Okay?"

Her eyes narrow and she bites her lip, and I'm not sure if she really buys it, and I'm thinking that maybe she expected me to protest, that maybe she was just suggesting something insane out of sheer morbid curiosity, and now she's genuinely surprised that I agreed so quickly, and she's thinking on the one hand *Is she serious?* and on the other *Maybe I should have asked her to do even more.* I work up my best crazy smile and say, "Sounds good!"

"Great."

*Yes, I've got her!* I'm thinking, or at the very least I've bought myself a little time to keep my job and get ahead in my classes or find a real job or get the hell out of town or *something,* but I can't let my smile get too big or she'll see right through me.

"Do you need any more of the—"

"No!"

*Damn,* I answered too quickly. She was trying to give me more of the stuff, and I knew I couldn't have that, couldn't handle it, couldn't trust my Bruce-Campbell-like hand not to start dumping it down my throat again. *Control the breathing, Ophie. Control it. You can't let her see you panicking like this.*

"I, uh, have plenty." Clear my throat. "I'm okay."

"All right, if you say so."

"I...do."

And that's it, I guess. And I'm thinking I should get out of here while I can, but somehow she's put herself right between me and the door, and I'm inching my ass toward the light, trying to escape the weight of her shadow.

"I should go. I'll be late for work."

She turns and goes behind her desk, and I jump down and bolt for the door, but I catch myself on the jamb, breathing hard, thinking *Don't look too desperate, don't look too desperate.*

"Um...so, question," I say.

"Yeah?" She's already slouching in her chair, clicking her mouse, smacking her gum.

"Any idea when we'll be done with the...experiment?"

"When I say we're done."

"Another week? A month?"

Doesn't look up. Clicking.

"A year?"

"When I say we're done."

I should go. I should go. "What if *I* say *I'm* done?"

Her eyes meet mine, and the gum-smacking stops. "I'll destroy you."

And I laugh. But she doesn't.

tues. jan. 18.
1:57 am.
triumphant

"You," Rachel's telling me, "are amazing." And she checks some things off on a clipboard and punches a few keys on her pager, and this might be the first time I've seen her smiling. It's weird, but tonight, I have energy, drive, I can actually get crap done. It's like I was telling myself before I came in, about how I need to take the right side, to push against death, to push as hard as I can, even if it wins in the end. So I focused. I attacked. I bit my lip and gritted my teeth and did everything they told me, and it feels amazing. "Where did *that* come from?" she's saying. "Where was this Ophelia the last two shifts you worked?"

I laugh.

"I mean, granted it's a slow night, but you've got us well ahead of schedule. Well done."

And I think for a moment that maybe things will be okay after all, that maybe I'm actually good at this, that maybe I can at least work here long enough to finish my degree, that maybe nothing bad will happen. That for the first time, I have a moment to breathe and I feel like I've earned it, and outside it's night, but in here the lights are buzzing bright in time with the stars.

She says, "Listen, I hate to ask, but..."

"What?"

She laughs and rolls her eyes. "Listen, don't take this as an insult this time, but child psych's got one of our gurneys again, and..."

"Go get the gurney?"

"Uh...yeah."

"Sure, absolutely," I say, and I charge up the stairs, three at a time, thinking *There is no way that this level of energy could possibly last*. I've had moments like this before, where everything seems finally perfect and I've found my groove and I think I can go on forever accomplishing things without even needing to sleep. It always turns out to be a lie. I always push myself too hard and then I crash. Or worse, sometimes I'll get so exhausted that I'll start to loathe my own accomplishments and start undoing them. Somehow, nothing has a more powerful draw on me than self-destruction.

So I make myself slow down.

This isn't just about riding a groove. It can't be. It has to be about consciously choosing to do what needs to be done. I'm starting to think that maybe that's what adulthood is— not going with the flow but *being* the flow, I guess. Directing the flow? I don't know. Something.

I'm back on the seventh floor now, and I push the door open into the cavernous hall filled with light and faces. Somehow this time it's less overwhelming. This time the endlessly recirculated air isn't choking me, and I breathe it in, and breathe it out, deliberately, just to show it who's boss. I stretch out my arms and I fill up the space, making it mine. *I'm not afraid of you, hallway full of paintings of old people.*

So, this isn't my dream job. But it is where I *am,* and it is where I can make a difference at the moment, and for the moment, that's enough. I won't be leaving in the morning having accomplished my every goal, but at least I won't have to slink back to bed feeling worthless and ashamed.

Is that success? I'm not sure.

What I do know is that the assortment of old, white, male faces staring at me from across the room look slightly less sinister this time around than they did the other night. Not that they're any more attractive, just a little less depressing, I guess. They may not have been the sort of people I would ever want to be in the same room with, but I guess the fact that they spent some money to build a hospital means something, right?

*I understand you guys.*

You didn't ask to be who you are and you didn't ask for your situation and you definitely didn't ask to be scary old guys. But you did something with it. You started a hospital.

Could you have done more? Maybe. I don't know.

(Could I do more?)

(Probably.)

I walk closer. I stretch out my hand, and trace the frame on a portrait. It's dusty on top and the corners are sharp like it's never been touched, and yet somehow it feels exactly like I expected it to. Edges and corners and a grain with a strange smoothness. And inside is the sad, tired face of a man who's seen more than he ever cared to. Close-up, isolated from the wall of staring faces, he's no longer creepy or intimidating—no longer a particle in a monolith of white, wrinkly flesh that threatens to topple over and drown me in a pool of sweaty money. Just a man whose name no one knows (except whoever etched it into the placard on the frame, I guess), whose only contribution to the world was to donate enough money to get his face on a wall but not his name on the hospital, who's rotting in a box somewhere now. And he couldn't even smile for the portrait hung in his honor. A sad, empty face, staring out from behind a thick screen of dusty glass. I trace his wrinkles in the dust, and as I do the portrait wiggles back and forth, swinging on a wire attached to the wall by a wobbly nail, and his face is nothing but a bit of paint on a canvas, and the eyes that are windows to the soul are just blackish blue dots with nothing behind them but stale air. A flimsy piece of fabric with paint smeared on top of it, and like everything else it will either stretch too tight or sag to oblivion till it's nothing but dust. And there's a hundred more of them just like him on the wall, just a hundred sad faces on a wall of a hundred people who never smile but just tried to do their best and now they're all dead.

Y'know. I assume.

I back up slowly, watching the face become part of the legion on the wall, watching the white wrinkliness in front of me expand into a massive panorama of well-intentioned death. I'm starting to see it. I'm starting to see why I shrink away from Sara, and I think it's because of the pills—the pills that starve your body till they beat you into a temporary idea of perfection, an idea that only exists because somebody's making money off of it.

Or maybe that doesn't make any sense. Maybe all of that is just the ravings of a mind struggling to dry out from a chemical that's twisted it to nonsense and refuses to relax its grip. Like when you wake from a dream that you're so sure was real that you're ready to call up a boyfriend you don't even have and break up with him, and maybe it takes you 20 minutes or even an hour to realize that it was all made up, and yet you still believed it even though it made literally no sense at all. Because you can't get out of your own head, no matter how much you want to. And then you think *Well okay maybe it wasn't real, but the fact that I dreamed it has to mean something, right?* as if there's some deeper reality your dreams are tapping into to show you the future or teach you some profound lesson, but then you read up on dreams and you find out that all they are is just your brainstem firing random impulses into a convoluted tangle of neurons. That's literally all dreams are, just electrons bouncing around in your head and your stupid brain thinking *Wow that's so deep,* even though it's the shallowest thing in the world. And then you think to yourself *If I can imagine something as stupid as my brainstem stuttering randomly means something, then how much other stuff am I imagining?* And you realize that there is literally no answer to that question, and that Sara is probably right that the universe is nothing but chemicals crashing into each other, except how do you even know for sure that *chemicals* are a thing.

*Which do you think is a bigger problem—that you're depressed, or that superstitions make you feel better?*

She has a point. Maybe I'll print that on a t-shirt.

Then the picture, the one I was tracing with my finger, falls off the wall and smashes on the floor, and it's nothing but glass and wood and canvas and paint. It's cracked now and he's staring up at me from the floor tiles, leaning halfway up against the wall, and I want to look away but I can't. It's suddenly twisted and I'm the one who twisted it and I need to get out of this hallway before someone who matters finds out.

I need to get the gurney and get back downstairs. Anyway, I have no idea how much time I've wasted standing here and thinking. My eyes are following the pools of light down the hall, hopping from one to the next, taking their time. Why am I afraid to look toward the child psych door? This whole time I've been up here, my eyes have been fixed on the faces on the wall, as if I'm afraid to look in the other direction, and even now, they still hesitate.

They're almost there when I remember what Kate was saying about my nails being buried in a door when she found me, and I want to look away and forget everything and pretend that I've never been up here before, but it's too late, I can't, and before I can do anything my eyes are latched hard onto the mass of beige-and-orange steel down the hall, covered in streaks and slashes with shreds falling off, covering the floor in orange-and-beige dandruff. And now I'm walking toward it, unconsciously, compelled by either horror or fascination (like there's a difference), and the streaks become closer and clearer till my face is pressed against the shredded steel, and my eyes dart up and down, running beige, and then down to the orange, and then to the silver ruts, where my nails dug down to the metal and left jagged memories of themselves that dance in the artificial light. My fingertips sting, remembering every scrape and cut and bruise, because I can't help but feel them when they're written in front of my eyes like this. I look at my hands, and the paint chips are gone now, but my nails are still broken and my fingertips still bruised and sliced. And I'm thinking that Kate obviously wasn't just blowing smoke up my ass, but why was I trying so hard to get into child psych?

And why does it make so much sense to me that the door used to be orange?

In my mind, I can't banish the image, one I barely remember, of a bright orange door the color of Halloween, and I'm screaming while they drag me inside it. I'm smaller and younger and the old people on the wall stare at me hard, banishing me to night after night in the violent grayness, and I'm crying now, till the orange-and-beige streaks are muddled in my eyes, running down my cheeks.

Remember to breathe.

I don't know what exactly I'm remembering. Nothing that makes sense. Just a jumble of neurons firing in my brain, painting images and sounds behind the streaks, and I muffle them hard and say, *Get ahold of yourself,* and I choke back the tears and think, *Only what's in front of you, that's all that matters.* I wish I believed it.

I scan my card.

There's a magnetic *clunk* like always, and the door is way too loud as it swings toward my face, and I jump out of the way just in time. The orange and the beige blur sideways and leave me with nothing to look at but the hallway that's always dark, lined with offices and frosted windows that bathe it in perpetual twilight, and I've walked it before, been dragged through it before, and I never want to pass through it again, but here I am.

I step inside. The air is cool but it's musty and stale, and my steps echo hard and they disappear fast, and I'm suddenly, weirdly, aware of my posture. I feel naked and awkward and stumble and stoop toward the door, till I say to myself, *Stop slouching so much,* and I straighten my back, but my boobs stick out weird, so I end up slouching back down. By the moment I get to the door at the end (like, a thousand years later), I feel doubled-over, like some old, crazy cat-lady. I wince as I pull on the handle.

It creaks, and the creak is the loudest I've heard, and I bend over backwards, turning my head and shutting my eyes. Shrinking away from the blinding light and the other thick doors and the blank children's eyes that stare out from the dark at all hours.

"Can I help you?"

That voice.

"Can I help you?"

And then there's silence. Till I look at that face, and *that face.*

"Ma'am?"

It's him. I remember that sneer and that face and those hands on my body, and late nights alone in my cell crying tears, saying *Please God don't let him come in.* And it's him, and he's here, and he's always been here, and he's staring me down, and he can't place my face, and I run.

I turn and my face hits the jamb as I fly down the hall, stumbling into the dark, and the twilight flies by, and I trip over the tile as the faces look on, sneering over their noses, and I hold up my hands to block them out as I fly past. Then my hand reaches out for the library door and it opens, unlocked, and I slam it behind me and crumple to the floor and cry into my knees for God-knows-how-long. The smell of the glue and the musty green carpet, and thick dust on everything from years-upon-years of no one coming up here. Footprints in dust, ten or fifteen years old, telling tales of a struggle. The feet look like mine, except smaller, and I still feel the callouses digging into my skin. Streaks from fingers in the dust on the book spines, gouges in the paper and nicks in the steel. Pain in my fingertips, scars in my throat dug by deep, feral screams, and I fall into dark, through the cold streaks of sweat, till I land on a stage in a spotlight five years ago. Up there, lit up, and in front of a crowd, and my dad and my mom in the dark, in their seats situated at opposite ends of the theater, and Sara somewhere in between them. (She's biting her tongue and I know that she is from the pain in my mouth.) My dress is miles long and my hair is done up and my nails are deep red, like the red in my blood that pounds hard in my heart every time I'm onstage. They're all looking at me, and I'm famous, important. I cry. Not real tears, just stage tears; the crowd hangs on my gasps and they hang on my sobs and I make them all feel things. They watch me. (It's power.) I pull on their eyes, dragging them from one end of the stage to the other, with my eyes and my fingers. Oh *Heavenly powers restore him!* I say, and they gasp. *I have heard of your paintings too, well enough,* he says. *God has given you one face and you make yourselves another.* He throws me down onto the floor, on the rough, black matte paint. *You jig and you amble, you lisp, you nickname God's creatures and make your wantonness your ignorance,* he says, but my face says far more than his words ever could. *Go to, I'll no more on 't. It hath made me mad.* I'm seething with breath. *I say we will have no more marriages. Those that are married already, all but one, shall live. The rest shall keep as they are. To a nunnery, go!* Then exit my Hamlet, the spotlight's on me, and the silence extends to the back of the theater till nothing is left but my spotlight. I gasp, and I choke, and all eyes in the room are now mine. *Oh,* I say, *what a noble mind here is o'erthrown!—the courtier's, soldier's, scholar's eye, tongue, sword, Th' observed of all observers, quite, quite down!* Then I pause here and gasp and I make them all beg for the lines coming next. (I look unprotected, but they know I'm controlling the room.) *And I, of ladies most deject and wretched, That sucked honey of his music vows, Now see that noble and most sovereign reason Like sweet bells jangled, out of tune and harsh; That unmatched form and feature of blown youth Blasted with ecstasy. Oh, woe is me, T' have seen what I have seen, see what I see!* And I crumple to the floor, and the crowd just sits silent, their mouths hanging open. The crumpling wasn't planned, and I never rehearsed it. Just happened. I gasp on the floor now, I'm gasping for real, while the crowd hangs on silence, and actors rush onto the stage. They yell and they scream, but no one is listening, they're (all of them) staring at me, on the floor, sobbing sobs that are real. I glance up and my mom and my dad sit up straight, with their mouths hanging open, both thinking, *God, what is it she's tapping into?* And Sara is gone from her seat now, and all I can think is *Where is she?* Then *Exeunt all,* and the audience gapes, knocked out cold by the silence, till the room rolls in waves of resounding applause. I ride on the waves, off the stage, to the girls' dressing room, where I have just two scenes to get changed and do makeup. I unzip my dress, and I hear her calm voice. *Nice performance,* she says. It's Sara. She's there in the door, and the lightbulbs (big orbs hanging over the mirrors) shine bright on her face, and her eyelashes turn into spidery shadows. Her red lips are curled, her deep-green eyes shimmer in half-dark, and all I can think is, *Where's everyone else?* The room is deserted—no Gertrude, no extras, just me and the twisted, red grin at the door. I tell her *Hi, Sara.* She says, *Won't you even say 'Thank you'?* I reach for my zipper and ask her, *For what?* and the chill in the air as she comes close to me is like ice-fingers up my bare back. I'm shrinking away, trying to hide my cold skin behind my thin locker door, but there's light peeking in through its slats, and it burns on my throat. She reaches around, fingers curled on the edge of the door, and her forehead and eyes peer around. She says *You could just tell me thanks for the compliment that I just gave you, or maybe*—and now she's so close I feel breath on my face—*or maybe for giving you pain you can draw from. For helping you live up to that stupid name that Mom gave you so you could receive that ovation just now. For making you into Ophelia. You're welcome.* Lights flicker, like flames. I say, *What do you mean?* and she shakes her head, slow, and she laughs at me under her breath. She says, *You don't remember at all, I guess, do you?* She smiles and says, *You don't remember the curtains I hung up to make our bed into our special O.R., and you don't remember the ways that I touched you, and you don't remember the way you attacked me, or any of those seven nights that you spent in the psych ward.* She chews on her lip, and I almost feel teeth, and the A/C kicks on and blows sleet in my face, while a clock ticks the seconds away till my entrance. She tells me, *Freud wrote about memories that people repress, but I didn't think anyone bought into that anymore. I thought it was bullshit like Oedipal complexes. Interesting.* Her eyes track my skin up and down, prick at hairs and at bumps. And she says, *That's okay. Guess it's not like it meant anything, way back then. Not at first, anyway. It was practice for being a doctor, I guess. Just exploring, I think. But then later, it did—it meant so much more. It still means so much more.* My eyes flit toward the door, but then there she still is, in my path, and I can't look away from her eyes. Two black pits in green pools, and they hold me in place, chain my feet to the floor. She says, *Hamlet is right, y'know.* (*What do you mean?*) She says, *Hamlet. He's right. In that scene, when he tears you apart. Throws you down on the floor. And I know you weren't acting, I might as well say. I know how real all of that was.* I try to say something, can't think of the words, and she tells me again, *He was right, just to treat you like that, just to tear you to shreds with his teeth. 'Cause that's how you show love. There are people out there who will lie to you, tell you that love's made of hugs and of kisses, of sweet, mucky selflessness. All of them, though, are dead wrong.* Her face is so close I taste salt from her freckles. She says, *Love consumes. It destroys. Love will swallow you whole.* And the next thing I feel is her warm lips on mine, and they burn me like blisters filled up with the sun, and she won't pull away. They stay there and roil with the heat of an army. Mine sink into hers and they twist to eternity, nothing but flesh, melting me, pulling me toward the center. Her teeth catch my lip as she's pulling away, and the sharp sting of blood says *Consume* and *Destroy,* and she's gone. I open my eyes and she's not in the room. And I think it's my entrance. I remember this night. It was five years ago, at the end of twelfth grade—but it's not senior year anymore. It's not happening again, just replaying in my head, just my brainstem. It's firing away with electrons. Asleep. I've been dreaming. I need to wake up. But I can't—I'm alone and I'm hollow, just standing half-dressed in a cold dressing room, thinking *What can I do if I'm trapped in a dream?* and the girl comes in. It's Cyndi, the one with the Ugg boots and highlights, the one I keep seeing, who once was a body and now she's a ghost, and she follows me everywhere (why does she do that?). She says to me, *Why are you down on the library floor?* I say, *What do you mean?* and she says to me, *Why are you on the floor, hugging your knees? There are battles to fight. Will you lie there forever, just letting your sister control you?* I say, *No I won't.* She says, *Then you need power, the strength to fight back. You're too weak, Oaf, you need to be stronger.* (But how?) And she tells me *You know how. You know what the source of your strength is.* She looks in my eyes with a squint that's two daggers, and I say, *Oh God, please not that.* But she grabs my hand hard, and she pulls me away from the room, through the wall, down the stairs to the basement. Behind my eyes' lids, I see lights flying by, and I can't make her slow down. I can't make her stop. And she drags me through bodies and darkness and throws me down hard on floor of the office that Sara works in. The orange of the rug stings my face as I slide on the floor toward her desk. *Open the drawer,* she says. I try to say, *Why?* but she says, *You know why. You heard what she said. She'll destroy you. And you need the strength to fight back.* I say, *But you know that I can't take this drug without losing control,* but she says, *Well, have you ever tried?* And there's silence that hangs in the air a long time because I'd never thought of that question. I ask myself, *What if she's right?* When I took it before, sure, it made me do things I regret, but I know what it does now, I've seen its effects. Maybe I can control it. I'll use it to keep myself safe, and that's it. I'll take it inside me and then I'll be stronger than her and use it to end her (just her) when she tries to destroy me. Because she *is* going to, she said she would and she will and I know that she will, and I need to make sure I'm prepared when she does. That makes sense. Right? I don't even know what makes sense anymore, and I'm breathing so fast, thinking *Maybe I'll nap on the floor?* but my hand's in her desk drawer now, fishing around, reaching out for the pills in the bright orange bottle. My fingers brush scissors, I think (are they bleeding?), but then they find plastic! It's round and it rattles! I wrap them around it and pull it out into the light, and it shines like glass fresh from a kiln, and I think *Am I sure that I'm wanting to try these again?* but she's saying *You do, yes you do, just don't think.* I open the bottle and swallow the pills and they're chalky and scratchy and claw down the sides of my throat as I push them down into me. It's so hard without water, to swallow, to take them inside, but I push and I feel them dissolve and I'm strong again. I look up at Cyndi. I ask her, *What now?* and she says to me, *They need to pay.* I say, *Who needs to pay? Sara? People upstairs?* and she says to me, *All of them. Every last one of them. They need to pay for the ways that they've hurt you.* And I say, *Okay,* and I look under Sara's cheap desk. There's a space heater waiting there for me; a thick stack of papers is sitting up top. It's easy, and simple, to turn on the switch and to leave the machine lying facedown on top of the papers and head for the door. When I get to the door, it's smoking already; by the time I get to my car, the sun is rising amid the thick flames.

## tues. jan. 18.
## 4:21 pm.
## tangled

"Ow."

I'm lying on the floor and I'm thinking *How did I get down here?* and my head hurts where it's been rubbing against the tile. I'm twisted in my sheet and my mouth tastes like smoke. I'm back in my room and the lights are on and Kate's standing over me, confused. I smell like death and my face feels bloody and I can't move my arms.

She's standing over me in skinny jeans, her spiral dreads pushed back under a bandana, laughing. My gut is doing some sort of weird reverse-vomit thing where it's trying to suck my lips in through my mouth, and somehow the room is spinning, even though the floor feels as hard as bedrock. Every joint I have is bent in a position I didn't know was possible, and the sun is slapping me in the face, while a TV squawks.

"When are you gonna get this whole 'sleeping' thing figured out?" she says, kneeling to help me get untangled.

"You'd think after five years of college I would have it down. Ugh, my head."

"What happened?" She tries to jerk a twisted sheet off my arm, but my elbow doesn't bend that way.

"I dunno. Nightmares. I don't really remember anything."

"What sort of nightmares?"

"Does it matter? Dreams aren't real, anyway—just your brainstem firing randomly—ow."

She jerks on a corner and says, "I know, I know. I've taken Psych 101, too, Phelia."

"Ow." She was jerking the corner the wrong way, turning it into a tourniquet.

"Whoops, sorry." She pulls it the other way. "Anyway, just because your dreams are random electrical impulses doesn't mean they mean *nothing.*"

"Doesn't it?"

"Why would it?" she says. "Everything your brain experiences is electrical impulses." I can finally move my right arm, but it's floppy and backwards. "You really don't remember what you were dreaming?"

I raise my free hand to my eyes to block out the sun. "I think something about...*Hamlet*. And a locker door. And a...space heater? I think? Ow." My left arm can move now. "Who cares?"

"Well, I'm just concerned that you haven't been entirely—oh my God."

"What?" I follow her eyes, and they're fixed on a building, and the building's on the TV, and the building's on fire.

"That's my—"

"Isn't that your hospital?"

I can't say anything, and my mouth is hanging open while my ears buzz with words like *fire started in the basement* and *appears to be an accident. So far the death toll is in the double-digits, and the number of injured in the hundreds, but the fire is under control.* It all seems familiar, like none of it is news, and the orange and red spit out from the black shell, and I lie on the floor and repeat, "Oh my God."

"Did you know about—?"

And she stops, abrupt. I look for the words for an answer, but the answer is *Yes,* and the answer is *No,* like I saw it in a dream, a dream I forgot, and I don't think I like what that probably means. I swallow it all, and I lie in the glow from the flame, and I tell myself over and over: "I didn't."

"Was your sister—?"

"I don't know."

The sun's behind a cloud now and the room is dark and filled with the orange from the screen, orange that flickers and bounces. My legs are still tangled in the sheet, but they're numb and I forget them. She finally says, "Y'know, it's weird."

"What is?"

She says, "Didn't Stalin supposedly say something like, *One death is a tragedy; a million deaths is a statistic?* Or something? Just a few days ago, there was a single corpse on the floor of our room, and it was horrifying. Now I'm seeing dozens of deaths on the TV, and it should be objectively worse, but my reaction is nowhere near as strong. It's just some pictures on a screen. It's like, I know I *should* care, but my gut's just not doing the same flip-flops."

I know she's just talking to fill the silence, but I tell her, "I know what you mean. One act of evil is horrifying. A hundred are just numbing." We sit there on the floor of the room, both thinking *What now?* because what can you say once you've admitted you feel almost nothing? I sit and I wait for my phone to ring, because I know it's coming.

After an ocean of orange, it does. It's there across the room, buried under the pillows on my bed, and its ringtone is muffled and tinny and quacky. I can't feel my legs, so I drag myself over the floor with my tingling arms. The sheet around my legs drags through the dustbunnies, and I get to the phone just in time.

"Hello?"

"Ophie? You're okay? Thank God."

"I'm fine, mom. Relax." It's my mom and I was sort-of hoping it would be anyone else, but it's her, and she's asking me about a million things, and all I really want to say is, *How is it you suddenly care about me when a week ago all you wanted was for me to get out of your house?* but I manage to bite my tongue and answer her hysterical, redundant questions as they come.

Then: "Have you heard anything from Sara?"

I pause. "No..."

"She's not answering her phone, and your father can't get ahold of her, either."

"Oh."

There are a thousand emotions right now, both *What if she's dead?* and *What if she's not?* and there's fear and relief and there's pain and there's guilt and there's chills, plus a sudden and desperate need to throw up. But I say none of that. I choke the vomit down and hang onto the phone, and the orange-glowing room spins around me. I look over at Kate, and she makes a face and mouths *What?* and I just shake my head, like *Shut up,* and immediately feel bad about it. "You don't know anything?" says a voice in my ear, and I jump because for a second I actually forgot I was on the phone.

"I—no.

And after some static, I hear, "Well, let me know the second you hear from her." And my phone is silent and it falls out of my hand and onto the bed.

My legs are still numb, but they're starting to tingle, like the orange TV flames are burning me alive, and I wonder how much longer the stupid news coverage can go on. *I get it, guys, there's a fire. They happen all the time.*

*I mean, right?*

Kate's still just sitting there, looking from the TV to her phone and back to me, her face changing from one shade of orange to another. Finally, I say to her, "Sara might be dead."

Her mouth hangs halfway open, somewhere in between *I'd better say something* and *I have no idea what to say.* Then she decides on, "Oh no. I'm so sorry."

I tell her, "You don't have to be," and my hands start untangling the sheets from my legs because there's nothing else for them to do. They're wound around them several times. After futilely tugging at one for a while, I add, "I'm not sure I am."

Orange silence, and then the news breaks for a commercial that's whitish and full of used cars and a fat guy yelling. It's so much louder than the news that we both jump, and she can't find the remote, and we both just pray for it to end. Then it goes to something quieter, a pinkish ad where single women sit around mooning over yogurt. She whispers, "What an awful thing to say."

"Is it?"

It's a serious question. I really don't know—is it so bad if she's dead? All she's done lately is manipulate me and pump me full of drugs. I don't feel sad, just—empty. Like I'm hanging in the air, about to fall into an endless, beige pit. (Is this what freedom feels like?)

I say, "Y'know what she said to me? Last night?"

Kate thought that question was rhetorical as well, and she's sitting there, just biting her lip and waiting for the answers, while the TV blasts noise into the gaping silence. It's words and music, but in the silent gap it just sounds like noise, like grinding teeth and pounding jackhammers.

And I think, *What would happen if you filled a concert hall with grinding teeth and pounding jackhammers? It would all just sound like the ocean.*

*Waves pounding on the shore.*

"She said she would 'destroy' me," I tell her.

"What does that even mean?" she says, finally, but obviously I don't know.

"I told her I was done. With the drug, I mean. She said I wasn't allowed to be. She doubled my dose, and she said that if I stopped taking it, she would destroy me." She finds the remote, finally, and turns off the TV. "I don't know what she meant."

"Maybe she was joking?"

"She never jokes," I say. "I've never heard her tell a joke." I jerk hard on the sheets, and my legs are finally free, and the air hits them like an electric slap. "I guess she does talk a lot about, y'know, *destroying* things, though."

"What do you mean?"

"Just stuff she used to say when we were kids. About how it would be fun to torture people. I mean, kids talk like that all the time, right? But they're never serious."

"I thought you said she didn't joke."

"Yeah, I guess." I'm trying to get up now, trying to push myself onto the bed so I can at least sit. My legs still won't do anything. "And there was something else she said to me once, back when we were in high school. I barely remember it—something about how real love isn't selfless. She told me that love *consumes* and *destroys.*"

"What does that mean?"

I'm up on the bed now, and I grunt as I plant my ass. "Just what it sounds like, I guess." With the fire from the TV gone, I suddenly realize how late it is. How dark it is. No stars through the slats in the blinds, just gray.

"Do you agree?" she says, and I wonder if it's a real question this time, like if she really needs to know how I feel about love, like it really somehow matters, or if maybe she's just trying to make a blunt point or fill silence. But the silence can't be filled by just those three words, anyway.

"I mean, why not, right?" I say. "Jealousy, divorce, revenge—aren't those the endgames of love? People talk about selfless love, but have you ever actually seen it?"

She's staring out the window. "I—I believe it's possible—"

"I mean, possible, sure. All sorts of stuff is possible. It's possible we're all just brains in vats. But in your experience? I mean, people *talk* all the time about love changing people, making them better. It's a nice thought, sure, but have you seen it happen? Like, ever?"

She opens her mouth, but nothing comes out.

"I mean, I'm just saying, every couple I've ever known has stayed together as long as they were getting something from each other. And once they weren't getting it anymore, they split up. Selfless love is a nice thought, I guess, but—"

I stop because she's gotten really quiet. Staring hard at the dark clouds out the window, like she's trying to hang onto the last shred of her beliefs, and at this point I'm just trampling over them, just to be a bitch. I should stop.

"Anyway," I say, "now I guess I don't have to worry about that anymore. But I'm out of a job again, as well."

She says, "Was the job important?"

"It was the only thing keeping me in school."

"But is school actually important to you?"

"Well, it's—I mean—why are you asking me all these questions?"

She takes a deep breath, and says, "Because you're not asking them of yourself, Phelia."

I sigh and I push myself to my feet. My shorts are tangled in my crotch. I tug at them, and the seams are like sawteeth, and I almost fall, but I catch myself on my desk.

"You still have that rosary?" she says.

I shake my head no, and I look at the floor so I don't have to look in her eyes, and I tell her, "Sara took it."

"She *took* it?"

"Yeah."

"And you *let* her?"

"I—I'm sorry," I tell her. "I didn't even have the chance to stop her. She was just going on about how I shouldn't let imaginary things comfort me, because that's even worse than being depressed in the first place, and then she just pulled it off of me and threw it somewhere. She was trying to help—"

"'Help'?"

"You don't understand," I tell her. "That's just how she does things. Love consumes, destroys. That's just Sara."

And she says, "She's wrong, Phelia," but her voice is so shaky small I can barely hear it. She chokes, clears her throat, and says—"I'm gonna find a way to show you how wrong she is." And then she's out the door, slamming it, and I'm left alone, just hanging, half-assedly, on my desk.

*I've done everything that's been required—*
*Stayed in school, studied hard, gotten hired—*
*But I'm starting to doubt*
*Just how things can work out*
*When my job, sis, and I are all—*

Ugh, *enough with the damn limericks.*

Get over it. Stop trying to force everything into rhythm and rhyme. It doesn't work that way. Nothing works that way, because nothing works, and *God,* I smell like death. I haven't showered in a week, and suddenly all I can think about are the dozens of lives I have smeared all over me, the blood on my hands and the skin under my nails.

I have to get clean. I have to get clean now.

I grab the bucket of body wash and shampoo from the floor of my closet, ignoring the dried splotch of blood underneath it, and run for the bathroom down the hall, where I duck into a shower stall and thank God it's deserted in here. I strip off my tank top and jerk the shorts off my legs and I twist the handle for hot water to blast myself in the face, just hoping to get the stink off of me.

I scrub my arms and my chest with the soap, but the water up here's super-hard, and it beads on your skin and refuses to run off and go down the drain, and the stink won't come off me, because what can wash water away? It's stuck to my arms with the sweat and the blood (is the blood really there, or am I going nuts?), and I think about when I was young and my mom used to talk about *cleaning the bathroom* or *cleaning my bedroom* or whatever else. And I'd think that that meant that the things in this world were all either just *clean* or just *dirty,* but later I realized that when I would clean things the dirt didn't just disappear, it just stayed where I left it, inside of the sponge or the rag or the mop, and no matter how hard I would scrub there was always some left. And even the gunk I would flush down the drain was still *somewhere,* it wouldn't just straight disappear, it was somewhere out there, even ended up (maybe) in fertilizer that they would spray on my food. And I started to think *Maybe 'clean' doesn't really exist. Maybe I've never seen something 'clean.' Maybe I never will. And was I ever clean? Will I ever be clean?*

Breathe.

It's like I was thinking yesterday, about how I still believe in these ideals—*clean* and *dirty, right* and *wrong*— even though everything in my experience tells me not to, that nothing exists in those sorts of binaries. I keep thinking about what Kate was saying about how I have a better moral compass than she does, but obviously that's not true, since I've killed more than a dozen people now. I wonder, can I be a serial killer and still have a good moral compass? Like, if I murder a dozen people, but I know it was wrong, is that better? Does that make me a better person than a murderer who thinks it was a good decision?

I have to laugh at that thought, because at the moment I don't have much to laugh at beyond absurd moral quandaries. When I stop laughing, though, I'm sure I hear something. A footstep, a cough—a human noise. Obviously it's not weird that there's someone out in the bathroom, because there are a lot of girls on this floor, but it is strange that the sound stopped the second I did.

No, I'm imagining things again. So glad I'm finally off this stuff. Once my system clears of it completely, then everything will make sense.

I grab my shampoo and massage it into my hair. It's that Herbals Essences stuff they brought back from the '90s, the stuff that apparently makes women orgasm in the commercials, but in the real world it just sort of foams in your hair. And in the hard water, if actually barely foams at all—it just sort of trickles down the back of my neck and makes the little hairs stand on end. I'm starting to shiver when I notice the outline behind the curtain.

There really is someone out there.

It wouldn't be weird if it was someone just washing her hands or peeing or fixing her makeup, but this girl is just...standing on the other side of the curtain.

I want to pull it back, peek around it, see what she's doing, but that would just be too weird. I can't make myself do it. So for the moment, she's just an outline in the frosted curtain, gray and blurry, like a yeti, and the breathing is strangely familiar. Like the sort of breathing I used to lie awake at night listening to.

Oh my God.

I'm backing away, as fast as I can, and wedging myself in the shower's back corner, and I'm naked and the water's turned cold. I can't explain the fear, can't tell you what I'm thinking, except *No no no no no.* And I feel her eyes on me, through the curtain somehow, tracking up and down me, saying, *Yes, I remember.*

I bury my head in the corner and let the water drip down my face, thinking *God, that's so cold,* and I shut my eyes tight, praying *Just go away.* There's a rattling, a tugging, a rustling. More breathing. My head in the corner, cold water on my skin, and I wait too long to open my eyes.

And she's gone.

The gray shadow, the yeti, isn't there now. Just a blank, grayish curtain that looks the same as before, and my tank top and shorts hanging right where I left them, still mostly dry. I shiver in the corner till the hot water returns and oozes through the ice on my back, taking forever to restart my heart and force the blood through my veins, like a thousand tiny bugs trying to squeeze through the spout of a ketchup bottle.

I stand under the warm water for a hundred and seventeen breaths, holding the shower handle for balance, counting hairs as they flatten against my skin, thinking *What's wrong with me?* Thinking that I must have imagined the whole thing, that if someone came in, she was just here to pee, that the breathing sounded exactly like—

But that doesn't make any sense at all. Even if she were alive, why would she be coming here to scare me in the shower? *That's stupid, stop imagining things.*

I just need to get out of this creepy bathroom and go back to my room and turn on all the lights and pile myself under blankets until I feel nothing but warm. I even have a can of soup that's been sitting on my desk since the beginning of the school year, and maybe I can finally open it up and microwave it and have a boring stay-at-home party by myself where I watch TV until I pass out.

By the time my hand finds its way back to the knob and the water turns off with a *kerchunk* and the last few drips are somehow louder in the silence than the rushing water was, I've managed to bury all thoughts of Sara, and the only thought on my mind is to hide in my bed and pretend this day never happened. I'm just now realizing that I forgot to bring a towel or a change of clothes, so I awkwardly shake the water off myself, and then slide back into my gross wifebeater and boxers. Then I pick up my bucket and head for the door, tracking puddles behind me on the grimy tile.

I stop dead in my tracks.

Ten steps down the hall, at the door to my room, in a black coat and hat, there's a cop, standing there, knocking hard on my door, looking down at his watch, and *My God, I guess everything's over.* I duck back inside the girls' room door, press my back against the wall, counting breaths, thinking *What do I do?*

The tile on the wall is a hideous puke shade of yellow that sucks all the heat out of me while I shake and I make myself breathe. He's still standing there at my door, like he's planning to camp out awhile. He's a young guy, short hair and a five-o'clock shadow. Looks nervous, determined. He's shaking a little; he leans on the wall, elbow out, looking down at his wristwatch again and again. And honestly, he doesn't look all that scary. Just kind of alone. He's here now for me, and I know that he is, and maybe (I'm thinking) I ought to go turn myself in. Would that be so bad? I have nothing to lose, anyway; maybe I should just tell him the truth, let him cuff me, and take me away. Because I can't just keep running forever, can't pretend that I haven't done all of the things that I've done. He looks nice enough. He probably won't even be that big a jerk about this. The worst that could happen is that he'll arrest me and take me downtown, maybe question me some. And maybe he's not even here to arrest me at all. It might be they don't even know it was me, maybe he's just come by here to feel around, that sort of thing. And as long as he doesn't see my disaster of a room, maybe he won't even be suspicious. He'll ask me some questions, and then he'll go, and if he needs me to come with him, I will.

It won't be so bad.

It even feels good, I'm telling myself, it feels good to come clean, it feels good to get all of that stuff off my chest, like a big, giant weight that I'll drop at this (chiseled) guy's feet. I take a deep breath, tell myself, *This is it. You're not ready, not prepared, basically in your underwear, but this is it and you're going to do it.* I look at him and think to myself how hopelessly dorky cop uniforms look, always at least ten years out of style, with unflattering lines and terrible fabrics, leather jackets that should match but don't, clip-on ties and fake buttons. I wonder about the stereotype how women are supposed to love a man in uniform, and I'm thinking *Which women are those?* The ones who are okay with dorks as long as they're powerful dorks, or maybe the ones who think their calling in life is to teach tasteless men how to dress? The ones (I guess) who yearn to get the man out of the uniform—not for sex, but so that they can put him in something that actually looks good, like a tux or a well-tailored suit or a pair of ripped jeans and a vintage tee. This one actually isn't too bad, looks like he might clean up pretty well, all things considered. A shave and a little less hair gel, and maybe learn how to stand without fidgeting so much, and he'd be pretty cute. I'm glad that it's him I'll be turning myself in to, and not some cynical old dude who's just here to collect a few final paychecks before retirement, or some chick officer who thinks she has to be a bitch to get respect. He looks kind of nice, really. Probably has a great smile that'll take the edge off of surrendering to the long arm of the law. Maybe he'll even thank me for being honest, or being a good citizen, or whatever. This won't be so bad. It's the right thing. I can do this. *Check your pocket.* (What?) *Check your pocket.* A voice behind me, one I almost remember, telling me to *Check your pocket.* I know that voice, and I know that hot breath on my neck, and I know the smothering heat of the fat man, and he's saying *Check your pocket* in my ear. I say *Why are you here?* but he says, *Check your pocket. Just do it.* My hand (trembling) lifts from the cold tile wall and it slides its way over my thigh and then into my shorts' tiny pocket. It wraps around something that's plastic and hard, and it's rattling, barely concealed this whole time, and it's pills. It's her pills, Sara's pills, in my pocket, the pocket inside of these shorts that I slept in, and they've been inside of them rattling against my right thigh this whole time. Right? I guess. That makes sense. Doesn't it? Anyway, they're there now, and his huge hands are squeezing my arms and his stale coffee breath's in my ear, and he's telling me *It doesn't have to be over.* I say, *What do you mean?* but I know what he means. I hold up the bottle in thick, buzzing light, and it dances like flame and it shines like stained glass. And the yellowy tile's lighting up with its glow and the rattle of little white pills shakes in rhythm with my cold, trembling hand. And the fat man who smells like sweat tightens his grip on my arm, and he twists it behind me, says *Time to fight back.* Then the other one's here; it's the hipster I've seen in the flannel and boots with the beard, and he's twisting my other arm, won't let me move, and the pills rattle loud in my ear where he's holding my hand, scraping flesh against flesh. I tell them I won't, that I'm done, that I'm free, but they say, *No, you're not.* Then the blond girl is here with her Ugg boots; they're crushing my toes, and they're grinding them hard in the muck on the floor. Her lips are so close that I'm tasting her gloss, and she says, *You don't have to give in. You don't have to quit now. That man in the jacket, he'll put you in cuffs, and he'll lock you away. You don't give in to that. You fight back.* Her fingers hook under the straps of my shirt, and her teeth flash like Sara's and say, *You just need strength to do it.* I choke on my breath till my nose drips with fumes, and I start thinking *Maybe she's right.* I see that as long as I'm taking the pills that I'm safe, that I'm strong. They're filled with a power that beats from the walls and caresses my throat and my shoulders and chest and my hips and my knees, and the chills go for miles. My throat itches for chalk and my guts squirm with acid; the ear-rattle tickles and tickles. Hold my breath, tell them *No,* that *It all leads to nothing, an endless black hole,* but they won't let me speak. (*If it all leads to nothing, then why do you want it so bad?*) I choke with her hands on my throat and their hands on my arms and the pills in my ear and I say, *You're not real!* but they pull on my arms and my legs and my hair and my teeth and say, *Prove it.* Their hands burn my skin and they tell me *You know that you want it,* and finally I break from the inside and tell them *I do.* The tears burn my eyes and my (strong?) arms collapse at my sides, and I choke on the thin, acrid air, and they're gone. I'm alone, but they're right, I can see that they're right, that as long as I'm strong there's no reason to give myself up. That no one can touch me or lock me away when I'm stronger than all of them. Freedom is violence and violence is pills. They rattle in orange, saying *Let me inside,* and I tell them *Okay,* and I untwist the lid. It *click*s and it *clack*s with a childproof heartbeat, and I tip it over, pour pills in my hand, maybe five (six?) of them. Can't really tell. So hard to count pills while I'm shaking with power and watching (transfixed) while my hand starts to rise toward my mouth, and it dumps them inside and they're burning my tongue, and it starts to convulse as they slide down my throat. One by one they burn down, and they stick to my insides and light up my blood with a thousand quick sparks. There's a girl in the mirror. She looks just like I do, with eyes that are hungry. Her bones are alive, and her veins look so sweet. She winks at me (gently), we both say *Let's go,* and we stalk down the hall, and she's long and she's lean, made of spindles and spikes and of teeth and of claws and she's me. And the cop in the hall, standing there at the door, he's so tiny and helpless. He screams, and my claws are a mile that twists through the air filled with sticky, sweet sweat, till all ten wrap around him and push him inside of my room. His eyes flash with fear and his hands reach for something, wave helpless like seaweed till I bite them both off with invincible teeth, and the blood flows like honey between them. His throat bursts wide open with the twist of a tooth, and he gurgles and chokes, as I chew on his flesh. Now he's dead at my feet, just a pile of bones and of skin and of meat, and the scent is of berries and peaches and lime, but I can't back away. I can't run. There's a small voice inside, in the back of my head, that says *Run, you should run now, it's over, he's dead,* but the hunger won't stop, and I can't stop the feeding. More and more in my mouth, more and more of his flesh, of his skin, of his blood, and of bones, and I eat and I eat, but the hunger goes on. It goes on till there's nothing but hunger, a pit, a black hole, crying loud for more meat. So I swallow and chew till I drown in the blood, and I'm swirling and sinking and gasping and waking and swirling and sinking and gasping and waking, and—

"Phelia?"

There's a voice, down the hall. It's a voice that I know. It's Kate, and she's there down the hall, and she's seeing me here now, with flesh in my teeth and the bones in my hands and the blood on my feet (on my face, on my arms, on my legs). And she sees everything.

*Oh God, what can I do?*

"Ophelia!"

And she's yelling at me, but there's nothing to say. I'm alone in the light with a pile of evidence, blood on my hands, and a buzz in my head saying *Shit, now you've done it.* A young guy's dead face staring up at my knees from the floor. And she's there, down the hall, with her mouth hanging open, yelling things like my name and *Oh God,* and there's nothing to do and there's nothing to say, and there's nothing but light piling up on the blood and the skin and the bones and the face. *God, that face,* once a face, now a mask, now a rubber expression with glass eyes and fish lips that bubble with blood, and I'm standing here thinking of what I can tell her, but no, that's just stupid, there's nothing to say, just get out while you can, just get out, *God, get moving! Just run!*

I look back at her face one more time, and her mouth's hanging open in cold disbelief and her eyes shine with night and her freckles are pale and I tell her "I—didn't—"

But there's no end to that sentence. Nothing but lies.

So I run.

**wed. jan. 19.**
**12:58 am.**
**alone. cold**

**I run until I don't know where I am.**

In this town, where I grew up, that takes a lot of effort—to find somewhere where I'm really lost, where I don't know where I am or what I'm doing—but I have experience with that. I'm a veteran of secret passages and hiding places and shaking in the dark praying no one will find me. I can blend into shadows till I'm nothing but air. And now I don't really remember the running, but I think I've been running forever because I'm so, so tired, and I finally fall down.

I'm not sure if I tripped over something just now or if my strength just gave out, but there's no point in running anymore. There's nobody chasing me, so I guess I'll give in to my burning muscles. I land on my face, in the dirt and the sand, and I breathe hard and gasp till my mouth fills with gravel. It's big, roundish pebbles, like a mouthful of teeth. I spit them out, slowly, trying not to bite down, and they clean out my mouth with a dull, earthy taste. (So much better than blood. So much better than bone.)

And the thought of that blood and those bones and that face makes my guts flop around till the vomit pours out of my mouth and my nose. I'm up on my hands and my knees, grinding them in the sand, while the blood and the bile spills out through my face, burns my eyes with its fumes, and they're acrid and sharp. Their smell turns my stomach. I turn away to breathe, and I fall onto my back.

I stare at the sky, and it's black and it's starry, with halos and clouds that say snow's coming soon. And the gravel beneath me is cold on my back, like a carpet of ice chips refusing to melt. I stare at my legs, and they're covered with blood, and they're bare, and I realize I'm still in my sleep clothes. A thin, tiny tank top, these same itchy boxers, the hair on my legs straight and proud in the wind. And I shiver.

Aside from the sky and my legs, all I see is a streetlamp, a decorative one like they only put up inside parks or in rich people's yards, but I think it's a park that I'm in, from the gravel that's digging cold pits in my back. Chills and hot waves rush fast through the sweat on my face.

And I breathe.

It's not a calm, peaceful breath, like you hear in a room with a roommate who's sleeping, or even the sort of rough, menacing breath that you hear in a scene in a lame horror movie where they say *Let's split up* and then all walk alone into dark, creepy rooms—it's a sputter, a sob, just a howling in pain, like a werewolf alone at the end of his big scene, crying out at the moon, not in strength but in weakness, looking down at his claws, thinking *What have I done.*

*What have I done.*

My mind isn't totally dark like before. Before it was jumbled, dark memories that dissolved in the light when I woke, but tonight there's no light to dissolve them. I cry loud, because all I can do to drown out the blood is to fill up my eyes and my ears with more violence, more noise. The noises are sharp and inhuman; they split through the sky while the tears sting my eyes and the snow falls. Giant flakes made of winter that first look like stars, but they're whiter than stars, and they drift to the ground faster than I expect. They land on my flesh, making pools among the goose bumps, but I don't even feel them on my blue, icy skin.

This is it, then, I guess.

I'm not trying to be dramatic, but the way things are, there's no reason I can think of to ever get up off of the ground. Where would I go?

The image is burned deep into my mind—of the blood, of the bones, and of Kate at the end of the hallway, just standing there, thinking *I knew it but just didn't want to believe it,* the drips from my hands as I ran for the staircase and stumbled out into the night crying out in the pain and the fear and regret.

So I can't go back there.

And what does that leave? My thoughts wander back to my mom's place, the one with the manicured lawn and the cheesy brass lion and the room up the stairs with the bunk beds with curtains and boxes I'm filling with books. The one that my mom dragged me up to that night and said, *Fill all these boxes, get out of my house.* I can't go back there, either.

So what can I do? There's nothing but me and this gravel, this streetlamp, this tattered wifebeater with brown-yellow pit stains and the cold, falling snow that blocks out the stars. I can't feel my skin anymore.

There's a Jack London short story they made me read in high school, where the main character dies of exposure. (That's seriously the whole story: *Guy dies of exposure.*) He says something about how it's not all that bad, it's like being numbed to death, or something like that. That's what I'm feeling right now, at least I think. My legs, turning blue, against the black of the sky, while the snow hits the ground and melts deep between pebbles.

And my back hurts.

There's a stabbing in my lower back and a crick in my neck and a sharp, shooting pain in my elbow, which I guess is what happens when you lie down in gravel too long.

Jack London was full of crap. I'm standing up.

What did the guy know about dying, anyway? He wrote "To Build a Fire" years before he died. And I guess no one had told him that life almost never gives in to death—it always fights back, whether you want it to or not. I remember reading, somewhere, that most people contemplating suicide won't actually attempt it if they aren't given a really easy opportunity. You hide the handguns or turn off the gas, no suicide.

Death is lazy. It only wins when it doesn't have to do anything.

I'm back on my feet now, and they're bare and they're numb, but I can still stand. The melting snow is washing the blood off my arms and my legs, and they're turning from a bright red to a vague gray-brown on my tank top and shorts. I catch some of the snow in my hands and smear it on my face. My hair is still wet from that shower, and it feels like it might be freezing, but I'm probably just being dramatic.

Still, though, I need to get inside soon. Half-naked and wet in the snow has never been a good combination.

I try to brush the melting snow off my arms, but it's falling too fast and I can't fight it. I look around and I see that I'm in the middle of a playground, one of those old-style playgrounds that were built before safety got trendy, with a giant, metal slide and cold, steel monkey bars, and dirty gravel that's sticking to my back. I reach awkwardly with my jagged nails and clumsy arms, trying to brush it off, but I can only reach about half of it. But I'm almost numb anyway, so I sigh and I sit on the gently turning merry-go-round. I lift up my feet and let it carry me. It's cold and it's steel, but I can't feel my butt, so I guess it's okay. I hold my feet up, and the thing just keeps turning, like it's pushed by a ghost in the stiff, snowy breeze. First the slide's drifting by, then the old monkey bars and a couple of lights; then I get a clear view of the houses around me. They're small but they're old, homes that would have been nice maybe 50-odd years ago, falling apart now. They've seen better days. The park is the same, with rough patches of dirt and some gnarled, old trees that stand black in the snow and twist roots through the ground. The merry-go-round just keeps turning, till she sits beside me and watches the night spin around us. It's the girl from the hospital, still in her scrubs, smacking gum with the streaky blond hair like before. She just sits there (she's silent), a ghost in the snow, which gets thicker and thicker, till she's just an outline of blond behind white. I bite on my tongue as the houses drift by and the playground creaks softly beneath all the snow, till I think we should speak, and I open my mouth to the white and say, *Rachel?* At first she won't turn, she won't look at my face, but she stares and says, *Hi there, Ophelia.* The breeze blows in my face, and I say to her, *What are you doing here, Rachel?* Without turning toward me, she says to me, *I go where you go, now, Ophie.* The wind pushes harder, then softer, then dies, and we creak and we squeak in the blinding-white snow till I finally tell her, *I'm sorry I started that fire. I'm sorry I burned it all down and you're here now forever with me.* She stares at the snow till her eyes are white dots, and says, *You just don't understand, Ophie. You think you do, but you don't. There were so many people—so many of them—who depended on it for their jobs, to pay bills, to pay rent, to get by. There were so many others who needed the place for their health and their lives.* And the wind pushes hard and the spinning speeds up, and she says, *Did you realize that ours was the one, only charity hospital here in our city? The only one open to uninsured patients? The poor and the homeless?* I tell her I didn't; she tells me, *Of course. You were too busy crying in the janitor's closet—just too busy pitying yourself to learn something. Too busy being the hero of your story to see that you're part of a huge, endless universe filled up with people who matter a thousand times more than you do. Too busy being your own special snowflake to see all the millions of similar snowflakes all falling around you.* I look all around, and the snow's getting deeper. It's up to my dangling feet, and my toes are dragging through it, making circles around the merry-go-round, but I don't feel the cold because of the numbness.

I look up and she's gone. Just a hole where she was, filling up with snow now. I push myself onto my feet, and I stand ankle-deep in the snow, and my head is still spinning. The snowflakes are streaks, like rods in the air shooting down past my eyes, and I can't feel my arms or my legs. I need to go somewhere, get out of the cold. The darkness gets darker, the whiteness gets whiter, and the buzzing in my head just won't stop. I think I hear a siren, but it's headed away from me, and it might actually just be an ambulance. I sit on the curb.

So what can I do? I don't have my phone and I don't know where I am. It's not like I can knock on anybody's door, looking like this. I can't go back to my dorm, can't go to my mom's. I guess I just have to walk till I find something. But my feet feel like they're on fire.

I try standing, try walking, but each step is like knives and my legs buckle under. Faces swirl in the snow and the streetlamps glow bright till there's nothing but white, and my blood turns to crystals that drag through my veins and, my mind's leaking out through my skin, and I think I'll lie down and give up and lie down.

And then there's a squeal.

A squeal of tires right next to my head that sounds familiar, because it's from a car that I drive every day, and it's my Escort and it's pulled up beside me. It's here at the curb and the door is wide open. The passenger door is hanging open for me. And a voice from the driver's side tells me, "Get in." It's a voice that I know.

And it's Sara.

# wed. jan. 19.
## 2:07 am.
## what

I stand in the snow, with my mouth hanging open, my skin turning bluish, the snow falling harder, the night spinning faster, my brain getting fuzzier, Sara just sitting there, holding the door, and she's telling me, "Get in, get in, just get in." Like she's some sort of Terminator, nude from the future, and glaring at me through her shades, mumbling (loud) *Come with me if you want to live, Oaf.* And I do want to live—*God, I do* want to live—but my sister (not dead!), in my car, is too much. I stand in the snow (like the Grinch from cartoons), thinking *What the hell happened, why are you alive, how'd you know I was here, why are you in my car?*

But I can't say those words because I can't say anything.

"Oaf? You hear me? You all right?"

"Uh—" Nothing to say and nothing in front of me but a hanging-open door and a passenger seat that I don't think that I've ever sat in. A sister with a facial expression I can't quite read, idling here on the curb, holding onto the brake while she's gunning the gas. And a roar from the engine that blends with blue smoke pluming out from the vibrating tailpipe, and I can't look away from the dome light that pulses and glows from the twitch of an old, broken wire.

And the radio's on.

*...still pulling bodies from the wreckage, with the snowstorm likely to slow down their progress. The fire department has traced the blaze to the basement, where it appears to have broken out by accident...*

"You getting in or not?"

In the dark, by the window, I see her gray eyes flash in the dome light, and the way that she's gunning the gas makes me wish I could run, but on the other hand it looks so warm in there. I look down at my seat, and it's soft because it's never been sat on, and it's not covered with crumbs like my driver's seat is. I tell myself *What have I got to lose?* and jump directly into the path of the heat blasting out from the dashboard.

"Buckle up," she says.

"What?"

"Buckle up." She pushes the button that locks all the doors, and she pulls on the stick and she stomps on the gas, and we fly under streetlights that whip through her grin. It shines in the light and then fades into shadows, and I realize I'm huddled up close to my door now, knees pulled to my chest and my seatbelt unfastened.

She's wearing her lab coat and scrubs like she was last night, and her stethoscope hangs from her neck. Her makeup is running, bags under her eyes—I can't even remember the last time I saw her looking this bad. Every night at my mom's she would always look perfect, but tonight she looks haggard, perhaps a bit manic, leaning over the wheel, jerking hard around corners. I watch houses fly by, and then shops, then more houses. I grab onto the door handle, pull on it hard (to escape? maybe just to hang on), but the child lock is on and the door doesn't open.

So many questions, but I can't open my mouth.

She goes first.

"What were you doing out in the snow in your underwear?"

I stare out the window, lick blood from my lips, and say, "It's not my underwear."

"What?"

"It's not underwear. I don't wear wifebeaters and boxers under my clothes, so it's not underwear." I thumb at the door handle again and add, "It's pajamas. It's what I sleep in."

"Oh."

She flies through a red light, her face glowing like fire, and I finally ask her, "What are you doing alive?"

"What?"

Just that one little syllable, like she's totally shocked to learn that I thought she was dead, like in her mind there's no way she could be dead, even though we all saw the fire and none of us have heard from her in almost 12 hours. "Have you called Mom and Dad?" I ask her.

"What?"

"Sara, are you even *trying* to listen to me? Where are you taking me, anyway?"

"Mom's place. Where else?"

"What? Why?"

"Would you rather spend the night naked in the snow?"

*I'm not naked.* I really want to say that, but it doesn't seem all that important in the grand scheme of things, so I just turn my head and look out the window till it fogs up from my breath.

The fog is full of grinning faces.

I finally say, "You *do* realize everyone thinks you're dead."

The words disappear into the fog, and I wonder if she even heard them. She jerks on the wheel and we fly under another red light, and the faces look fiery and bloody. She says, "Why would they think that?"

"Will you stop answering my questions with questions?" I want to punch something, but instead I just sink farther into the door and start drawing an *H* in the window fog. "What are you doing out in the middle of the night in my car?"

"I gave you this car," she says, "remember? You think I didn't keep a key?"

So many non-answers. "Well, what happened to your Jag?"

"This car was closer."

"'Closer'?"

"Yeah." I start drawing a backwards *E* next to the *H.* "What are you doing there?" she says, looking over her shoulder.

"Uh—nothing. It's stupid." I erase it with the back of my hand.

"Well, stop." She jerks the wheel again.

We're out of the city now, and the streetlights thin out till we're riding in nothing but darkness, and it's hard to see anything but the whites of her eyes and her teeth. She's gunning the gas even more. "Why haven't you called Mom and Dad? They're freaking out."

She shrugs like I just asked her what her favorite color is. "I left my phone in my office. Besides, there are certain advantages to having people think you're dead."

My head wants to ask her, *Like what?* but my gut's saying *No, no, no, no, oh please, just get me out of here, break down the door if you have to, oh please.* I hug my knees and say nothing.

"Anyway," she says, "I was near an exit when the fire alarms started going off. I didn't have the chance to go back for anything, but I made it out fine. I've been lying low ever since."

*Lying low where?* is the obvious question here, but again I don't say it, and even with the heat blasting at me I still can't quite feel my fingers or toes. My shirt and my shorts are both still soaked.

She says, "So—" in her best small-talk voice, but then she stops and says nothing and just eyes me up and down in the darkness like she's trying to make sense of my tawdry appearance. *Oh God, watch the road.*

I'm trying to think of a plausible explanation for how I look, like *I was in a fight,* or *I was sleepwalking,* or *My roommate kicked me out,* but nothing I can think of makes sense except maybe *Your damn pills turned me into a murder-zombie and now I've got nowhere to go and you're not helping by dragging me to the last place I want to be.* But there's no point in saying any of that, so instead I just ask her, "How did you find me?"

"Huh?"

"How did you know where I was, Sara?"

She coughs a little, bites her lip. "Who says I did?"

She shuts the radio off, and there's suddenly silence where there once had been noise, and I clear my throat to cover the dead air. "So you were just driving around, randomly, in my car, in the middle of the night?"

"Well—" and she slams on the brakes and I fly into the dash and I think I might have dislocated something. "We're here," she says. And the car's in the drive of my mom's looming mansion, and she unlocks the doors as the security light snaps on.

# wed. jan. 19.
## 2:59 am.
## the dread of something

**It's getting worse.**

So many gaps in my memory, where everything's fuzzy and minutes or hours or whole days are missing. I'm here in my bed now, the one I grew up in, awake and alert and unable to silence the static that swirls in my eyes. I think I remember a car ride with Sara, pulling into the driveway, but after that, nothing. I must have come inside and climbed up the stairs and sunk into my bed, but there's none of that I can remember. I was in my own car, in the passenger's seat; now I'm buried in blankets (but still so, so cold) and there's nothing but gray in between. I twist with the sheets and my plush toys, the unicorns, dragons, and dolphins I owned as a kid, and I'm eyeing my room through the gaps in the curtains. These curtains. I thought I had hung them when I was in high school, but now that I see them with newly-awake eyes, I think I remember they weren't my idea. What was it she said, that one night in the dressing room, something about how she hung them but I couldn't remember? I'm trying to think of why Sara'd hang curtains, and memories flood back of the move to this house when the ceiling seemed high and we begged Mom for bunk beds, and *I get the top bunk,* she told me. And all I could think at the time was that it wasn't fair, the way she'd be on top with a view of the whole room and everything in it, and I would be stuck underneath, staring down at the floor or the gray underside of her bed. Then she hung up the curtains and closed off my view of the whole world except for her face, and she smiled and told me and told Mom the curtains were there for a game we were playing, but it never felt like a game when she came in at night. *I'm a doctor,* she'd say, *and I'll make you feel better.* She always was lying, she never once did. And after, she'd leave, and I'd shake in the dark, with my dragon and unicorn tight in my arms, and I'd pray to *forget, just forget.* I guess that I must have, because if I hadn't, then I wouldn't be here. I wouldn't be jumping in cars she was driving at midnight, or taking the pills that she shoved in my pocket. It's weird how the things that you want to forget are the ones that you probably ought to remember—for instance, that night in the dressing room, burned in my dreams, when she breathed in my face those four words: *Love consumes, love destroys.* Now I shake in the dark and I tell myself, *I don't believe it,* but nothing I've seen in my soul's telling me she was wrong. Like that night at the bar with the boy and the beer and the girl who stormed out and the way he just sat there and stared at my boobs and I told him to buy me a drink. Now why would I tell him to do that, unless all I wanted to know was if I could get things out of him with my assets? And he was the same—all he wanted from me were the things that I could do for him. And the girl who stormed out was the same way as well, thinking *If I can't own you, I don't want to be with you.* I say to myself that if that's what love is, maybe Sara is right—love consumes, it destroys. I look in my arms, at the toys from my childhood, the bears and the cute unicorns and the dragons. The dragon's the oldest, the one that I've had since before I could walk, and he's missing his eyes and his fur is worn ragged, and each time a new piece fell off and went missing, my mother would tell me, *It happens. It's just 'cause you love him so much, Ophie.* Each time I'd cry, but I'd drag him behind me regardless, and think that *My mom must be right,* because if she was wrong, that meant I was a horrible monster. (*Dragon, I love you, and I will destroy you.*) If my mother was right about stupid plush toys, maybe Sara was right about people as well, because how is there even a difference? Clichés people spout about how someone likes them for *just who they are* are all just what they sound like, just greeting card bullshit. It's warm it's fuzzy and makes people feel good, but everyone knows that if we just loved people for being themselves, then we'd all just love everyone all of the time, because what else can anyone do but keep being themselves? All the old people dying in hospice, with dozens of grandchildren, none of whom visit, are being themselves, and nobody loves them for *that*. And hell, since I'm on a roll, no one loves cheesecake just because it continues existing. They love it for what they can get out of it, and not by just spending some quality time with it, either. Love consumes, it destroys. And I think about Mom and I think about Dad, how they both chose to split up as soon as they had what they wanted to get from each other. I was young when it happened, I didn't understand, but I think now I do, and I think I can see why this house feels so empty. I think it's the love, the real love, not some greeting-card love. Through the gaps between curtains, which are narrow by design, I see half-packed-up ruins of dead adolescence, one whose funeral's been playing on loop for (I guess) several years now, and maybe it's time to accept that. Open boxes of books filled with titles that drip with the vain purple prose of a time that's long dead, posters hung on the walls, dangling loose from their corners, with rock bands on them, bands I barely remember, the sort that seemed brilliant a few years ago, but are now just some hair and some teeth. And they all look so miserable, scowling as if they just learned what death is and they think that they might kind of like it. The signature feeling of true adolescence—*Adulthood must blow, so I guess I'll just jump headfirst into this chasm of death, because death is so cool.* Just ink on a page, just a mixture of yellow, magenta, and cyan, that looks like a face but is really just paper and chemicals, wrinkling and rotting even now as I stare, and behind it a wall. Ten years (or so) now, since I hung all these posters, and almost as long since I purchased an album by one of these bands, and it's funny to think that they've probably moved on with lives no one knows about—all driving minivans, office jobs, babies. And some of them, by now, have probably died, and I wonder if death is the velvety dreamland they droned about (corpse-robot voices that howled from the grooves in my iPod, now rotting itself somewhere, deep in a landfill, dissolving back into the world, just like everything else). Does it mean anything that the agent of death, the new one, the one who's been called on to mete out predictable ends to the ones now alive, has become me? Or am I just one in a long line of conqueror worms, just an endless progression of lonely devourers, called on to do the inevitable? I'm reminded of something a drug dealer said to me once, that if she were to stop selling meth, someone else would just do it, and life would go on, and it all made no difference. Those doomed to death, or to deadly addiction, would be where they are without anyone lifting a finger to help them, and all things eventually tend toward the grave, and the only real choice is to sweep up what wreckage we can as we all stumble toward it, or not. And that's all I am now, a blind wreckage-sweeper, now etched into history—me, cancer, AIDS, the *Titanic,* the Plague, all of us are just peas in a fungus-smeared pod, history's janitors, mopping up breath for a living. There's nothing unholy in being the id, in taking from people what never was theirs, what they never had earned and they wouldn't hold onto, regardless—virginity, innocence, health, money, life. Life is nothing but chance in the time-space continuum, hiccups and spasms inside of a corpse, just a big stack of chemicals, all of which used to be dead, and they're all headed that way again. And if my teeth are chosen to help them along, then I guess that's all right—I'm performing a much-needed service that some of the worms in the world just aren't up to. A small, tiny voice in the back of my head still says I should fight it, and what was it Kate said, about moral compasses, how I might have one that's better than hers? But that's bullshit. I see that it is now, and lying here listening as snow turns to rain, then to sleet, then to ice mixed with lightning and thunder, I see that there's nothing but death in the universe, everything ending with whimpers, not bangs, and that only a fool would choose life over death when all life will surrender to death in the end. There's a scene in *The Exorcist* where the two priests talk about why a demon who has all the powers of hell would waste time on invading a little girl's body, and one of them says to the other the purpose is just to embarrass—to damage and insult the form of a human, to take away hope that a good God could love it. I guess that if God and those demons are real, it all sort-of makes sense, but I can't get away from the thought that the whole thing's a huge waste of time, that the real human form will destroy and embarrass itself, if you give it enough years to get the job done. If we all just wait to watch cute people die, we'll all see what a joke superego, society, manners (all that bullshit) are—that death is the final, unstoppable force, and that anyone fighting against it is nothing but flotsam awash in a grotesque tsunami that drowns life in darkness, with nothing beyond. I lie in my bed and absorb all the thunder I can, and I revel in all the new freedom I've found in embracing the death and becoming the id. *All surrender to me in the end*—but if death is the end (if it's *really* the end), then I can't understand why the dark of my bedroom is swirling with ghosts. The fat man, the hipster, the girl with the Ugg boots, and Rachel, and dozens that I haven't seen before, weightless and wandering in between boxes and tracing their hands on my posters (to scoff at the fake, packaged death sold to teenagers). Moaning and singing in time with the thunder, a symphony (silent) that's filling my ears. I see them in swatches and stripes and in blinks, in the slats between curtains that hang from her bed, just a glimpse of a face (or a back, or a hand), and the faces are angry or sad, pressing out on the walls, or in on my curtains. And I so want to pull all these curtains aside, to reach out and to tear them all down from the bed and look into the faces, ask *What do you want?* maybe *Why are you still around? Leave me alone!* or just share the same breath and feel the same dark, but I can't move my arms and I can't reach the curtains, although they're just inches away from my face. My arms are tied up in the dragons and unicorns, buried in memories, unable to move. So I shake under blankets for hours (maybe years?), watching ghosts slowly pick through the ruins of my life, till the lights all go out in their eyes, one by one, and I'm left in the black with just one who remains. She's the one who (I know now) I'll never escape, the ghost who will haunt me in life and in death, and her black silhouette stands and waits in the dark, and

262 ~ Luke T. Harrington

the lightning cracks (loud), and her Cheshire-cat grin's looking in, through the curtains, right at me. I tell her I know that she's not really there, that she's really asleep in the room down the hall, where she went after parking the car in the driveway (I think?), but she's still at the end of the bed, looking at me with something like hunger. (The love that consumes, the love that destroys.) It's time to play doctor the way that we would back when I was a kid. She's climbing inside now with eyes that flash lightning and teeth filled with thunder, and all I can do is just wait for the pain. Close my eyes and imagine I'm back in the kitchen (my mom's) eating dinner, a year ago, picking politely at Mom's mac 'n cheese, wondering who the hell makes mac 'n cheese filled with onions (my mom does). The lights in the kitchen are bright and they're yellow, the three of us silently watching the snow as it fills the backyard. The teakettle whistles for no one, since no one wants tea, but my mom always makes it regardless. We all ask each other the same boring questions we ask every time we're together. My mom says to Sara, *Your research—so how is that going?* and Sara looks cold and won't even get up to go pick up the teakettle off of the heat, and it's making her wince with its shrill, piercing scream, and she tells her *I'd rather not talk about it.* My mom stabs the tray of asparagus, wilting and pungent, and tries to fill silence by filling her plate with a vegetable she doesn't want, as if buckets of foul-smelling pee will make up for this hour spent avoiding real talk about life. She turns back to Sara and says, *Is it really that bad? 'Cause I thought that you said you were right on the verge of a breakthrough,* and Sara says *Stop. Please. The last thing I need is a mix of I-told-you-so's and I'm-so-sorry's. The rats are all dead and the trials are a bust and I'm not even sure Yale still wants me around. Now just leave me alone— doesn't Oaf have a life we can all scrutinize?* Then they both look at me, by the window, still picking at noodles and onions and cheese, and I sigh and I say to myself (in my head), *Hey, you can't be a teenager slouching at dinner, you're past 22 now, you can't just regress to your old and embarrassing self every time you come home for a weekend or night.* But there's nothing to do now, with both their eyes on me, but let them both know the attention's unwelcome. My sighing and eye-rolling take me and pin me down into a slouch, like a sad, teenaged ghost that's possessing my body and forcing it into contortions of apathy. All I can do is regret it as soon as it happens, but now that it's out there, there's no way to grab it and pull it back in, and it hangs in the air like the ghost's foul fart, adolescence's last gasp in someone who's just now discovered adulthood is nothing but *Insert tab 'A' into slot labeled 'B'* in an endless attempt just to postpone the inevitable. If I still can't banish my teenagey angst, maybe that's just because it's the only response to the world that makes any sense. *Don't say that,* my smart adult brain is chiding my lizard-brain, but I can't keep the argument up for too long, since I can't think of reasons she's actually wrong about life, and I say to myself, *When did you get so cynical, anyway?* And still they're both sitting there, waiting for me to say anything, something to fill up the silence we live in. They sit and they stare until Sara gets up and excuses herself. And she walks down the hall, and we watch her until she gets swallowed by dark, and then Mom turns to me yet again and repeats what she said. And I say, *Well, you know that I dropped education,* and she clears her throat and she tells me, *I know.* We sit and we pick at our food, and I watch the moon rise on the snow-filled backyard and mix glitter from snow with the sharp, jagged shadows cast long by my swing set (it's strange how the things that I loved as a child look scary and alien now). She hasn't looked up from her food this whole time I've been staring outside, and I say, *Please excuse me,* and get up and walk down the dark hall as well. We haven't turned lights on in hallways for years, ever since the day Sara came home from third grade and she told us about the perpetual energy crisis. I'm not sure if leaving the lights off in places does much to avert the apocalypse; anyway, she was insistent, and soon we all grew used to walking down pitch-dark-black hallways. Like always, we pass in the dark, and her eyes and her smile both light up electric, but this time she stops, and she looks in my eyes, and she says to me, *My rats are dead, Oaf.* I tell her *I know,* but she takes a step closer and says, *Don't you want to know why?* I look toward the bathroom (so close but so far), with a light she left on to illumine the darkness (or maybe to flip a huge bird at her youthful ideals), and then back to her face, which is inches from mine, with a deep, reddish tongue that sticks to her lips, and I tell her, *I guess it's because your big dream drug is poison.* She says, *No, it's better,* and takes a step closer, and traps me against the white wall that looks black in the dark. *It's better than that, so much cooler than that.* I tell her, *That's great, but I just need to pee,* but her eyes lock on mine and she says to me, *They all turned violent, Oaf. Every last one of them—murderers.* The breath from her words is like ghosts, and it hangs in the air as a gray requiem for things best left forgotten. Her smile is so big and so white that the dark can't contain it. She leans in so close I smell grease in her pores, and she tells me, *They all figured out different ways to escape from their cages, and then they found victims and tore their throats open and ate them. The cages all smashed apart, blood everywhere, it looked like a horror flick, Oaf. First the ones I was giving the drug to attacked my control group—they picked them off one-by-one (fish in a barrel), and then when there weren't any more easy targets, they turned on each other and mutually murdered themselves in a big battle royal that went on for days. I watched it all happen. They slaughtered each other and ate the remains until only one of them was left standing. And that one left standing, y'know what he did?* And that last bit of steam-breath, the one from the *did?,* just hangs in the air there in front of my face, just a sour puff of cold breath that's dripping with sweat and that's shaking with anticipation. I finally tell her, *Okay, I'll bite, what?* And that cold Cheshire cat grin lights up in the steam and she says *Are you sure that you want to find out?* and I nod (though I'm actually not, but what choice do I have?), and her nose brushes mine and she whispers *He ate himself, Oaf.* She watches my face to enjoy my reaction, and adds, *There was nothing else left, no more fights to be won, no more murders for him to commit, so he gnawed at himself till he died on the floor in a big pile of rat bones.* She smiles. *You almost had me going there, Sara,* I tell her. *But none of that makes any sense. There's no way you would sit there and watch them destroy both your lab and your research, and I don't believe that story at all.* She says, *Suit yourself, I just thought you'd enjoy it,* and, dumbstruck, I ask her, *Enjoy it?* and she says, *Well, yeah—that's why I didn't step in to stop all the carnage. 'Cause watching was fun—lots more fun than conducting the study had been. There was nothing more boring than weighing those rats and their food every day, making notes of the tiniest changes, pretending they matter. Pretending that drugs make a difference in life when the people who take them will all end up dead in the ground, anyway. That rat? He was right. He was right all along. And the one (only) reason that people pretend otherwise is that it makes them feel better. I know that it's soothing,* she says, *to pretend that your life has meaning. But Oaf, you've been studying English for years now, so you must have noticed by now: the words 'meaning' and 'end' are synonymous.* She hovers too close, till I'm smelling her lip balm (it's cherry and cold in the dark, humid air); then she turns and she walks down the hallway back into the light, toward my mom and her table. I shiver from all the cold steam in the hallway, and walk toward the light, and it's blinding and yellow and forces my eyes open—

*Sometimes I'm alone in my bed*
*(And it feels like the past is killed dead);*
*Other times, I'm awake*
*And my world starts to shake*
*And I can't get her out of my*

I'm in my mom's kitchen and sitting at the table with a pen in my hand and a poem in front of my face, and I say to myself, *Dammit, I said no more limericks,* but there it is in front of me, and my next thought is *Hey, I finally wrote something,* and then I think, *How did I get down here?*

I must have been sleepwalking again. It's dark in the kitchen, but a ghostly white is pouring in from the yard that's filling with snow, and the windows are beaten with sheet after sheet of ice, while lightning and thunder crack the sky and rattle old memories in the attic. I'm trying to sort through the images that remain at the back of my mind, and I realize I've lost track of time completely. I think it's still the same night, the one when Sara picked me up from the old playground and drove me here, and—

All I can think of are teeth and steam. The night's a black hole, like the universe after its last star burns out. I was in my bed, and now I'm at the table, and I guess I must have written something in my sleep, but the rest of the night is a sucking chasm. I'm still trying to sort through it all when I'm suddenly awash in the flashing glint of light from her eyes again, because she's standing right behind me—

"What's that?"

I hear the curled lip in her voice, a sneer twisted around my ear that makes me shiver while I rush to cover up my loopy handwriting. Her fingers are on my shoulders and they're icy like frozen cold cuts. I look up through the dark air and I can barely make out her face. "What are you doing up?" I ask her.

"What's that page in front of you?" she says.

"It's—nothing." I start folding it, awkwardly, into triangles and trapezoids, but her sharp nails snatch it out of my hands and uncrumple it to read it in the illumination from the lightning that pounds on the windows. The flashes reveal half-seconds of smiles and sneers, and her glassy pupils shrink with each flash and then swallow darkness again.

"Don't quit your day job," she says, as she recrumples it and squashes it into the already-full kitchen trash, and the air is momentarily filled with the odor of week-old chicken. She opens the fridge and her face is lit (suddenly) with a yellow light, and the sound of Tupperware slamming into other Tupperware rattles in between peals of thunder. "But then again," she says, "you actually wrote something, so I guess that's a milestone, right?"

I try to think of something witty to say, but she's right, and anyway what's the point of arguing with a half-illuminated ass sticking out from behind a fridge door? I look at said ass, draped in way-too-expensive pajama pants that only people who spend a lot of time worrying about being comfortable when they're unconscious buy. They've got an unfortunate cutesy pirate print on them, and I wonder who they were made for—rich girls who wish they were pillaging the high seas (and presumably never learned about the filth and disease involved in that pursuit)? She jerks a Pizza Hut box off of the middle shelf and I hear a plastic container of something clatter to the floor.

"The thing about life goals," she says, "is you have to actually work to make them happen." She rips a triangle of congealed milkfat off of the greasy cardboard, bites off half of it, and chews.

"Because you worked so hard toward your medical aspirations?"

"Y'know what? Yeah, I did. I just had a thesis advisor who was out to get me—ugh, this is terrible," she adds, cramming the rest of her pizza into the trash as well. "What are you doing up, Oaf?"

"What are *you* doing up?"

"Checking on you, obvs. Big sister stuff, you probably wouldn't understand. Why are you out of bed?"

"Just...couldn't sleep, I guess."

"Nightmares?"

"What?"

"Nightmares. You used to have them all the time when we were kids. You remember, right? You would wake up in the middle of the night, screaming and sweating. And then I'd have to...comfort you." She picks pizza crust from her teeth as she collapses in the chair next to mine and leans over the table. "You ever hear of something called 'Universe 25'?"

"Called what?"

"'Universe 25.' I was just reading about it the other day. There was this guy who built 'universes' for mice to live in—just, like, little mouse habitats. He built 25 of them, and he called them 'universes,' so the 25th one was 'Universe 25.'"

"So?" I'm twisting the pen in my hands between my fingers, and I can't help but notice how sharp it is as she leans in close and the lightning dances across her face.

She says, "Universe 25 was designed to be a mouse paradise, with everything a mouse could ever want. Unlimited food and water, a perfect 68-degree temperature all the time—plus the whole thing was completely self-cleaning. The mice didn't have to do anything but eat, sleep, and fuck. Sounds awesome, right?"

"I guess."

"Except that it *wasn't*." She wipes a greasy hand on her expensive pants, and leans in so close that I can count her pores. "Within a couple of years, the whole thing had turned into absolute shit."

My back is flat against the wooden bars of my chair now. They're digging into it hard. "What do you mean, 'absolute shit'? What's that mean?"

"Cannibalism. Constant, random violence. Weird pansexuality. Mothers eating their young, everyone humping inanimate objects, hundreds of them who would just pile up in the middle of the enclosure and then start eating each other out of sheer boredom. Once all of their problems were taken care of, they turned to self-destruction."

"Why are you telling me this?" I say, and the thunder and rain and snow all fall silent, till there's only a pale, white glow drifting in through the windows.

"I just thought it was interesting." She leans back and starts cleaning her nails.

"'Interesting'?"

"Yeah," she says, "isn't it? You take care of all of someone's problems, you say, *I'll handle your food and your water, your hygiene, everything, and all you have to do is whatever the hell you want,* and how do they respond? They say, *Oh, okay, I guess I'll destroy myself, then.* You set people—well, mice—free to do *literally whatever,* and they're like, *Oh, cool, death sounds good, I haven't tried that.* Given a truly free choice, we choose death. Makes you think." A long bit of lightning illuminates her nails and gives her a chance to really dig hard under her left pointer finger. "Darwin, y'know, he thought life existed to survive and reproduce. The end of life, in other words, is life." She bites her tongue and winces from the pain. "He was wrong, though: the end of life is *death.* I mean, isn't that obvious? The only purpose of any of this comes from the fact that it *ends*—and deep down, we all know it. The mice knew it. That's why heaven always turns into hell. Always."

I jump when the long stretch of lightning is interrupted by its own thunder, and the house rattles from the basement up. Then the sleet starts beating the windows again.

"And how do I know?" she says, leaning in till all I can see are her eyes, which in the dark are just black pits. "Universe 25."

She takes my hand and picks at it with her perfectly painted, perfectly sharpened nails, and her tongue flicks hard against her teeth when she says these last two words:

"Love destroys," she reminds me. Then she drops my hand, hard, and it lands on the wood, and she slinks away into the dark.

I squint into the black, trying to follow her with my eyes and see where she's going, but now the light from the lightning is gone. Her pale, ivory back disappears into the gray almost before she even stands up, and I'm left alone, listening to small bits of ice playing bells on the window, their soft little *plink*s all dissolving to thick sheets that build till the snow in the yard's just a fuzzy impression of faces pressed up on the glass. They're the faces of ghosts like the ones from my room, the ones I saw wandering in between the door and my curtains, but now they're outside. They want to come in, and I tell them they can, that I'm lonely and scared, that their sad, desperate faces are better than nothing, but all they can do is press harder and harder, saying *We should come in, but we're scared of her, too.* So I sit by myself in the dark while the wind whistles hard. I can see every hair on my arms and my legs standing up in the glow from the faces outside, and I'm slowly aware of the filth from the rags that I'm wearing (again), and I think I might need a hot shower. But still I can't stand up, can't bring myself even to lift up my hand and reach into the dark, just because I'm afraid of the things that might wait there to touch it. Damn these long winter nights, won't the sun ever rise? I'm beginning to see that the night is all hers, that the dark and the winter and whatever's left when the universe ends all belong to the ones who are willing to kill, to the ones who believe in the nothingness coming, embrace it and love it, and know how to use it to fill all their needs. Love destroys, love consumes, love devours like the black holes that spin at the centers of galaxies. When all things are finally, totally dead, only those who still know how to swallow, consume, are the ones who will still keep on going. I see now that life is a zero-sum game, that the ones who survive are the ones who are able to steal life from others, that *love*'s just a word for the power to take, and my thin, wasted form (well—at least sort of skinny) that's flopped in this rickety chair is the proof that she's now nearly taken what little I had. I say to myself that I have to fight back, that I have to *love* back (ha!), to turn myself into the thing that she always has been—just a sucking black hole that devours its loves right along with its hates—if I want to survive. *Now I am become death, destroyer of worlds.* Isn't that what that one guy, the nuclear physicist, said when he set off the bomb in the desert? *I am become death, destroyer of worlds.* I think it's a quote from the *Bhagavad Gita*, and isn't it possible Hindu philosophy's right about this one? That life, love, and hate, and the grave are all one? That to love is to kill, and to kill is to love? I can still feel a tiny amount of her drug in my blood—just a few chalky pieces that scrape on the sides of my veins. A powdery strength that's dissolving, not gone. I know where she sleeps, and I still hear the beat of her heart, just the way that I did every night when we shared the same room and her breath and her heart woke me up in the dark. But now I'm awake, wide awake, while she sleeps, and I think that I have enough strength in my veins left to finish this game that she started, to end her before she ends me. If everything's death, and if *I am become death,* and if she's been right all these years about love and death being the same, then one more makes no difference, just nudges the universe toward its inevitable fate. Her blood will be blood, whether it's in her veins or poured out on her bedsheets, regardless of whether it glows rosy-bright in her cheeks or it paints them in scarlet. *I am become death, destroyer of worlds.* In light from the window that glows off the snow, my frayed, broken nails are all sparkling, all ten of them, broken and bloody, but ready and waiting and thirsting in ways that I now understand. I stretch them in front of me, into the darkness, emboldened now with the new promise of blood, and not blood from a stranger, but blood from a love who'd be proud if she knew. Deep in the dark, I feel ghosts rub against them, the ghosts of the things that once lived here before, all the millions of years before placid McMansions existed, and ever will live on, for millions of years or more, after the last of them crumbles. The Something Alive that my mom tried to scrub from the last of the plastic perfection—it still sticks to things and occasionally jams in their corners, requiring a scrub or a wipe (what a terrible word). But the tools that you clean with absorb all the dirt (they don't send it to hell!), and it just sits inside them forever. Now I see, Mom, the answer to all the things growing, the things that destroy sparkling dwellings by *living*—the molds and the fungi, the termites and ants—the solution's not cleaning, not making things sterile; it's utter destruction. It's love and it's death. And it's not in the gray-beige of matte-painted walls; it's the orange of flame and the deep black of entropy churning forever. Now the ghosts from the windows are all here behind me, there's hundreds of them, and they're lifting me up—it's like floating on clouds made of darkness, or wearing a dress with a vaporous train that stretches behind me for millions of miles. And I say, *Up the stairs!* and my army, my ghosts, my train made of lightning and thunder, all lift me up over their rarefied heads and I float on a pillow of vapor and smoke up the stairs, sharpening nails on my teeth. We float by my room, it's the one with the posters in shreds on the walls and the old, dirty curtains surrounding my bed, and we float past the bathroom that glows with a nightlight that lights up a toothpaste-flecked mirror I once used call Bloody Mary (but she didn't come because all ghosts are lies). Then finally my sister's room, there on the right at the end of the hall, where the steam-breath that once filled the curtains from my bed now leaks out beneath her closed door. The white of the steam is the pale light of life, and it's swallowed up fast by the black that's behind me and pushing me forward, my ghosts. *You say love destroys; are you ready for love? All those years when you talked on and on about death, saying it was the only true meaning of life, are you ready to look those words hard in the face? Are you ready to chew them, to feel their blood run down your throat and become you?* Now I am become death, destroyer of worlds. *With your pills inside me, an army behind me, I'm ready for love and I'm ready for death, and are you?* We push on her door, me and all my ghost army, we push on her door till it breaks off its hinges, and fill up her room with our black, inky darkness. It presses on her from above, sinking down, till it chokes out the white and her breath disappears. And I look at her face, and it's pale, and it's white, and her eyes have turned gray, and there's blood on her teeth. She breathes in the black of the death and absorbs it, and somehow her eyes both light up in her sleep, and she doesn't wake up, but I feel her eyes on me. She sleeps with her eyes open, Sara, she sleeps and she breathes with her dull, gray eyes open, and now I can see that my one chance is now, that I won't get another chance after this moment to give her a taste of the death that she says is life's meaning. *You ready?* I ask her. *You ready for Vishnu, for Jupiter, Chronos? It's now, Sara, now, when time swallows you up, because I AM BECOME DEATH, DESTROYER OF WORLDS.* The lightning outside flashes loud, shakes the windows, and lights up her face with gray skin and gray eyes, and it lights up my nails, and it's time for some blood. I reach for her throat, through the black and the white, for the gray, pulsing skin hiding deep in the mist. I reach from my perch up on top of the black, but like chess she retreats and slips into the white. Either she's sinking down now or I'm floating up, but somehow my hands never quite reach her throat. And I see now that I can't destroy the life beating inside my own veins, that the love that destroys swallows everything with it, beloved and lover, the blood, and the air. And there's nothing to do now but open my eyes, and I see I've been dreaming again. I'm back in my bed, in the dark of the night and the smothering curtains, and she's on my chest, and she's pinning me down, and there's nothing to do but stare into the gray of her eyes till the sun finally rises.

**wed. jan. 19.**
**11:24 am.**
**snowed in**

**The sun's finally up.**

It took forever to rise, and I counted the seconds, or I would have, if I had had any idea of how fast or slow time was moving last night. Somehow the night turned into weeks. The solstice was almost a month ago, but the nights still get longer and longer.

But now I can see the sun—bits of it—through the gaps between my bed's curtains. It's not yellow and bright like the sun in the spring; it's a pale, whitish glow that's been filtered through miles of clouds and two inches of ice on the window. I lay here for hours last night, trapped, just watching the ghosts, with their skeletal faces, all slowly dissolve from the deep midnight black into lingering gray, till the last of the twisted, white grins disappeared, chased away (for the moment?) by pale winter sun.

And once they were gone, I started to breathe again.

I still feel hands around my throat, even though there are none. I have memories of last night—dreams and impressions, anyway—and some bits feel more real, and some bits feel more like fantasy, but I have no idea which was actually which. All I can do is huddle in the corner while images of life and death dance around me, and wonder if the shadow play means anything at all, or if it's just the last flashes of a brain that's shutting down.

Those pills are still rattling in my pocket.

I slide them out and look at the orange bottle over again, let it catch the light and shine it around my bed, catching the old, stale clouds of her breath. The bottle rattles in my hand because I can't hold it still, and the clattering whisper tells me ugly stories about the past. In the orangey light, I can see my arms are covered in scratches. There's still a voice somewhere at the back of my mind saying *You need to get off this stuff,* but at this stage, what would even be the point? I still feel those pill fragments scraping around the inside of my veins, and I'm not sure I could sort them out from my blood, even if I wanted to. I can't imagine life without all the faces I'm used to seeing now.

And when (if) I go off of it, what, exactly, will disappear? What if the wrong parts of my memory, the happy parts, crumble away, and I'm left weak and alone, with nothing? Somehow the parade of mutilated memories and twisted faces seems preferable to the gray abyss of life's mundanity.

I know that that's stupid, that it's obviously the ravings of a drug addict who spent way too much time rewatching Tim Burton movies in high school, but it's all I have left. I've stood on the edge of the chasm of adulthood, and I've seen that I can either give myself to the world or give the world to myself, and at the moment I can't think of a single reason to do the former. I'd rather ride this roller coaster than get out and push.

Does that even make sense? It makes sense in my head. I'm just saying, I need to use up the people and things around me, before they use me up. These pills used to frighten me with the way they'd make me see things that weren't there, but now it's starting to grow on me. At least it's not boring and disappointing like real life is. Maybe being followed forever by the ghosts of the people I've harmed is better than being alone. Better than living in constant fear of seeing Sara's—

Face.

I scream.

I'm instantly embarrassed, because the face I'm looking at is my mother's. It's poking in through the curtains and looking confused to see me here. She honestly doesn't even look that much like Sara, more like me, really, maybe halfway between us, if that. Her eyes are still blue, like mine used to be, before the pills hollowed them out.

"Hi, Mom. Sorry."

"You all right, Ophie?"

"Yeah, I just—I wasn't expecting to see you there. Sorry."

"What are you doing here?"

"I—" I stammer because I'm still trying to decide what I *am* doing here. The preceding night is a blur of cold faces, cold pizza, cold blood, and something about rats, or was it mice? Gray blood all down my front and icy gravel all over my back, half-naked in front of my mom, strangling a stuffed unicorn till it vomits rainbows. And those boxes from a week (a year?) ago are still sitting on the floor, half-full of books, and it's hard to even remember who I was back then. A bitter college girl whose biggest worry was paying the bills, and now here I am, an animal quivering in the corner and licking the last bits of blood from my teeth. She's wondering why I haven't been back to pick up the rest of my stuff; I'm wondering why I'm still not locked in a cage somewhere. How do you bridge *that* gap? "Sara brought me here."

"Sara?" There's a dumbfounded look on her face, utterly confused and maybe even a little bit offended at hearing the name. And then I remember that she still doesn't even know Sara's alive—still doesn't think Sara's alive—wait. Is Sara alive? I saw her last night, but my memory of last night is a pile of weirdness, and the more that I poke at it, the more it unravels into a mass of bewildering black goo.

"Uh—yeah—she picked me up at the playground around midnight, and—" This is making even less sense than I thought it would.

"Ophie, are you all right?"

"I...think so." I'm trying to hide my torn, dirty wifebeater and my blackish-tasting mouth. She pulls the curtains aside and sits on the bed.

"Sara's not here," she tells me, and I think, *No, she has to be.* I can still see the white of her teeth and the gray of her eyes, burned into the backs of my eyelids, like the cat's face in the back of Alice's woods. I stared at them all night till the sun melted them away, and they were the realest thing I'd ever seen. But I know that doesn't make any sense.

"I saw her last night. I talked to her."

"Are you sure you're okay?"

"I *think*..." What was it she said, about there being advantages to faking your own death? "Maybe I'm a little confused."

"It's *your* car that's out in the driveway, Ophie."

"She said—" she said that it was closer. That she still had a key. Does any of this make even a little sense?

"She said what?" My mom's looking really concerned now, like she's wondering if maybe she should find me some friends in white lab coats. She puts her hand on my knee and I wince. It feels cold against my snow-soaked legs, even through the blankets.

I shrink deeper into the corner. Breathe deep and squeeze my unicorn. I say, "I guess you never did hear from her, then."

She sighs—a sigh weighed down by years that I only partially understand. "I stood outside the wreckage for hours yesterday," she tells me. "I watched as they dug out body after body."

"No Sara?"

"No Sara. And she hasn't called, either. If she were alive, she would have at least called, right?" She clears her throat. "I just—"

She's crying. My mother is crying, and I can't remember the last time I saw her cry (maybe never?), and now she's not even trying to hide it, she's just hunched over her knees, shaking, head in her hands, making new wrinkles on her face. And here I am in the corner, still trying to hide, still trying to make my blood-soaked near-nudity invisible.

Some of this blood on me might be Sara's.

It's awkward. Embarrassing. Strange and distracting, to see her hunched over and shaking like this, with a quivering nakedness pulsing in her veins. For years I've been coming here, week after week, holding it as symbol of things that I hate. A vast, empty shell made of brick and wood, ten or twenty times bigger than it ever should have been, huge and foreboding and smothered in money. Angry, defensive. A monument unto itself. But the shell was distracting me, up until now, from the kernel of humanness hiding inside.

I see her there now, in the light from the snow, in pajamas, no makeup, no heels and no dress, just a body (of flesh and of skin and of bone), and she's staring at death, looking right in its face, and she's seeing what I've seen (but closer, with age). She's scared, she's upset, and she's sifting through feelings she's known that she has, but ignored for so long, beaten down by a thousand and one disappointments, with no one who knows what it feels like to be her, unable to cope with the hollow inside, except dressing up, smiling, pretending as hard as she can that most things are okay. Long nights in the dark, carving wrinkles in flesh in deep solitude, wishing that things had been different—I see all that now, behind wrinkles and glasses, her blue eyes and brown hair, her wide hips and short, stubby fingers.

She's me.

Older and sadder, more stretch marks, regrets, but she's shaking with feelings I know well. The deep, indescribable sorrow of death's endless hunger. The knowledge that pure inky blackness lies waiting for all of us. First it claims people you love, and then, finally, you. She's staring in death's eyes and hearing it tell her, *Yeah, I took your marriage, and I took your daughter, and soon I'll take you, and have fun doing jack-shit about it.*

Does she even know?

Does she even realize she's sitting right next to death's angel? That *I* am the death that she's shaking her fist at? That death's not a demon with black wings and fangs, it's a burnt-out coed wearing shorts and a tank top? See, death's claimed me too, Mom. It's got both your daughters. We're deep in its claws, and we've been there forever, since long before the hospital fire. The blackness you're staring at waits for us all, but I'm halfway down into it, graciously being allowed to help pull others down till it sucks me deep into its nothingness, too. Lucky enough to be used till it's done with me.

This whole situation feels so familiar, though.

Crying on the edge of the bed. Pajamas and tears. Life and death.

I was caught in this same space just three days ago, when I sat on the bed next to Kate and I cried and she held me. She told me about making choices, or something, how she had this theory—I think she was right—that our actions are always in favor of life or in favor of death. That even if, in the end, death wins, regardless, that life is still something that's worth fighting for. That the choice to create or build up is a meaningful one, maybe even if all your attempts fail or nobody notices. That the ones who bring death are the ones who make history, but the ones who bring life are the ones who taste sweat from God's face.

I sit up.

"What are you doing?" she says, as I wrap my arms around her. I'm holding my breath, and I'm gritting my teeth, thinking *This might be wrong,* since it's been several years since I hugged my own mother, but the hell with it, right? She's rigid, confused, but the shock soon wears off— she relaxes, leans in, and we're both so, so cold, but somehow our shared heat feels warmer. Two small flames alight under mountains of snow, and the (real) threat of being extinguished seems lessened, somehow.

I don't know how long we stay sitting like this, with my head on her shoulder, her tears in my hair, but it's just long enough to melt some of the snow (just a bit). And the fog on the window pulls back, and the sun sneaks back into the room. It's still gray, but it's brighter.

She whispers, "Thank you," and hugs me back, and her arm around me is alien and familiar. She swallows, relaxes, chokes back a few more tears, and says, "It's been years since you did that. Maybe decades."

"I not sure I can remember doing this, ever."

She says, "You used to run up to me and say, *Mommy, hugs!* when you were really little. It was cute." She squeezes me again, wipes away a tear. "But everything was happier back then." She snorts. "*God,* listen to me. I sound like a damn Lifetime movie." She holds me closer, and I collapse into her. "You're all I have now, Ophie."

I laugh.

"Don't laugh, I'm serious. Promise me nothing will ever happen to you."

"I—Mom, how could I possibly promise that?"

"Just—please."

"Okay, I—I promise." Because, what else can I say? *I'm sorry, Mom, I've already sealed my fate? I've already signed a Faustian pact with the Reaper (except not really even Faustian, because I'm getting exactly jack-shit out of this deal)?* There's nothing for me to do but just burrow deeper into the folds of her pajamas and say, "I'm sorry about Sara."

She sighs. "It's not your fault. It's just the way things are."

*I know what I did.* "But I know she was your favorite." Damn it—why do I always say the wrong thing? But I can't take it back now.

But she just laughs. "Are you kidding? She was *never* my favorite. Ophie, you were my favorite."

"Uh—" And what can I say in response to that? I'm completely disarmed by the casual way she tossed it off, like we're a couple of middle-aged women knocking back martinis over lunch. I laugh at her. "You're not supposed to say stuff like that to your kids."

"But what difference does it make now?" she says, and I have to concede the point. "She's gone, you're an adult, I don't have to play parenting games anymore. I don't *want* to—I was always terrible at them, anyway. I want to be honest. *God,* for once in my life, I want to be honest."

"You do? Like, really?"

She winces a little. "Yeah," she says. "I do."

"Then can I ask you something serious?

"Okay."

I bite my lip. Hesitate. But I have to know. "Why are you kicking me out?"

She laughs. Rolls her eyes. "I'm *not*, Ophie. You haven't lived here in years. I just asked you to clean out the room you *used* to live in. Is that really so bad?"

I don't know what to say to that.

She says, "I understand how you feel. This is a great room. I know you worked hard at making it perfect."

"Wait, you *like* my room?"

She laughs. "Yeah."

"I think teenaged me just rolled over in her grave."

She laughs again and she says, "Well, maybe that's the point. Adolescence can't last forever." Wind kicks up snow and beats on the window, and she adds, quietly, "I'm case-in-point on that one."

"What do you mean?"

"This is the really embarrassing part," she sighs. "Turns out I'm broke. I thought if I cleaned your room up a little, maybe I could rent it out, or something."

"Oh." And she's right that that was the embarrassing part, but it's embarrassing for me, not for her. I've been worrying about my perfectly mounted posters and perfectly calibrated carpet color, and she's freaking out over how she's going to pay the bills. It hurts to be told I'm so selfish, especially since she doesn't even have to say it.

She says, "I've been so stupid. Did I ever tell you why I kicked your father out in the first place?"

"You never talk about that."

She sighs. "I wanted to write."

"You what?"

"I wanted to write. Like, to be a writer. Or whatever. Embarrassing, right? He wasn't supportive enough of my writing for me, and things went south from there, and then I kicked him out. It was so stupid. And here I am, 15 years later, with nothing to show for it. A bunch of pages in a drawer." She lets go of me now, drops her head into her hands, rubs her temples the way only menopausal women ever do.

I say, "Mom, I didn't realize, I—I never knew. Writing, huh?"

"Naming you after a Shakespearean character wasn't enough of a clue for you?"

"I—"

"I guess it says a lot about me that I named you after someone so self-destructive," she says. "I could've named you Regan or Portia, but no. I went with the one who goes crazy and kills herself. God damn it."

(All these years, I've been thinking of her as a woman who only exists to collect alimony checks and buy shoes.)

"I kicked him out because I *knew* he was wrong, that if I had more time, more space, I could write something great. If I'd kept him around, he could have at least kept tabs on whatever I was spending so much money on every month, but no, he wasn't supportive enough for me. So I just took his alimony and shut myself in a room and banged away on a keyboard for a decade and a half and came up with jack-shit."

"Mom, why haven't you ever mentioned this before?"

She reaches out into the air, like she's going to find an answer there, but obviously she doesn't, and finally she shrugs and says—"I was embarrassed, I guess. I mean, how embarrassing is it to say to someone, *I want to be a writer?* I didn't tell anyone because I was scared of being scrutinized. It doesn't even make sense. I mean—who was I writing for, myself?" She chokes. "But that completely cut me off from people—from reality. You see what I mean? Self-destructive. It's a streak all the women in our family have."

My thoughts dart for a moment to Sara, who might be dead, or maybe-possibly alive. And also might be here, or maybe-possibly somewhere else. But they don't linger on her for long, because I see that my mother is crying again. Shaking, pouring out regret in front of me, for the first time in years, and I wonder what I could possibly do to help. There are voices in my head saying, *She's just whining* and *She did this to herself,* but I see something now that I never saw before: she's trapped in her own skin. A victim of her former self, with no easy way out.

Like me.

I don't know what to do, but I know I should do *something.* And I feel like even knowing that is a step in the right direction. "Mom," I say, "about those pages in the drawer..."

I catch myself trailing off, and she's obviously waiting for me to finish the thought, because she says nothing.

"I...I'd be happy to read them, if you'd like me to."

"But they're not any good," she tells me.

"Why don't you let me decide that?"

She glances at me sideways with a look that says *I can't believe you're not laughing at me,* and she says, "You actually want to read my stuff?"

I tell her, "Why not? You wrote it so people could read it, right? Unless you'd rather leave it in a drawer."

She rubs her eyes and says, "Well—I guess that's a good point," and she stands up, as if she just remembered how. "Let me show them to you." Takes my hand, pulls me to my feet.

"Right now?"

"Why not? It's not like we're going to accomplish much else today, buried under four feet of snow."

I say, "Okay," and I'm thinking how weird it is that I'm about to spend a day with my mom, and the sun is peeking through the clouds for the first time in days, and the ice on the window shatters the beam into a million yellow gems, filling the room. And in the corner of my eye, I see the girl with the Uggs.

Wait. No. Not now.

She's at my left, and the boy's at my right, the one with the beard and the flannel and jeans, and the fat man's behind me, and Rachel's behind my mother (who fades in and out). The walls are dripping, and the windows are jagged, and the whole room is beating in time with my heart—everything in the universe, tied to my pulse, pulling in, pushing out. I taste blood on my lips, and I reach for the pills.

No.

Not now.

*Are you all right?* I hear a voice say, drowned out by the rushing of blood, and I can't tell who said it, and the room fills with bodies. A thousand eyes shrouded behind yellow sun, staring at me and licking their lips, and I say to myself that I have get out, have to leave, get away from my mother before something happens to her. I swallow and choke.

"I, uh—need to shower—" somehow I said it, I pushed the words out, and I feel the surprise on her face and say, *Sorry, I smell,* and I push on the floor with my feet, which like water slips under them, struggling through thick air and trying to push past the dead, veiny hands reaching out for me as mine shoots toward the doorframe. I push into the bathroom and slam the door shut, pressing hard with my back to make sure it stays closed, while I choke on my breath. And in the next room, I hear my mother hesitate before shuffling sadly downstairs.

## wed. jan. 19.
## 3:36 pm.
## fog

**I'm standing in the shower now,** blasting my closed eyelids with almost-scalding water while plumes of steam rise around me and tease at the goose bumps that never go away. I'm trying to wash the day-old filth of corpse off of me, but somehow the steam just amplifies it all, and the smell is like rancid meat that's been warming all day in a Crock-Pot. My mouth is dry and no matter how much hot water I swallow it still has that metallic blood taste stuck to it. But as long as I keep the water blasting into my eyes, they glow red, and the faces almost disappear. I collapse into the wall and let it hold me up because there's no strength in my knees. I gasp quick breaths of the hot, filmy air, and it sticks to my lungs like glue in a tube, and I listen to the sounds in the walls. Feet. Echoing. In the walls. I won't open my eyes, because if I do, I'll see faces again. Will it always be like this, from now on? The faces that won't go away, the urges to swallow the pills and drink blood? Addiction's not something I've dealt with before, so I don't even know where to start thinking through it. And the more I think about how deep I've sunk into helplessness, the heavier my lungs get, and then my eyes snap open and I realize I'm sliding down the wall. I reach out to stop myself but the tub faucet rushes up to meet my face. My lip's bleeding when I hit the wet floor, and I watch the red spiral around the drain in a twisted, nauseous bullseye. I have to look away. My eyes follow the grimy water spots that never wash off up the length of the shower curtain, looking for light to center my spinning brain like a moth's, but behind the curtain all I can see are silhouettes. The ghosts that follow me everywhere, won't leave me alone, won't let me go, won't let me look away. They used to not be real. I used to see them only sometimes, and I knew they were imaginary. But now I see them everywhere, and they never disappear, and I wonder if maybe they're imagining me.

"Stop! Go away! You're not real!"

*You're dead, you're not real, stop following me.*

They shrink away, a little. I bite my lip to stop the bleeding and blow water out my nose. But the footsteps in my head don't go away (in the walls, in the attic?), and I just want to be alone, by myself, alone, but I don't think that I ever will be again. I reach up into the steam, and the faucet cuts my hand (twice) before I have a grip on it, and I pull myself up to my knees. I kneel in the water and tears mix with blood, and they run down the drain, and I beg for it all to just stop.

I don't know how long I stay here like this, because seconds turn to hours and ounces to gallons, but the red water turns pink and then clear. Then I reach out for the faucet and shut it off and drops drip down the drain in the echoing silence. My hair hangs in matted strands across my face, and the white-and-black stripes bob up and down, and in the cavernous tile, no one can hear me crying. I can feel the house heaving under the buckling weight of the snow—white and gray layers of ice crystals entombing us in our own home, like the layers of rock that turned the dinosaurs into goo. If no one ever digs us out, we'll die here, and then we'll just be puddles of petroleum waiting to burn. No one will ever care that my mom was a writer or that I was a murderer; we'll go back to just being carbon molecules cycling through the system, dug up and burned and pumped into the air (the water, the soil), until maybe the last bits of us become part of someone else.

*You're not special, snowflakes. People say you're unique and no two are the same, but none of it matters. If you hadn't buried me alive in my mom's house, some other dumb snowflakes would have, so stop acting so smug about it. And then you'd all melt and disappear anyway.*

God, it hurts.

Hurts to carry all this guilt. Hurts to be unable to tell my mother the truth. Hurts to know that she's unwittingly hiding a killer in her own home. Hurts to know that I betrayed Kate's trust and I didn't tell her the truth when I could have, and now she knows because she found out in the worst possible way, and she probably called the police last night (of course she did, why wouldn't she have?), and it's only a matter of time before the roads are clear and they're knocking on my (mom's) door. Maybe I should just crawl back into bed and shut everything out and sleep away my last few hours of freedom. With any luck, I won't wake up.

And I'm about to do that, but that's when I hear the piano.

It's a song that I've heard before; Sara used to bang it out all the time. "Take the 'A' Train," by Duke Ellington, but it's different from how she used to play it. There was a mechanical exactness in her strokes—it was a sequence of notes timed just as Duke had recorded them, programmed precisely into her hands and executed like a surgeon. She used to play it all the time, like she got real pleasure from hitting the same notes over and over again, never deviating from the head or changing the tempo. I've been sick of it for years.

But this isn't her.

This is someone different, someone who likes to ride a groove, to improvise however she wants. Notes that bounce, notes that dodge in and out from the melody, tripping over each other in an awkward and thrilling ballet of pent-up emotion, somehow (miraculously) sliding up and down the keyboard. It sounds like Kate's slide guitar.

But—?

I know it's not my mother because my mother doesn't play—just keeps the baby grand around because it looks nice. And it's not Sara because Sara's never played like this, ever. It doesn't make sense, though, that Kate would be here, that she'd be playing my mom's piano like nothing had happened last night. And it really, obviously, doesn't make sense that she'd manage to get here when every road in town is blocked.

And yet, there it is, someone (*someone!*) banging away on the keys in a style distinctly Kate-like while I sit on the floor of the tub brushing wet hair out of my face and feeling sorry for myself. I rub my sore eyes till the tub floor turns green and then purple and then white again, and the music keeps playing, darting back and forth and doubling in on itself, like someone who doesn't really know the song and doesn't care. And somehow, it steadies the quivering room, till my mom's knocking on the door, saying, "Ophie, you all right in there? There's someone here to see you."

Somehow that's enough, and I jump up, through the curtain, grab a towel from the wall to wrap myself in, and it's one of the "good towels," but who cares, and I'm stumbling down the stairs, out into the living room where Kate is making the piano sing.

She's sitting there, in snow-covered boots, her spiral dreads bouncing up and down and her scarf swinging back and forth while her mildly clumsy fingers stumble over the keys. It's obvious she doesn't play piano all that much, that she's just blowing off steam, and there's a determined half-scowl on her face that tells me being any better would mean less catharsis, less to hear. It still makes no sense that she's sitting in my mom's living room, but it takes me forever to return to that thought because I can't look away from her fingers, and it takes her a minute to look up and see me, but then when she does she says my name and she runs across the room and I'm in her arms.

"What are you doing here?" I ask as she squeezes my towel and I fumble, trying to keep it around me.

She says, "I had to come after you," as if that makes perfect sense and explains everything. And she hugs me again and says, "Do you want to get dressed? You look cold."

"Uh—okay."

"Okay?"

"Okay."

I ascend the stairs to my room in a daze, entirely confused by what just happened. The old high school clothes in my closet fit me again, though they're admittedly a little childish. Studs and spikes from a misguided attempt at being edgy. I find some jeans that aren't too worn and a t-shirt with the name of a band on it that's not too embarrassing, and I open the door to let Kate in. She raises her eyebrows a bit when she sees the band on my shirt, but that's okay, and she sits in the middle of the floor, cross-legged, like story time in kindergarten.

I sit on the edge of my bed. The sun's back behind the clouds and ice is overtaking the window again, covering it in crisscrossed bars that remind me I'm trapped like an animal. It's snowing more, and the snow has already piled up high on the windowsill, and now it's just bouncing off. She's looking up at me from the floor, surrounded by half-full boxes, the shadows from the bars of ice playing across her face. She takes a breath, and she swallows.

"I've...got a lot to say," she says.

"I've got a lot of questions," I admit.

She says, "I imagine, but—let me get this out. This is important." Clears her throat. "I guess I'll start at the beginning." And she bites her lip and she picks up a paperback from one of the boxes—my Lovecraft collection—and plays with its dog-eared cover. And finally, she says, "I like horror movies...a lot."

"What?"

She laughs, awkward. "I'm sorry," she says. "It makes absolutely no sense to start the conversation there, does it? I'm—I'm trying to work my way toward my point. It's hard—you'll have to be patient with me." She half-opens the book and she flips a yellowed page back and forth between her hands, and sighs, and says, "What I'm trying to say is, I've seen all sorts of weird violence on movie and TV screens. I've seen every zombie movie ever—and yet, somehow, that didn't prepare me at all for what I saw last night. Even, like, a little, y'know?"

"I—"

"No, it's okay," she says. "I get it. I see it now. Honestly, I don't know why I didn't see it before. I guess I was just blinding myself to the truth on purpose, y'know? I didn't want to think that my roommate was capable of something so disgusting. I like to assume the best of people, and it's always a mistake." She's dog-earing a page. "It's the drug, isn't it? It doesn't just make you act strange—it makes you kill people."

I try to think of something to say, but honestly, what can I say? *Yes, I'm secretly a zombie? Sorry about that?*

She says, "Did you know?"

"I'm—I've been figuring it out. Slowly."

"And the fire at the hospital?"

"Yeah, I'm pretty sure that was me."

And then there's silence.

I'd like to fill it, but with what?

"Well," she says, flipping pages, "that's uh—that's quite a body count." She's staring at the floor, no doubt wondering why she came here. As am I.

I'm biting my split lip. The blood is sweet, and it's sour, and I wish it would stop flowing.

And then, quietly, under her breath, I hear her add, "I really like musicals, too."

"Uh—what?" Such a weird thing to say, but I don't laugh, mostly because I'm just struck by how bizarrely convicted she sounds about this.

She says, "I'm sorry, this all sounds so stupid now that I'm saying it out loud." She's picking at Lovecraft's pages with her purple nails, calmly. She's so weirdly comfortable in this room, like she's forced herself to forget that I'm a danger to her life and everyone else's. Her breathing is even. "I was thinking about these things the whole way here—rehearsing this conversation over and over. It all made so much sense in my head, but now that I'm saying it out loud, I realize that it's nonsense. Y'know that feeling?"

"Every day of my life."

"Then I guess I'll keep trying," she says. "*Man*—the truer something is, the harder it is to put it into words, y'know?" She shuts her eyes and scratches her forehead like she's trying to free an idea, and she asks, "When you tell someone you like musicals, what's the first thing that they say?"

"That they're cornball?"

She opens her mouth in a frustrated grin, and she breathes through her teeth and says, "Yeah, but more specifically. Everyone who doesn't like musicals has the exact same complaint about them. At least, in my experience. Any idea what I'm getting at? Try to help me out here, so I know I'm not crazy."

"You mean, like, *People don't break out into song in real life, so why would you want to watch a movie where they do?* That?"

"Exactly!" she says. "Exactly. That. I've heard it a thousand times. Pretty much every time I admit to liking musicals."

I kind of want to say, *That's why most people know better than to admit to liking musicals,* but I think better of it. She's looking up into a corner of the ceiling, like she's trying to find the next few words there, like she's still not sure anything she's saying makes sense.

She says, "But it's really weird to me that I never get that reaction when I tell people I like horror movies. Y'know? Like, no one ever says *Horror movies are so cornball. People don't rise from the grave and feast on human flesh in real life, so why would you want to watch a movie about it?* No one ever says that. And that's really interesting to me—that it's so much easier for people to accept flesh-eating zombies than a little bit of singing and dancing. Y'know?"

I admit that I hadn't thought about that before now. I feel like I should say something to fill the silence, but I'm too busy considering the point.

"I've been thinking about this," she says, "and I've decided that I don't think musicals and horror movies are really all that different, y'know? Musicals take powerful emotions and turn them into something beautiful. Horror movies take powerful emotions and turn them into something ugly. But otherwise, they're the same. They just go in opposite directions."

She stops for a minute, and I can tell this is the moment where the conversation gets harder, where the point she's been trying to make turns to vapor that can't be wrapped in words, can't be nailed to the air. And I can't say anything, but I'm thinking *Keep trying.*

And finally, she says, "I don't know what I'm trying to say, exactly. I guess that—well—I mean, I believe in heaven. And I believe in hell. But you know that."

*Keep trying.*

She sighs. "I guess what I'm trying to say is that I can't believe that what we experience directly is all that there is. There are things above our reality and things below it— things that are more real than we are. I mean, otherwise, how do you explain things like horror movies and musicals? Why do images so far removed from our experience resonate with so many people?"

I could probably explain them a thousand other ways, but *Keep trying.*

"What I'm saying is, animals adjust to whatever reality you present them with. If you start kicking your dog every day, pretty soon he'll just accept that his purpose in life is to get kicked. If you feed him a steak every night, he'll decide he exists to eat steak. Whatever there is, there is, y'know? That's how animals think. But people aren't like that. They're always reaching above, reaching below, trying to touch the transcendent and the sublime. And I know that doesn't prove anything, but it's just what I've been thinking about lately."

She's not breathing, just waiting, waiting for me to say something, anything to assure her she's not just filling the air with craziness. I think she has a point, that there might be something to it, but I can't find the words.

Finally, she says, "And again, it's so weird to me that people are so much more accepting of horror. That no one says, *That's stupid, zombies and ghosts aren't real.* That people are somehow more okay with using their imaginations to create hell than to reach for heaven. I just wonder why that is."

"I don't know."

She says, "I don't know either, exactly. At least, not in a way I can put into words without sounding really trite and blasé." She breathes, plays with my book, then throws it on the floor and adds, "But I'm realizing something: that you can respond to ugliness by creating more ugliness, or you can respond by trying to do something beautiful. Horror begets horror unless you reach for heaven, y'know?" She sighs, like she finally it all out. "Anyway, that's why I came here, I guess."

She's leaning forward now, brow furrowed, eyes looking up at me, waiting for a response, some validation, something, anything. I say, "How'd you even get here? I mean, with the roads all blocked?"

"I walked."

"What?"

"I walked," she shrugs, like she's embarrassed, and maybe she is. "It took me all morning and most of the afternoon."

"Even driving, it takes forever to get here."

"I know." She breathes. "Maybe I should tell you what I've been up to in the last 24 hours."

I say, "Yeah, I think you should."

She sighs, she gets up, she walks over the window. Leans on it (hard), her hand on the sill, while the snow and the sleet push back on her shoulder.

I listen.

She says, "I don't think there's any way to really describe what it felt like, last night, to walk in on you standing over a mutilated corpse. Like I said, a thousand horror movies couldn't have prepared me for it. Somehow, seeing you, standing there, gnawing on a human leg bone, was nothing like seeing a zombie in a Romero flick do it. There's just no comparison."

The sleet pounds hard on the window, like dirt being thrown on a coffin.

"To be honest—and I know this will sound really petty now, but—I was still really mad at you for losing my rosary. But then I saw you there, completely out of control, just tearing another human being apart like an animal, and—well, it's weird, but what I felt was actually *pity*. Is that weird? No, I mean, *pity*'s not quite the right word, but, like—well, I felt bad for you. Not right away, I mean—obviously, first I was just shocked and horrified, and then I was pissed. I was pissed that you would do something so disgusting, but I was more pissed that you hadn't even tried to tell me the truth. And then I was pissed that you were running away, but then I started thinking, like, *What would I have done if I were her?* and the answer was *Probably the exact same thing,* which to be honest was a terrifying thought. I mean, back when we hid that body? Cyndi, or whatever her name was? That was *my* idea. We all do stupid shit and then try to run from it."

Her hand slips off the windowsill and she turns back and looks over the posters on my walls. I'm pretty embarrassed by most of them, but she doesn't say anything.

"I've only taken a couple of physics classes," she says, "so don't let me act like I'm Stephen Hawking or anything, but I was reading the other day that relativity theory would tell you that the passage of time is actually an illusion. We think this moment is happening *now,* but what's *now* is entirely arbitrary. Time's just another dimension, and *right now* and *tomorrow* and *three years ago* are all coexisting in some sense. Our future selves are all looking back at us, shaking their heads sadly, and our past selves look forward at us, laughing, like *Ha! We screwed Present Self good!* or whatever. Y'know? I mean, I don't think that's the way it really works, but the point is, we're all basically victims of our past selves. I'm not saying we aren't responsible for our own actions, because obviously we are, but it's also true that we can't undo them. It doesn't matter what lessons we learned, or didn't learn, from our pasts—we're still stuck with them. It doesn't matter who we are right now; we've all done stupid shit that comes back to bite us in the ass. God knows I have."

She sinks into the one chair in the room, the one my mom used to read to me in when I was little, and a mushroom cloud of dust explodes into the air.

"Obviously," she says, "I didn't think about the situation all that deeply at the time, because I had a dismembered corpse sitting at my feet. And obviously my first instinct was to call the cops. But clearly I didn't."

"Why not?"

"I'm trying to explain why," she says. "I really am. Like I said, I felt bad for you, as stupid as that sounds. And I knew you were only doing what you were doing because of your sister's pills, and I wanted to make it right. So—well—I—sort of—hid a body for you. Again."

She's studying my face, trying to see how I'll react, but I have no idea what to say, what to do.

"I'm not exactly proud of it," she says, "but I hid the body in my closet. I picked it up, piece by piece, and I threw it all in my laundry basket. Then I mopped the blood up from the floor. And then I stood there, looking at the shiny, perfect tile, thinking *What the hell have I done, and what the hell do I do now?* It was surreal."

She's looking at me like I'm supposed to validate her actions somehow, like I'm supposed to tell her she did the Right Thing. "Kate, why the hell would you do that?"

"Do you remember what I said to you last night, Phelia? Just before I stormed out?"

"Uh—" It seems so long ago now.

"I told you Sara was wrong about love. About love devouring and destroying. I promised you I'd prove to you that she was wrong, remember? So—after you ran off, I was standing over that pile of blood and bones, and I thought maybe, just maybe if I did something truly selfless, like hide a body, for you, you'd see that—I mean, I know it doesn't make a whole lot of sense. Obviously, I wasn't thinking super clearly at the time. I was running on adrenalin, what can I say?"

"That's—that's—wow."

"I know."

"And I'm not sure it was really selfless if you did it just to prove a point."

"Yeah. But it *wasn't*, y'know? I mean, there *was* that, but I also was afraid for myself, obviously, and, well—I was worried about you."

"Why, though?"

"I don't know, you've just—you've given me someone to talk to, to sort through things with. You're not the only depressed super-senior bouncing around campus, y'know?

I mean, in the back of my mind, I knew I was just postponing the inevitable, but it seemed like—I don't know—I just—"

"I get it," I tell her.

"You do?"

"Well, I mean, sorta. It's either the sweetest or most horrible thing I've ever heard, y'know?"

She slides up onto the arm of the chair and says, "I know, right? That's kind of where I am right now, too. I mean, when we hid that first body, we were just covering our asses, but this was different. I knew you had done it, and I still chose to hide the evidence. At the time, it felt like the Right Thing to Do, but the further I get from it, the uglier it seems, y'know?"

She picks up a toy off my bookshelf—a sparkly My-Little-Pony-knockoff unicorn, one that I haven't thought about in a decade. She tosses it from hand to hand. It's shedding sparkles on her lap.

"That's the thing about being Catholic," she tells me. "People say that Catholic theology is 'incarnational,' that we're all supposed to be Christ to the world, to absorb its evil and create some good, but then when you try, you see what an ugly, messy thing it is, and how inadequate your own attempts are. It's not a Beautiful thing or a Good thing, at least not on the surface. It's more like being elbow-deep in someone else's blood. This time, literally."

"That's sick."

"I know, right?" she says. "But I'm starting to see that that's how things work. And anyway, it really only describes half the problem here. I'm obviously not in a position to absolve you for the mortal sin of eating a police officer—I mean, I didn't even know the guy. He's got a family, friends, a job—people who need him. I'm starting to see what that line means, though—*Behold, I make all things new.* Remember that one? I can't erase a debt that's not owed to me, but if I owned literally all the money in the world, I probably could, y'know? I've been trying to make things right myself, but I'm seeing how futile that is. All I can do is strap myself in for the ride."

She's combing the unicorn's mane with her nails.

"But anyway. I tossed the body in my closet and cleaned up, and after that I realized that I'd better get out of there as fast as I could. I would have called you, but I saw that you left your phone on your desk, so I got in my van and I just drove. Once I'd put enough distance between myself and campus, I just pulled over to the side of the road and slept in the back. And then in the morning, I thought I should probably try to find you, so I Facebook-stalked you on my phone till I found your mom's address. By then my van was buried in snow and it wouldn't move, so I just got out and I started walking."

"What if I hadn't been here?"

"I dunno."

"Well—" I have no idea what to say to any of this. It's like a musical wrapped in a horror movie. "Thanks for finding me, but—what do we do now?"

She's pulling on the unicorn's legs, pulling her front legs and her back legs in opposite directions, like she's trying to draw and quarter her. She says, "I don't know. I wish I did. I can't just leave a body in my closet and you can't just hide here forever. They're both terrible hiding places, for starters. But I am sure of one thing."

"What?"

"You *need* to get off these pills."

"I—" and I swallow—"I don't know if I *can,* Kate."

She sits in silence, and I stare at the dragon on my bed in the fading gray light. And then I hear her whisper, almost inaudibly, "The human heart is a factory of idols."

"What?"

She shakes her head like she's waking from a dream. Looks embarrassed. "It's a quote from John Calvin," she says. "A Protestant theologian." She looks down at my unicorn and adds, "I heard it somewhere a year or two ago, and I always kind of wondered what he meant." She stands up, tosses the unicorn on the chair, and goes back to looking at my posters. Closely, without judgment, like she's looking at the tiny dots of ink. "I think I'm starting to understand now, though. That people are wired to 'serve' things. That no one exists just to exist. That we all worship something, or serve something, or fight for something, and it's usually the wrong thing."

I find myself sliding off the bed onto the floor, till I'm finally sitting on my black carpet, with my back against my mattress. The book she was playing with earlier is sitting next to me, open to "The Call of Cthulhu." I tell her, "I keep seeing things."

"What sort of things?"

"People. And—and memories."

"What sort of people do you see?"

"I think they're ghosts."

I pick up the book and read the words, *The most merciful thing in the world, I think, is the inability of the human mind to correlate all its contents.*

I tell her, "They're the people I've killed. I didn't realize that at first, but their faces have gotten a lot clearer lately. They follow me everywhere, and they talk to me."

"What do they say?"

"All sorts of stuff. Sometimes we just chat. Sometimes they help me, give me advice. And sometimes they tell me to...to do things."

"'Do things'?"

"Yeah, like the stuff that I've been doing. Killing people. It sounds kind of stupid, now that I've said it out loud."

"Not *that* stupid," she says, and she sits on the floor next to me and takes the book and closes it.

"I mean, I'm seeing things that aren't real. That's *pretty* stupid."

"Well, what's *real*, right? Maybe only you can see them, but that doesn't make them imaginary. And maybe they *are* imaginary, but that doesn't mean they don't *mean* something. It's like what we were saying about dreams: maybe physiologically it's only your brainstem firing randomly, but that doesn't mean it's *only* that."

She leans up next to me against the bed and sighs.

She says, "I'm Catholic, Phelia. I believe there's more to the universe than just atoms bumping up against each other. I could be wrong, but maybe I'm not, y'know? *There are more things in heaven and earth than are dreamt of in your philosophy,* right? I know you're a fan of that one."

"How'd you know?"

"Are you serious? Because, you carry it with you everywhere."

"Yeah, I'm actually kind of embarrassed about that."

"Don't be. I get why it fascinates you. Mystery, ambiguity—it's a work you can think about your whole life and still not fully understand. And, I mean, it makes a good point, right?"

"What point is that?"

"That partial ignorance is no excuse for inaction? I mean, that's the point of *Hamlet,* right?"

"I guess. Maybe?"

"I mean, he spends the whole play hesitating, just because he's not 100% sure what the truth is. Even though all the available evidence points to only one thing. And he pays with his life for it. I mean, I'm just saying."

"I always thought it was about the Oedipal complex. Y'know, like everything is."

She laughs.

"Wait, I never told you, did I? I totally made our Shakespeare prof squirm the other day."

"What'd you say to him?"

"Um—I just pointed out that there's never been any real evidence for the Oedipal complex, and that only English profs care about it anymore."

She laughs. "And what'd he say?"

"Well, y'know, he just—he pointed out how prevalent it is in literature. And then I told him *that* was bullshit because you pretty much only see it in post-Freudian modernist lit, and he stammered a little more, and—Kate, I have to ask you something."

"Oh?" Her eyebrows go up a little, surprised by my suddenly serious tone. And actually, there are so many things I have to ask her. But let me start with the easiest one. Relatively speaking, I mean.

"Do you—do you think Freud was right about sexual abuse? Like, that neuroses are rooted in repressed memories of it?"

"The seduction theory?" she says. "You realize that even Freud abandoned that one, right?"

"Yeah."

"I mean, if something is too far-fetched even for Freud, then—"

"But, I mean, is it possible?"

"A *lot* of things are possible."

"Kate, I don't know what's real or what's imaginary anymore. I don't even know if you're really here, if we're really having this conversation. But I keep having these memories—of a week spent in a psych ward, of Sara's face in the dark, of hands on me, of things inside me, of—it's—it hurts so much, Kate."

I fall into her arms, and she's warm and she's soft and she smells like smoke. And she holds me as the last rays of the gray sun disappear and another long winter night begins. In her arms, it's warm and it's safe.

I don't know how long I spend in here, buried in her heat and soaking her scarf with my tears, but in the end I look up and tell her, "Thanks for believing me."

"Of course."

"I know it doesn't make a lot of sense."

"It's like I told you the other day," she says. "Pain is pain, y'know? I've lost too many friends to callous skepticism."

"You don't think I'm crazy?"

"I can't *afford* to doubt you. Neither of us can." She bites her lip. "That guy friend I told you about? The one who got raped by a girl? He's dead now."

"You mean—?"

"Suicide," she says. "OD'd on some pills. And, I mean, I don't know if it was *just* because I laughed when he told me, but—"

Now she's crying too, and I pull her in, and we sit on my floor sharing what little warmth we have. "You think I might be right, though? About the things I'm remembering?"

She says, "Well, here's what I know: there's no shortage of people in the world who see everyone else as a means to an end—who just want to wring whatever power and pleasure they can out of other people, y'know? I remember reading that one percent of all people are complete sociopaths—with no empathy for others at all. And I'm pretty sure the rest of us just differ from them by degree."

"Is that what Sara meant? When she told me that love destroys?"

"I guess."

"Do you still think she was wrong?"

But Kate doesn't say anything—just holds me till the first star forces its way through the clouds.

I say, "So what do we do now?"

She looks at me and says, "I think the first step is to get you off the pills. I'm not an expert on addictions—nicotine aside—but I understand cold-turkey is usually the best way."

I'm rattling the pill bottle in my pocket.

"Will you give me the pills?" she says.

My hand wraps around them and squeezes them hard, and the plastic is strong and smooth on my skin.

She says again, "Will you give me the pills? Please?"

I feel the plastic starting to crack.

"Please, Phelia."

I hand them to her.

I'm completely surprised. It was easy. Easier than it should have been. And she takes them and drops them in her purse and says, "Well, I guess that's done." She pulls the zipper closed and says, "What now?"

"I don't know."

We sit in the dark and she rattles her purse, and it sounds like the sleet on the window. "Well," she finally says, "we're not going anywhere tonight, I guess. Are you hungry?"

I say, "Maybe. I'm not sure. I've kind of forgotten what hunger feels like."

"Maybe your mom's hungry. I can cook."

"Good, because she can't."

She laughs at that, and I laugh, and I look at her and she looks at me, and she stops and says—"Didn't your eyes use to be blue?"

"What?"

"Your eyes. When we first met, they were blue. I remember. Now they just look really...gray."

And my mouth drops open and I say, "Oh my God."

"What?"

"Oh God," I say again, because now everything makes sense, and I have no idea what to say, what to do. The gray eyes. That was the one missing piece, but it all makes sense now. I stand up, and I'm holding the sides of my head, trying to think what to do, and I only now realize I've been backing away from her when I run into the wall and the heat from my burning face is sucked out the window.

"Phelia, what's going on?"

"I—I'm not sure—she's here, Kate, she's here." I look toward the ceiling, where I heard her footsteps before. "She's here, oh God, she's here."

"Who's here? What are you talking about?" She stands up now, too, but she's afraid to come near me, and my gray eyes turn bloodshot.

"Sara," I tell her. "She's here. She picked me up last night, and she was in my car, and she was acting so strange, even for her I mean, and then she was gone in the morning and I told myself that I must have imagined it, that she was dead, that she died in the fire, that she wasn't actually here. But she's here, Kate, and I think that she's taking the pills, that she's on her own drug, and I know because her eyes were gray last night, just like mine turned gray, and I saw them, and I don't know what she'll do."

"Phelia, calm down. Nothing you're saying makes sense."

"No, you're not listening, this makes perfect sense. I don't know why she'd do it, but who knows why she does anything? Maybe she saw the way the drug was making me act and wanted to see what it was like to be on it? Or maybe she's trying to prove that it's safe? I knew it, I knew I wasn't crazy."

"Are you sure? Because you sound crazy."

"No, she's here. And I have no idea what she's going to do to me. To any of us. What do we do, Kate? We could all die tonight."

"Phelia," she's saying, "just calm down. I don't think she's here. Why would she be hiding in your house? That doesn't make any sense."

"I know, right? Exactly. Nothing she's going to do makes sense, because she's taking the pills. She's going to be exactly like me, trapped in her own nightmare world, seeing things that aren't there, and she'll kill people. She'll kill *us*. I don't know what to do." More noise from the attic.

"Ophelia—"

"Don't you get it? We have to get out. We have to leave."

"Where would we go? The roads are completely blocked."

"Oh God, you're right." And now the darkness is pouring in from the window, overpowering the single lamp in the corner, and my throat is starting to close and my eyes land on her purse. *The pills.* (What? No.) *The pills.* It's the cop, the young one with the freckles, and he's standing behind me and he's whispering, *The pills.* I look back at Kate and she's saying *Who are you talking to?* and to my left is the girl with the Uggs, saying *You need to get the pills. Remember when we killed the cop? What you need is the pills. Take the pills, kill Sara, it's all over.* Then the fat man has my arm in his beefy hand, and he says, *Get the pills, now,* and I look to Kate's face, but it's fading away. I say, *No, I can't, I just finally now got them off of my hands, please don't make me, not now,* and I turn and the hipster, the one with the beard in the flannel, is standing there, saying, *We're almost done. Just get the pills. Take the pills one more time, and we'll end this, okay?* (But why are you back? I was free, you were finally gone, please just leave me alone...) And then in my ear, Rachel's voice in my ear: *You can do this, you're almost done, just take the pills and we'll end it forever.* I'm looking toward Kate, and her gray, blurry face is filling with fear, and she's biting her lip till it bleeds, and I tell her, *I need those pills back.* She says *What? There's no way,* but I say, *I'm not asking.* She runs for the door, but it's all in slow motion. My ghost friends and I drag her down to the floor, and they all hold her down while I yank on her purse, and the leather first stretches but finally breaks, and then tampons and lipsticks explode to the floor while the cracking pill bottle flies into my hand. I squeeze till the orange explodes into flames and a shower of pills. And the pills fill my hands and my hands fill my mouth and I swallow the handfuls of whiteness. And now as the light fades away and the room disappears, I think, *This is how it was supposed to end.*

## wed. jan. 19.
## 11:53 pm.
## clear for the first time

**When I open my eyes I don't know** how much time has elapsed. The darkness is gone now, but nothing looks quite the same as it did. The ice is gone from the windows and the fog is gone from the air, and my nails are a thousand miles long, like the claws of a rat in a trap. I'm alone now, I don't know what happened to Kate or Rachel or Cyndi or the fat man or any of my friends, but I still can hear Her in the roof, in the walls, in the nails in the furniture, and I see now that She's always been there, the screws holding my bones together. I have to extract Her, with tweezers, or pliers, or fire. I may have to tear my own flesh from my bones, but I have to remove Her, I have to. My bedroom is dark, a darkness like nothing I've seen. It's a sopping blue blanket that's sticking to everything, a smothering blue blob that feels like Her love. It presses down on me, demanding my breath, and it's holding me down while it stares in my eyes, but I won't let it hold me, I promise I won't. I wrestle it off with the strength in my veins and I force myself onto my feet. My heels dig down deep in the carpet. I'm ten miles tall and the room, with its dark, sinking memories, can't drag me back to my morass. I see now that what Kate was saying, that death and that life are opposed, that they're separate, was bullshit. They're two sides of one coin, and you can't embrace one without kissing the other. Her death, Sara's death, will feed into my life, and there's no contradiction. Each life ever lived has been built on a thousand or ten-thousand deaths, and there's no choice except to make sure that your own life is built on the deaths of all others. I'm a mouse in your trap now, dear Sara, we're both mice, awash in the flesh of the mouse-crush of old Universe 25, and you must know that

I'll be the one down here grabbing your leg and then pulling you into the dark, where I'll pick all the flesh from your bones before you get a chance to start feasting on mine. It's dark and it's sweaty and hairy down here, Sara, smells like a pile of mouse flesh that's rotting, but these are the mice that survive through the excess of excess; the ones who can cause the most death live the longest. You think you can win at this game built on shadows and memories and ghosts and (my?) death, but as long as you're here it's still amateur hour. You know that it is. Let me show you the pain, let me show you each second of anguish you gave me, in double. I'm tearing the curtain down, dropping it (rough) on the floor, because now I won't hide from my pain. I'm embracing the Worm, even as (in the drama) he feasts on my flesh. I won't be the Actress. I will be the Worm, and the Worm always wins, and I will be the Worm. I burrow through floor and through walls and through ceiling. The wood tastes like earth and the earth tastes like flesh, and I send out my thoughts. *Hi there, Sara. I'm here. And I'm not in the past anymore. And I'm coming for you, and I'll pick your bones clean. And I know you can hear all my thoughts, and I'm coming for you.* The walls shake, the floor shakes, they pound with Her footsteps—the ones that I'd hear every night when She'd come down to see me. I remember Her back then, ten thousand feet tall, and constructed from stethoscopes, bubblegum, sinews; long, manicured claws that would reach through my curtains and fill my performance with cannibal Worms. But the teeth and the claws won't touch me this time, and my flesh is like steel and my eyes are like fire. I snake down the hall and I pour myself up through the door to the attic, the one that my mom never opens, the one filled with memories we've banished for good. Lab coats and notebooks and footie pajamas, spices and plush toys and dump trucks and Barbies. Everything piled in a dark, blackish mass, which bleeds jagged shadows down into the floor, while the walls stab asbestos deep into my lungs. I see Her again, just a bright Cheshire smile that appears in the corner, and then it fades out and fades in another, and then I'm inside it and dodging Her teeth. *Where are you? Come out.* And Her voice, like a thunderous whisper, beats out from the walls and the boxes of memories: *I am out. I'm in you, around you, and through you. The pills in your veins and the screws in your bones. You said so yourself. So why are you trying to find me? I've always been here.* I claw at my arms till the blood turns to rivers, but can't dig Her out of my bones. And I swing at the boxes with arms made of night, and the blood and the stars splatter hard on the cardboard and knock over pages that spill on the floor, where the crayon and the rats mix together. I reach for the smile in the dark that's Her face, but it's only the star stickers, bright in the dark, on a ceiling they tore down a decade ago. And Her voice, small and infinite, drifts from the corner; it's dripping with violence, Her words driven under my fingernails, spikes with a hammer. I try to escape, out from under the weight of the words bleeding pain in my ears, but my sheets are like concrete, my limbs are like twine. I say, *Go away, please just leave me alone,* but Her breath pins me down, and I soak through the mattress, the bedframe, I'm liquid. I'm black blood that seeps through the cracks of the floor and the pipes and the bedbugs and roaches. I land in my mom's room, the one that I'd run to when She gave me nightmares, grab onto the bed, the edge of her mattress, and pull my chin over it, feeling the scrape of the quilt on my throat. *Hey Mommy? Hey Mommy.* The snoring is filling the dark; they're the snores that I always imagined were monsters down under her bed, but were always my mother just breathing the dark in and out, and yet this time it's different. It's deep and it's angry, and liquid is fresh on the sheets, still hot in the black. It drips down my chin and then onto my feet and the carpet and stains both my hands, and the snoring's not coming from Mommy. It's higher and darker and wetter and deeper, and eyes are above me, high up toward the ceiling. They stare like two lamps dripping wet with fresh blood, and the red Cheshire grin grabs me hard and inhales my attention. I see Her, ten-thousand feet tall on the mattress, with teeth miles long like a rat's and a skeleton smothered in fresh, jagged rust, and Her mouth is deep-dripping the blood of my mother. I stare in Her eyes now; they're galaxies-wide and the Earth is revolving around them. They're spinning in nighttime and flashing like quasars, electrons and teeth and planets and stars. I quiver on rubbery bare feet (pajamas?) and watch as Her mouth gapes wide open with comets and caskets. There She is, in the dark, with all suns revolving around Her. She's swallowing kings and devouring kingdoms. *I am become death, destroyer of worlds.* She *is* the darkness, the shadows oppressing the room that push hard on the windows until they all shatter, and light from the streetlamps is sucked deep inside Her. A dark singularity, heat death incarnate, the owner of all of me, grabbing for more. Ten tongues, thirty claws, twisting through the dark, toward me, and I'm three feet tall and dive into the closet. The smell of the dust and the pine and the solitude, dense, yellow light, and the choke and the hiss of the furnace, and She never finds me in here, never knew of the deep, secret tunnels. I dive into Hefty bags filled full of clothes, but Her tendrils are right there behind me. *No, wait, you can't do this! My tunnels were where I was safe, you don't know about them, you can't find me in here!* But the teeth and the claws and the eyes are all scraping my heels, and I dig through the plastic and cotton (a rat or a worm), snake my way through the memories like water as tentacle mouths bite my feet. There's nothing left now, no part of my soul that She hasn't invaded. I swim through the night, through the sea of old board games, white dresses, and thrown-away novels, and drag myself (choking on memories) out onto a beach made of concrete, and crash through deep rug burns and doors into darkness. It's cold and it's black, and it smells like cadavers and metal and fast-dripping water. I scrape my nose open on steel as I rise, till my eyes meet a sea of dead, cold, graying flesh. *You knew that She'd do this, Oaf—knew all along She would chase you back here—that the morgue was the one, only place this could end. You're just one more to add to the pile of the dead in Her sanctum, a trophy to hang on Her wall. You know this is the place, Oaf, the palace of death where we all end up when it's all over, but you just gave in so much sooner than most. You can't inhale death and expect not to choke. You can't do that, Oaf, and now that She's trapped you, you've learned that too late.* She roars through the wall like an army of storms and of teeth and of knives and of hooks and of thunder. A freight train with headlamps that suck all the light and the heat from the room, till the mouths of the dead give their last drop of moisture up into Her. I try hard to run and trip over my scrubs, while my ID badge loops on a table. She's a black, gaping mouth that's as wide as the night, and She sucks glowing dust from the stars on the ceiling, sucks light from the cold winter sun, and sucks heat from the coffee, guitars, and the cigarette smoke, and sucks teeth from my dad's peanut-goal-kicking smile. It chews through the SpongeBobs adorning scraped knees and the block towers built when the sun showers started. It burns through the songs in my head and the book in my pocket, the crunch of the snow and the glow of the stage lights. Her tongue is a hundred miles long and it's sharp. I push myself forward, tear thin, brittle skin from the concrete, till bones crack and teeth bleed deep-red, like the *Exit* sign glowing—*the Exit sign!* High on the wall, like a weak eye that's smothered in whiskey and blinking at black tar and long, empty nights. I tear bones from sinew and jump over corpses that fly through the air toward the Nothing behind me. I slide over sharp, rusty drains, through a blunt, sideways hail made of bathroom scales, scalpels, and teeth, lips, and gums, till I find my two feet and I sprint for the exit. I sprint for the red, because red leads away, to the hallway, away from the black fog of Her. I reach for the door while Her teeth and Her lips scrape my back and my thighs and my skull, and I jerk it wide open and slam it behind me, and stare at the light—but it's strange and it's gray. It's a gray that I've only seen once, and a smell burns my eyes in a way that I can't not remember. The four white-gray walls that I spent that long week in, the ones with the bars and the small slot for eyes, and the huge, sweaty fat man with strong, meaty hands. And the *clank* shakes my bones as She latches the door with Her tongue (and Her claws, and Her spines, and

Her eyes), and everything's white now and everything's gray, and I look to the sun filtering in through the window for hope, but the light is too weak and the cold is too strong, and I see now that this is the way that She planned it. That through all the night, She was chasing me here, to the room where my soul has been locked up forever. That through all my life, this was where it was leading. The sun's rising now, just to show me the truth, and She swallows the room, and She swallows the light, and She swallows me, too, and inside Her is nothing but gray.

(Gray forever.)

(purge)

# thurs. jan. 20.
# 7:50 am.
# it's over, isn't it

**My head is starting to clear** as the sun rises over the prairie and fills my cell with the awful, gray light that I know now I'll never escape. I've been dragging it behind me for years now, so it was only a matter of time before it swallowed me whole.

There's a pounding in my head that won't stop, and won't even do me the favor of finding a consistent rhythm. My hands are shaking and so are my feet, and I'm dressed in clothes I haven't worn since high school. A t-shirt with a band on it I haven't listened to in years, and a pair of too-tight jeans with a spiky belt. I don't quite remember putting them on, but it seems like I've been wearing them forever and not at all.

I'm waking from a nightmare, something about the air becoming a galaxy and then a freight train, something about the blood in my veins eating me alive. My arms are covered in deep lacerations, and my shirt and my jeans are torn a thousand ways, and the shredded face on my shirt looks like mine. What year is it?

Everything's quiet.

I've been in this room before. It's the gray one they shut me away in the night that I tried to hurt Sara. But this isn't back then, and hasn't it been years since then? These clothes were the ones I was wearing back then (I think), but they look older and tighter and somehow they're itchier. Dust and loose threads are invading my veins.

I feel like I should stand up, but I'm not sure I can move.

I'm afraid to look up at the window, because I loathe what it does to the sunlight—the way it filters all the radiance from the bright-yellow glow till it's nothing but a dull-gray scarf of dust landing heavy on the floor. The cold tiles beneath me are whitish with flecks of every color, probably made from the scraps of linoleum left over on the floor of the tile factory. Every color of the rainbow mixed into puke.

I vomit on my hands.

When I'm finally done with that, I wipe the reddish bile on my torn shirt and pants while I try to remember how and why I'm here. I remember talking to Kate in my old bedroom—what was she doing in my house?—and then I got chased through the dark. I keep thinking Sara locked me in this room, but that makes no sense at all. I burned this building to the ground. She died in the fire.

I think. Right?

From where I'm sitting, in my vomit-soaked corner, I can see that the door, the one with the single slot for my eyes to peer through, is shut tight, and presumably locked as well, but I guess I should at least try it before I give up and pass out in my vomit-puddle. I feel my guts slosh around inside as I push myself to my feet, like my intestines have been hanging loose for a week. And my feet are bare, and the tiles are cold and they're covered in sunlit dust that clings to my leathery, winter-skin soles. Every step is pain.

I trip forward across the bent shadows of bars on the floor and I reach for the door as I stumble. It's solid and filled with concrete, just like I remember. A thousand pounds of door, expertly engineered to keep 12-year-olds in. The lines worn in the paint by my fingernails are still there, or are these someone else's paint-gouges? I push and pull on the door, but it's not moving, and my muscles ache, burn, and drip red on the floor. I pound with my fists, but the door makes no sound, doesn't move, doesn't shake, just absorbs every punch (every kick) and gives pain in exchange.

Then my eyes land on the slot, the one in the door I spent day after day looking through, waiting hundreds of hours for something to change, but all that I ever could see looking through was the fat man's bald head. It seems lower now, and I have to half-crouch to see through it this time, and somehow the crouching hurts more than the pounding, but slowly my knees and my back bend, and I finally can see through the wire-laced glass—and I scream and fall backwards. Pain shoots through my skull, lighting up my hair (jagged and wild), and the backs of my eyelids turn red and then yellow.

Those eyes, the ones that stared at me through the dark every night, floating (wild) above the Cheshire cat grin, now lit up and crackling with jagged, red veins, and they twitch and they quiver, unable to focus on anything more than my pores. Staring in, staring back at me, pressed against glass, blinking hard in the dawn while the fog from her breath rises slowly, in pulses. From the floor I can't see them as well, but they're there, in the glass, staring in through my skin and my bones, and they shake. They stare into me, and I stare into them, while the sun inches into the sky. But the light is still gray, like her breath.

She licks her dry lips, and she finally says, *You're awake.*

Her voice is ethereal, quivering a little. It soaks through the concrete and steel like a liquid. Slow, like it's trying to find its way in, but I hear her.

*Good,* she says, and the glass puffs up with the fog, just for half a second. As soon as the word disappears, it turns blue-clear again, while a few wisps still lazily cling to the wires.

I try to find words, to get up from the floor, but I stare and I can't look away from her eyes, and my mouth tastes like blood and like salt and like dirt, and I choke on my tongue, and I gasp in the cold and wet air, and it stings in my throat like the gray of the sun. Is the floor shaking?

The memories from last night are (sort of) returning. A chase that began when I took back my pills from Kate's purse; then it led through the attic, the past, and the wreckage. I chased; then she turned and she chased after me; then she caught me and locked me in here, in this cell. I chew on my tongue, trying to think of what happened to Kate and my mom, till it bleeds and the blood runs out over my bruised bottom lip and it adds itself into the pool on the floor. And her eyes (which still quiver) stay framed in the glass of the door's tiny window, while I find myself backing across the tile floor, crab-walking drunkenly through blood and through vomit. Closing my eyes (but she won't go away), and I clench brittle fists till my knuckles pop (loud).

*I was starting to think you'd never wake up,* she says. *You took so much of the stuff. I had no idea what sort of effect it would have. But I'm pleased with what I've seen.*

*What are you doing to me?* The words slip out of my mouth, angry and loud but feeble and choking, desperate to escape my throat but terrified of the sweaty winter air. The fog on the window recedes for a moment as she takes a deep breath and thinks over the question. And somehow I see her smile through the door, through the concrete and steel.

And she says, *Well, that's an interesting question, Oaf, because I haven't actually done anything to you. I got you a job. I did that. You're welcome, by the way. But you took the pills. You're the one who chose to down them like shots at a frat party. You're the one who chose to use them as an all-purpose problem-solver. You're the one who decided that murder was an appropriate response to your fear.*

I say, *That's not fair,* but she stares at me through the glass, biting her lip and twitching her eyes till I can feel her pupils bouncing around in my skull.

*Isn't it?* she says. *I gave you the pills but you chose to take them. You're the one who chose to take them when you burned down the hospital, and you're the one who chose to take them when the cop was at your door, and you're the one who chose to take them when you heard me in the attic. If it wasn't your choice, whose was it? If you aren't calling the shots here, who is?*

*You are, obviously.*

*I was hoping you'd say that,* she says, and I see her eyes disappear, leaving nothing but empty, blue space in the slot that once held them, and I squeeze my head (hard) between cold, scabrous hands, trying to stop it from throbbing. Somewhere above me are birds yelling loud, and their sharp, piercing screams dig into my ears while the room spins.

*Let me out.* The words are a yell in my head, but only a whisper in my mouth, getting lost somewhere in the dried blood and the caked-on dirt. *Let me out!* Then I'm at the door again, this time on my knees, but pounding with my fists, and they both make no noise when they strike the immovable wall that it is. Just like my voice, the thump of my fists stops dead just outside of my skin and collapses to the floor where it rolls in the gray like a marble in a maze. I pound until I can't feel my hands anymore.

*What are you doing?*

That wasn't Sara's voice. It was Rachel's, and in the corner of my eye, I see her scrubs and her sneakers, and she's standing there next to me, even though I was alone just a second ago. But the more I see people fade in and out, the more normal it seems, and I'm thinking maybe I'm the same way. Maybe I exist as long as someone needs to talk to me, and then I fade into the ether again. How would I know otherwise?

*What are you doing?* She says it again, gently, and her voice whistles like a breeze, and I think to myself that I owe her an answer.

*Trying to get out. To escape. Leave me alone. Just let me pound on this door.*

*What are you trying to escape from, though?* she says.

*The hospital. Obviously.*

*But don't you remember? The hospital burned down.*

*Of course I remember,* I tell her. *I'm the one who started the fire. But here we are. Now just let me pound on the door, it's all I have left.* And I pound on the steel till my head fills with concrete.

*You're not listening,* she says. *Have you tried looking through the little window?*

*Of course I have. All I can see through it are her eyes—*

*But she's gone now,* Rachel says.

I grab the bottom of the tiny frame with my shaking fingers and drag my eyes into place so I can see through the wired glass, and the flame-red blur drifts in an out of focus, till it finally sharpens into an orange carpet, and a faux-wood desk, and a bathroom scale. Not the white, sterile room I expected, but the one in the basement, the other room that haunts my nightmares. Sara's office. And she's sitting inside, hunched over her desk, facing away, filling the room and the room filling her.

And down by my feet is a shape that's familiar. A translucent loop of blue beads and a cross. Kate's rosary, peeking just half a bead under the door, but it's catching too much of the gray sun to miss. *It's there for a reason. It must be.* I reach down and grab it and pull.

It won't move.

A foot coming down and an eye in the window. She's back at the door, with her foot on the beads, and I hear her voice pounding through concrete. It's louder this time. *Yeah,* she says, *it's there for a reason. That reason is because I threw it on the floor the other day and I accidentally kicked it just now. Both were random, stupid accidents.* I sink down the door, sliding hard against it with the shreds of my t-shirt, and catching my skin on each tag of the nail-shredded paint. She says, *Weird, though, isn't it, that these two rooms are right next-door now? That our happy memories are finally joined together and we can spend eternity in the prisons we've built for ourselves? I can't think of anything I'd rather be doing, Oaf. We'll sit here and watch the minutes of our lives tick away.*

*That's your plan? To sit here and wait for death?*

And she sighs and she says, *Oaf, who says you always need a plan? All plans end the same way: you die. And anyway, what's left for either of us, now that we're both murderers?*

The images from last night flood back in a swirl of supernovas, and I gasp. *It was all real, then. When I saw you standing over Mom's body, that was—*

She says, *Yeah, I'm starting to think that it was real. It was so strange from the inside, so much stranger than I expected. In my head, it's still a jumble of images, but I'll never forget the taste of her blood or the sound of her scream. Now I know why you love this stuff so much, why you can't get off of it, even when you want to. Now I am become death, destroyer of worlds.*

*Where did you hear that?*

*You say it all the time,* she says, *when you're sleepwalking. You said it the other night when you were standing over my bed.* And when I gasp, she adds, *Yeah, I was awake. But I knew you'd never kill me.*

*Why—why would you think that? How could you know that?*

"Because I *own* you," she says. "Because you're mine."

*What?*

"You still don't get it. You still don't remember that you promised you'd always be mine. That you *belong* to me. That's why I had to bring you here. Now we'll be together forever. There's nothing between you, me, and the embrace of death."

*But—*

"Love consumes. Love destroys."

*And Mom?*

"Just a casualty of love. Love, death, life, hate—they're all the same thing, just expressed in different ways. Why do you think I've been making you kill, anyway?"

*What?*

"Why do you think I made you kill, Oaf? You think I didn't know what effect the pills would have on you? You think I forgot what happened to my rats? You think I had hope for this drug? That I thought it would make me a gazillionaire or something? You think something that was so disastrous in animal testing would ever have made it to market?"

I'm tracing the scratches in the door with my fingernail and it fits perfectly.

"I just wanted to know what would happen if my chemical got inside of you. How your body would react. If I could turn you into one of my rats. It's been a fascinating experiment."

*But—*

"You just don't seem to understand that you're *mine.* Why do you think I got you fired at the publisher? At the middle school?"

*Wait, you—*

"It's because you were trying to get away from me. Don't think I didn't know. It's the same reason I sabotaged your stupid play senior year. The same reason I withdrew your application from NYU."

*You—?*

"I realized that the only way to keep you to myself was to turn you into something that only I could understand. To climb inside you and teach you to destroy. To kill. So I did. And now you're mine forever. Now we've shared something no one else can ever share. And since no one will understand you anymore—since they'll all hate you now—you'll have to stay here with me. It'll be just like the pretend games we used to play, but now it's real. We're in danger, and the only people we can trust are each other. For real. Forever."

I stare into the gray behind the blue, and I've never seen her eyes smile like this. I search for something to say, but the words aren't coming because I know that she's right—that there's no hope anymore and there hasn't been for a long time. That she owns me (body, soul, mind), and she probably always has. That I'm swallowed by the gray.

"I admit I was surprised, at least a little," she's saying, "that you started killing so quickly. I mean, the rats did, but rats are rats. They're stupid. You, though—well, you talk about *right* and *wrong* a lot. I thought the whole moral compass thing might get in the way. But it really didn't."

I look for Rachel, where she was standing, but all she is now is a pile of charred bones.

"It's weird," Sara's saying, laughing to herself, picking under her nails, "how everyone has their moral principles, and yet they're all so eager to violate them. Y'know? Everyone's just looking for an excuse. For some of my classmates in med school, all it took was for there to be a good grade or some funding on the line. For you? Just the right mix of chemicals."

*That's not the same thing!*

"Isn't it? We're all just chemicals interacting with chemicals, aren't we? Isn't money just a chemical, setting off more chemicals in your brain? Maybe you didn't choose how you'd react to the pills. *Maybe* you didn't. But y'know what? My classmates didn't choose how they'd react to money and grades. It's all just chemicals setting off chemicals."

My hand is still on the beads, still pulling, and I honestly don't even know why. Just for something to hold onto, I guess.

"Unless you want to believe in the soul," she says. "I assume that's why you're still yanking on this crappy plastic necklace—because you still want to believe in the soul, right? That the human mind is more than just a bunch of electrochemical reactions? That deep down, we're really moral creatures? That there's meaning to everything? That you have some sort of consciousness higher than the random firing of your brainstem?"

The question just hangs in the air like concrete, halfway through the door, halfway into my skull, and it won't budge no matter how hard I try to dislodge it.

"But how is that even a little bit comforting?" she says. "Is it really reassuring to think that you have a consciousness higher than the chemicals in your brain, and yet you *still* gave in to them? Because, *without* a soul, you're just a victim of chemistry. But *with* it, you *chose* to commit those murders. Which hypothetical universe do you prefer, Oaf?"

I inhale to answer, but I choke.

"But anyway, it was less than 24 hours, wasn't it? Before you killed for the first time? I think it was that night, right? After that last dinner we had at Mom's? You were packing up the stuff in your room—I was out in the hall, watching—and you passed out. But then you got up and made sort of a beeline for the door. It was strange because I thought you had woken up at first, but then I realized you were still asleep. Well, kind of an altered state of consciousness, I think—not asleep, but not awake, either. But anyway, you got in your car and started driving—it was the weirdest thing—and you headed back toward campus. I was following you in my Jag, obviously. And then when you got there, I was thinking maybe you would just go to

Ophelia, alive ~ 323

bed, or something, but instead you just sort of started wandering. And then you cornered a guy—just some random guy, I guess—you cornered him on the skywalk, and you strangled him against the wall. It was awesome.

*Awesome?*

"Don't be so righteous, you've watched plenty of horror movies. It's a thrill to watch a murder. It's a rush. Everybody knows that that's true, it's just that some people aren't ready to say it out loud. But anyway, it was at that point that I realized I should probably hide the evidence. I didn't want you getting caught before I had full control over you, and I definitely didn't want your little indiscretion to get traced back to me. So I took the body and slid it into one of my drawers down here. It was only after the second murder that I realized you would come up with the exact same idea. Great minds think alike, am I right?"

*Uh—*

"Of course, when you decided to burn down the hospital—which, *wow*, by the way—that was kind of impossible to cover up, obviously. But I took the opportunity to become a little dead myself, which was probably the best decision I ever made. Now the collections agencies can't find me, so, thanks for that."

*Um—*

"I was a little worried when you swore the stuff off, but I knew that if I kept it in front of you, you'd eventually come around to it."

*What? How could you know that—*

"Because you want the same thing everybody else wants, Oaf. You want *power*. We all do. We all want to see people cower in fear when we walk by. Everyone wants to take the people they love and lock them up forever, and everyone wants to take the people they hate and destroy them, and at the end of the day, what's the difference, Oaf? Either you *do* have a soul, in which case you chose evil a long time ago, or you're just a bunch of chemicals, in which case, who cares? Why cling to comforting lies when you can just have what you want? You never *really* quit the stuff, so I know you agree with me on this, whether you're going to admit it or not."

*I don't.*

"Oh, please, Oaf. It's over. You're *mine* now. You can drop the act." Her breath fogs the window till her eyes disappear, and she adds, "We can finally be honest with each other. Now what do you *really* want? Drop the bullshit about wanting to be a teacher or a writer, and just tell me what you *really* want from life. And think fast, because there's probably not too much life left."

*What difference does it make?*

"I just thought it'd be fun for a laugh. But we all know you'll just tell me you want to be a writer again, because you can't even be honest with yourself. So just go ahead and say it."

*I'm not going to say it for you.*

"Fine," she says. "I'll say it for you, then. *I want to be a writer, Sara!*" She laughs. "Cracks me up every time I hear it. Don't get me wrong, the world needs writers—I mean, I guess it probably does—maybe—but I've never even seen you set pen to paper. You don't want to be a writer, you just want to *tell people* you're a writer, so they'll think you're cool." She coughs. "It all comes back to power. You want to feel cooler than other people, so that you can have power over them. Just like everybody else does."

I want to say, *No, you're wrong, and that's stupid,* but I can't make myself say it. Can't push the words through my dry throat. I'm turning them over and over in my head, trying to see them from an angle that tells me she's wrong, but my thoughts get lost in the gray.

Why do I smell coffee and cigarettes?

*And what is it that YOU want, Sara?*

"What?"

*You heard me. Answer your own question. What is it you want?*

The window fogs up and her eyes fade away, and she says, "We both know what I want, Oaf. I want *you*. I want you to admit that you love me and you're mine forever."

*No.*

"What?"

*No.*

"Stop mumbling. Speak up."

"NO!"

"There you go!"

"You want to know what I really want, Sara?"

"Yeah."

"Are you sure?" I say.

"Yeah," she says. "Tell me."

"Okay. I want to cause you every bit of pain you've caused me. I want to add your body to my pile, but I want to do it as slowly and painfully as I can. I want to hear your screams until you beg for your life to end. And then I want to keep you alive, and in pain, for as long as I can." I'm coughing up blood. "That's what I want, Sara. That's what I really want."

Her eyes get wide in the blue, and at first I think it's fear, but then I see the corners of her enormous smile, and she laughs and says, "Finally we're getting somewhere. Finally we've gotten past all that bullshit repression. It's like I keep telling you, Oaf: love, hate, hugging, kissing, strangling, killing, fucking—it's all the same thing. They're all infinite sides of one infinite coin that the universe has been flipping since before you and I were even a thing." And she winks and she disappears again. And the blue fills with red, and my nails slide down the paint till my face mashes into the vomit and blood on the floor, and my eyes sting with acid and leak red into the brown.

*What are you doing?* The voice comes from a pair of boots next to my face, and I don't have to look up to know that the hipster lumberjack whose name I never learned is back at my side.

"I'm dying."

*You're dying?* he says. He sounds skeptical.

"I'm dying," I tell him. "I'm giving up because there's nothing left for me to do. I'm Ophelia. I have three jobs to do in this production: show up, freak out, and die. And I've done the first two, so this must be my death scene. Now leave me alone. You've never been any help."

*But—*

"Get away from me!"

And he whispers, *Look in front of you,* before he walks away into the heavy, gray air.

I force my eyes open. The gray light stings hard, and my breath tastes like acid from inside my guts, but I choke, and I gasp, till the room is in focus. In front of my eyes, and refracting blue sun into all of the corners of the room, are Kate's rosary beads, lying with Sara's foot off of them now. My hand's saying *Pick them up, wrap me around them,* and I still feel the pits and the valleys dug into my hand from the last time I squeezed them.

And so, I'm back where I was mentally just a few days ago, wondering *Is there a chance Kate might be right?* Wondering if saying, *Oh, Virgin Mother, pray for me!* will actually result in a virgin mother praying for me. Probably not. Sara's probably right that there's nothing more than chemicals reacting with other chemicals, and she's definitely right that if there *is* more than that, that that's even worse—just a bigger burden to bear. She's probably right about everything.

But she might be wrong.

*There's more to the universe than just atoms bumping up against each other. I could be wrong, but maybe I'm not.*

What have I got to lose?

I don't know why I feel so weird about wrapping my hand around a dull piece of plastic and string. If there's nothing in the world but chemicals and reactions, then this string of beads is harmless. A security blanket. Something to squeeze till it makes me feel better about my march toward the grave. And yet the trepidation is shaking my bones, as if it really matters, but I know that it must just be my brain doing weird things to keep me distracted while it finally shuts down. Is it childish to reach for a security blanket, or is it mature to admit there are plenty of things I don't know? *There are more things in heaven and earth than are dreamt of in your philosophy.*

Okay then.

I reach out, I wrap my hand around the beads, and I pull them back, and I hold them close, and I wait. The acid steam in front of my face goes into my lungs and out, and each time I breathe it stings more than before. I breathe my own breath and taste my own vomit, till the pain and the cold turn to numb and to black, and the thought that something miraculous still might happen is the last of the absurd ideas that I banish from my mind.

It's not like the black is unwelcome.

When your dreams are nothing but horror, the right not to dream is a right that you'll fight for. The ability to shut your eyes and see nothing but the backs of your eyelids is a need that's inescapable. I thank the blackness, over and over, for making everything go away, and I savor the numbness of the fuzz spreading through my brain, thinking that even if I'm not more than a handful of atoms, at least maybe I'm less. Maybe I'm just a low hum in a radiating chaos, enduring an occasional fit of unpleasant consciousness. And every moment I drown in the sea of black is one more bit of freedom from her voice scratching on the steel and the concrete, worming its way into my ear like a tongue.

*What are you doing?*

It's the same question again, but in a different voice this time, one made of bits and pieces that still aren't quite assembled together, still floating in the dark, daring me to catch them, sort them out, combine them. Like some musical notes jumbled at the bottom of a page of empty staffs, or like some sharp Legos lying on the floor in the dark. Not quite an intrusion into my sleep (like an alarm clock), but just a gentle voice waking me, a character in the dream I wasn't having. A sun coming through blinds or a wind beating hard against the strong side of a warm house. I piece it together and I see that I know the voice, know it better than anything I've heard all morning. Not music or a Lego castle, not a whisper from a fiction, but soothing and sharp, like a glass bottleneck sliding up and down the neck of a guitar.

"Kate?"

The darkness in my eyes rolls back, and I'm looking up now, and her face is ringed with light that ignites her dreadlocks and sharpens her freckles into deep, black punctuations. She gasps at seeing me half-naked and filthy, but she's here (somehow?), and she's trying to smile. *What are you doing?* she says again.

I tell her, "I'm trapped here, Kate, I'm trapped in this room. Sara locked me in here, in this room in the psych ward, with burnt bones and rats and my blood and my vomit. I don't understand how she trapped me in here, but I'm trapped and I can't tell what's real, and I just can't escape," and she tells me, *Calm down.* "What?"

*Calm down.*

"How can I calm down? I can't think, I can't see straight, I don't know what's real, and you're probably not real, even, I'm seeing things and I keep hearing voices—just so many voices. I wish you could help me, but I'm too far gone, Kate. Just please go away. Just please. Go away."

*Phelia, all you have to do is walk out.*

"What? What do you mean? I don't understand, you're not making sense, I can't breathe, I can't breathe, and she's waiting out there, and she's going to hurt me, she thinks that she owns me—Kate, you have to help me, I don't understand—"

*Oh, Phelia—how can I make you understand? How can I make you see what's real?*

She stares into my eyes with her boundless brown pools that quiver with tears. And I see her lips trembling. She's mouthing some words, some words from last night (it seems so long ago), and the words are familiar and cut through the sun.

*It's not a Beautiful thing or a Good thing, at least not on the surface. It's more like being elbow-deep in someone else's blood.* And she shudders and chokes back a gag, and she pulls off her shirt.

As the gray sun lights up her brown curves, she kneels down beside me and touches the shirt to my face, and it soaks up the blood and the vomit. Her shirt smells like coffee and sweat and tobacco, the smell of an addict who's stayed awake all through the night, probably running down dark alleys, shouting my name, and it finds all the dried bits of bile on my face, and it gently removes them. I watch them all fall as wet, wobbly scales, on the ground. And then when I'm clean and my pores taste the air, she tosses it off in the corner of the room, and she lays down beside me, and wraps her arms around me, and holds me in the afternoon light. I cry on her skin, and she cries in my hair, and we lie on the floor in the muck till we're finally warm.

It's been hours of lying here, crying and thinking of nothing, and I say to her, "Thank you."

She thinks for a minute and finally tells me, *I think that I might understand now. Maybe a little, at least.* And the sun's disappeared from the window, the gray in the room's gotten duller, and she stands back up and she holds out her hand, and she says, *Are you ready to go now?*

"Where?"

*It's time to leave,* she says.

"How? I'm so confused."

*Just walk out.*

"I don't understand."

*Just walk out.*

I look at her face, and it's gold in the gray, there are tears in her eyes, and she's tugging my hand (gently), not toward the door, but away, toward the back of the room. But I can't pull my eyes from the heavy steel door and its tiny blue window.

Her eyes fill the slot again (Sara's cold, gray eyes). They laugh.

"Where are you going, Oaf?"

"I—"

"There's only one way out, y'know."

"But—"

"It's through me," she says. "You know it's always been through me."

My hand's falling empty as I push toward the door and I say, "I don't think you want that, Sara." I press my eyes against the glass, and I stare into hers, and I say, "I don't think you want that at all."

*Phelia, please just look up—*

"Oh, I do," Sara says. "Come get me. Come destroy me like you promised."

*Please, just look up.*

"Open the door, then," I tell her. "Just open the door, and I'll tear you apart—like I should have last night, and the night before that."

And she whispers, "Okay."

I hear the bolt *click*, and then slide, and it's heavy. Kate's saying, *No, Phelia, oh, please just look up,* but it's all just a buzz in my head and I swat it away. The bolt pounds the door and then grinds hard against it. I hear a latch *click*, and the door opens wide, and there's Sara.

That gray pair of eyes and the body attached to them, standing in front of me, daring me (begging?) to strike, to attack. To open her veins and to pour her out onto the tile and the rug filled with mildew. I see now that she's not the voice that I heard in the attic, and she's not the goddess who swallowed the sun in my mom's room, and she's not the freight train who crashed through the wall with the black, gaping mouth.

She's me.

The door is a mirror, and through it, I see not ephemeral monsters or willowy demons, but just a young girl with the same scars that I have, the same stone-gray eyes, and the same ratty hair. It was never a secret that she was the pretty one; now, though—hunched over, with scars on her arms, and her bones sticking out of her skin, and her clothes torn to shreds, hanging off of her limp, corpse-like figure?

She's nothing but me.

There are bits of her—bits of her pill, I mean—scraping inside of my veins still, and making my nails itch, and whispering, *Kill her.* But now that I find myself caught in this mirror, I see for the first time that she has the same scars that I do. That these bones in front of me might have done terrible things (and they have), but that mine have as well, and that now she's just standing here, shaking and baring her throat, just a victim of who she once was, in the past. A victim of atoms? A victim of soul? Does it matter? I see now it doesn't—not to me, anyway. I see now that I and my atoms (my soul) all need grace (and depend on it, really), and I can't deny that, not even to someone who's standing in front of me, begging for justice.

I've killed her before (in my sleep, in my nightmares), and somehow the pain was still there when she died in my hands. I'm starting to see, if this figure in front of me dies here right now—this small jumble of atoms that calls itself *Sara*—that it'll be just like the ghosts in my dreams. That her body (her atoms) will fall to the floor and leak fluids deep into the rug, but her soul will still haunt me, will follow me everywhere, staring at me while I sleep, sucking hard at my veins like a vampire.

There's nothing to do but let go.

I admit that I don't quite know how. I admit that a lifetime of pain and regret and some half-repressed memories are hard to let go of. I admit that it's hard to let go of revenge while she stands here and quivers and begs me to take it. Still, something inside of me (not the pills—*something*) is saying if not for grace, I'd have been dead long ago. That I can't undo dung-heaps of wrong from the past (like a single not-killing would make up for Stalin, or even my own checkered history), but to the extent I can influence time, space, and matter in front of me, maybe my goal should be shining a small piece of light. That I don't quite know how, but that *Dammit, I'll try.*

I look into her eyes, and they're gray just like mine, and I ask myself, *What can I do?* And behind me again, I hear Kate's voice much clearer now (not incorporeal), telling me, "Phelia, look up. Phelia, please just look up."

I look up.

I crane my head upward, exposing my throat to the cold and the sweat, and I see that there's nothing but blue sky. There's nothing above us—no ceiling, no roof—just a blue sky, a clear day, and sun shining yellow and melting the snow on the ground up above us.

And now I can see how Kate got in here.

Behind me, and above me, a makeshift staircase of burnt, blackened rubble leads down toward the wall with the one tiny window that's been the room's only source of light until now. The building collapsed in the flames, but somehow this one room fell through the rubble, survived, and landed in the basement, next to Sara's office (which, except for parts of its carpet, is charred beyond recognition). Above us is nothing but black, twisted wreckage, wrapped in thousands of rolls of yellow *Caution* tape, and beyond that I can make out red and blue flashing lights and the sound of a siren or two.

We're the tragedy "Man," in two acts (insanity and death), unfolding in the round.

I look up at the pathway that leads to the surface, the one that Kate took to get down here, and I see it's not something I could climb on my own. With two of us, though (or with three), we can easily help each other up. Kate looks into my eyes and holds out her hand, and says, "It's time to go." And Rachel, behind me, says, *It's time to go,* and the fat man to my left says, *It's time to go,* and the hipster with the beard and the girl with the Uggs and the cop with the freckles all agree, and my mother, who's been standing in the corner, says *It's time to go.*

And I guess that means it's time to go.

I look back toward Sara, and I see now that she's just a charred pile of bones, and she probably has been for days, and I think that she's only been talking to me because I wouldn't let her rest. And I know it's not much, and I know that it's hard to accept that I mean it (even for me), but I say, "I forgive you," and I bend down, with the rosary in hand, and I set it on top of her femur. (I think it's her femur.) Then I say, "Goodbye, Sara," and Kate takes my hand, and we pull each other up from the rubble and into the sun. And my knees are scraped, and my skin is cold and sweaty and bloody, but someone wraps me in a blanket, and I fall asleep (hard) in the back of a car.

## thurs. jan. 20.
## 4:27 pm.
## sleeping. in a cop car

**The seat is hard, and it smells like vomit,** but I don't mind.

I'm sleeping, in the sun, for the first time in weeks. Not a nightmare sewn from memories or a heavy, black blanket, but just a warm, peaceful nap in the afternoon's last light.

The road makes the seat rumble low in my ear, and the tires crunch snow between their teeth. The sun's yellow and warm and it sticks to everything like melted butter.

And it's so strange to me to think that the sun's always shining.

Not just when I see it, I mean—not just in the day. Even though I'm asleep right now, it's still shining. Somehow I know, because I can see it (feel it) through my eyelids.

And a hundred million miles away, it's in the process of destroying its own core, crushing its own atoms, just to make light and heat.

(For me.)

(And also for everyone else, I guess.)

(But right now? I'm pretty sure it's mostly for me.)

I'm starting to think that Sara was right. That love devours and destroys. Sometimes, when you love someone, you really do end up devouring her. You really do destroy her.

And sometimes, you destroy yourself, for her.

I like the second kind of love better...

**sat. aug. 20.**
**2:16 pm.**
**caged**

**I'm sitting alone, in a padded cell**, bouncing a rubber ball against the wall. It's one of those giant SuperBalls, the kind that when you first see them you think are going to be even better than the small ones, because, well, they're bigger, but then when you throw one you find out it actually bounces *less* high and *less* fast than they do. Maybe because it's heavier?

The padding on the walls doesn't help, either.

I've kinda lost track of how long I've been here at this point, but it's not because I'm crazy. Really, it's not. Once I got off the pills—once I really dried out—I stopped seeing things.

Well—with a handful of exceptions.

I'll spare you the details of my formal arrest and trial, but it turns out I'm *a danger to myself and to others!* or something, at least for now, so they put me in here for close observation. And it turns out that not all psych wards are horrible, abusive hellholes, and I'm actually fairly happy here. The doctors and nurses are nice, and the food's not bad, and I have plenty of time to be alone with my thoughts.

Well, sometimes.

The short version is that the nightmares stopped. I never saw Sara's face again, never recovered another terrible memory, never again felt the urge to kill. I slept in my bed every night, never sleepwalked, and once I got through the worst bits of kicking the habit (tremors, scratching, the whole deal), I never craved the pills.

But the thing is, the ghosts never went away.

Everything else went back to normal. Sleep went back to being a soothing, black abyss, occasionally punctuated by a happy dream about puppies or being naked at the grocery store. Meals went back to being the best time of day, all the spirals and fuzz turned back to right angles, and human blood stopped being so damned delicious.

But sometimes at night, I'd wake up, and the girl with the Uggs—Cyndi—she'd be standing in the corner, just looking at me with her big, sad eyes. Just standing there, like she was waiting for something.

Or sometimes it would be Rachel, sitting down at the end of my bed, looking down at her feet, eyes wet with fresh tears. And when I'd say her name, she'd look up, take a breath, and then disappear into the blackness.

Once it was my mother. I woke up, and she was leaning over my bed, staring into my eyes, her nose almost brushing against mine. I confess to screaming that time. And when I did, the nurses all came running, and my mom disappeared into thin air, and of course then I looked crazy in front of the whole loony bin.

They didn't speak to me anymore, I guess because I didn't have any more words to put into their mouths. They'd just sit there, or stand there, staring at me, refusing to go away, even once my blood started testing completely clean of the drug. Actually, I was seeing them more and more as the weeks went on, until it was starting to feel weirder when they *weren't* around.

I took the rap for Kate.

I felt a little conflicted about it, but I really couldn't think of a good reason that she should have to be punished for my crimes any more than she already had been. So the first chance I got, I confessed to absolutely everything, insisting that I acted alone. Then later, as soon as she and I were alone together, she tried to argue, saying that what she had done was wrong and she deserved to serve time for it, but I pointed out that now was a lousy time to be growing a moral compass, especially when she was so close to graduating (I mean, you might as well finish, right?); then she relaxed a little and said *Thanks,* and I said something cheesy that I don't remember anymore.

Sometimes she comes and visits me here. She'll bring her new guitar, and she'll play me a few songs, or she'll bring a deck of cards and we'll play a game, or she'll bring a book and sit on my bed and read to me—some poetry or a mystery or sometimes a bit of theology when I feel like humoring her. She told me she was thinking of joining a convent. I understood why. I wish she wouldn't.

One night she finished reading and she put the book aside and we just lay there on my bed, staring at the padded ceiling. The silence was kind of nice, so I didn't want to disrupt it, but when I saw the bearded guy's ghost standing in the corner, I freaked out and screamed, and pretty much ruined the moment.

*Who are you talking to?* Kate said, and I told her, *Remember how I told you once that the pills made me see ghosts everywhere? That the people I had killed followed me around and talked to me? They never went away. They're still standing around, staring at me, almost all the time, and they never say anything, and there's nothing I can do to get rid of them.*

And Kate said, *Well, what have you tried?* and I thought about it, and I finally said, *I guess pretty much nothing,* and she laughed at me and said, *Well, maybe you should try something.*

I asked her what I should try.

She said, *Phelia, you're always talking about how you think of yourself as a writer. Have you been writing at all lately?*

And I realized that she was right—that I suddenly had nothing but time on my hands, and if I didn't use it for writing, then that was on me, and only me. I was out of excuses. So I asked one of the nurses if I could get some paper and pens, and I started to write. I wasn't writing poetry, or stories, or anything like that—just a lot of letters.

I started with a letter to Rachel's parents. Basically, a letter saying I was lucky to have known such a hardworking patient transporter, and that I felt awful for my actions, and that if there was any way I could take them back, I would. And I told them that I knew it probably didn't mean much, but that if there was anything I could do, to please let me know.

And then I mailed it.

It was far from the best thing I'd ever written, but it felt like a small amount of weight—one ghost's worth, y'know?—had been lifted. And after that, I never saw Rachel's ghost again.

So I kept writing. I wrote to Cyndi's parents, and I wrote to the bearded hipster guy's mom (it turns out his name was "Daniel"), and with each letter I sent, there was one fewer ghost in the room. Usually, I never heard from the recipients, but some of them actually wrote me back, and I read every letter and kept them in a drawer. Most of them just said *Thank you,* and a couple cursed me out, and there were one or two that actually asked me for something. I think one of them, believe it or not, asked me for prayer, which was weird, but not necessarily in a bad way. Kind of flattering, really, that someone would imagine that God would actually listen to me. Because, I guess, what else can you do when your spouse has been murdered? You pray, or you ask someone else to pray for you.

People are strange. But good-strange.

And the other request I got was even weirder, if you can imagine that. I guess I must have mentioned in my initial letter that I sort-of thought of myself as a writer, because the woman I sent it to wrote me back and asked me if I would write her son, who I murdered, some poetry. It was weird, but I told her I would be honored, and I hoped what I wrote would help heal some of the damage I had caused. It took me almost a month to get the sonnet I wrote for him right, but when I was done, I stepped back and looked it over, and I honestly I didn't think it was too bad. I kept a copy of it for myself, and I sent one to her. And then when she wrote me back to tell me how much better she felt after reading it to her son's grave, I think I finally sort-of understood what writing is for.

At that point, I found it hard to stop writing. When I wasn't eating or sleeping, I was at the tiny desk in my room, putting words onto pages. Stories and poetry and essays and everything else. I wasn't sure what to do with any of them, but I started passing them around to the patients and staff at the ward, because why the hell not? Some of them made people laugh, and some of them made people cry, and some of them made people roll their eyes, which is how I learned that not everything I write is awesome.

And that's okay.

But I kept writing letters, and with each letter, another ghost disappeared. A couple of recipients actually wrote me back more than once, and believe it or not, I made a couple of friends that way—we send letters and occasionally talk on the phone, and it's weird to think that I murdered these people's loved ones, but they tell me that having a relationship with me actually eases the pain, and who am I to argue? Everyone has their own weird way of grieving, I guess. Some people turn to prayer, some to copious amounts of alcohol, and some become pen pals with their daughter's murderer.

It's sort of like Kate was saying to me that one time, about how there are really only two forces in the universe. There's death and there's life, and if Sara were here she'd tell me that they're actually one and the same, but then I'd have to ask her, *So why do they feel so damn different?* Because, the thing is, death is huge, and it's strong. A gunshot to the face, a hundred knife wounds in your gut, a collision with a train. Death is big, and it's violent, like the emptiness of space, or like pounding your fists on the wall till they bleed. I spent a week as death's unpaid intern, and it's a job that I never want back, because killing a person is an arduous task. It takes everything out of you. It tears you apart from the inside.

Life isn't like that.

Life is tiny. It's weak. The things that bring life are small and they're subtle, like coffee and sonnets and glass bottlenecks held loose against the strings of guitars. Like sunlight and rain and a single SpongeBob Band-Aid on a child's knee.

Life is tiny and weak, and the weird thing is that life wins in the end, anyway.

I carried death with me wherever I went for half a dozen days. And it's true that a lot of people died because of my actions. But the thing is, even more people survived. And for the people who survived, life went on, and when they asked me to, I was able to push their lives forward a little, with phone calls, and sonnets, and even a stupid little prayer. I still don't think I believe in God, but shouting into the darkness seems preferable to just accepting it.

I still think about the heat death of the universe sometimes—how everything will have to die eventually. But it occurs to me that the universe is such a huge, powerful thing, and life is such a tiny, weak thing, that honestly, the universe doesn't stand a chance.

But anyway, I kept writing letters, till all the ghosts disappeared, except one.

The one who remains is my mother.

I keep flashing back the last conversation I had with her, when I told her I would look at her writing. Her face lit up, like she had been waiting her whole life for someone to say that, and then instead I banished myself to the bathroom, just to avoid killing her.

And then, y'know, I killed her anyway (which explains why her ghost looks so pissed).

I honestly didn't know who I could write to to apologize for her death, since her only remaining family member is me, and I doubt I could ever forgive myself. It's like what Sara said about how either what I did had no meaning at all, or I did it because I *wanted* to. The first possibility is terrible, and the second is even worse, and neither leaves any room for forgiveness.

I didn't know what else to do, so I sent a letter to my dad. And a few days later, he called me.

Despite everything, he was happy to hear from me, and he made sure to tell me how much he had enjoyed catching up with me back in January, and that he really wanted to show me something, and could he come by some time?

And I had no idea what to say, so I said sure.

So here I am, waiting for the man who left me so many years ago, hoping he'll come bringing some good news and not just a lot of anger and confusion.

*Behold, I make all things new.*

And now there are footsteps in the hall, and even though my room has no windows, I still recognize the sound of my father's feet. Even if it's been years—really, more than a decade—I remember their sound in the hall, strong and rhythmic, with purpose, like waves on the side of a ship, gently rocking me to sleep.

A nurse knocks to be polite, and then she unlocks the door, and my father is standing there with a laptop, half-smiling and awkward, and still in his lab coat and stethoscope. And without even thinking, I jump to my feet and say, "Daddy!" and throw both my arms around his neck and just hang there, smiling up at his stubble. I realize that's a strange thing to do—I know this is a man I've barely talked to in years—but I'm starting to see how short this life is, and if I don't love now, then when?

I remember his smells (slightly boozy, cologne). I remember his voice with my head on his chest. And he's all that I have now; there's no way I'll let myself waste him. He says, "Glad to see you too, Ophie," and he hugs me back (awkward, sincere). When I finally relax and allow him to speak, he says, "Ophie, I've been going through your mom's stuff—somehow, legally, I ended up responsible for her estate—and I've found pages and pages of stuff that she wrote. Did you know about all this?"

"Well—" I say—"she mentioned something to me about it just before she, uh, y'know. But I really don't know much, no."

"It's really good," he says.

"Seriously?"

He says, "Yeah, I think so. I've been reading it—but, I mean, you know more about writing than I do."

I look into his eyes, which are blue like mine, and I'm happy the gray in mine faded away and my world shines the same color as his now.

And he says, "Anyway, it's good stuff, I think, but a lot of it is half-finished. I was wondering if maybe you could help me go through it, and maybe the two of us can cobble together something that might be worth publishing."

I tell him, "I'd like that."

And he's almost surprised. "Really?" He laughs. "Can we get started now?" And we sit at my desk, and he opens the laptop, and I see now how life can go on. Tiny words on a page—insignificant things that somehow contain my mom's soul. He shows me her work, and we read it together, and I think that he's right—that it's good. And that somehow, despite all the death that's occurred—that I've caused (why mince words?)—there's a glimmer of life shining bright in this room. And a glimmer is all that you need.

Because life grows, like a weed pushing up through the sidewalk.

And I look in the corner, where my mother is standing, and she smiles.

And then she fades away for good.

# Acknowledgments

Obviously the first round of thanks needs to go to my wife Julia, who was the first person not to laugh at me when I announced my intention to write one of those "novel" things I'd heard so much about, and whose experiences in the medical industry inspired some of this book's episodes. Without her longsuffering support, I probably wouldn't have written a word, in this book or anywhere else. Then again, I already dedicated the book to her, so maybe I don't need to belabor the point here. You're pretty cool, wife. I like you.

I owe nearly as many thanks (but not quite as many— don't get greedy, you guys) to Ben and Rachel Bausili, who have been in this book's corner from the moment they first knew about it, and have provided me with incomparable amounts of advice, support, cheers, jeers, love, and friendship. I don't know where I or my family would be without the two of you, but it would no doubt be a much darker place.

Third, I must give special thanks to my brother Thadd, who has been my friend and confidant for as long as I have known him, and my muse and artistic collaborator for much of my adult life. Thanks for believing in my creative ability before pretty much anyone else did, kid. You still owe me a screenplay.

Blake Collier, my first and possibly biggest fan, who provided no shortage of encouragement when I was trying to sell this thing.

Everyone who read previous drafts of this novel and offered feedback and support: my dad, my sister, my brothers, Joe Valasek, Evan Derrick, Ryan Dunlap, Ryssa Laucomer, Megan Timperley, Daniel Bergman, Dana Wimmers, Dallas Koehn, Scottie Moser, Ian De Jong, Pr. Hall, April-Lyn Caouette, Nicole Harrington, Nicholas

Tieman, Jessica Buller, Jeffrey Mays, Rachel Uhrenholdt, Carol Mathias, Joe Rubas, Brad Carter.

Everyone at Christ and Pop Culture, a writing community where I have found no shortage of friends, advice, encouragement, and opportunity to grow as a writer.

The good people at Cracked, who gave me my first real writing break.

Eric and Stephanie at Post Mortem, for giving me this opportunity.

My mom and dad for conceiving, birthing, and raising me. Hope you don't regret it too often.

Apologies to anyone I forgot. I'm a jerk for forgetting you.

And special thanks to anyone who actually read this far. Hi, mom!

# POST MORTEM PRESS
## www.postmortem-press.com

## About Post Mortem Press

Since its inception in 2010, Post Mortem Press has published over 100 titles in the genres of dark fiction, suspense/mystery, horror, and dark fantasy. The goal is to provide a showcase for talented authors, affording exposure and opportunity to "get noticed" by the mainstream publishing community. Post Mortem Press has quickly become a powerful voice in the small genre press community. The result has been five years of steady growth and successful endeavors that have garnered attention from all across the publishing world.

CPSIA information can be obtained
at www.ICGtesting.com
Printed in the USA
LVOW12s2217130716

496174LV00009B/911/P